KU-274-198

**By Christie Golden**

*Star Wars: Fate of the Jedi: Ascension*
*Star Wars: Fate of the Jedi: Allies*
*Star Wars: Fate of the Jedi: Omen*
*Ravenloft: Vampire of the Mists*
*Ravenloft: The Enemy Within*
*Star Trek Voyager: The Murdered Sun*
*Instrument of Fate*
*King's Man and Thief*
*Star Trek Voyager: Marooned*
*Invasion: America*
*Star Trek Voyager: Seven of Nine*
*Invasion America: On the Run*
*Star Trek the Next Generation: The First Virtue* (with Michael Jan Friedman)
*A.D. 999* (as Jadrien Bell)
*Star Trek Voyager: The Dark Matters Trilogy, Book 1: Cloak and Dagger*
*Star Trek Voyager: The Dark Matters Trilogy, Book 2: Ghost Dance*
*Star Trek Voyager: The Dark Matters Trilogy, Book 3: Shadow of Heaven*
*Star Trek Voyager: Endgame* (with Diane Carey)
*Warcraft: Lord of the Clans*
*Star Trek Voyager: No Man's Land*
*Star Trek: The Last Roundup*
*Star Trek Voyager: Homecoming*
*Star Trek Voyager: The Farthest Shore*
*On Fire's Wings*
*Star Trek Voyager: Spirit Walk, Book 1: Old Wounds*
*Star Trek Voyager: Spirit Walk, Book 2: Enemy of My Enemy*
*In Stone's Clasp*
*Warcraft: Rise of the Horde*
*StarCraft: The Dark Templar Series, Book 1: Firstborn*
*StarCraft: The Dark Templar Series, Book 2: Shadow Hunters*
*Under Sea's Shadow* (eBook format only)
*Warcraft: Beyond the Dark Portal* (with Aaron Rosenberg)
*Warcraft: Arthas: Rise of the Lich King*

Fate of the Jedi

# ASCENSION

Fate of the Jedi

# ASCENSION

CHRISTIE GOLDEN

Century · London

Published by Century 2011

2 4 6 8 10 9 7 5 3 1



First published in Great Britain in 2011 by
Century
Random House
SW1V 2SA

www.starwars.com
www.fateofthejedi.com
www.randomhouse.co.uk

Addresses for companies within The Random House Group Limited can be found at:
www.randomhouse.co.uk

The Random House Group Limited Reg. No. 954009

A CIP catalogue record for this book
is available from the British Library

ISBN 9781846056918

The Random House Group Limited supports the Forest Stewardship Council® (FSC®), the leading international forest certification organisation. All our titles that are printed on Greenpeace approved FSC® certified paper carry the FSC® logo. Our paper procurement policy can be found at www.randomhouse.co.uk/environment

Printed and bound in the UK by
CPI Mackays, Chatham, ME5 8TD

Book design by Elizabeth A. D. Eno

This book, my last entry into this amazing nine-book adventure, is dedicated to those who walked it right alongside me:

Aaron Allston
Troy Denning
Shelly Shapiro
Sue Rostoni

The co-creativity of this team has been and continues to be nothing short of phenomenal. Thank you for letting me be a part of it.

# Acknowledgments

In addition to the awesomeness of my fellow writers and editors, I wish to also thank the following:

Leland Chee
Pablo Hidalgo
Jeffrey Kirby
David Moench
David Pomerico
Joe Scalora
And the 501st

May the Force be with you!

# THE STAR WARS NOVELS TIMELINE

## OLD REPUBLIC 5000–33 YEARS BEFORE *STAR WARS: A New Hope*

***Lost Tribe of the Sith****
- Precipice
- Skyborn
- Paragon
- Savior
- Purgatory
- Sentinel

**3650** *YEARS BEFORE STAR WARS: A New Hope*

***The Old Republic***
- Deceived
- Fatal Alliance

- Red Harvest

***Lost Tribe of the Sith****
- Pantheon**
- Secrets**

**1032** *YEARS BEFORE STAR WARS: A New Hope*

Knight Errant

Darth Bane: Path of Destruction
Darth Bane: Rule of Two
Darth Bane: Dynasty of Evil

## RISE OF THE EMPIRE 33–0 YEARS BEFORE *STAR WARS: A New Hope*

Darth Maul: Saboteur*
Cloak of Deception
Darth Maul: Shadow Hunter

**32** *YEARS BEFORE STAR WARS: A New Hope*

**STAR WARS: EPISODE I**
***THE PHANTOM MENACE***

Rogue Planet
Outbound Flight
The Approaching Storm

**22** *YEARS BEFORE STAR WARS: A New Hope*

**STAR WARS: EPISODE II**
***ATTACK OF THE CLONES***

**22–19** *YEARS BEFORE STAR WARS: A New Hope*

The Clone Wars
The Clone Wars: Wild Space
The Clone Wars: No Prisoners

***Clone Wars Gambit***
- Stealth
- Siege

***Republic Commando***
- Hard Contact
- Triple Zero
- True Colors
- Order 66

Shatterpoint
The Cestus Deception
The Hive*
MedStar I: Battle Surgeons
MedStar II: Jedi Healer
Jedi Trial
Yoda: Dark Rendezvous
Labyrinth of Evil

**19** *YEARS BEFORE STAR WARS: A New Hope*

**STAR WARS: EPISODE III**
***REVENGE OF THE SITH***

Dark Lord: The Rise of Darth Vader

***Coruscant Nights***
- Jedi Twilight
- Street of Shadows
- Patterns of Force

***Imperial Commando***
- 501st

***The Han Solo Trilogy***
- The Paradise Snare
- The Hutt Gambit
- Rebel Dawn

The Adventures of Lando Calrissian
The Han Solo Adventures
The Force Unleashed
The Force Unleashed II
Death Troopers

*An eBook novella
**Forthcoming

## REBELLION
## 0–5 YEARS AFTER
## *STAR WARS: A New Hope*

Death Star

**0**

**STAR WARS: EPISODE IV**
***A NEW HOPE***

Tales from the Mos Eisley Cantina
Allegiance
Choices of One
Galaxies: The Ruins of Dantooine
Splinter of the Mind's Eye

**3** *YEARS AFTER STAR WARS: A New Hope*

**STAR WARS: EPISODE V**
***THE EMPIRE STRIKES BACK***

Tales of the Bounty Hunters
Shadows of the Empire

**4** *YEARS AFTER STAR WARS: A New Hope*

**STAR WARS: EPISODE VI**
***RETURN OF THE JEDI***

Tales from Jabba's Palace
Tales from the Empire
Tales from the New Republic

***The Bounty Hunter Wars***
- The Mandalorian Armor
- Slave Ship
- Hard Merchandise

The Truce at Bakura
Luke Skywalker and the Shadows of Mindor

## NEW REPUBLIC
## 5–25 YEARS AFTER
## *STAR WARS: A New Hope*

***X-Wing***
- Rogue Squadron
- Wedge's Gamble
- The Krytos Trap
- The Bacta War
- Wraith Squadron
- Iron Fist
- Solo Command

The Courtship of Princess Leia
A Forest Apart*
Tatooine Ghost

***The Thrawn Trilogy***
- Heir to the Empire
- Dark Force Rising
- The Last Command

X-Wing: Isard's Revenge

***The Jedi Academy Trilogy***
- Jedi Search
- Dark Apprentice
- Champions of the Force

I, Jedi
Children of the Jedi
Darksaber
Planet of Twilight
X-Wing: Starfighters of Adumar
The Crystal Star

***The Black Fleet Crisis Trilogy***
- Before the Storm
- Shield of Lies
- Tyrant's Test

The New Rebellion

***The Corellian Trilogy***
- Ambush at Corellia
- Assault at Selonia
- Showdown at Centerpoint

***The Hand of Thrawn Duology***
- Specter of the Past
- Vision of the Future

Fool's Bargain*
Survivor's Quest

*An eBook novella
**Forthcoming

# THE STAR WARS NOVELS TIMELINE

## NEW JEDI ORDER
## 25–40 YEARS AFTER
## *STAR WARS: A New Hope*

Boba Fett: A Practical Man*

***The New Jedi Order***

Vector Prime
Dark Tide I: Onslaught
Dark Tide II: Ruin
Agents of Chaos I: Hero's Trial
Agents of Chaos II: Jedi Eclipse
Balance Point
Recovery*
Edge of Victory I: Conquest
Edge of Victory II: Rebirth
Star by Star
Dark Journey
Enemy Lines I: Rebel Dream
Enemy Lines II: Rebel Stand
Traitor
Destiny's Way
Ylesia*
Force Heretic I: Remnant
Force Heretic II: Refugee
Force Heretic III: Reunion
The Final Prophecy
The Unifying Force

**35** *YEARS AFTER STAR WARS: A New Hope*

***The Dark Nest Trilogy***

The Joiner King
The Unseen Queen
The Swarm War

## LEGACY
## 40+ YEARS AFTER
## *STAR WARS: A New Hope*

***Legacy of the Force***

Betrayal
Bloodlines
Tempest
Exile
Sacrifice
Inferno
Fury
Revelation
Invincible

Crosscurrent
Riptide

Millennium Falcon

**43** *YEARS AFTER STAR WARS: A New Hope*

***Fate of the Jedi***

Outcast
Omen
Abyss
Backlash
Allies
Vortex
Conviction
Ascension
Apocalypse**

*An eBook novella
**Forthcoming

# Dramatis Personae

Abeloth
Allana Solo; child (human female)
Ben Skywalker; Jedi Knight (human male)
Darish Vol; Grand Lord of the Lost Tribe of the Sith (human male)
Drikl Lecersen; Moff (human male)
Gavar Khai; Sith Saber (human male)
Han Solo; captain, *Millennium Falcon* (human male)
Haydnat Treen; Senator, member of the triumvirate governing the Galactic Alliance (human female)
Ivaar Workan; Sith High Lord (human male)
Jagged Fel; Head of State, Galactic Empire (human male)
Jaina Solo; Jedi Knight (human female)
Leia Organa Solo; Jedi Knight (human female)
Luke Skywalker; Jedi Grand Master (human male)
Padnel Ovin; Senator from Klatooine (Klaatoinian male)
Saba Sebatyne; Jedi Master and member of the triumvirate (Barabel female)
Tahiri Veila, escaped convict (human female)
Vestara Khai; Sith apprentice (human female)
Wynn Dorvan; member of the triumvirate (human male)

*A long time ago in a galaxy far, far away. . . .*

# ASCENSION

# Chapter One

COUNCIL CHAMBERS OF THE CIRCLE,
CAPITAL CITY OF TAHV, KESH

THE SUN BEATING DOWN UPON THE STAINED-GLASS DOME OF THE Circle Chambers painted the forms of all those assembled in a riot of colors. Yet it was not hot in this large room; regulating the temperature was child's play for such masterful users of the Force as the Sith assembled here.

It was an emergency meeting. Even so, formalities were strictly observed; the Sith were nothing if not meticulous. Grand Lord Darish Vol, the leader of the Lost Tribe, had summoned the meeting less than a standard hour earlier. He now sat upon a dais in the very center of the room, elevated above all others, enthroned on his traditional metal-and-glass seat. While there had been sufficient time to don his colorful formal robes, he had not had time to sit and permit his attendants to paint his gaunt, aged face with the vor'shandi swirls and decorations appropriate to the meeting. Vol shifted slightly on his throne, displeased by that knowledge, displeased with the entire situation that had necessitated the meeting in the first place.

His staff of office was stretched over his lap. His claw-like hands closed about it as his aged but still-sharp eyes flitted about the room, noting who was here and who was not, and observing and anticipating the responses of each.

Seated on either side of the Grand Lord were the High Lords. Nine members of the traditional thirteen were here today, a mixture of male and female, Keshiri and human. One, High Lord Sarasu Taalon, would never again be among that number. Taalon was dead, and his death was one of the reasons Vol had called the assembly. Seated in a ring around the dais were the Lords, ranked below the High Lords, and standing behind them were the Sabers.

Several of their number were missing, too. Many were dead. Some . . . well, their status remained to be seen.

Vol could feel the tension in the room; even a non-Force-sensitive could have read the body language. Anger, worry, anticipation, and apprehension were galloping through the Chambers today, even though most present hid it well. Vol drew upon the Force as naturally as breathing in order to regulate his heart rate and the stress-created chemicals that coursed through his body. *This* was how the mind remained clear, even though the heart was, as ever, open to emotions and passion. If it were closed, or unmoved by such things, it would no longer be the heart of a true Sith.

"I tell you, she is a savior!" Lady Sashal was saying. She was petite, her long white hair perfectly coiffed, her purple skin the most pleasing tone of lavender. Her mellifluous voice rang through the room. "Ship obeys her, and was not Ship the—" She stumbled on the choice of words for a moment, then recovered. "—the Sith-created construct who liberated us from the chains of our isolation and ignorance of the galaxy? Ship was the tool we used to further our destiny—to conquer the stars. We are well on our way to doing so!"

"Yes, Lady Sashal, we are," countered High Lord Ivaar Workan. "But it is *we* who shall rule this galaxy, not this stranger."

Although the attractive, graying human male had been a Lord for many years, he was new to his rank of High Lord. Taalon's untimely demise had paved the way for Workan's promotion. Vol had enjoyed watching Workan step into the role as if he had been born to it. While Sith truly trusted no one but themselves and the Force, Vol nonetheless regarded Workan among those who fell on the side of less likely to betray him.

"She is very strong with the dark side," High Lord Takaris Yur offered. "Stronger than anyone we have ever heard of." That was quite a statement, coming from the Master of the Sith Temple. Few on Kesh had as extensive a knowledge of the Sith's past—and now their present as they expanded across the stars—as this deceptively mild, dark-skinned, middle-aged human. Yur had ambition, but, oddly for a Sith, it was largely not personal. His ambitions were for his students. He was content to teach them as best he could, then set them loose on an unsuspecting world, turning his attention to the next generation of Tyros. Yur spoke seldom, but when he did, all listened, if they were wise.

"Stronger than I?" said Vol mildly, his face pleasant, as if he were engaged in idle chitchat on a lovely summer's day.

Yur was unruffled as he turned toward the Grand Lord, bowing as he replied.

"She is an ancient being," he said. "It seems to me foolish not to learn what we can from her." Vol smiled a little; Yur had not actually answered the question.

"One may learn much about a rukaro by standing in its path," Vol continued. "But one might not survive to benefit from that knowledge."

"True," Yur agreed. "Nonetheless, she is useful. Let us suck her dry before discarding the husk. Reports indicate that she still has much knowledge and skill in manipulating the Force to teach us and future generations of the Lost Tribe."

"She is not Sith," said Workan. The scorn in his melodious voice indicated that that single, damning observation should be the end of the debate.

"She is!" Sashal protested.

"Not the way *we* are Sith," Workan continued. "And our way—our culture, our values, our heritage—must be the *only* way if our destiny is to remain pure and unsullied. We risk dooming ourselves by becoming overly reliant on someone not of the Tribe—no matter how powerful she might be."

"Sith take what we want," said Sashal, stepping toward Workan. Vol watched both of them closely, idly wondering if Sashal was issuing a challenge to her superior. It would be foolish. She was nowhere near as powerful as Workan. But sometimes ambition and wisdom did not go hand in hand.

Her full diminutive height was drawn up, and she projected great confidence in the Force. "We will take her, and use her, and discard her when we are done. But for love of the dark side, let us take her first! Listen to High Lord Yur! Think what we can learn! From all that we have heard, she has powers we cannot imagine!"

"From all that we have heard, she is unpredictable and dangerous," countered Workan. "Only a fool rides the uvak he cannot control. I've no desire to continue to sacrifice Sith Sabers and Lords on the altar of aiding Abeloth and furthering her agenda—whatever it might be. Or have you failed to realize that we don't even truly know what that is?"

Vol detected a slight sense of worry and urgency from the figure currently approaching the Circle Chambers. It was Saber Yasvan, her attractive features drawn in a frown of concern.

"Only a fool throws away a weapon that still has use," countered Yur. "Something so ancient—we should string her along and unlock her secrets."

"Our numbers are finite, Lord Yur," Workan said. "At the rate Sith are dying interacting with her, we won't be around to learn very much."

Vol listened as Yasvan whispered in his ear, then nodded and, with a liver-spotted hand, dismissed the Saber.

"Entertaining as this debate has been," he said, "it is time for it to conclude. I have just learned that Ship has made contact with our planetary defenses. Abeloth and the Sith I have sent to accompany her will not be far behind."

They had all known to expect her; it was, indeed, the primary reason the meeting had been called. All eyes turned to him expectantly. What would their Grand Lord decide?

He let them stew. He was old, and few things amused him these days, so he permitted himself to enjoy the moment. At last, he said, "I have heard the arguments for continuing to work closely with her, and the arguments to sever ties. While I confess I am not overly fond of the former, and have made little secret of my opinion, neither do I think it is time for the latter. The best way to win is to cover all angles of the situation. And so Kesh and the Circle of Lords will invite Abeloth to our world. We shall give her a grand welcome, with feasting, and arts, and displays of our proud and powerful culture. And," he added, eyeing them all intently, "we will watch, and learn, and listen. And then we will make our decision as to what is best for the Lost Tribe of Kesh."

Sith Saber Gavar Khai sat in the captain's chair on the bridge of the *Black Wave,* the ChaseMaster frigate that had once belonged to Sarasu Taalon. Filling the viewscreen was the spherical shape of his homeworld—green and brown and blue and lavender. Khai regarded the lush planet with heavy-lidded eyes. For so many years, Kesh had been isolated from the events of the galaxy, and Khai found he had decidedly mixed feelings about returning.

Part of him was glad to be home. As was the case with every member of the Lost Tribe, he had spent his entire life here until a scant two years ago. Deeply embedded in him were love for its beautiful glass sculptures and purple sands, its music and culture, its casual brutality and its orderliness. For more than five thousand standard years, the Tribe had dwelled here, and with no other option, had—as was the Sith way—made the best of it. The ancient vessel *Omen* had crash-landed, and the survivors had set about not merely to exist in this world, but to dominate it. And so they had. They had managed to both embrace the Keshiri, the beautiful native beings of Kesh, and subjugate them. Those who were deserving—strong in the Force and able to adapt to the Sith way of thinking and being—could, with enough will, carve out a place for themselves in this society.

Those who were not Force-users had no such opportunities. They were at the mercy of the ones who ruled. And sometimes, as was the case with Gavar Khai and his wife, there was mercy. Even love.

But most often, there was neither.

Too, those who gambled to increase their standing and power and lost seldom lived long enough to make a second attempt. It was a very controlled society, with precise roles. Everyone knew what was expected of him or her, and knew that in order to change their lot, they would need to be bold, clever, and lucky.

Gavar Khai had been all of those things.

His life on Kesh had been good. While, of course, he had his eye on eventually becoming a Lord—perhaps even a High Lord, if opportunities presented themselves or could be manipulated—he was not discontent with where he was. His wife, though not a Force-user, supported him utterly. She had been faithful and devoted and raised their tremendously promising daughter, Vestara, very well.

And Vestara had been the most precious of all the things that had belonged to Gavar Khai.

Discipline was something every Sith child tasted almost upon emerging from the womb. It was the duty of the parents to mold their children well, otherwise they would be unprepared to claim their proper roles in society. Beatings were the norm, but they were seldom motivated by anger. They were part of the way that Sith parents guided and taught their children. Khai had not looked forward to such aspects of discipline, preferring to explore other methods such as meditating, sparring till exhaustion, and withholding approval.

He had found, to his pleasure, that he had never needed to lay a hand on Vestara in reprimand. She was seemingly born to excel, and had her own drive and ambition such that she did not need his to "encourage" her. Khai, of course, had goals and ambitions for himself.

He had greater ones for his daughter. Or at least, he once had.

His reverie was broken by the sound of the comm beeping, indicating a message from the surface.

"Message from Grand Lord Vol, Saber Khai," said his second in command, Tola Annax, adding quietly under her breath, "Very prompt, very prompt indeed."

"I expected as much, once he received my message," Khai said. "I will speak with him."

A hologram of the wizened Grand Lord appeared. It had been some time since Khai had seen the leader of the Lost Tribe. Had Vol always seemed so fragile, so . . . old? Age was to be respected, for to live to an old age meant a Sith had done something very right indeed. But there was such a thing as *too* old, and those who were too old needed to be put down. Idly, keeping his thoughts well shielded, Khai wondered if the renowned Grand Lord was getting to that point. He saw his white-haired Keshiri second in command staring openly at the hologram; doubtless Annax, with her near obsession for determining weakness, was thinking the same thing.

"Saber Gavar Khai," said Vol, and his voice certainly sounded strong. "I had expected to speak to Abeloth herself."

"She is on Ship at the moment. Do not worry, you will see her when she arrives on Kesh," Khai said smoothly. "She is anxious to create a good first impression."

"I take it that since you are the one speaking to me, she has selected you to replace the late High Lord Taalon in our . . . interactions with her."

"It has not been said specifically, but yes, Abeloth has turned to me since Lord Taalon's death."

"Good, good. Please then assure Abeloth that as she is anxious to create a good first impression, after our people have worked so closely and sacrificed so much for her, we are also desirous that our first meeting go well. To that end, we will need time to prepare for such an august visitor. Say, three days. A parade, showcasing the glory that is the Lost Tribe, and then a masquerade."

Khai knew a trap when he saw one. As did Annax—who quickly busied herself with her controls so as not to look too obvious as she listened in—and the rest of his crew. As traps went, this was blatant. Vol was testing Khai's loyalties. To force Abeloth to wait three full days before being received was to tell her her place. To keep her waiting, as one might a Tyro summoned for interrogation about his studies. Yet Vol would deny such, simply saying that he wanted to make sure everything was just right for their esteemed guest. And with the Sith's love of ceremony and showcasing, the statement had the dubious merit of perhaps even being true.

Vol was waiting for Khai's reaction. He was trying to figure out where the Saber's loyalties lay.

And Khai himself suddenly realized, with a sick jolt, that he himself didn't know.

Abeloth had doubtless sensed the conversation and was monitoring

Khai's presence in the Force. For all he knew about Ship, she also had the ability to monitor the conversation itself. He addressed himself calmly to the man who ostensibly ruled the Lost Tribe of the Sith.

"Abeloth will be disappointed to hear that preparations will take so long," he said, keeping his voice modulated. "She might even see it as an insult." Out of Vol's line of sight, Annax was nodding.

"Well, we wouldn't want that, would we?" said Vol. "As a fine example of a Sith Saber, you will simply have to assure her that this is done out of respect. I trust you will be able to do so."

Slowly, Khai nodded. "I will."

"Excellent. You have always done well by me and the Circle, Khai. I knew you would not fail me now. Give my best to Abeloth. I look forward very much to our meeting. I have heard certain rumors, and am anxious to hear from you how Vestara is performing on our behalf."

The hologram disappeared. Khai leaned back in his chair, rubbing his chin and thinking. He heard the soft chime that indicated an incoming message and was instantly alert.

"Saber Khai," said Annax, "Abeloth wishes to speak with you privately." Her bright eyes were on him, her quick mind doubtless racing two steps ahead, wondering about the outcome of this particular conversation.

Khai nodded. He had expected this, too. "I will receive her in my quarters, then."

A few moments later, he was in the austere captain's quarters of the *Black Wave*. He took a moment and steadied himself for the interview. Settling down at a small desk, he said aloud, "Transmit."

"Patching her through, sir," Annax replied promptly. Idly, he wondered if the Keshiri was eavesdropping. He had expected a holographic appearance, but Abeloth chose to communicate through audio only.

"Saber Khai," she said. Her voice sounded better than it had when they'd made their agreement to work together; stronger, more in command. Less . . . wounded. Khai slammed down that line of thinking at once.

"Abeloth," he said. "I have heard from Lord Vol."

"I know," she said, confirming what he had suspected—that she had sensed the conversation already. "It did not go as well as you had expected."

"Say rather it did not go as well as one could have hoped," Khai corrected.

"I do hope that he is not denying me the chance to visit your world after all," said Abeloth.

"Quite the contrary. He has insisted that Kesh, and primarily Tahv, be granted three days to prepare for your arrival, that the Sith may welcome you as the honored guest you are."

"You suspect he is lying?"

It was a very dangerous game Gavar Khai was playing. Above all else, he wanted to ensure his own personal success—nay, simple survival, if it came to that. He had always been fiercely loyal to his people, but his experiences with Abeloth had also opened his eyes to the vast power she could wield. Ideally, he could bring the two together, but he had to always be aware that conflict could again erupt between Abeloth and the Lost Tribe.

And if that did happen, he needed to make sure he was on the side of the victor.

While lies were useful, sometimes the truth could be even more so. So he told the truth. "I do not think he is lying. It is a cultural tradition to have great celebrations for momentous occasions. There are always parades and parties and so on. And certainly, Lord Vol is very well aware that choosing to ally with you is an extremely important moment for the Sith."

"But three days seems like a long time to ask so apparently honored a guest to wait." There was irritation in her voice, and he could feel it, cold and affronted, in the Force.

"Such preparations do take time," he said. "I do not know what he plans."

And that much, at least, was as true as the sun rising, although Tola Annax probably could give him a list of possible ideas.

"Very well. We shall give Lord Vol his three days. I must admit, I think I will enjoy seeing so elaborate a celebration. It is good to be honored and respected."

"Indeed. It will be a joyous occasion. I have been told that there will be a parade and afterward a masquerade."

A moment, then a chuckle. "A masquerade. How fitting. Yes, I will definitely enjoy this."

"I can safely say it will be unlike anything you have seen before."

"Of course. I am sure so isolated a world must have developed unique traditions." The way she said *isolated* made it sound like *backward.* Khai forced down any hint of resentment at her condescension.

"This is your world, Saber Khai," she continued. "I know you have other family besides your daughter. You will be visiting before the celebration?"

"I am the leader of this flotilla," Khai said. "I had not planned to, no."

"Do," said Abeloth. It was couched as a suggestion. Khai knew it was not. "And any others you think would appreciate the chance to visit should do so, as well. I do not think that I will be tarrying overlong."

"As you wish," said Gavar Khai, wondering, for the hundred thousandth time, just what she meant.

# Chapter Two

KHAI ESTATE, KESH

THE NIGHT WAS BEAUTIFUL. THE MOON WAS HUGE AND FULL, CASTING a silvery blue glow on the land surrounding the Khai estate. Gavar Khai leaned on the balcony of the master suite, naked save for a pair of light, billowy trousers. His black hair was undone from its usual topknot and flowed loosely about his shoulders.

He looked down at his cybernetic arm, lifting it slowly, clenching and unclenching the fist. The technology was excellent. It looked in all respects like a real arm. It had complicated sensors, so that all tactile sensations were replicated. And in many ways, it was superior to a flesh-and-blood arm. Now that he was mastering the use of it, he realized that he would soon become stronger and faster with it than with his real hand. If such were the case, then the "disfigurement" so frowned upon by the Lost Tribe would be recast in the light of an advantage.

But . . . it was still a false hand. And when he had caressed his wife's body with it an hour earlier, her skin had not felt the same.

It was not a flaw—no senseless accident had caused its loss, but rather a fight with one of the most powerful Jedi who had ever lived. And yet, he could not shake the feeling that it should not have happened.

Khai sighed quietly, looking out again over the landscape of rocky hills and stubborn trees that grew, albeit twisted, in the arid environment. Directly below him he heard the pleasant flow of water from a large glass-and-ceramic fountain.

Typically, he found the sound soothing. Now, when he thought of the word *fountain,* all he could recall was the Fountain of the Hutt Ancients on Klatooine. It had been the epitome of arrogance and foolishness for Taalon to want to harvest a piece of the thing. It had led to the unnecessary loss of several members of the Lost Tribe. Normally, such a thing would not concern him. But he could not help but wonder if perhaps, had they had another ship full of Sith, they might have been able to triumph over and properly subdue Abeloth after all, rather than being in the unpleasant position of trying to strike an alliance with her.

Yet . . . this could be a good thing. If she were, indeed, more powerful than the Lost Tribe—

He sensed his wife's wakefulness and concern, heard the soft pad of bare feet as she came up behind him and slipped her arms around his trim waist. Absently he covered one of her hands with his cybernetic one. Her cheek pressed against his back.

"Why does my husband not rest soundly in his own bed?" Lahka asked quietly. "Surely he is not worrying about the event to come."

Gavar did not answer immediately. He sighed, then turned to face his wife and gather her in his arms.

"I am, yes," he confessed. "There is much riding on how things go tomorrow night." He glanced up at the moon and amended his words. "Tonight."

She smiled up at him. Lahka had not a speck of Force sensitivity in her. Normally, that would have made her automatically undeserving of his affections. But Lahka had other extremely worthy qualities. She was intelligent, patient, and knew how to keep secrets. And she was beautiful, as beautiful as any Keshiri woman, though she was human. Even now, well past her youth, her soft smile moved him. She had proven a good mate and mother, and he had missed her.

Her eyes searched his. "You are worried about our daughter," she said.

Gavar tapped her nose lightly. "And you tell people you aren't Force-sensitive."

"I am Gavar-sensitive," she said, humor warm in her voice, "which is perhaps even better."

They had not spoken of Vestara until now, and Gavar found that he yearned to unburden himself of the worry. No one in the galaxy knew Vestara as well as he and Lahka did. Perhaps she could shed some insight.

So standing on the balcony, his arms around his wife, Gavar Khai spoke quietly of the challenges he had set their daughter. Of her success, or possible failure. Of killing High Lord Taalon. Lahka didn't protest, or seem upset in any way. Both her daughter and her mate were powerful dark side users. He was the one best suited to guide Vestara, not she. But Gavar knew she loved them both, and he welcomed the chance to speak freely.

"She loves this Jedi boy?" Lahka asked.

"While he is yet a boy, he is already a Jedi Knight. Their equivalent of a Saber. And yes, I believe she does."

"Do you think she could sway him? He could be a powerful asset to the Tribe, and it sounds like he will treat our daughter properly—with respect and care." Lahka had the correct priorities—first the Tribe, and then their child.

"I fear he might sway *her*. Sometimes I think she is truly my daughter, a fierce and proud Sith, as I have trained her to be. And sometimes I think she is on the verge of betraying all of us."

She gave him another one of her smiles, almost radiant with love. "Not our Vestara. She knows her duty. To the dark side, to the Sith, to the Lost Tribe, to us. Even if she falters, I have faith she will not truly fall from the path."

He pressed his forehead to hers, sighing softly. "I hope you are right," he said. He did not have to elaborate. If Vestara betrayed them, his duty would be to slay her. And Lahka knew it.

Wordlessly, Lahka lifted her mouth to his and kissed him. Her fingers curled around his cybernetic arm, and she led him back into the bedroom.

Gavar left her again once she had fallen asleep, quickly donning his robes and slipping out. He walked the halls of his own home as if he were a stranger, seeing everything with new eyes. Was this truly his glorious home, filled with art and high ceilings and musical instruments? He paused in front of Vestara's room.

He thought of the day that he had knocked on this door, knowing what Vestara did not—that soon she would begin her training at the Temple. He remembered bringing out Muura, telling the puzzled young Keshiri female that her services would no longer be needed.

Muura had known better than to ask for a reference. She had left quietly, after Vestara had departed. He had not been ungenerous; Muura had clothing, and food for several days. And he had alerted one or two of his friends who had daughters that she would be departing. If they were interested in employing her, they would find her. Regardless, Muura's time as a servant in the Khai household had come to its logical and inevitable end, and they both knew it.

Unable to resist, Gavar opened the door and looked into his daughter's room. Lahka had kept it as if the girl had only just left and might one day return, though Khai knew that would never happen save for brief visits.

The windows were closed against the cool night air, but the drapes were open. By the soft light of the moon, Khai could see everything. His gaze wandered to the beautiful glass vases, once filled with flowers; to the overstuffed bed that had not been slept in for a long time; to the dresser and mirror where Muura used to prepare Vestara. It was calm and orderly without being severe.

Here he had embraced his only child as she departed for her destiny; here, he would always see her, her strong body and lovely face adorned with vor'shandi markings, wearing an exquisite dress, standing straight and tall although he knew she was nervous.

It had been so promising a beginning for her . . .

Khai took a long, last look, then quietly closed the door. He trailed his fingers against the smoothly polished stone of the walls as he left the main house. Massive doors opened with a twitch of a finger, and a moment later Gavar Khai was standing outside in the cool night air. He took a deep breath and looked out over his lands. Then, knowing where he needed to go now, he turned to make his way down a winding stone road.

The Khai family was nowhere near the wealthiest on Kesh, but they had done well enough. Vestara would have inherited everything upon her parents' death, and would have become a wealthy and powerful woman. The estate would have made her wealthy; her innate ability and shrewdness would have taken her very far in Sith society.

Would have.

Still could?

Gavar Khai did not know, and this not knowing ate at him, fueled the restlessness that would not let him sleep, even in his own bed next to a devoted wife.

It was a good thing, to be clever enough so that others did not guess one's motives. He had been proud that Vestara had misled the Skywalkers—even the vaunted Luke Skywalker—sufficiently well that she was still in their company. He had been excited at the thought of bringing so talented a Force-user as Ben Skywalker over to the dark side—firmly at the side of a Sith woman.

A Sith woman who had killed a High Lord . . . a High Lord who was becoming something . . . *else*. Had that been treachery, or loyalty?

Was Vestara still playing the game they had arranged?

Was Sith Saber Gavar Khai the father being duped, not Luke Skywalker?

For the life of him, Khai could not tell. He growled softly, following the road down to the stabling area. The stables were, on the exterior, as beautiful and ornate as the great house itself. Off to the side, there was a gated area for riding beasts such as the shumshur and the muntok, and in the center, tall and rectangular, was the aerie. He stood in front of it and flicked a finger, moving the heavy bolt on the great door that kept the uvak confined, and entered.

Vestara was playing not only with her own life and reputation, but with those of her father. Of her very lineage. If she failed to turn Ben Skywalker and enable the defeat of his father, then Gavar Khai would bear the brunt of the reprisals from Lord Vol and the rest of the Circle. And if she actually was swayed by the persuasion of the boy—

"It will not stand," he said aloud.

He stood in the center of the aerie. It was quite dark inside; uvak were diurnal creatures, and enclosing them in a dark space usually put them right to sleep. He had kept the door open, and a small patch of moonlight was the only illumination. Inside were two tall columns, vanishing into the darkness. The roof, now firmly shut, was retracted during the day and the beasts were allowed to fly, within limits; a collar affixed to their legs would emit a painful shock if they drifted too far from home.

There were two uvak in the Khai family. Gavar had one and Vestara, when she was much younger, had honored the family by causing a hatchling to imprint upon her. Tikk, she had named him, for the clacking sound his beak had made as he crawled out of the shell. Gavar had watched the hatching, had watched his daughter exert her will to make the creature come to her instead of to another Sith youngling.

She'd loved Tikk. He had known, as she did not, what might happen to the beast when Vestara had chosen him to bear her to the Temple for her apprentice training.

When Vestara had arrived at the Temple, her new Master, Lady Rhea, had appeared about to give an order to have Tikk slain. Vestara reacted properly—by not protesting. Lady Rhea, pleased, had spared the beast.

It was an old tradition, a sort of hazing, never spoken of to those who had not already experienced it. Khai had known to expect it, and when he had been asked afterward if he wished to recover Tikk from the Temple, he'd realized his daughter had passed her first test.

He gazed up at the column that served Tikk for a nest. Khai used the Force to enhance his ability to see in the dark; from this vantage point, Tikk seemed to be slumbering deeply. With a slight tweak of the Force, Khai leapt upward, landing softly beside the uvak. Tikk was curled up beak-to-tail, his wings folded over his body like a blanket.

Khai watched him for a moment, then glanced at the other pillar. His mount was also asleep. Khai extended his real, living hand to the other uvak and gently, unobtrusively, guided the creature into a slumber from which she would not awaken for several hours. Satisfied, he reached out to pet Tikk's long, sinuous neck, sending calm to the creature. Tikk stirred slightly, opened one eye, and made a rumbling, purring sound before closing the eye and falling even more deeply asleep.

Tikk had been a loyal mount, serving Vestara well, as she had served the Sith well.

Gavar Khai no longer knew if she did so or not.

There was a *snap-hiss* as he lit the lightsaber. A soft red glow bathed Tikk's sleeping features. A heartbeat later the uvak's head toppled down to land with a thud and a slight crunch on the stone floor. Tikk's eyes were still closed.

The death had been accomplished with no pain to the creature, and Khai was glad of it. Tikk had done nothing to warrant suffering. Khai extinguished the lightsaber, nodded to himself, and Force-dropped to land gently.

He could sleep now.

# Chapter Three

TAHV, KESH

TAHV HAD NOT SEEN SUCH A CELEBRATION SINCE THE SITH HAD FIRST departed its soil to conquer the stars.

The famed City of Glass, as it had become known through the centuries, had been active day and night ever since Lord Vol had announced that a great celebration would be thrown to honor Abeloth, the Friend of the Lost Tribe. Crafters had used the Force, bribery, coercion, and threats to fashion commemorative fireglobes to encircle the entire city. Each fireglobe—a glass-and-metal sphere that contained something illuminating, be it a candle, a glow stick, or a naturally luminous living creature—was unique. Nothing was mass-produced, and each advertised its maker in some fashion: with a particular design, a unique coloration, or, more crassly but possibly more effectively, a name etched into a pane. A few of the glassmakers had quite literally worked their apprentices and journeymen to death.

Special shikkars had been crafted for the occasion, too. There would be much maneuvering out of the public eye for a preferred position for everyone in Tahv, be they craftspeople, politicians, or ordinary Sith citizens—although no one in a Sith society would ever consider him- or herself ordinary.

Delicacies were brought in from across the planet and from other worlds. More than a few vessels met with unfortunate accidents, and their competitors expressed sympathy while rushing to fill the void with their own products. Those who had a noted touch with their brushes were in high demand for the most beautiful, most elegant vor'shandi skin paintings, and tailors scrambled to meet the sudden need for "the most gorgeous robe on Kesh, do you understand?"

Money was changing hands; reputations rose and fell hourly. And the Sith thrived on it.

At last, all was in readiness.

Three standard years earlier, there had been a large, open stretch of land to the north of Tahv. Neither conducive to growing crops nor attractive enough to build houses on, the area had proved ideal for expanding into a port for space-traveling vessels—a thing the Sith Tribe had never before needed, and which had arisen haphazardly in different stages. Work had begun shortly after the arrival of Ship, the mysterious, seemingly sentient Sith training vessel that was older than any of them could imagine. Under Ship's guidance, the Lost Tribe had created a rudimentary port and soon had vessels that needed room to dock.

Now the landing area was filled with ChaseMaster frigates, the honored Ship who had started it all, and throngs of Sith. Most were simply eager to welcome their loved ones home, if only for a brief visit. Some were there to analyze behavior, actions, and feelings in the Force and report back to their Masters. Some were there with orders to follow and assassinate.

All were there to see Abeloth, who had arrived in Ship's strange innards, and who alone did not choose to land. Ship hovered about fifteen meters in the air, a spherical shape with two pointed extensions above and below it, and two bat-like, membranous wings extending to either side. In its center, looking like a hideous eye, was a circular screen.

Abeloth waited, of course, until the last possible moment; until after every frigate had been emptied of its crew, until the last celebratory note had been played or sung, until Lord Vol had stood on a hovering dais in splendid, heavy formal robes for an uncomfortably long period of time. On the ground, standing next to his wife, Gavar Khai watched, a slight frown on his face.

At last, slowly, like a creature awakening from slumber, Ship's "eye" grew transparent, and then opened.

Abeloth floated out.

She did not need a dais, and wore no heavy robes. She wore, indeed, seemingly very little, which somehow managed to cover her more than modestly; a diaphanous draping that caught the breeze and fluttered just so. She had chosen her golden-haired female form, with wise gray eyes, and a slight smile was on her lips. She lifted her arms and tilted her head, and the breeze played with her flowing fair locks as she floated gently to the ground. Khai glanced at Vol. He neither sensed nor saw discomfort in the old man as he rode the dais to the ground next to Abeloth, but he knew that Vol had to be annoyed, at the very least.

It was going to be a very interesting day.

The two powerful Masters of the dark side landed almost simultaneously, a meter away from each other. Abeloth waved to the crowds, who were applauding enthusiastically, few of them as aware as Khai was of the tension between the two leaders. Vol, as the host, made the first gesture, moving toward Abeloth with hands outstretched. She turned pleasantly, smiling, and clasped his hands in her own.

"For far too long," Vol said, his voice carrying easily, "the Lost Tribe has slumbered on Kesh. While this is and will always be our true home, it is but one of many, for soon worlds uncountable shall be ours. The last three years have seen staggering changes. And today marks perhaps the most significant one since Ship first appeared in the skies of Kesh, informing us of the galaxy that awaited us and assisting us in freeing ourselves from the confines, however pleasant, of our world."

He turned his sharp face with its prominent, beak-like nose again to Abeloth, smiling with what seemed like genuine warmth. "On this day, we, the Lost Tribe, welcome one who was once our enemy. We are powerful and strong, and so is our honored guest. By allying with Abeloth today, we lay the foundation for a brighter future for our younglings. The universe is vast. But soon it will be ours—the Lost Tribe's and Abeloth's. Our enemies shall fall beneath us or flee in terror, and the Sith, with our dear friend by our side, will rule everything that catches our eye. I ask you, my fellow Tribe members—join me in welcoming . . . *Abeloth*!"

He suddenly dropped Abeloth's hands and raised his own in an inviting gesture. From every direction, birds suddenly emerged in a flurry of color and rapidly beating wings. Each of them carried a small flower, and they dipped and darted over the crowd, releasing their colorful, sweet-smelling gifts.

Khai recognized the flower. It was called the Sith Victory. It attracted not flying insects to pollinate it, but ground insects. It emitted the sweetest scent of its brief life not when it bloomed on the bush, but when it was pinched hard, or better yet crushed under one's foot.

Laughing, Lahka caught three of the lovely yellow flowers, crushed them, and sniffed happily at the scent.

The flower was commonly known, and everyone was destroying the blooms all around Khai. Abeloth looked a trifle puzzled, lifting a blossom to her delicate nose and shaking her head at the lack of scent. Khai watched as Vol instructed her, and she gave a slow smile, pinching the flower with exaggerated vigor.

A shudder of apprehension shivered through Gavar Khai, and he wondered if the Sith Victory flower was aptly or poorly named.

The parade that followed was spectacular. All the returning Sith and, of course, the guest of honor rode through the ancient, twining streets of Tahv as dusk fell. Some rode the great, gentle beasts of burden called shumshurs; others preferred to sit atop hoversleighs of some sort. The beautiful fireglobes, each as unique as a snowflake, hovered along the path, lighting the way for the twining line of celebrants.

Abeloth and Lord Vol sat together on a particularly exquisite hoversleigh. Carved from vosso wood in the shape of a bird of prey and decorated with precious gems and stones, it moved like a living thing. It turned its head this way and that, clever technology implanted so that its eyes blinked, and occasionally it opened its beak to emit a sharp cry.

"How enchanting," Abeloth had said when she saw it. "Your craftspeople are quite deft. Perhaps I shall take one such vehicle for myself, as a souvenir."

"Something similar, perhaps," Vol had said, giving her a smile that was both indulgent and predatory. "But nothing quite as lovely as this one, I fear. The competition among artisans here in Tahv is legendarily fierce and violent. I regret to inform you that Master Dekta Amon, the undisputed expert artisan who fashioned this lovely hoversleigh, seems to have disappeared."

She had turned, arching a blond brow. "Indeed? Most unfortunate."

"Not for those in possession of his few masterpieces," Vol had said.

She had regarded him steadily for a moment, unblinking. "Well, then," she said, giving him an equally charming and equally false smile, "I might simply have to have yours."

They had laughed. Onlookers not sensitive to the Force would have noticed nothing. Those who were Force-sensitive would have detected only good cheer. Lord Vol knew they both would have been dead wrong.

Abeloth seemed to be enjoying herself. Vol watched her with the sharpness of the bird of prey upon whose likeness he rode. Lord Darish Vol was no casual observer of others. He had not climbed as high as he had, nor lived as long as he had, without being superior to any who would challenge him. He had lost count of the assassination attempts and political ploys that had been thrown his way over the last eight-plus decades. But he had learned from each one. And so he played the good, benevolent host smoothly while taking stock of all he saw.

Abeloth was very attractive, and most appealing. All present, even the throngs of observers crowding the capital city, knew that she was able to shift her shape. It was a fascinating ability, and Abeloth obviously enjoyed giving demonstrations of it. There were three appearances she seemed to prefer: two human, and one Keshiri. All were female, though Vol was well aware that she could also impersonate a male. She cycled through them as the need arose, judging her audience well: pretty but natural-featured Girl with Brown Hair, cultured and lovely Fair-Haired Woman, and a Keshiri who took even Lord

Vol's breath away, aged as he was and aware—thanks to the reports—of her true appearance.

Night fell while the parade slowly moved through Tahv. The artificial lights that normally kept the city illuminated had been ordered to stay off, so that the thousands of fireglobes might sparkle all the brighter. As the parade reached its termination point—it had taken a serpentine path from the north side of Tahv to the south—the participants emerged to find a bevy of small, floating disks. Each disk would safely lift two or three dozen beings high into the air, and each had a small staff of two or three Sith Sabers controlling it.

Vol Force-leapt a not-insignificant distance from the hoversleigh to the disk, then turned to Abeloth. "Come join me," he said, "for the finale of the parade. And then . . . our masquerade."

Abeloth smiled prettily, then floated—she did not even need to leap—to stand beside him. As she drifted through the air, her features changed. The hair grew dark, coarser, and curlier, and her face broadened slightly. Only her eyes seemed the same: gray and unfathomable. He smiled at her, acknowledging her shapeshifting with a nod, and, spreading his arms, lifted the dais upward.

Tahv was now laid out before them, the fireglobes outlining every one of its streets and adorning the tops of the walls that encircled the city. It was a view that might inspire awe in even the most jaded, Vol thought. He felt a quick stab of pride in his homeworld and his people—both the Lost Tribe and the purity of its line, and those Keshiri who had earned their places as powerful Sith.

This woman beside him, if woman she could even indeed be called, was a tool to help them to greater glory. And the instant she outlived her usefulness—well, then she would have outlived everything.

A sudden sparkle of lights shattered his reverie as the fireworks display began. Abeloth watched, strangely enraptured, clapping her hands like a little girl as the pyrotechnics—all directed by the Force to form pleasing shapes and designs—exploded all around her.

Vol found it a peculiarly disturbing image.

The masquerade would be the final event of the busy day. The next day, Abeloth and the Circle would have a formal meeting in the Circle

Chambers, where the finer points of their alliance would be negotiated. Tonight, however, was ostensibly for enjoyment, entertainment, playful deception, and frivolity; in reality for continued observation, assessment, duplicity, and plotting.

In other words, it was a quintessentially Sith-like event.

It would be held in the great hall of the Sith Temple. As was most of the Temple, it was cavernous and dark. But unlike the majority of the spaces frequented by the students, which tended to be austere and forbidding, this hall, which saw large gatherings of a usually celebratory or otherwise pleasant nature—graduations and theatrical productions such as tonight's—was somewhat more congenial. The walls were still looming rock, carved from the mountain itself, but there were portraits of prominent former students on the walls, marble mosaics inlaid in the floor, and illumination that was more festive than practical.

The guests were powerful Sith, human and Keshiri, male and female, all at the top of their fields. They were present because Vol wished to either reward them or observe them. The Lost Tribe generally eschewed droids, even though many had come their way in the last few years, regarding their skills and talents as inferior to those of living beings. Most droids had been dismantled, their parts and pieces utilized to improve the weapons and vessels that were deemed so important in the larger picture of galactic Sith conquest. Therefore, human and Keshiri servants, clad in masks but not in costumes, wandered the floor offering beverages and tidbits.

Those Sith who had received an invitation to what would perhaps be the most coveted occasion for years to come had gone all-out with their costumes, spending small fortunes and making tailors and artisans work without cease for the last three days. The result was an overabundance of finery, with so much jewelry, rare metals, and ornate glass masks on display that the eye grew tired of observing.

Lord Vol had anticipated as much. He wished his own choice of costume to send a message; one clear, but not blatant. He would not make an appearance until his oh-so-honored guest did. A full hour after the masquerade had begun, Sith Saber Gavar Khai was announced. He did not bring his wife; she had not been invited. From a private room, Lord Vol watched as Khai entered the room.

"Well, well," he said, "I see that Khai remembers his mythology."

Gavar Khai stood in black from head to toe; not unusual for one who always preferred traditional Sith robes. But this time he wore a cloak of black feathers, each one sporting a jewel, and his mask was a sharp beak.

"The Dark Tuash of Alanciar," said Ivaar Workan, standing beside Vol. "An interesting choice."

"The question is, is the Harbinger's news for us, or Abeloth?" mused Vol.

There were two Tuash'aa of Alanciar in Keshiri folklore, a Dark One and a Bright One. The Tuash'aa were giant birds, believed to bring messages about the coming of the Destructors. The Bright Tuash brought word that the Destructors had either been defeated, or else had chosen not to trouble a world. The Dark Tuash—

"I imagine," drawled Workan, "we will find out. And look—his lovely lady is not far behind him."

Workan did not refer to Lahka. He referred to Abeloth. Vol sighed.

"She does like to make an entrance," Vol said, not without a trace of admiration.

Abeloth did not simply make an entrance. She made the perfect entrance. The doors were flung open, and wind rushed in, quite literally ruffling Khai's cape feathers and disturbing the costumes of several other Sith in the immediate vicinity. The "wind" took on form and color, swirling until it took the shape of a woman seemingly made of ice and air, glittering and beautiful, larger than an ordinary human female, regal and commanding. Her hair was gold, her gown silver, her mask the purest, glistening, icy white.

She hovered for a minute, acknowledging the applause, and floated gently as a feather to the stone floor.

"Fallanassi illusion," Vol said at once.

"She learns," Ivaar Workan replied in his pleasant voice. His face was calm, benevolent appearing as the two Sith watched Abeloth.

"She does. But then, so do I. Come," he said, rising. "Let us go greet our honored guest."

And so it was, when the hour came to welcome Abeloth to the masquerade, Lord Darish Vol, leader of the Lost Tribe of Sith, greeted Abeloth in long, plain brown and tan robes, with only a black mask imperfectly hiding his recognizable features.

The crowd parted, murmuring uncertainly at first as they recognized his ensemble, then breaking into appreciative laughter and applause that swelled until the entire room was cheering. Vol turned, waving and smiling slightly, giving them a bow.

"Lord Vol," said Abeloth, her voice artificially warm. "What an amusing costume . . . though no one would ever mistake you for a Jedi."

*Nor would anyone mistake you for an ally,* Vol thought, but he kept his musings flawlessly concealed. He smiled amiably, quirked a finger, and a goblet of something purple and rich-smelling floated into his hand.

"I trust you find it as amusing as I do. When you reach my age, amusement is a precious and rare thing. Saber Khai. A pleasure to see you. An interesting choice of costume."

"The Dark Tuash of Alanciar was my daughter's favorite story of the Return," Khai said.

"You dress to honor her." Another flick of the finger, and goblets floated to both Abeloth and Khai. "I take it, then, that she is performing well for us still."

"So well that for a short time, even I was uncertain as to which side she was on," Khai said. Truth; Vol could sense that much. But then, those of the Khai line had always been masters of hiding their feelings.

"No longer, though?" Vol sipped the tangy beverage, quirking a white eyebrow. "Even though she murdered High Lord Taalon?"

The room seemed to become very still. Khai smiled thinly. "She did what she thought best for the Tribe," Khai said. "Sarasu Taalon was . . . rapidly becoming an unfit leader. He would soon have been of no use to anyone."

Abeloth sighed. "Such a pity."

"We have dissolved our alliance with the Jedi"—Khai said the word as if it left a bad taste in his mouth—"and have allied with a far superior being. Vestara will bring us the Skywalkers, with the young one eating out of her hand."

A hint of something—then it was gone. Khai was not lying, not exactly, but not all was as he painted it.

"Good, good, this pleases me, all of it," Vol said, smiling benignly at both of them. "Abeloth—you had the pleasure of working with

High Lord Sarasu Taalon, and our esteemed Saber Gavar Khai. There are others I wish to introduce to you."

He beckoned them forward, seemingly trusting and proud of the Lords and High Lords as he introduced them: the petite and pretty Lady Sashal, the poised and distinguished Workan, and "our true host, High Lord Takaris Yur. He is the master of this Temple, in charge of guiding our younglings properly along the path of the dark side."

Abeloth smiled beatifically at them all, though there was a flash—just the merest fraction of an instant—when Vol sensed something so alien that even he felt unnerved. "Such a pleasure. I trust, High Lord Yur, you are proud of the younglings you have trained."

"Indeed," Yur said, inclining his head. "We are the purest possible Sith lineage."

"Vestara was one of your students?"

"One of my finest."

A smile, so sweet it would drown the insect that flew to it for sustenance. "She appears to be excelling at her current assignment."

"A teacher could hope for no more."

"No," Abeloth said. "To see the younglings excel . . . to know they are devoted to the principles one instills in them . . ." Again the strange flicker that sent a chill down Vol's spine. "Well . . . one could die happy then, couldn't one?"

And Vol realized that, suddenly, Yur saw what he had.

"Your timing is excellent," Vol said, changing the subject. "The masque is just about to begin."

She froze, turning slowly toward him. "I thought a masquerade was a sort of costume party," she said.

"It is! But a masque itself is a play. Theater. It is all about pretending to be something you are not." He smiled pleasantly. "If you will accompany me, I assure you I have the best seat in the house reserved for you."

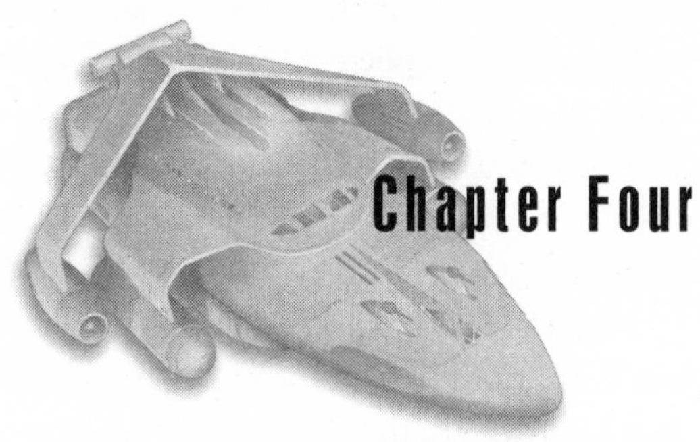

# Chapter Four

SEVERAL MOMENTS LATER VOL, ABELOTH, YUR, WORKAN, SASHAL, AND a handful of others who were no doubt patting themselves on the back at being selected for the honor sat in an elaborate box, peering down at the stage. Others took their seats, the vast room filled now with the eager murmuring of an anticipatory crowd.

The room went dark. A moment later there was a bright light on the stage, and a perfect, albeit much smaller, replica of the *Omen* hovered there, about to crash precariously into a perfect, albeit much smaller, representation of the Takara mountain range. Some of the most attractive Keshiri whom Vol had ever seen played their own ancestors. They exaggerated their primitiveness, wearing scandalously little in the way of clothing made of animal hides as they pointed up at the Sith vessel and exclaimed, "What is it? It is far too large for any bird or uvak!"

Vol did not watch the play. It was broad, stylized, and while the actors were likely perfectly adequate, it was a piece of propaganda. He watched instead the being for whom the play had been written.

Abeloth gazed at the stage, her golden brows lowered in a frown, her lovely mouth thinned. At last, she turned to Vol and asked, "This is a piece of your mythology, is it not? Like Saber Khai's black bird?"

"No," Vol replied. "It is a slice of our real history. This play will show how the *Omen,* filled with our ancestors, came to crash on Kesh, and how the Lost Tribe was welcomed as the Protectors."

Her voice, mien, and presence in the Force revealed nothing. "Protectors?"

"Surely you know the story," he said. "When the *Omen* first arrived on Kesh, our forebears were welcomed and regarded almost as divine beings. You see, the Keshiri believed that—" He broke off and leaned forward, addressing Khai. "Gavar, I can't believe you failed to enlighten our guest on the single most important part of our history!"

Caught off-guard, Khai still managed to shield his feelings. "It is our present and future I chose to discuss with Abeloth," he said.

"And yet here you are, dressed as a Tuash!" Vol clucked his tongue disapprovingly. "For shame!" He returned his attention to Abeloth.

"I suppose it falls to me. You see, the Keshiri had an ancient myth about magical and powerful beings called the Protectors. The Protectors would defend and save the Keshiri when the feared Destructors eventually returned. The Destructors, according to ancient Keshiri myth, periodically descend on inhabited worlds to wipe out civilization and return all beings to their natural, primitive states."

"A legend," Abeloth said. "As accurate as a giant bird, black or white, foretelling safety or doom."

Vol shrugged. "Perhaps. Perhaps not. We have conducted our own research. Such a planetwide catastrophe has been visited upon this world at least once."

"You disappoint me, Lord Vol," Abeloth said. "I had not thought you so susceptible to stories told by primitive beings. The events you speak of are natural disasters, nothing more."

"Be that as it may, I think you know the point of why the original Sith embraced it."

She smiled slowly. "Indeed. It would have been foolish not to exploit such an opportunity. One might think that the Keshiri would have resented your ancestors for perpetrating such a deception." She turned to Lady Sashal. "Lady Sashal. You were lied to and taken advantage of."

Sashal gave her a slight smile. "Our ancestors were," she said. "Not I. While the humans of the Lost Tribe and the Keshiri are different races, no one has ever been excluded from achieving high rank if she can prove herself worthy. You yourself worked with Sarasu Taalon. It is merit, not genetics, that enables one to rise or fall in our culture."

"Yes," said Abeloth, "I did work with Taalon." Vol noticed she left it at that. Sashal apparently did not notice, and continued.

"The arrival of the Lost Tribe helped my people. They brought civilization—medicine, technology, art. And now both Keshiri and the Tribe stand together as Sith, poised not only to guard against the return of the Destructors, if they do exist, but to do far more—to conquer the galaxy. It is our destiny. And you can be part of that."

Abeloth did not bother to hide her amusement, and Lord Vol shook his head inwardly at the delicious irony. Lady Sashal was the staunchest advocate Abeloth had in the Circle. And yet she had, apparently obliviously, just treated this powerful being with condescension. No, Lady Sashal might have her political machinations going full force, but she was foolish. He would not discount her, of course. Vol never discounted his enemies until they were dead. Sashal might be stupid . . . but stupid beings could still be very dangerous.

He realized he actually might be grateful to the petite Keshiri female. Sashal had distracted Abeloth, who was clearly enjoying toying with her, and he could observe this potential enemy more readily.

So very often, he mused, stupid people, though dangerous, were useful.

## LORD VOL'S ESTATE

Four hours later, there was a meeting. It was not held in the Circle Chambers, but rather in Lord Vol's private residence, and he was the only one physically present. He did not make the amateur's mistake of underestimating Abeloth, nor the power she might wield over certain members of the Tribe who had once been sent to capture her and instead had brokered an alliance.

Vol was the single most powerful individual on the planet. He had also amassed more than a fair amount of wealth over the years of his rise, because he had observed early on that often wealth was an asset to obtaining power. He did not, however, accumulate it for himself. Sarasu Taalon might have lusted after beautiful objects or beings, but Vol saw such things only as stepping-stones to tightening his control and solidifying his influence. His estate was lavish and lovely, his public rooms subtly speaking of his wealth and fine taste, but his private rooms were as bare as the apprentice quarters of the Sith Temple.

He sat now in a chair that was comfortable but simple, and he was surrounded by five holograms. Of all the number of the Circle, these were the only ones he truly trusted.

Well, he amended as he settled down with a cup of something hot to warm his old bones, trusted as much as the Grand High Lord of the Lost Tribe of Sith *could* trust.

Workan, of course. Yur—as neutral as any being could be and still walk the dark side path. Jesko Umarn and Ysadria Kaladris—lower in rank but rising swiftly, hungry for power and recognition and wise enough to ally with the one who could give these to them. And Sammul Sharsa, an older human woman, the widow of a former Lord; she had been chosen to step into his position after his recent—and, unusually, natural—death. They had had two children, one of whom was an artisan, the other a Saber.

"So," Vol said without preamble, sipping the steaming beverage. "Tell me your thoughts on this evening."

They did. He listened, interrupting each as they spoke in turn only with questions for clarification.

Some of them shared his opinions. Some did not, and he respected those opinions as well. He had not risen to this position—and stayed for so long, almost unchallenged—without understanding that dissenting opinions were often the most valuable.

It was Workan who brought up Vol's greatest concern. "I am unsure about Gavar Khai," he said. "Per your request, I have spoken with some of his compatriots. They have expressed concern over the girl Vestara's true loyalty, and fear that therefore Khai's own loyalty might be compromised."

"Few dote on a child as openly as Khai did Vestara," said Sharsa. She, apparently, did not have undue difficulty with overly doting upon her children.

"Vestara Khai was chosen by Ship," Yur countered. "Many more Sith than just her parents expected great things of her."

The usage of the past tense did not escape Vol. "We will deal with the issue of Vestara Khai's treachery or service later," Vol said. "Abeloth and Gavar Khai's connection with her is the pressing matter. Kaladris—you were the one who debriefed our returning Tribe members. Give one or two the duty of keeping an eye on Khai and reporting back. It may be the father, not the daughter, who is turning traitor."

There were more discussions, and plans, and then at last it was time for sleep. Vol would never admit it, but he tired more easily the older he grew. More and more, he found himself needing to take a few moments to utilize the Force to refresh himself. If only one could completely renew an old body, he mused. But he had to settle for knowing that his age was still more an advantage than a liability.

Part of his before-bed routine was meditation. Tonight he eased himself down on a simple woven mat located in a corner of the bedchamber. On the mat was a single candle in a glass holder. Vol made the most minute of movements with his index finger, and the candle flared to life.

He concentrated on the flickering little flame and reviewed the evening, settling things in his mind so that his dreaming self could focus on gnawing on the problems. He went back over the last few days in the same manner, reviewing the information he had gleaned from speaking with several of the Sith who had returned with Abeloth. Not all of them were undecided, as Gavar Khai seemed to be. Some of them had astonishing insights and information, and had been eager to inform their Grand Lord of all they knew in return for earning his favor.

And some things they knew were fascinating indeed. Like someone methodically planting seeds in fertile ground, Vol recalled all that had transpired in the past few days, gently tucking the seeds of information into the good soil of his subconscious and patting down gently. At last, tired from the busy few days and that night's event, he rose, sighing as his bones emitted audible creaks, and slipped between the comfortable sheets.

He was glad there were at least a few hours before the meeting with

Abeloth in the morning. Trances were certainly useful, but natural, simple rest was sometimes even better.

Sleep found him quickly.

And so did something else.

He stood, alone, on the lavender shores of the ocean, lightsaber held in one gnarled hand. The heat was oppressive, the sun beating down on him more strongly than it did even in the height of summer. His robes were heavy, far too heavy, and he became aware immediately that this was much more than a simple dream.

She stood facing him, wearing her lovely Keshiri visage like the mask she had worn tonight. But this time, she was deliberately permitting the mask to slip.

Vol had seen much violence, deceit, ugliness, and brutality in his day. He had seen, and sometimes committed, deeds such as evisceration of the body and torture of the mind through the power of the dark side. He had seen bodies explode into tiny fragments, watched powerfully intelligent people reduced to gibbering idiots when their minds were destroyed thought by thought.

And he shrank back in horror now at the monstrosity revealed to him.

Before him was a nightmare. Her hair was long, twining tendrils of hideousness, her eyes sunken and yet bright as tiny stars, her mouth widening, widening, until it split her face. She laughed, the tendrils reaching out both physically and in the Force.

"Silly Vol," she said. "To imagine, even for a moment, that anything human could even conceive of the vastness that is Abeloth, let alone trap me for your own tiny-minded purposes. Now you shall die, and your world shall become mine. I shall be unto them Protector and Destructor both, and there is nothing that you or any of your little friends can do to stop me."

The tendrils were on him now, slithering into his mouth, his ears, his nose, caressing in a strangely appealing manner even as he cringed back in loathing.

It was a dream, he knew, but it was more than a dream as well. And even in such an in-between place, Vol knew what he had to do. It terrified him, but the thought of being destroyed without a fight by this vile *thing* terrified him even worse.

He had to dive inside that mind.

He took a precious second to wrap the Force around him like a blanket, then unshielded his mind and opened it to Abeloth.

In her arrogant glee at the ambush she had performed, she was reckless. She surged forward, violating his mind, unaware that this was precisely what Vol wanted. She had given him entrance, and he wasted not a heartbeat in opening up to the ugliness that was within. Like a thief with the law on his heels, Vol plundered swiftly, with no care for delicacy or of discovery. And he found unexpected riches.

Anguish. Loss that ripped and tore at the heart of all that was Abeloth. Betrayal. Need—*need!*—for companionship, for love, for someone, anyone, any*thing,* to adore her and to never, ever leave. To *stay* with her forever . . .

*—Don't leave me don't leave me don't leave me—*

Something that was part of her, that she had loved with all that was in her, was gone, gone beyond finding again, and someone would pay, and she would be loved and idolized and worshipped, it was right, it was what should be, what would be—

He felt her astonishment, and then fury, and knew he was discovered. The tendrils were no longer coyly teasing and caressing. They were violent and brutal now, wrapping about his throat, invading his body. He resisted and went on the attack. There was a wound, visible as something black and bloody and infected, in what passed for a soul or a heart of this monster. And he went right for it.

*No one loves you. You are ugly, and disgusting, and if you ever thought anyone did care for you, you were tricked and lied to, and they laughed at your gullibility.*

A blast of Force anger buffeted him, but he rooted himself against it and continued.

*You will never be loved. You will never be adored or cherished. Only feared and hated. And there is nothing you can do, no words you can speak, no one you can become to change that. Luke Skywalker was appalled at what you were, when he truly saw you. He follows you, not as a young gallant, oh no, but to kill you and put the universe out of its misery.*

She convulsed, writhing in pain in the heart of the Force, reacting to his relentless attack on her wounded area as if he were ripping at an infected cut in the physical world. Her attack on him changed from a desire to harm to a desire to escape. Elation filled Vol. He only hoped he could survive long enough to deal the killing blow.

*You live causing revulsion, you will die that way. You will die* now—

He threw everything he had into the attack, slamming his Force self into the psychic, oozing wound as if he were punching a lacerated torso.

*NO!*

Her pain exploded and hurled him back, releasing him, but causing the most exquisite agony Vol had ever experienced to race through every part of his being.

Vol surged forward out of the dream so quickly that he hurled himself from his bed and landed hard on the floor, where he lay gasping, weak, so weak, sweat-soaked and terrified. He—used to manipulating objects in the Force, leaping great distances, crushing things with a thought—had not the strength of a new-hatched uvak. It was an effort to lift his head, to push himself up off the floor, and the muscles quivered from that simple strain.

Grunting, he dragged himself to a seated position, muscles trembling. It would have to do—rising, let alone walking, would take several more minutes. He summoned his last drop of energy and sent forth an urgent demand to Revar, the young Sith Saber who attended him. Four seconds later Revar burst into the room, lightsaber illuminating the darkness and the younger man's worried face with an eerie red glow.

"My lord," Revar cried, lighting the room with a gesture at the same time he deactivated the weapon, "what happened?" He rushed and eased the old man up onto the bed.

Vol opened his mouth, but could not speak. Finally, he rasped, "Abeloth . . ."

"She was here?"

Vol shook his head. "No. In . . . dream . . ." He knew that he sounded senile, but he also knew that there were marks on his body that Revar and others could see. "My ship—take me to my ship. And awaken the Lords," he said, alarmed at how feeble he sounded. "And the defenses—the city . . . she is going to . . . to make the city pay . . ."

Revar wasted no more time on questions. Using the Force, he lifted his Master as gently as possible, then, holding on to him, Revar raced, with Force-augmented speed, toward the hangar atop Vol's estate. There was always a small personal vessel at the ready; one never knew when the Grand Lord might wish to depart on short notice.

As they fled, Vol began to weep. Revar was disconcerted, but not so much that he did not pay close attention to the mumbled words.

"Nothing can hold her . . . Fool to think I could use her . . . What *is* she? . . . Mistake . . . By the dark, the greatest mistake I have ever made . . ."

Abeloth had been wandering the City of Glass when she had attacked Vol. She had been enjoying the calmness and prettiness of the place illuminated by the fireglobes, and had been idly thinking about what she might do with it once it came under her control. Should she make this her base, from which to rule the galaxy? It was quaint and charming. Or should she give it to those who had served her well, as a reward?

Too, the attack on Grand Lord Vol had been in her mind the moment Ship had begun to head for Kesh. She had wanted to strike here on this world, from the center of this place of which he was so proud; to show Vol and the others that nothing they held as precious was safe from her. She knew he was a powerful Force-user and strong with the dark side. And that, she could have handled.

But he had tricked her, had used a technique that his antithesis had used on her not so long before. He had learned the uprooting technique of the Theran Listeners, as had the despised Skywalker, and used it with even less care than that Jedi had.

He had—

Abeloth screamed from a mouth that slashed her face in two. Unable to retain her form, unable even to *notice* that she had not retained her form, she thrashed and howled as tentacles erupted from her torso and her face shifted like melting wax. Her anguish used the Force as a weapon, as she had so often before, but this time she was barely aware that she was releasing nearly inconceivable amounts of Force energy upon a city that was completely unprepared for it.

There were several dozen beings within immediate range, some sleeping quietly in their beds. Most were with their families.

They imploded. Farther away, others awoke in agony as their bodies were turned inside out and chunks were ripped from their bones.

The entire city was attacked by a wind filled with glass shards, each a shikkar driven by a single purpose—to hurt anyone, anything, living inside the City of Glass. They were the Lost Tribe—they would suffer, all of them, as their leader had made her suffer.

The shards melted as they pierced flesh, spreading white-hot, painful death. The buildings, made of metal and glass, dripped slowly toward the ground, smothering those unfortunate enough to be dwelling inside them.

None of it harmed Abeloth, though she would not have noticed if it had. She barely noticed when she was lifted from the street where she lay convulsing up into the night air, and a large shape that looked like nothing so much as an angry orange eye sped toward her.

## ABOARD THE *BLACK WAVE*

Gavar Khai had chosen to spend the night on the *Black Wave* rather than with his wife. He had informed her of this prior to departing for the masquerade; as a good Sith wife she accepted that her husband had his reasons, and obeyed.

So it was that Gavar Khai survived long enough to become a widower.

Abeloth's agony wrenched him out of a sound sleep, and he heard the angry klaxon of an alert blaring through the ship. He threw on his robes and raced to the bridge, to find his crew, some only partially dressed, all bleary-eyed and terrified, in their seats.

"Saber Khai!" yelped Annax. "We felt Abeloth—she is—"

And then all of them fell silent. Except for those who screamed. A wave of pain swept over them; no, not a *wave*, nothing so weak as that. A tsunami, comprising the anguish and fear and physical torment of thousands of beings.

It was both nauseating and delicious. Khai had never experienced anything like this. Fighting to keep his eyes opened, he stared at the viewscreen. A moment earlier it had shown Tahv, quiet, peaceful, outlined by the normal lights of a city at sleep. Now flames were engulfing some areas of the city and—

"Melting," he murmured. Abeloth was melting the city. He shook himself quickly. Recovering his composure, he snapped, "What's the status of the landing area north of Tahv?"

Her fingers flew. "Some damage, but . . ."

He knew without being told. Those ships that were still functional were going to attack the frigates, believing they had sided with Abeloth.

Had they?

"They're taking off," he said. "Evasive action. Where's Ship?"

He felt it, cold, focused. *Abeloth is safe. We must depart immediately,* Ship said.

Khai hesitated. He knew he stood at a crossroads. He could choose to be a proud and loyal member of the Lost Tribe of the Sith—what he had been all his life. He could side with Grand Lord Vol, defend his world, his culture . . . his wife. He could order the fleet to turn on Abeloth right now. All of them together might possibly be able to destroy Ship. Whether it would destroy Abeloth was a complete, and terrifying, unknown. Or they could depart, firing as they went, and cast their lot in with her.

"Sir?" prodded Annax. "They're close to being within firing range. The other frigates are demanding orders. What do you wish us to do?"

He made his choice.

*We will come,* he thought, and felt Ship agree.

*Follow me.* Then the strange construct that was Ship withdrew from his mind, and Khai felt suddenly empty.

"Shields up. We stand with Abeloth," he said. "Ship—"

"—is sending coordinates," blurted Annax as numbers crawled over her screen.

"Follow them! Tell all vessels to retreat!"

The *Black Wave* suddenly rocked as she was fired upon. Khai glanced at the small screen in the captain's chair and saw two small blips representing ChaseMaster frigates flare, and then vanish.

"Return fire!" he ordered. At once the frigate dived, firing, and Khai had the satisfaction of seeing one of the attacking vessels blown into small bits. His faint smile faded somewhat. Who had been in that vessel? Someone he knew, doubtless; there were not so many Sith in the Lost Tribe fleet that he would not at least recognize the name.

They were the enemy now. He closed the door on any regret he might have felt, however fleeting. "Attention, Abeloth's fleet," he said, and there was no going back from that statement. "We are under attack by the Lost Tribe of the Sith. Coordinates to our next destination have been downloaded to each of your vessels. We will rendezvous there. Any vessel that does not retreat to those coordinates, and does not immediately attack those from Kesh who have now chosen to become our adversaries, will be deemed a traitor and fired upon accordingly."

He closed the channel. "Tola, is everyone changing course?"

"Negative, sir, the *Dark Dancer* is still stationary."

"Hail them." She did so. "*Black Wave* to *Dark Dancer,* why are you not moving to the coordinates I have given you?"

Silence.

"Destroy it," Khai ordered. "They have chosen poorly."

She glanced up at him. "Sir, the *Dark Dancer* suffered a hit. They may not be choosing to disobey. The damage could have rendered them unable to move, or affected their communications systems."

"Then that is their bad fortune, and the Force is not with them this day," Khai replied. "I cannot take the risk of anyone under my command turning against us. Obey my order, Annax, or else I may deem you a traitor, as well."

Her eyes widened slightly, then she squared her broad shoulders. "Yes, Captain."

Gavar Khai watched, cold and unflinching, as the *Dark Dancer* went from being an intact, if damaged, vessel, to being nothing more than flotsam, jetsam, and pieces of once-living flesh.

The ship rocked again. "Annax, make that jump to hyperspace," Khai growled.

"Trying, sir, but I—"

"Do not *try. Do* it."

Her fingers flew. A third explosion made the *Black Wave* tremble, and he could see the console light up with reports of casualties from all over the ship.

And then, blessedly, the white pricks of light that were stars stretched out, elongated into lines, and they were gone.

# Chapter Five

GAVAR KHAI SAGGED AGAINST THE BACK OF THE COMMAND CHAIR, closing his eyes for a moment.

They had escaped. He winced slightly as he realized he had used the word to describe leaving his homeworld—the place that had birthed and trained him.

"Saber Khai?"

He didn't answer Tola Annax at once, as another realization shook him to his core. He would never become a Lord now. He had just severed all ties to everything he had ever known, and he was now a traitor. He swallowed, reaching into the Force to compose himself and find some measure of calm.

"Yes, Annax?"

"We won't be able to go back, will we?" Her normally sharp eyes were distant, her broad shoulders set, as if she were already carving out her future actions.

"No, we will not," he said, as if he himself had not wrestled with the same feelings that were now clearly occupying Tola. "We have made our choice. We were sent to subdue Abeloth, but she has proven too strong for us. We returned to Kesh in good faith. Lord Vol decided to attack Abeloth alone, for whatever reason, and failed. When we left with her, we sealed our fate. Are you having second thoughts?"

That got her attention, and she snapped out of her reverie with a little start. "No, sir, of course not, sir!"

It was too quick a reply to be sincere. Khai knew, as he knew Tola Annax knew, that the word from the Tribe was that Abeloth had attacked Vol. But he decided to turn the identity of the aggressor around. Better for his crew to think that Vol had violated the agreement and suffered for it, while the innocent Abeloth moved on to greater things. Better to think they had chosen rightly, because even if anyone felt they had not, there was nothing to be done now. The fabled City of Glass lay in molten ruins, its Grand Lord crippled, though not killed. Nothing, no abasement, no apology, nothing could return anyone in this fleet to favor in the Lost Tribe.

Ever.

He felt a faint brush of approval in the back of his mind—Abeloth sanctioned the revision of history.

"The true essence of the Lost Tribe will be preserved," Khai said. "And as allies of Abeloth, we are much closer to achieving our destiny of ruling this galaxy."

"Of course, sir. I am in complete agreement with you. Sometimes, the useless chaff must be forced away if the seed is to grow."

Annax's voice was sincere and strong. Khai didn't believe her for a moment.

"What now, sir?"

Khai realized he didn't know, but he had to take action, some kind, any kind, or else he would be deemed weak by his own second in command.

"Hail Ship and tell him I would speak with our mistress in my quarters," he said firmly. It was the first time he had used the term, but it felt appropriate. Abeloth needed to believe that all of them were on her side. Of course, all of them were. They had to be. And even as he rationalized it coldly, Khai found himself glad of the events. There was something . . . *pure* about Abeloth, purer than the elaborate masques and traditions of the Lost Tribe. This was no glamour, no false dazzlement he was experiencing. He had seen Abeloth at her best and worst, had fought against her and with her. He would never have imagined events would turn this way but . . . he was not unhappy that they had.

Annax nodded brusquely, her fingers flying as she went about her task.

Khai opened his mind to the Force, calmly content in his thoughts, so that Abeloth would sense him immediately and know the gist of his intentions. She was, of course, ensconced in Ship once more, cradled in its strange embrace while she healed.

He felt her mental touch immediately upon entering his quarters, even before he heard her voice over the comm. It was, as before, strangely slurred.

"You wish to know my plans," she said.

"As much as you care to share with me, that I may best serve you."

He felt tired humor from her. "So, you are firmly on my side now, are you not?"

"You know I am. Any bridges that I once had are surely well and truly burned."

"Good. You will not be a Lord of the Lost Tribe, Gavar Khai. You will be something greater. Something infinitely more important. I need someone by my side I can trust."

"I would be that being, Mistress."

"Your ambition pleases me. See that your wisdom is as true, and there is nothing we cannot accomplish."

"The Lost Tribe thought too small," Khai said. "I can see that now." It wasn't the complete truth, but it was true enough so that he could believe the words as he spoke them. "You are far greater than anything Lord Vol could become, and I am not a fool, to blindly follow a leader simply because I have always done so."

"You are right in your expanding vision," she said. "And you are smarter than Taalon. You see without having to be altered."

Despite himself, Khai shuddered.

"My path—I am not sure. It is possible that your daughter has revealed the location of Kesh to the Skywalkers by now."

Khai shifted uneasily. "I still do not believe my daughter is a traitor," he said.

"Be that as it may, it is possible," Abeloth said, a touch sternly. "Do not attempt to lie to me and deny *that.*"

"I . . . cannot," Khai said simply.

"And having allied with the Skywalkers before, the Lost Tribe, with so-called Grand Lord Vol smarting from his defeat, might attempt to do so again. We must not allow ourselves to be traced. I . . . need time to recover, and to decide the next course of action. Lead them on a merry chase, Gavar Khai."

"I shall do so," he said. He thought about how such an order would be received. Tola Annax would enjoy it, at least. Despite her eccentricities, there was a sense of play about her. Annax would be amused at the thought of leading a Sith fleet to random places, simply on a whim, if only so she could occupy herself with pondering what might happen, and how best to counteract anything negative. Amusement was a good thing for morale, he thought. Soon enough, Abeloth would recover. Khai took a breath to speak, then paused.

"What is it?"

"If I may be so bold . . . what are your plans concerning the Jedi queen?" he asked. "Might not that be our next step? Our initial attempt to assassinate Tenel Ka did not meet with success, this is true, but we are closer than we have been at establishing the true identity of this female. Perhaps we could continue to—"

"No." It was a flat, firm, almost sullen response, and brooked no argument. "That pursuit is of the past. That was Sarasu Taalon's fantasy and fear, and it need not concern us now."

Khai knew when he had been put in his place, but some instinct prompted him to protest. "But surely, a Jedi queen would—"

"A moment ago, you accused the Lost Tribe of thinking too small," Abeloth said tartly. "You are in danger of tumbling back into that way of thinking, Khai. It is easy and comfortable and familiar, but it will not get you what you crave. When my plans are finally put into motion, if there is indeed a Jedi queen still alive, she will be as a small buzzing insect compared with the power and greatness I shall wield."

Khai's heart suddenly skipped a beat. He could almost feel his mind opening. He was awash in sudden joy and fear and awe, and he felt sweat break out on his forehead. How unspeakably audacious he and the other Sith had been, to think of taming and breaking Abeloth. If she thought of this powerful Jedi queen that Taalon had been so adamant about destroying as little more than a buzzing insect, what had she thought of them? Of him? She could destroy him with a thought. And yet, she needed them . . . wished them . . . *him* . . . to be a part of her inevitable triumph.

And it *was* inevitable, he realized. Overcome with this revelation, he sat down hard on the bed and, with an effort, reined in his emotions.

He knew she knew all that he was feeling. And yet, she chose to move forward with the conversation courteously, as if his revelation had not happened.

"Besides, I do not wish to run even the slightest risk that my plans will be revealed. If the effort to kill Tenel Ka is traced back to me, it could hamper my effectiveness. No, that fear died with Taalon. There is a greater destiny, a truer one. The Sith will rule, Gavar Khai, rest assured. But you will rule alongside *me*."

ABOARD SHIP

Abeloth sat huddled in Ship's interior. She had not revealed to Khai or anyone just how badly wounded she had been by the attack on Kesh. Vol had much of the power of Skywalker, combined with experience, and it had been a devastating encounter.

She had harmed him, too, though. Almost killed him. And she had destroyed his precious city, unleashing her outrage and fury on the site of her shame.

In the end, though, she would recover. And she would be stronger for the experience. In the meantime, she would absorb and learn all she could.

Abeloth had turned Ship into a circular display of images, asking him to show her newsvids from everywhere he could think of. And so, simultaneously, Abeloth beheld dozens of images. She learned of slave revolts, of murders, of coups. She learned of wars, and treaties, and natural disasters. She wanted to know everything she possibly could about this galaxy that, once she recovered, she would dominate and bend to her will.

She felt a flicker of amusement, watching the reports about the Fountain of the Ancients, knowing as she did exactly what had transpired on Klatooine. She gazed, unmoved, at the horror of a tsunami on a world that had fully a quarter of its population swallowed by the devastating wave, observing the grief and carnage as she watched famine turn bodies into living skeletons.

She watched holodramas, interviews—

Interviews . . .

Abeloth instructed Ship to pause, to focus on one of the scenes. The others faded out, their brightly moving images replaced by the dull, old-blood color of Ship's interior.

The speaker was a Chevin, an elder of his species, conducting an interview in what appeared to be a newsvid. But his kindly, wise, large face was not what had attracted her attention. She had been galvanized by the being he was interviewing, a female of another species with which Abeloth was unfamiliar. As she watched, her eyes unblinking, Abeloth inquired of Ship as to the nature of this species.

Ship responded by filling her mind with images and history, which Abeloth absorbed at once even while listening to the interview.

The female was of a species called the Jessar. Their planet, Qaras, had recently undergone the upheaval of a revolution. The Jessar had risen up and overthrown their masters, a species called the Minyavish, who had enslaved them for thousands of years. As such things went, while it was not exactly a bloodless coup, it was nonetheless remarkably civilized and constrained. The images flashed in Abeloth's mind at lightspeed, of peaceful protests, one single strike in the night on the seat of power that resulted in only a few dozen casualties, a new government that forbade retaliation against the Minyavish even as it joyfully celebrated the dream of freedom.

And this female was the heart and mind of the entire affair.

Her name was Rokari Kem. Upon initial perusal, she did not look like the leader of millions who led a rebellion to topple a reign of a thousand years. Rokari Kem was slightly built, humanoid, with elongated limbs and a tranquil demeanor. Her skin was a lovely shade of blue, her hair—long and straight and shiny, falling almost to her hips—blue-green and woven with colorful ribbons. While she listened to the question from the Chevin interviewer, Kem appeared almost languid, so still was she as she concentrated. And then she spoke.

"But you see, Perre," Kem said, her large green eyes wide as she leaned forward and gestured with her three-fingered hands, "words *are* important. In and of themselves, they are simply noises, or symbols etched on stone or in the sand!"

"So you *are* censoring free speech, as the Minyavish government in exile has stated?" questioned the Chevin.

She looked sad rather than angry, and shook her head. "No. Because we respect words far too much. My people have a long tradition of never speaking anything that is untrue, as you may know."

"That seems—hard to believe," the Chevin—Perre Needmo, well-known holonews star—said, his eyes kind even as he expressed his dubiousness. "Deception seems to be a part of every being, in some form or another, whether it be intentional or not."

Rokari Kem smiled, her great green eyes crinkling, her small pert nose upturned. "We do not even have a word for it in our language. If words cannot be trusted, what then? All we believe in spins into chaos. The Jessar creation myth tells us that with the naming of things, they came into being, and the Jessar were charged with never violating the creative power of the word."

"Rokari—"

She waved her hand, smiling. "Please—call me Roki. Everyone does."

"Roki, then. Let me ask about your Silence oath," he said. "I've heard about this. Slaves who were planning to escape never lied about their intentions. Instead they stayed silent, even when they were beaten to death. Is that right?"

She nodded sadly. "Even when it might mean the deaths of themselves or others, they never spoke what was not. They simply chose not to speak at all. Some Minyavish understood this, and were merciful to their slaves. Others were not. And it is this history, this—" She struggled for words. "*This* is why I have insisted that the Minyavish depart our world. There is too long a history of hate, of violence, between our peoples."

"Some would argue that it is their world, too," said Perre Needmo.

"It is," she said at once. "It is both our worlds. But we have only ever shared Qaras as masters and slaves. The Jessar do not know how to be other than slaves when interacting with the Minyavish. And with those who enslaved us still on our world . . ." She sighed and shook her head, the colorful ribbons catching the lights of the studio.

"No, Perre. We must be alone, to discover who we are when our heads are not bowed. And we cannot do that while our former oppressors are still on Qaras. Nor can the Minyavish truly wash themselves clean of the stain of what they have done while they still gaze upon us."

Her voice had grown stronger, though it was still melodious. Abeloth watched raptly, not wanting to take her eyes off Roki Kem.

"This is the best thing for both Minyavish and Jessar. For us both to discover how to heal. For them to depart the world they know as masters, and find a world where they can simply be themselves. And as for us, the Jessar need to know how to be on Qaras as a true, active part of it—not as property."

Her voice broke on the last word.

"You seem like such a peaceful being, Roki," Perre Needmo continued. "Yet you condoned violence."

"I did," she replied unflinchingly. "But the coup came only after every other peaceful method of obtaining our freedom had been attempted. It was, in the end, our last resort. To this day, I regret that it had to come to that. We did the best we could to avoid bloodshed. I have met with the families of the Minyavish who died in the coup, and told them how deeply we regretted what we had to do."

That seemed to catch Needmo off-guard. He blinked his large eyes and took a moment to clear his throat. "How . . . was that received?"

"Not well, I fear. And I understand. But I do not lie, and so, eventually, I believe with all my heart that they, too, will understand." She smiled, gently, her green eyes warm with hope. "When they see the peace that must come with having no one to dominate, to own and dictate to—they will understand that their loved ones died for a precious cause."

"I must say, if anyone can make them believe that, I think that would be you."

She laughed—a sound light and bright as sunlight, sweet as water flowing. "I would say, rather, I would not *make* them believe—I simply have absolute trust that they will."

"Now, the latest I have heard is that you are to be departing for Coruscant to join the Senate of the Galactic Alliance, is that correct?" Needmo asked.

"Very true. I'll be departing Qaras soon."

"It seems to me your people will miss you greatly," Needmo continued. "Some say that you are the heart of this new order."

She smiled, her face softly radiant. "Oh, no, I should hate to be that. My entire philosophy rejects this. Everyone has something special, something truly unique, to contribute. I had what was needed at the time it was needed, nothing more or less. Those who stood by me for so many years are as able as I am to guide my people. I do not say *lead*—simply guide."

"It will be very interesting indeed to see what you bring to the Senate, Rokari Kem. I would say a breath of fresh air, but that would be an understatement. Thank you so much for being with us here on *The Perre Needmo Newshour*. We'll close out this segment with a long shot of the celebrations still going on in Qaras. For those of us who do not understand Jessaran, I will say that the song's refrain is this: 'Peace, welcome, Roki Kem is your mother. Come, children, come, come home.'"

It was nearly twilight on the world, Abeloth saw, and there was no cheering, no wild celebrating—simply dancing, if you could call it that.

Other leaders might be idolized, worshipped, adored.

Roki Kem . . . was *loved*.

*Peace, welcome, Roki Kem is your mother. Come, children, come, come home . . .*

# Chapter Six

OFFICES OF THE CHIEF OF STATE, CORUSCANT

IT WOULD, ACTING JOINT CHIEF OF STATE OF THE GALACTIC ALLIANCE Wynn Dorvan vowed, be a calm, productive, and organized meeting.

He realized even as the thought formed that it was likely to be doomed within the first five minutes. Little was calm, productive, and organized these days, other than Wynn Dorvan himself.

The recent Jedi coup that had overthrown and imprisoned Admiral Natasi Daala had also led to his unsought and frankly undesired promotion. Alongside Master Saba Sebatyne and Senator Haydnat Treen, Dorvan was one of three who had the cumbersome title of Acting Joint Chief of State. Thus far, it had worked surprisingly well, which was a good thing considering how much remained to be properly sorted out. The planet of Coruscant alone had more than enough needs to attend to, having been rattled by the unexpected transition of power, peaceful though it was, right in its heart. The ramifications of that event were still rippling throughout the entire Galactic Alliance.

One would think that this might be enough of a whirlwind of "things to deal with right now" issues for one term. Dorvan had discovered the hard way that one would be wrong. The recent flood of revolutions taking place across the galaxy was a positive step, of course. Dorvan was pleased to see slavery, an abominable institution no matter what sort of spin a government might want to put on it, cease on so many worlds. What was less positive was the chaos that inevitably followed in the wake of such a profound change.

Some of the uprisings had been extremely violent, and the "governments" that sprang up were little better than the ones they replaced—occasionally worse. Much worse. Centuries, sometimes millennia, of oppression had rendered many former slaves thirsty for revenge, and the reports of atrocities that were coming in sometimes made his assistant, the extremely sensitive-natured Twi'lek Desha Lor, very upset. Dorvan was slightly more jaded than the younger female, but he found that even he could be haunted by nightmares of what he had learned.

Other uprisings had been less destructive in terms of lost lives or property damage, but were no less of an upheaval. The change turned a world topsy-turvy, no matter how positive a change it was.

Too, with all these new governments being set up, there was a flood of applications to the Senate as worlds that had been denied because of the practice of slavery suddenly found themselves meeting the criteria for acceptance. And while that was largely the Senate's purview, thankfully, Dorvan still had to be involved. Everyone seemed to need his full attention, right this moment, urgently.

It was all quite wearying.

He closed the door to his office and strode down the hall to the meeting room, a small case full of datapads in one hand. His pet chitlik, Pocket, moved expertly from his shoulder to the spot for which she was named and curled up. Absently, Dorvan reached up a hand and gently patted the small, warm lump. He knew that most people considered his affection for the little marsupial to be either an eccentricity or an affectation. He didn't much care. Pocket was the ideal companion for someone in his position—mild-tempered, undemanding, and comforting.

And trained to use a litter box—also of vast importance.

Desha Lor was there, smiling brightly at the assembled beings. She wasn't like Dorvan—not in the slightest—but he was wise enough to realize that that wasn't necessarily a bad thing. Despite his initial misgivings when she had originally been assigned to him, and his irritation at what seemed to be a hypersensitive personality combined with hopeless naïveté, he'd come to value what she brought to the table. She'd learned to manage her reactions to injustices and tragedies without losing her personality, and that sweetness had given Dorvan a more appealing "face" in the eyes of the public. He relied on her instincts when it came to dealing with people, and she hadn't steered him wrong. And when his workload had more than quadrupled in the last few weeks, she had stepped in and quietly, almost unobtrusively, begun to manage—and manage well—things that did not need his immediate attention. Besides, Pocket cooed when Desha petted her.

Other familiar faces greeted him. Former GA Chief of State and Princess Leia Organa Solo, Jedi Knight, subbing for Saba Sebatyne. The always cheerful and astute Senator from Kuat, Haydnat Treen, the third member of the "triumvirate" currently governing the Galactic Alliance. Representing the active military were the steady and reliable Gavin Darklighter, commander of the Galactic Alliance Marines; General Merratt Jaxton, large, square-jawed, square-bodied Chief of Starfighter Command; Admiral Sallinor Parova, acting naval commander in Admiral Bwua'tu's continued absence, and Bwua'tu's Bith aide-de-camp Rynog Asokaji, who was always either here taking notes for his comatose boss or else at his bedside.

Present also for the first time in a long while was the recently recalled chief of staff of the GA Army, General Stavin Thaal, so tall and powerfully built that one might have mistaken him for a Chev. With his physique and sheer size, buzz-cropped gray hair, tanned skin, and watery, intense blue eyes, he would have been striking even without the thick scar that ran the length of his entire throat. Some years earlier, an assassin had slashed Thaal's neck, leaving him alive but unable to speak with his own voice. Now a deep, cold droid voice issued from a device implanted in his throat when he had anything to say. It was unnerving, and Dorvan rather suspected that Thaal enjoyed the reaction he got.

Also in attendance were two well-known figures serving in a thus-far purely advisory capacity: Tycho Celchu and Carlist Rieekan. Both men had white hair, although General Rieekan had several years on the other man. Both had even temperaments and were known for thinking things through before speaking. And both were unquestioningly devoted to the Galactic Alliance, as well as having good connections with the Jedi.

All in all, it was a selection of decent beings. Dorvan nodded at those assembled, taking off his coat—gently so as not to disturb the sleeping chitlik—and hanging it on the back of his chair. He nodded his thanks to Desha as she brought him a cup of caf.

"Thank you all for attending," he said. "We've got to stop meeting like this."

A ripple of amusement went around the room. "No, we really do," Dorvan said, completely serious. "The frequency of these so-called emergency meetings needs to slow dramatically."

"Well, they'd hardly be called emergency meetings if we could predict them, now would they?" said Treen.

"If *everything* is an emergency, then *nothing* becomes an emergency. The Galactic Alliance is beyond being spread extremely thin, and I am most uncomfortable with that thought. We must prioritize, or else something that will turn out to be the most important thing of all will never be noticed."

There was unhappy murmuring. "Well, then," said Jaxton, "what do you propose we do?"

"We focus," Dorvan said. "And we get down to business right now." He thought he saw a small smile curve Leia's lips. Whether it was approval or amusement, he didn't know. He liked and respected Jedi Solo, and valued her input and support. While Dorvan was well aware that she was present largely because of her connection with the Jedi, he was nonetheless grateful that he had someone to consult who had been in the same position in which he now found himself. Nothing against Saba Sebatyne, but there had been moments when her unfamiliarity with politics—and politicians—had frustrated all three parties involved.

Dorvan reached for the pile of 'pads Desha had neatly arranged at his seat, took a bracing pull of unsweetened caf, and picked up the first one.

"Today," he said, "we have fourteen different worlds applying for membership in the Galactic Alliance. Let's begin with B'nish and its representative to the Senate, Kameron Suldar."

B'nish was one of those planets that, like something kept on the highest shelf of a seldom-opened cabinet, was there, but was not particularly noticed or thought about much. It had come forward only recently with its application to join the GA. B'nish had supported slavery, but nothing too egregious—or too forward-thinking—and, inspired by the uprisings on Blaudu Sextus and Klatooine, had decided that the time was right to end the institution and move toward becoming more active in galactic affairs. What little the GA had learned about Kameron Suldar painted the human male as pleasant and easy to work with, and nobody could summon much enthusiasm one way or another. The upshot was that if no one had any objection and things looked promising, B'nish would be permitted to join the GA.

And so it went. Dorvan was determined to get through all of them. They were listed in the order in which they had submitted their formal application. Sometimes, he noticed, the difference was minimal. Planet Number Fifteen to submit, Aloxor, had missed being Planet Number Fourteen by eighteen and a half standard seconds. The tower of data cards, which seemed to teeter rather precariously on his left, consisted only of those that dealt with the Galactic Alliance application. There was an entirely *separate* pile on his desk, which Desha would retrieve once this portion of the meeting was completed, that dealt with the Senate. And there was another pile after that.

Normally his bureaucratic heart would beat faster at the process, but there was simply so much, and it was all so important, Dorvan could not help but feel that he would be shortchanging *someone* in the end. That, or missing something important as he had warned, which was worse.

With the compartmentalizing ability that was one of his strengths, Dorvan mentally folded up his worries and tucked them neatly into a corner of his brain for later attention.

Consensus was reached fairly quickly on Xilxash. It was a small, backrocket world, notable largely for its agricultural contributions, particularly a succulent fruit called brul, which was all the rage in the best Coruscanti restaurants. The new government had toppled the old fairly easily; it seemed that most of the current "masters" of Xilxash felt that they would benefit more from having slaves as contributing citizens who could be taxed rather than as property that cost money. They offered nothing odious in their proposal and much that was positive.

"The fact that I'm very fond of brul has nothing whatsoever to do with my approval of their application," said Dorvan, with one of his rare expressions of humor. Everyone grinned, and the motion to accept the application passed unanimously.

Dorvan picked up the next data card and grimaced inwardly. This would probably need a second cup of caf all on its own.

"Klatooine," he said, and everyone fidgeted. "We've all heard the holonews on this one. Their recent liberation was highly controversial. Jedi Solo, you and Captain Solo were on Klatooine very recently. Can you share your insights into the current atmosphere there?"

Leia nodded. Elegant streaks of silver ran through her rich brown hair, making her look wise and dignified without detracting an iota from her beauty.

"As I am sure all of you know, this was a world that had willingly enslaved its population to the Hutts for twenty-five millennia. The treaty, known as the Treaty of Vontor, stipulated that the Klatooinians would serve the Hutts if the Hutts would protect their most sacred site, the Fountain of the Hutt Ancients." Leia looked around, making eye contact with those assembled. "It seems the Sith accidentally did something of a good deed. They violated the fountain to get a sample of the glassine structure called wintrium, and because the Hutts did not act in time to prevent the blasphemy, despite an official ruling that the Hutts did all they could do, emotions won out and the Klatooinians rebelled. They have taken to calling that attack and the riots that overturned the treaty the Violation and Liberation. Unused as they were to governing themselves, Captain Solo, and Queen Mother Tenel Ka of Hapes, and I were asked in to assist them."

"According to your report," Dorvan said, consulting it as he spoke, "the Klatooinians seemed to have a difficult time of it."

It was, as was often typical of Dorvan, an understatement. In addition to the Klatooinians unexpectedly being forced to deal with their sudden freedom, peace talks recently held on their world had been violently disrupted by an assassination attempt on the Hapan queen, Tenel Ka.

"They did, and they are far from having a peaceful, well-run government. But they are on their way, and I believe that they can contribute a great deal once they can get past their rocky start."

"I assume, then, that whoever they are choosing to represent them is among the more . . ." Tycho Celchu almost physically searched for the appropriate word. " . . . civilized of the Klatooinians? Perhaps one of their Elder Governors?"

"Unfortunately," Leia said, "the members of the Klatooinian Elder Governors were deemed to be too out of touch to truly represent the new spirit of Klatooine."

"I trust they have come to no harm?" Treen asked.

"No, they have not. The Klatooinians respect their elders far too much. The chancellor and the governors have been removed from all positions of power, but they have not been harmed or even imprisoned, despite what some of the more impulsive of the populace refer to as 'collaboration' with the Hutts."

Glances were exchanged. As expected, the military representatives—Jaxton, Thaal, and Parova—seemed wary and skeptical, but many other heads were nodding. Dorvan was relieved to hear what Leia had to say. A realist, but neither a pessimist nor an idealist, he had no illusions that abolition of slavery would always be a happy and pleasant transaction. Violence and chaos were more the norm than peaceful transitions of power, so any instance of a populace showing restraint toward a governing body associated with the "masters" was always welcome. Particularly from the Klatooinians, a species not exactly known for gentleness and pacifism.

"That's a very positive sign," Dorvan said. "You think they can build on this?"

"I do," Leia said firmly. "They are interested in taking their place in the Galactic Alliance. We have much that we can share with them and teach them, and they have a great deal to offer in return."

"If they can calm their riled populace," put in Darklighter. Leia nodded.

"Jedi Solo, you've been a diplomat from your youth, and I think everyone around this table respects your opinion. If you think we should admit them into the GA now, that is sufficient for me," Dorvan said. Most of the other heads nodded. "Now, who is the current government of Klatooine putting forth for representation in the Senate?"

Leia calmly pressed a button, and a hologram appeared in the center of the table. It depicted a particularly gruff-looking Klatooinian, who stooped despite a clearly powerful build and had a glower on his canine face. He sported scars on what little olive-green skin was visible beneath his long robe. Elegant and simple, the robe contrasted vividly with the veritable armory of weapons he wore about his person.

Dorvan raised an eyebrow. "Padnel Ovin?" he said, sounding slightly incredulous. "The leader of a terrorist organization?"

"Han and I got to know him very well during our time on Klatooine," Leia said calmly. "And yes, the Sapience Defense Front, or Ovin's Sand Panthers as they were known informally, *were* terrorists . . . or freedom fighters, depending on how one looks at it. But let's take a look at the actual history of the Sand Panthers. Grunel Ovin had ideals for his organization, and he enforced them. The money came from donations from former slaves or enemies of the Hutts and, admittedly, some piracy against their masters." She gave Rieekan a look. "Was the Rebel Alliance any different forty years ago, Carlist?"

He gave her a wry smile. Rather than answering, he simply waved her to continue.

"The targets were limited to shipping, corporations that traded in goods manufactured or otherwise supplied by those enslaved to the Hutts, and the military resources that protected those corporations. That was it. Civilian targets were strictly off-limits."

"What about the civilians who had the bad luck to simply be employed by those corporations?" said Parova.

Leia regarded the admiral evenly. "Everyone sitting at this table understands the concept of collateral damage and acceptable losses. With so many millennia of slavery bearing down on their people, the Sand Panthers still did all they could within their power to minimize civilian casualties. Make no mistake, this was a war."

"Be all that as it may, Jedi Solo," said Dorvan, trying to bring things back on track, "the duty before this group now is to determine if Klatooine should officially join the Galactic Alliance. As you said, you have met Padnel. What is your opinion?"

"He's a brave being, as his brother was, and knows how to inspire those who follow him."

"He seems rather . . . martial," said Jaxton, who ought to know. "An odd one to represent his people in peacetime."

"He is respected by his people, and if we agree that Klatooine is deserving of membership, he is their choice to represent that world to the Senate. I believe his heart and his passions are in the right place. He wants to do right by his people, even if that means learning an entirely new way to go about it."

"The Klatooinians have thrown off the bonds of slavery that have lasted twenty-five thousand years," Dorvan said. "They have won the right to run their world as they see fit, within the restrictions of Galactic Alliance membership. If they have chosen to send Padnel Ovin to represent them, we shall welcome him as we would welcome any other duly elected Senator." He eyed Leia and asked, "He was duly elected according to law?"

Leia nodded.

"I wonder if Klatooine *is* actually ready to formally become part of the GA," Rieekan said. All heads turned to him, listening. He leaned forward, his hands frail and liver-spotted but his eyes alert and intent. "If they're not, granting them membership could be a very negative thing for all involved. It would be much harder for them if we are forced to end their membership than if we take our time in granting it."

"I can understand your concern," Leia said. "But in a way . . . this new freedom they have . . . it's something they've been working toward for twenty-five thousand years."

"Then they can wait to get it right," Rieekan continued.

"No, sir," Leia said firmly to the man she had once served under. "The formal membership will tell the Klatooinians that after so long believing themselves only worthy to serve the Hutts, they have the right to come to the table with others. To sit down and have their voices heard by a body they respect. If we deny them that right based on nothing more than our opinion rather than looking at the facts, then this moment, this opportunity, unique in their history, will be lost."

"Jedi Solo," Dorvan said quietly, his eyes more intense than usual as he regarded her, "you have the finely honed instincts of a politician and a diplomat. You have years of experience. And you have the Force. In your opinion, are the Klatooinians ready for the challenges that being part of the Galactic Alliance will offer them? Particularly, do you think this former warlord is ready to sit down and solve problems with conversations and insights over a cup of caf rather than with weapons?"

Leia did not reply immediately, and Dorvan had not expected her to. She sank back thoughtfully, her eyes unfocused, her lips pursed. After a moment, she nodded firmly.

"I do believe it. He is certainly rough around the edges. But he loves his people and will learn to do what is right for them." A smile curved her lips. "Although he seems fonder of arguing for argument's sake than most."

"He should do just fine in the Senate then," Dorvan said drily. "If Klatooine continues to behave within our laws, it is welcome. Any further objections?"

There were none. Even though she was a Jedi, and even though not all agreed with her politics or her actions from time to time, everyone present respected Leia for the service she had given throughout her entire life. Her certainty was enough for them.

For now.

"Moving on," Dorvan said, taking the next datapad. He smiled slightly. "Well, this conversation should go a bit more quickly. Next up for membership is Qaras, and as all of us have heard by now they are submitting Rokari Kem to be their Senator."

"Qaras does have its share of difficulties to overcome, but at least they have her going for them," Darklighter said.

"It's a world divided, though," Tycho said. "I feel a bit bad for the Minyavish. By all accounts, they were not unduly violent toward the Jessar, and yet Kem is forcing exile on them. They've gone from being lords and masters to not even being welcome on their own planet."

"The government is apparently working with the Minyavish to help them relocate," Gavin said. "And frankly . . . I can't blame the Jessar for not wanting them around." He looked over at Dorvan. "What information do we have about how this transfer of power is really working?"

In other words, mused Dorvan, what do our spies have to say about it? "It does seem that all is as it appears," he said. "It is indeed a world divided . . . but both leaders seem to support the conclusion that separation is a good idea, and the transition is going as smoothly as can be expected. I imagine that Kem is probably going to request assistance with the issue, but that's a matter for the Senate to vote on. Our duty today is to decide if we wish to accept Qaras into the GA, and I for one see no reason not to."

There were nods around the table. As situations went, this was among the less sticky, and the atmosphere eased somewhat. Dorvan was convinced he even caught Carlist Rieekan smiling at one point.

Of course, the day was still young.

# Chapter Seven

MOFF DRIKL LECERSEN'S ESTATE, CORUSCANT

THIRTEEN AND A HALF HOURS LATER, HALF A WORLD AWAY FROM GA headquarters, a meeting very similar to that which the joint Chief of State had hosted was transpiring. As at that earlier conference, the attendees were all powerful beings in the world of politics. There were victuals and beverages provided for their enjoyment, and the meeting's itinerary was identical to that of the earlier meeting.

It was there that the similarities ended. It was well past the dinner hour, but those assembled were used to odd hours and still odder places to gather. This place was not as peculiar as others had been; it was a private residence, set on several acres of very expensive property, with a discreet landing field nearby.

Moff Drikl Lecersen smiled at his guests. He was seated at a large table carved of dark red wood, its heavy presence dominating the spacious room. The table was covered by an exquisite cloth, spun from the silk of the rare saass worms of G'haris. Each dish and piece of cutlery cost more than a civil servant such as Desha Lor could expect to make in a year, and the assembled guests appeared quite at home. Fur rugs made of the pelts of various exotic creatures covered the cold Ithorian marble floor, and knickknacks from all over the galaxy adorned various shelves and sideboards.

Lecersen was at the head of the table, of course. At his right hand was Senator Haydnat Treen of Kuat. Today, at the after-dinner gathering that would also serve as a going-away party for Lecersen, Treen wore a lovely blue-and-silver robe that matched her hair perfectly. It was formal, yet relaxed, and an indigo scarf was tied just so around her elegant throat, not only for style, but also to hide the fine network of wrinkles on the slightly sagging skin.

Seated next to her was General Merratt Jaxton, who had arrived mere moments earlier. His hair, too, was gray, but the Chief of Starfighter Command had fewer years and fewer lines than the others seated at the table. And, it seemed, more appetite. He had filled his plate with a great deal of small fried fish cakes and tiny slices of nerf steak with grilled mushrooms.

He, in turn, seemed dwarfed by the imposing General Stavin Thaal, who looked like he should be chewing on durasteel rather than the delicate pastries that appeared little more than crumbs in his large hands. The movement of his scarred throat as he swallowed was almost hypnotic, and Lecersen dragged his attention away to regard the guest on his left—Coruscant's own Senator, Fost Bramsin. Age had not been as kind to Bramsin as it had to Treen, and he was bowed with the weight of the years. He still had a good appetite, but his hands trembled slightly as he poured cream into his caf to enjoy with a piece of traditional Bespin cloud meringue cake.

Beside the Senator was the acting naval chief, Admiral Sallinor Parova. Like the other heads of the military, she was still in uniform, crisp and efficient looking as she sipped her caf.

The talk was pleasant, filled with lively chatter, humor, and the sound of forks and knives scraping against dishes as those gathered enjoyed their rather late supper. When the serving droid came to clear the empty plates away and refill cups of caf—rich and dark and headily aromatic, the best that could be found—Lecersen knew it was time to get down to business.

An E-3PO protocol droid hastened up with datapads, which it diligently handed out to the guests. They wiped their mouths and put their napkins down, ready to direct their full attention to the matters at hand. After all, fine as Moff Lecersen's caf, pastries, and nerf steaks were, that was not why they had come.

"You're certain Dorvan doesn't know we have access to this?" Bramsin asked, carefully picking up his datapad and perusing it.

"If he did, we would not be having this pleasant gathering," Lecersen said.

"I cover my tracks," Jaxton said. "Don't worry. He's got no idea."

"Always so careful!" Treen said brightly. "I like that about you, General. I do." She turned to address her fellow Senator. "Such a thing *is* a possibility, but it would be a very long-term way of misleading or flushing us. Chief of State Dorvan's position is rather delicate at the moment. If he suspected our compatriots in the military of anything, it would behoove him to move quickly, not put something extended into play when he might not be in office long enough to follow up."

Lecersen nodded absently, seeing no need to comment further. He was quite certain they remained safely undiscovered.

"The only break we seem to have caught recently is that we three survived the purge," Jaxton said. He popped a pastry into his mouth and washed it down with a swig of caf before wiping his fingers on the fine linen napkin and picking up the 'pad. "I intend to milk it for all it's worth. This is the list of what Dorvan's cabinet discussed earlier today. I'll tell you—"

"*We* will tell you," Parova interrupted. Her voice was pleasant, but there was a brief flash in her dark eyes that told Lecersen that, while she was the junior member of the little group of conspirators, she did not intend to stay humbly in the background.

Jaxton met her gaze. A muscle tightened in his jaw, then he nodded. "Of course. Several of us were present at the meeting. We will tell you where the cabinet fell out on each issue. But that's really secondary. What the six of us need to do tonight is to see if there is any being or any situation that we might turn to our benefit. Let us begin with B'nish, which I'd never heard of until today."

"Don't feel bad about that," Treen soothed, reaching across the table and patting the younger man's hand. "There's no need to apologize. Very few of us had."

Jaxton glared at her. "I wasn't apologizing. If I haven't heard of it, it's because there's not anything worth hearing. This is a completely ineffectual world. Look at the stats. Basic agriculture, midlevel technology, no extreme political views. They even solved a slavery issue in a civilized way. I don't think there's anything to really exploit here."

Lecersen opened his mouth to agree, then paused. He had called up an image of the Senatorial candidate put forth by B'nish, one Kameron Suldar. Suldar seemed pleasant enough, but there were wrinkles etched in his face that were not laugh lines. His gaze was clear, his head held at a certain angle. Lecersen had not gotten as far as he had in politics without being able to read body language.

Even just in a single, frozen image.

He handed the pad to the protocol droid and said, "Eethree, run the hologram this image was taken from."

"Certainly, sir."

Glances were exchanged, but those present knew better than to question. They leaned forward as the small hologram materialized in the center of the table, next to the carafe of caf and the cream, curious to see why Lecersen had seen fit to bring this to their attention.

"It is with great appreciation, humbleness, and a sense of duty that I accept the nomination to represent my planet in the Galactic Senate."

The voice was strong. The handsome face, framed by neatly trimmed gray hair, showed both passion and restraint. Lecersen thought he even caught a glimmer of tears in the eyes, but that could have simply been the lighting.

"For too long, we have kept to ourselves. We have grown too comfortable with our situation. But now, it is time to leave that comfortable rut. My friends and fellow B'nishi . . . the only difference between a rut and a grave is the depth of the hole."

A cliché, no doubt, but one that clearly got a warm reception, judging from the sound of applause. Suldar nodded, lifting a hand to call for silence, smiling.

"Freeze, right there," Lecersen said.

The droid obeyed. And there it was—a glint of something very not-selfless. Something that bespoke pleasure in what he was doing, and a quiet understanding and appreciation of the power he now held.

"Do you see what I see, Senator?" Lecersen mused, turning to Treen.

"Oh, indeed I do," said Treen. "That looks like someone who might be right at home at this table. Why, he looks a bit like you, Fost, when you were younger and full of fire." Bramsin looked pleased.

"Come now, Drikl," scoffed Jaxton, looking at him incredulously. "You can get that from a single paused hologram? If you caught me at the right moment, I could look like either a god or an imbecile."

"This is true," said Lecersen, not adding that he thought the latter more likely than the former. "However, this new Senator bears watching. And you, my dear, are in an ideal position to do so."

Treen tittered.

They moved quickly through the list that Dorvan himself had handled, possibly quicker than the Chief of State had done, as their concern was much more focused.

"Ah, Klatooine and the oh-so-diplomatic and charming Padnel Ovin," purred Lecersen. "Can we use or turn him, do you think?"

"Nonhuman," grumbled Bramsin, refilling his caf. "I, for one, don't want to work with him."

"Neither do I," Parova put in. "I've served under a Bothan long enough. I thought I was going to develop allergies. I'd just as soon not associate with a dog."

"I know the type." The voice was deep, metallic, and ominous. Everyone turned to regard Thaal. He so seldom spoke, it was always worth listening to. Thaal didn't miss the mixture of fascination and revulsion on the faces of the Senators, who had not spent much time around him recently, and a smile of amused contempt curled his lips.

"His bumbling and noise should do us a roundabout favor. He will be a welcome distraction, if nothing else. The newsvids will adore either bashing or praising him, because he is so terribly colorful. Subtler things will escape their notice."

"One hopes," said Treen.

"One does hope, and one should make sure that it happens," Lecersen said, the barest hint of warning in his voice. Treen smiled cheerfully.

"All of these planets abolishing slavery reminds me of when the Empire fell," Bramsin muttered. "All the chaos of those liberated worlds celebrating and throwing everything out of order. It's making things very difficult."

"Difficulties are often opportunities in disguise," Treen said. "We've already determined a possible ally and a potential distraction."

"If I ever get my hands on whoever is responsible for creating and organizing the Freedom Flight, I'll choke the life out of him," Jaxton continued.

Lecersen, Bramson, and Treen exchanged glances. Then the Moff turned his attention back to Jaxton.

"I suppose, since I am safely in my own home with droids poised ready to stop you, that now might be a good time to tell you that *I* am the one behind the Freedom Flight," said Lecersen.

He smiled inwardly. It took a great deal to shock Jaxton, and the man was now staring like a slack-jawed idiot. Parova, too, looked startled, but she managed not to gape, and a small smile turned up the corners of her full lips. Stavin Thaal revealed his surprise only with a quick flash of his pale blue-gray eyes; otherwise, his expression remained unchanged.

"You're the mastermind behind this?" Parova asked.

"*Mastermind* is not quite the correct word." Lecersen nodded to the droid, who poured him another cup of caf. "You should all know by now that I make it my business to know what is going on in as many places as possible. One never knows when the perfect opportunity will arise. Intelligence reached me some time ago that there were small, isolated events involving rebelling slaves on a few distant worlds. Nothing that would attract any real attention from anyone. When I looked into it, I realized that it could potentially be turned to my advantage."

"Unleashing this madness on the galaxy?" Jaxton's voice was rising. "This is something I'd expect from the Solos, or someone else of that temperament, not from a Moff!"

Lecersen refused to let Jaxton's sputtering rattle him. "Think about it," he said. "Think of what a fire wasps' nest it could become for any politician who had to deal with it—especially someone who opted to come down on the quote-unquote morally wrong side of the situation. Someone like Daala."

Jaxton's expression changed. "Ah, now I see."

"Mmmm. When Senator Treen first approached me," Lecersen continued, "she very wisely recommended that we have a crisis ready to erupt at some point. What was it you said, my dear? You were working on some useful potential crises, and perhaps I could, as well?"

"Indeed, I believe that was precisely how I phrased it."

"Well. It turned out I had a perfect crisis all ready to erupt."

"So . . . it was in existence before, but now you're running this show?" Jaxton pressed. "What happens if it is traced back to you?"

"As I believe I just said, no, I'm not *running the show,* and tracing anything back to me would be quite impossible. I organized a few things at the outset, and then let it do what it would. The late little Devaronian interviewer who was so passionate about the Freedom Flight had it quite right—the chain of command is clear only for a few links." He sighed, glancing at his caf.

It had worked splendidly—for a while. The attempted assassination of Admiral Nek Bwua'tu, which Lecersen, Bramsin, and Jaxton had also arranged when it became clear that he would not willingly join with them, coincided beautifully with the greatest surge of the various uprisings. At first, Lecersen had lamented that Bwua'tu had survived, but the tension that the coma coverage had generated in the public eye had also played into their hands.

Daala had made some bad choices while under both of these pressures. She had brought in Mandos, generating sympathy for the Jedi, whose Temple had been laid siege to, and the other worlds, such as Blaudu Sextus, when she had ruthlessly put down the rebellions. The attack on Bwua'tu had also kept her from thinking as clearly as Lecersen knew she could.

Despite those auspicious moments, however, the pesky Freedom Flight had taken on a life of its own. Like a child, it had outgrown its original form and was asserting its independence. There was no way Lecersen could manipulate or even direct anything at this point.

"It pains me to admit that it has gotten rather beyond our control. But not all plans perform perfectly, and it has done a great deal of damage to Daala's administration. If those inconsiderate slaves had stopped there, all would have been well, but alas, the GA is now being flooded by shiny new advocates for their worlds."

"Ah, ah," Treen chided cheerily, "there can be opportunities there too, Drikl. Every cloud has a silver lining."

"And nearly every world has someone who can be corrupted," added Parova. "Such as Kameron Suldar, if all goes well."

Treen actually clapped her hands like an excited little girl. "I do look forward to meeting this fellow," she said. "I have the *best* feeling about him."

They worked their way through the rest of the list, but no likely candidates for corruption or opportunities for additional crises presented themselves. The droid hummed up, topping off cafs.

"When do you depart for Imperial Space?" asked Jaxton.

"In a few days," Lecersen replied. "I have some loose ends I need to tie up here, and a few favors I need to call in, but that shouldn't take too long."

"Where will you be heading, specifically?" Parova inquired.

"That, my dear, is one of the loose ends." He gave her a genial smile.

"We shall hold the fort until your return," said Treen.

And he had no doubt that they would.

The hour was growing late. Jaxton, the last to arrive, was the first to put his napkin down and push his chair back. "Dorvan's scheduled another obscenely early meeting tomorrow," he said.

Parova sighed and rose, as well. "Merratt unfortunately speaks the truth. We have only a few hours to snag some sleep."

"Then perhaps you should have gone lighter on the caf," Treen chided.

"Are you kidding?" said Jaxton. "With the brewed swill we've got to look forward to tomorrow morning? I'm going to enjoy the good stuff while I can." Parova chuckled and nodded her head in agreement.

"When things are settled, I promise you I shall introduce you all to my supplier," said Lecersen, rising and taking Jaxton's outstretched, meaty hand and giving Parova a courteous bow. "We can't possibly have a proper Empire fueled by bad caf."

Thaal rose in silence and shook Lecersen's hand, nearly crushing the other man's fingers. And in silence, he headed for the door. Lecersen flexed his fingers and eyed him speculatively.

"I should be heading home, as well," said Treen, rising as the generals and the admiral left. "As should . . . oh dear."

Bramsin had fallen asleep in his chair. Gently, Treen tapped his shoulder, and amid protests that he was just "resting his eyes," she and E-3PO located the venerable Senator's hat and coat and escorted him to the small speeder that had brought him there. Treen gave them a cheery wave as the door closed behind her.

Lecersen hadn't lied. There were several favors to call in. In the morning, he'd contact his old friend Porrak Vansyn. He'd opted not to include Vanysn in his little "group," as the younger Moff didn't really have much to offer. Now, however, he was certain Vansyn would aid him in establishing a base of operations.

He turned his mind to another one of the loose ends. He sank back in his chair, reached into his pocket, and unfolded the piece of flimsi E-3 had delivered to him a few hours earlier.

"I found it tucked in the flower bed by the the gate, sir," the droid had said. "Do you wish to peruse the security vids?"

Lecersen, rather alarmed that someone had felt confident enough to walk up to his gate and place an old-fashioned note in a flowerpot, did indeed wish to peruse the security vids. He had watched, eyes narrowing, as they showed nothing more sinister than a small human village child on a hoverbike approaching the gate, looking admittedly wary. His—or her—face was turned away from the cam, and he or she wore gloves, gripping the note hard, edging up to the gate, shoving it into the dirt, and then hastening away. No doubt with a bit of effort he could uncover the identity of said child, but there was little point. He was certain that the youngling had been put up to it, perhaps with the promise of some credcoins or treats, and would not be able to identify the real culprit.

The note was written in block letters, in Basic, and read simply:

WE HAVE SOMETHING TO DISCUSS THAT WILL BE TO YOUR BENEFIT. I WILL COME TO YOU.

"Come if you like, my mysterious friend," murmured Lecersen. "Walk freely into the rancor's lair."

# Chapter Eight

ABOARD THE *JADE SHADOW*

"WELL, THEY CAN'T SIMPLY HAVE JUST DISAPPEARED," JAINA SOLO SAID. "I mean—that was a lot of ships. They've got to be somewhere."

"Physics would dictate that," Luke Skywalker replied, rubbing his eyes wearily. "But I get the feeling that Abeloth and the Sith aren't great believers in physics."

"All can be bent to one's will, if one's will is strong enough," said Vestara Khai, looking up from a game of dejarik. Luke's son, Ben, had dug up the program and was instructing her in its finer points.

"That some kind of Lost Tribe Sithy saying?" Ben retorted, but he was grinning and the words had no sting. Vestara smiled back at him.

"Nope," she said. "I just made it up. Do you like it?"

"No," Luke said sharply, even though the question was meant for Ben. He was in no mood to patiently indulge teenage flirting, which the conversation was perilously beginning to resemble. "Vestara, you could do a great deal of good if you'd simply tell us where your homeworld is instead of inventing platitudes."

Vestara's eyes, warm with mirth as they regarded Ben, turned cold for a moment.

"*Good*?" she repeated. "Master Skywalker, I'm Sith. I don't 'do good,' remember? Or at least, that's what you keep insisting."

"She's got you there, Dad," Ben said. He examined the board, frowning a little as Vestara moved her molator two squares, where it proceeded to attack Ben's houjix.

"Yeah," Jaina agreed. "She does." While Luke's niece was only present in holographic form, she had apparently been following the conversation. Luke fought the urge to scowl.

"You would have me believe that you have turned your back on such things," Luke said. "That you are working with *us* now, not the Sith, nor Abeloth. As such, I think you'd be more willing to help us."

Vestara's eyes flashed briefly, but she did not rise to the bait. "I have helped as best I could without becoming something I despise," she said quietly, wrapping a surprising amount of dignity around her like a cloak. "I may not agree with what this strike force is doing. But that doesn't mean I want to turn them over for Jedi-approved genocide."

"Hey, wait just a minute, Ves—" Ben began. Luke lifted a hand for silence, and for a change, Ben obeyed the unspoken command.

"Jedi," Luke said, his voice just as soft as Vestara's and just as intense, "do not condone or participate in genocide. We've been on the receiving end of it. Or didn't you know about that?"

"Oh, I know," Vestara replied. "And I know from what Ship told us that Order 66 was issued by a Sith, and carried out by a Sith who was your own father. If anyone has reason to hate my—" She caught herself and corrected. "—the Sith, it's Jedi—and you. You are making my argument for me. Why in the *universe* would I willingly lead you to my world when I know you will feel obligated to kill everyone?"

No one missed the slip. But that in and of itself didn't necessarily ring warning bells for Luke. Even if Vestara had truly had a change of heart—which he didn't for a moment believe—old habits died hard. They *were* her people, and had been all her life. It would be a long time before she thought of them in any other way.

"Look," Ben said, glancing from his father to Vestara, the dejarik game completely forgotten, "we're getting off-track here. The Sith we're all agreed we want to find are the members of the former strike team. I know you want that, too, Ves. We also need to find Abeloth."

She nodded. Anger still radiated off her in the Force, although anyone with eyes could see it easily in her body language. Luke supposed he'd feel the same.

"I'd tell you if I knew anything that would help you find Abeloth or the strike team," she said. "I think you know that. But I was never included in their grander plans, and it's been far too long since they even trusted me with minor information. I've told you all I know."

And she had. Luke could sense her honesty—in this, at least.

"I believe you have told me what you know," he said, equally as honest. "But now it's time for you to tell me what you *think*. Give us your best guess. You know these people, in a way we don't. If you have any theory, any idea about where they might go or what their next step might be, I would ask you to tell us. Any starting point would be welcome."

Vestara seemed mollified, and her body posture eased slightly.

"Well," she said slowly, glancing at Ben, "if we don't know where they were planning on going now—which I don't—we might want to think about where Sith have been in the past. The Lost Tribe cherishes its own history and hungers to learn more about other Sith, and they would want to learn all they can."

Ben was nodding. "That makes sense for the Sith, but what about Abeloth? I get the feeling she's going to go for the greatest source of either power or beings she can take advantage of."

Luke and Jaina nodded. Luke frowned for a moment as a thought occurred to him. "Vestara . . . do you think they would travel together?"

She opened her mouth to object, then closed it for a moment, looking pensive. "The original plan was to capture and enslave her. That's why they initially joined with you. I . . . I don't know. If they think it would be a good decision, then yes, I suppose they might do so."

It was not a pleasant thought—Abeloth and the Sith, working together, but the more Luke sat with it, the more right it felt.

"If they're traveling together, it would be Abeloth who would dictate the direction. And we don't know enough about her yet to hazard a guess where she might go."

"So we're right back where we started," Ben said glumly. Vestara had just lost her Kintan strider, one of the most powerful pieces in the game. He moved quickly to take advantage of an opening only to have Vestara, the novice, find an opening herself to take Ben's own Kintan strider and two other pieces.

"Ship." It was the hologram of Jaina that had spoken the single, galvanizing word. All eyes turned toward her.

"What about Ship?" Luke asked.

The small figure shrugged. "Ship is the one thing both Abeloth and the Sith truly have in common. Although she's commanding him, we know that Ship doesn't seem overly fond of her. I picked up on that when I dealt with him, and Vestara's confirmed it. He exists to serve Sith and train their younglings. Abeloth doesn't fit into that programming, and yet he still serves her."

"He has to," Vestara chimed in. "He doesn't want to. He doesn't like her at all."

"In the end, Ship is still a vessel," Luke said. "He will always obey his programming, whatever his personal preferences. We know that about him, and that gives us an advantage." He had never liked the tendency some had of referring to Ship as a male. Ship was a construct, not a living being.

"Well . . . that depends on how you define his programming," Vestara said. "Ship wants to help the Sith, and he is programmed to do so. But he must also obey one with will enough to command him. Abeloth is simply too strong for him to disobey right now."

Luke eyed her for a moment. "He would come to you if he could, wouldn't he?"

She nodded.

"Even if you were helping us?"

She hesitated, then said, "Yes. I think so. He wouldn't like it. He would come, even if just to try to get me back onto what he sees as the right path. But I'm a Sith youngling, and well—not to brag, but he sought *me* out. I do think I have a bond with him."

Luke glanced over at his son, who had been quiet through this part of the conversation. Ben, too, had once had such a bond with the ancient vessel. During the time when Ben had been his uncle Jacen's apprentice, and therefore had been walking the line between the dark and the light side, he had encountered Ship on Ziost. The Sith had once been powerful on that world, and the miasma of dark-side energy had lingered among the ruins that marked their former presence and lain heavily in the shadows of the woods.

Ship, hidden deep in the bowels of Ziost and forgotten for millennia, had called to Ben, sensing in the then-fourteen-year-old youth the brush of the dark side.

Sensing a Sith apprentice.

Ben had responded, utilizing Ship as a way to get off the forsaken world. He had not fully understood at the time that Ship was using him in the same way. He had managed to exert the force of his will over the vessel sufficiently to pilot it, and retained enough of that will not to succumb to its mentally whispered urgings. Far from achieving the unity that Ship and a dark-side apprentice could have had, Ben had essentially ditched the training vessel as soon as he could—giving it to Jacen as a gift once the younger Skywalker had safely returned.

Ship had not seemed to like Jacen, and had allied itself with a different dark-Force user shortly afterward. Luke found himself wondering what Ship's dislike of Jacen meant, then shook it off. It was not relevant, not anymore.

"If we can find Ship, then we'll find Abeloth," Jaina was saying. "And if he's managed to escape her somehow, then he'll have sought out the Lost Tribe. We could find one or both of our targets by shifting the direction of our search to finding *him* instead chasing *them*."

"That's a great idea, Jaina," Luke said. He was a little embarrassed he hadn't thought of it himself. "Ben, Vestara—you've both been inside Ship. Jaina, you've encountered him twice, and the second time you gave a good account of yourself. The three of you put your heads together and see what you can come up with."

"I'd also like to utilize what resources we have back at the Temple," Jaina said. "Have someone start pulling whatever research we've got on Ship."

Luke nodded. "Get right on that. Anyone in particular you'd like to work with?"

Jaina cocked her dark head, considering. "I think if Natua Wan's available, I could work with her. I know that most of the Jedi Knights affected by Abeloth are still having a close eye kept on them, and since I'm the one who brought her in when she snapped . . . I'd like to let her do something to feel useful."

Luke nodded, pleased but not surprised that this had occurred to Jaina. He would have felt the same way. Even though it was certainly not the fault of the "Jedi crazies," he knew that there was still a pall cast over Jedi Knights who had been, in the end, victims. Letting Natua Wan help with research would give her something positive to do while keeping her in the Temple.

"Let's get right on it, then," he said.

"But first," Ben said firmly, deactivating the holographic game in which he had been soundly trounced, "lunch."

JEDI TEMPLE, CORUSCANT

Natua Wan understood, completely, the reticence with which she had been allowed back into Jedi society. She had harmed innocents—coming perilously close to killing more than one—destroyed property and livestock, and threatened the entire Solo clan.

Everyone knew that she had believed, truly believed, that they were all imposters. That she had been unwittingly and utterly under the control of Abeloth, a being so powerful and dangerous that Grand Master Luke Skywalker had joined into an alliance with Sith to fight her. And they all knew that Natua Wan was cured.

But they still worried, and Natua couldn't blame them. Even if it meant that, unofficially, she was still under observation.

She'd bridled at it at first, but the very practical Markre Medjev, the current chief librarian of the Temple, had pointed out that Jedi needed patience and compassion. After a time, they would all come to believe in their hearts, not just their minds, that the "crazies" were truly cured, and she and the others would again be sent out on assignments that required absolute faith in their abilities. She'd sighed, nodded, and resigned herself to the situation.

Natua had always been quick-tempered and, while intelligent, could hardly be called "studious" by even the most charitable of her teachers. Embracing where she was as Medjev had suggested, she had actually volunteered to stay at the Temple and assist Master Cilghal with some of her research. Cilghal had been surprised, but pleased, and had taken great pains to acquaint the Falleen with most of the librarians, who were delighted to have someone to take into their care.

It was . . . odd, but rewarding. So when Markre Medjev himself took her aside and said, "I have had a specific request for your services," she was quite pleased.

"Who needs what?" Natua asked.

Medjev smiled. There was a twinkle in his dark eyes as he replied, "Jaina Solo needs help researching the Sith. It seems that they want more information on Sith history in general and Ship in particular. You'll be doing a great deal to help Master Skywalker and the fleet locate both the Sith and possibly Abeloth, too. Jedi Solo asked for you by name." It was clear that while Medjev was trying to appear nonchalant, the chief librarian was bursting with pride.

Natua's eyes widened. She had not been surprised when she, along with most of the others who had suffered under Abeloth's control, had not been permitted to depart with the Jedi fleet. But now it didn't matter. Jaina Solo, who had fought her at the Coruscant Livestock Exchange and Exhibition, had asked for her help. Natua still remembered, with deep shame and regret, how Jaina had said, "I don't want to hurt you." Natua's response had been, "But *I* want to hurt *you.*"

Even though her natural inclination was to fight rather than research, Natua Wan would never, in a thousand years, do anything but gratefully accept Jaina's overture.

Besides . . . she knew Jedi weren't supposed to focus on revenge, but she felt a deep sense of satisfaction in knowing that she could take part in tracking down the being who had so violated her mind.

Natua grinned at Medjev. "Tell Jedi Solo that it would be my honor to assist."

# Chapter Nine

ABOARD THE *JADE SHADOW*

The list of places that Jaina, Natua, Ben, Luke, and Vestara had come up with read like a Top Ten Worst Places to Vacation, Ben thought as he looked at the names.

Dromand Kaas. Ziost. Krayiss II. Khar Delba. Korriban. And it went on and on. Ben didn't know a lot about the specific history of each planet, but he was more than familiar with some. Like Ziost.

He watched with not a little unease as Vestara read almost hungrily about the history of her—hopefully—former people. She methodically crunched a muja fruit, studying silently while they ate lunch in the galley.

Finally, uncomfortable with the silence, Ben said, "Your soup's getting cold."

"Hmm? Oh, right. Thanks." She took a single spoonful and resumed reading.

Ben fidgeted, then said, "So I thought you'd already be familiar with a lot of these places. Maybe even tell us about some new ones."

That got her attention. She looked up from the datapad. "A lot of them are familiar. But the *Omen*'s data bank did suffer some damage, and a great deal of information was lost. Remember, we didn't really have the technology until recently to recover lost data. And Ship was much more interested in bringing us up to speed on the current state of the galaxy than on its history. So yes, a lot of this is new to me."

"Interesting?"

She gave him a level gaze. "Of course it is. Knowledge is power, Ben, and I know you know that. I was born a Sith, even if I've changed my mind about a lot of what they stand for and who I want to be. I bet even you think this is interesting."

He couldn't deny it. "Well, yeah, it is. But it's kind of like watching a ship crash. You can't take your eyes off it, but you don't really like what you're seeing."

She shrugged. "Perhaps. The nature of this is nothing new to me, only the details. And don't worry. I've got plenty of information on ancient Sith planets to share with you." She waggled the 'pad. "This is definitely incomplete."

"Ancient Sith planets, but not Kesh," Ben said.

Vestara sighed and put down the 'pad. "I've been thinking about this," she said. "I know that there's a very good possibility that Abeloth and—and my father's team have retreated to Kesh. But what I told Master Luke still stands. I'm afraid if I tell you where it is, every Jedi in the galaxy is going to converge on it and blast it back to the date that the *Omen* crashed. I can't do that, Ben. I just *can't*—and neither could you if you were in my situation."

He stared into his soup. It was good soup, as such things went, with generous chunks of nerf meat and vegetables, but it was not holding his attention. Which was highly unusual, and a sign of how troubled he was by the direction the search was taking.

"I guess you're right."

She reached over and squeezed his arm. He glanced up from the soup and found her smiling. "Thank you for that."

He gave her a crooked grin in return, then it faded. "But

still . . . by choosing not to tell us, you're putting all of us at risk. What if she *is* there? She's got to be stopped, Ves, you know that."

"I do. But not at the expense of my whole world."

Ben didn't know what to say. He wanted to argue that it wasn't genocide the Jedi were after, just . . . destroying Sith. But it sounded like the whole planet had become Sith, even the non-Force-users. He couldn't give her a promise that only the "bad people" would be targeted and destroyed, because as far as Jedi like his father went, *all* Sith were bad people.

She looked thoughtful for a moment, the datapad forgotten. "Unless . . . " she said, then shook her head. "Never mind."

"Unless what?"

She hesitated, gnawing her lower lip for a moment. Ben again found his eye drawn to the tiny scar, the single perfect imperfection in a face that otherwise, to him, had no flaws. "Unless . . . you could give me a promise that my people—those who haven't cooperated with Abeloth—would be safe."

He stared at her mutely, his blue eyes sad. She smiled, her own brown ones resigned. "See? I didn't think so. The only way for that bargain to work would be if I had a chip to bargain with. Which . . . you might be able to give me."

After so much time in her company, Ben was getting used to Vestara's subtle shifts in the Force. He was on the alert now, sensing that, contrary to what she wanted him to think, what she was about to say was something that had been on her mind for some time.

"Go ahead."

"Trust . . . comes hard. But this would be something each of us could use against the other—if we had to, of course."

"Of course." He leaned back and folded his arms, his face impassive.

"I would consider revealing to you the location of my world . . . if you would tell me who you think is this Jedi queen."

He almost laughed. "There's a difference, Vestara. Kesh is real. It exists. The Jedi queen is likely just some kind of figment of Taalon's fevered imagination."

"You know," she said, her voice equally conversational, "I somehow don't think so. There's at least a kernel of truth in it, or else you and your father wouldn't have reacted so when it came up." She leaned her chin on her hand, smiling at him.

Ben considered the trade-off she was proposing. For about a nanosecond. And in that nanosecond, he came to the painful realization that at least for now, he didn't trust Vestara Khai, though he badly wanted to.

"If you're telling the truth," he said, "the best *we* can hope for is maybe—maybe—finding Abeloth and the Sith fleet. The best *you* could hope for is murdering someone very important to the future of this galaxy who might actually exist. And if you're lying, and I actually did give you information—if there was any information to give—you would have everything and we'd have nothing."

Vestara did not seem at all put out. She actually smiled. "Ben, I can see why Ship was drawn to you. There's the making of a fine Sith in you, you know that?"

"Let us not devolve into insults," Ben said. Vestara Force-tossed her muja fruit core at him, which he easily deflected. He wanted to be angry, but he couldn't be. This was where they were, plain and simple. He was frustrated, but unsurprised, and he found that it did not stand, and never had stood, in the way of his liking and caring about her. He still believed she was edging her way over to the light side, but she wasn't there.

At least, not yet.

"Well, now that you've had a chance to read about these," Ben said, dragging the subject back on track, "where do you think Ship would be most likely to go?"

"It's hard to say. Perhaps Ziost?"

Ben shook his head. "No," he said firmly. "There was nothing for him on Ziost. That's why he wanted me to free him, so he could get away from it."

She looked at him, no doubt picking up on his discomfort. "Sure you're not saying that because you don't want to go back there?"

The initial retort died on his lips. It was a fair question. He took a minute to think about it. "I'll be honest," he said, finally. "You're right. I *don't* want to go back there. I don't really *want* to go to *any* of these places. But my wants are irrelevant. If I thought Ship would take Abeloth there, I'd be the first to investigate. But think about it. If there was anyone there on Ziost who would be important enough to Ship or Abeloth, that being—or those beings—would have already freed Ship long before I got there."

She nodded. "Good point. Well, what about—"

"Korriban's our best bet," came a female voice. They both looked up as Jaina strode in and without preamble set about making a meal for herself.

It was still odd, having Jaina aboard the *Jade Shadow*. After her transmission earlier, she had come to join them in person as well as spirit. It had been a while since Ben had been in such close proximity to his cousin for anything more than a family visit. He was glad to be working with her, but he knew that she, like his dad, was . . . well, to say "highly skeptical" of Vestara was putting it mildly. And yet, she had made a point of including Vestara in all the conversations.

"Why do you say that?" Vestara asked.

"It's the homeworld," Jaina said, pouring two cups of caf. "Most of these other places do have *a* history for the Sith, but Korriban's *the* history. It's logically the place we should visit first."

Vestara lit up like an exploding sun in the Force for just the briefest instant. Ben's heart sank.

"We can send others out to explore some of the possible sites, but me, I'd like for us to go to Korriban," Jaina continued, taking a sip from her cup. She acted as if she hadn't seen Vestara's reaction. Maybe she hadn't, thought Ben. He was more attuned to Vestara than either Jaina or Luke. He might have been the only one who noticed it.

"I would like to accompany you when you explore it," Vestara said.

Jaina didn't bat an eye as she moved to leave with the steaming cups. "I think you should."

Ben was certain that he could literally *hear* his jaw drop.

"You told her *what*?" Luke was accepting a cup of caf from Jaina, and nearly spilled it as she told him what she had said to Vestara.

"You heard me," Jaina said, plopping into a chair opposite her uncle. They were meeting in Luke's quarters with the doors closed, so there was no chance of their being overheard.

"You want me to take a Sith, whose trustworthiness seems to depend on the time of day, the season, and the phases of whatever moons happen to be nearby, with us on a potentially dangerous mission to the Sith homeworld."

"That's about right, yes," Jaina said.

"Please give me a reason for why you think this is a good idea in any way, shape, or form."

"I'll give you more than one," Jaina said. "First, it's because she's a Sith. She grew up with this, Luke. Like I grew up in a family of Jedi. Her culture is obsessed with its history, and she probably knows more about the ancient Sith, their technology, languages, and maybe even alchemy, than we do. If her own safety and life are on the line, she'll tell us what she knows if we run across anything useful."

"Set a thief to catch a thief," Luke said, rather glumly.

"Something like that," Jaina said. Her face split into an impish grin. "You know it always works when we send my dad out after people with shady reputations."

"Can't argue with success," Luke said, allowing himself a small smile.

"Two," Jaina continued, "Ship really does have a bond with her. That means if we get her near him, even if we can't find him, he'll be able to find her."

"Why does that thought not fill me with delight?" Luke asked rhetorically.

"It should," Jaina said, ignoring the sarcasm and choosing to address the question literally. "Even if he attacks, he'd be showing himself. And that's what we want, right?"

Luke was forced to agree. "You make a persuasive argument."

"Jag must be rubbing off on me," she said. "In all seriousness though, Vestara Khai is a unique asset. We should make use of her."

Luke sighed. "I am still very, very leery of bringing her along with us. I think it's asking for trouble." He had been looking down at the rapidly cooling cup of caf, but now he lifted his eyes to her. "She's Sith, Jaina. Not just a dabbler, not a victim, not a fallen Jedi. Born and raised in an entire community of Sith. I'm convinced she's not going to throw that aside and wholeheartedly join us, but I know Ben still thinks she can be redeemed."

"There are those," commented Jaina drily, "who still think you can't be redeemed. Or Grandfather. Or Aunt Mara. Or Kyp Durron, or—"

Luke held up his hand. "Point made. But those were different."

"Were they? Or do you just want to think they're different because you're worried about your son getting hurt?"

Luke opened his mouth to retort, then closed it again. Jaina was right. His very quickness to respond negatively was proof of that. While Jedi did have to make split-second decisions over life-and-death matters, they were also not supposed to react emotionally, or to rush down a path recklessly. And he was doing precisely that.

"I do worry about Ben," he admitted. "He's a strong young man. And wise—much wiser than I was at his age. And no, you don't have to agree with me," he added as Jaina drew breath to speak. They smiled at each other. "I don't think for a moment she'll bring him over to the dark side. But I think he might get hurt—physically and emotionally—because he wants this so badly. He cares for her, Jaina. I can feel it."

"Which means she can, too, most likely," Jaina said. "I don't want to get overly sentimental here, Uncle Luke, but—don't underestimate the power of love. It's pulled two family members back from the dark side already. Ben may be sixteen, but he's not a fool." She leaned forward, her dark eyes intense. "Maybe if he believes she's redeemable . . . it's because she *is.*"

Luke was silent. "All right," he said at last. "Vestara can come with us to Korriban. But we are going to be watching her every minute."

"Of course we will. And drink your caf, it's getting cold."

# Chapter Ten

LUKE WASN'T HAPPY ABOUT ANY OF THIS. NOT ABOUT NOT KNOWING where either Abeloth or the Sith were, not about having to visit Korriban and other Sith-steeped locales, and especially not about having a Sith girl with them on said jaunts.

She was a danger. Luke knew it. Was there a chance that Ben and Jaina were right, that Vestara could indeed be won over to the light side of the Force? Of course there was. There was always hope. But there were also odds. And Luke knew that the odds were stacked—heavily—against that possibility.

He had at one point, years earlier, banned all navigation data regarding Korriban from Jedi computers, and asked the Galactic Alliance to do the same. Now that decision came back to bite him. Jaina had set Natua Wan the task of going through ancient, locked-up records in order to find anything of use. Luke half hoped the Falleen would fail in her task, but she—along with, presumably, more able researchers—had uncovered sufficient information for their purposes.

The closer they drew to the ancient Sith world, the quieter they all became. The only one who seemed excited about the prospect was, of course, Vestara.

Luke had pressed her to tell him what she knew about the place, considering that at one point she had had access to the *Omen*'s data banks, and somewhat to his surprise, she agreed.

"The term *Sith* actually refers to a species of red-skinned beings who were native to Korriban," she began. "The Sith today are descendants of Jedi who chose to follow the dark side of the Force rather than the light side. There was a war in which the Dark Jedi were exiled. They arrived on Korriban and, much like my own people with the Keshiri, were received almost as gods because of their ability to harness and direct the Force. They assumed the name *Lords of the Sith,* not because they *were* Sith, but because they were their masters. They figured out a way to mingle their DNA with that of the Sith natives, and gradually that species became extinct. I myself might have some Sith DNA."

Out of the corner of his eye, Luke noticed an expression that might have been a wince flickering over Ben's face.

Vestara continued. "The Sith had strictly defined castes—a slave caste, a religious caste, an engineer caste, and a warrior caste. There was no transitioning from one to the other." She smirked a little. "That is, I think, where the Lost Tribe is superior. When we arrived on Kesh, we did not believe in such divisions. Any Keshiri could rise according to his ability with the Force—as you have seen."

"And that makes you better?" Jaina asked. She leaned against the bulkhead, her arms crossed. She was regarding the girl with, if not open hostility, at least healthy dislike plain on her face.

"Yes," Vestara said simply. She looked at Luke. "Surely you agree, Master Luke. Or do you think it's better to deny beings the right to grow and achieve simply because of their birth?"

It was an argument Luke could not win. "Next you'll ask me when I stopped beating my son. Neither is preferable, Vestara. There is no better or worse; there is only the dark side." And if she were truly moving to the light side, he thought, but did not say, then she would understand that.

Vestara did not react, merely continued. "The Sith Empire thrived, until its discovery by . . ." She cocked her head, thinking, biting her lower lip in concentration and looking like an ordinary girl trying to recall her lessons. "Gav and Jori Daragon. That discovery led to the Great Hyperspace War, which I understand the Sith lost. It was during that time that the *Omen* crashed, and I'm afraid I don't know very much after that."

"Ship didn't tell you?" Luke couldn't read Ben, which was unusual for him. He didn't seem overly skeptical, nor innocently inquiring. Ben was, Luke realized, in his *gathering information* mode. His time with the Galactic Alliance Guard had taught him the value of a methodical approach, one in which all evidence was considered. Ben was doing exactly that—asking questions, listening, and observing.

"Some," Vestara said. "But there were many other things that Ship thought were more important. The Sith have a varied and complex history, and Ship wished us to live in the present, not the past. We spent more time learning about how things are currently in the galaxy."

"Like learning about me and Dad," Ben said, again speaking in a calm, impartial voice. Investigating.

"Yes," she answered, unruffled. "You would have done the same, would you not?"

"I . . . suppose I would have."

"All you really need to know about the Sith on Korriban is that we believe they haven't been there for some time," Luke said. "The place has become a burial ground. It's more important for us to be aware of potential dangers we might encounter."

"The burial-ground aspect is itself a great danger," Vestara said quietly. "The area will be strong with the dark side. And . . . I am told that things can be created with the dark side of the Force."

Luke nodded. "That's true. The general catchall term is *demon*."

"Works for me," Ben said. Luke could tell now that he was making his voice even with an effort. Ben had had a close brush with such "demons" on Ziost two years earlier. No doubt he was recalling those long days and nights as he spoke.

"There are other, less spectral dangers as well, though," Luke said. Both Ben and Vestara looked suitably solemn as Luke called up a hologram.

The creature resembled a rancor—if rancors had sharp spines bristling down their backs and large tusks. "This is a terentatek," Luke said. "They can be found in several places around the galaxy, but they originated on Korriban. Some say they are products of Sith alchemy. Others think they were simply rancors twisted with dark-side energy. Regardless, they are aggressive and deadly. Those claws," he said, indicating the enormous three-fingered hands, "and their tusks are poisonous. Since they like to live in caves and other places where dark-side energy is strong, and since that's exactly where we'll be going, we might run across some."

He touched another button. This time, the beast that appeared looked like a canine. Sort of. Its eyes were red and glowing, and its paws had sharp claws. A whip-like tail lashed as they watched it.

"This is a tuk'ata," Luke said. "Also known as a Sith hound. They are guardians of the tombs."

"Which, don't tell me, is exactly where we're going," said Ben.

Luke nodded. "They also live on other worlds, but they originated here."

"Sounds like Korriban exports a lot of things," Vestara said.

"I've seen one," Jaina said. Her arms were folded across her chest as she regarded the beast. "On Yavin Four. They're sentient—at least somewhat. I've heard that it can understand the ancient Sith language. In this case, it understood gratitude, at least. It left us alone after—after Jacen healed it."

There was an uncomfortable silence. Luke again thought what a tragedy that the young Jacen Solo, with his great heart and gentle love of animals, had somehow—and inevitably so—become Darth Caedus.

There were more things to beware, most of them lurking in caves in or around the Valley of the Dark Lords. Bat-like shyracks dwelled in the darkness of the caves. Reptiles thrived on this world. Clay-footed wraids, also found on the desert world of Tatooine, lumbered the sands of the planet. The waters housed dark-side dragons with the onomatopoeic name *hssiss,* and the sand was rife with pelko bugs. These insects were attracted to Force-sensitives, and their toxin produced a numbing effect that, depending on how many swarmed upon one, could paralyze.

"Let's see," Ben recapped. "Dark-side demons and dragons, Sith hounds, mutated rancors, deadly bats, and paralyzing bugs. Sounds like business as usual."

Vestara gave them all a sudden grin, reached under her seat, and produced a small spray canister of droch repellent. "We're ready for at least one of those creatures," she said, and even Luke found himself smiling.

KORRIBAN

A few hours later, none of them was smiling as Luke brought the *Jade Shadow* into Korriban's atmosphere.

They passed over a settlement, a dilapidated spaceport surrounded by small clusters of buildings that made up a sort of village. Luke knew this place better than he would have liked; there was no need to get involved with the locals. If the Lost Sith Tribe were hiding here, the locals would either not know or be too frightened to reveal anything of use, and he had no desire to make his presence here more public than it had to be.

"It's so . . . barren," Vestara murmured as they flew over the desolate place.

"Welcome to what happens to a planet steeped in the dark side," Jaina said. "Use, abuse, and discard. That's the Sith for you."

"But our world is not—" Vestara fell silent. Ben gave her a quick glance, though it was hard to tear his gaze from the disturbing but oddly compelling sight of this rocky and sandy world. She still kept anything about Kesh that might reveal its location a closely guarded secret. Ben supposed he couldn't blame her, and in a way welcomed the reminder that, funny and smart and beautiful as Vestara might be, until she could truly prove otherwise, he had to be careful around her.

It was not a reminder he enjoyed.

They were heading right for the Valley of the Dark Lords. "It's the most logical place to begin our search," Luke had said. "The holy of holies for the Sith. If they're hiding here, they'll gravitate to the place that has the strongest dark-side energy—and that's the valley."

Ben shivered slightly. He could feel it, and knew everyone else could, too; a sort of heavy, sinister tugging, as if his clothes were weighted with water, dragging him down to the depths. He'd felt this before, on Ziost, and this time was very glad to have his father and cousin as company.

And, odd as it seemed, Vestara. This was a rare chance for her to prove her loyalties—one way or the other—and if she was truly, as Ben believed, coming over to the light side, her knowledge would be a gift and not a curse.

A gift from the dark side. How about that?

Her face was alert, attentive, and unlike Luke, Jaina, and Ben himself, she appeared to be utterly comfortable with the energies wafting up from this ancient world. He recalled seeing a similar expression on her face on Klatooine, when the turbolift had stopped on a floor that was home to several establishments that provided very *exotic* entertainments catering to the less savory desires of beings, and he felt again the shadow of doubt fall cool on his heart.

He shook it off. This place would indeed challenge Vestara—but it would challenge the three Jedi, as well. Mistrust, fear, suspicion—all those were tools of the dark side. Ben was sure this place would like nothing better than to cause division among them, turn them against one another, make Vestara feel that she had no place with the Jedi.

Ben wasn't going to let that happen.

"With all that dark-side energy swirling around, it's going to be hard to tell if there are any Sith down there at all," he said. "Particularly if they know how to hide themselves in the Force."

"I won't know for certain, but I might be able to help there," Vestara said. "I know many of the Lost Tribe members who came on the mission. I might be able to discern their presences more easily than you can."

Luke nodded. "Another reason we're allowing you to come with us," he said. He tweaked the controls slightly, and Ben saw they were heading directly toward a notched mountain. As it grew larger in the viewscreen, Ben felt his stomach tighten as the light, dim to begin with, grew even darker around them. As if some thick, toxic cloud was blocking the light and air. Which, Ben mused, it kind of was.

The single mountain turned out to be merely the dominant one over a whole range, a dark and ominous massif that towered over the valley below it.

At the mouth of the valley, there was a ruined citadel. And lining the walls of the valley, some distance back so they towered alone, were enormous stone statues of various figures.

Some of them were hooded, their heads bowed, ominous even as they seemed to be obeisant; more symbolic figures than any representation of an individual. Others were clearly meant to represent specific Dark Lords—towering, prideful, sending chills along Ben's spine as he looked into empty carved eyes. Steps led upward into what he knew were sealed tombs.

Sith from the luckless slave caste had been sealed in there as well, to tend their masters in the afterlife . . . once they themselves had died. Dozens slowly starved to death, or were perhaps aided on that journey by tuk'ata, which were also sealed inside the tombs.

All in all, even if the place hadn't been wrapped in the smothering feeling of dark-side tendrils, it would have been unsettling. Ben realized he was clenching his fists as his father brought the *Shadow* in for a landing near the citadel ruins.

Luke didn't rise immediately; he looked at each of them in turn. "No splitting up or wandering off. We stay within sight of one another at all times. Use your comlink to speak to anyone who isn't right beside you. If you notice anything, either simple physical evidence or something you sense in the Force, report it immediately. Are we clear?"

The last was blatantly addressed to Vestara. Her nostrils flared with annoyance and for an instant she was bright in the Force with it, but it faded quickly as she nodded along with Ben and Jaina.

The door slid open, the ramp extended, and three Jedi and one Sith stepped out onto the sands of Korriban.

# Chapter Eleven

GALACTIC SENATE MEDCENTER, CORUSCANT

FOR A MOMENT HE THOUGHT HE WAS STILL IN THE NIGHTMARE. THE nightmare of fighting for his very life against two Jedi who had gone mad—

*—they weren't Jedi. Or else he wouldn't have been able to—*

*—to do what?—*

—two humans who had attacked him. Cut off his arm with a lightsaber. A green one. Funny what the mind remembered. He recalled grasping his own severed arm, which still held a blaster, and firing at his attacker.

Then the antiseptic sterility. The sounds of voices, muffled, the words indistinguishable but the voices recognizable. Natasi's, rich and warm. Rynog Asokaji, aide-de-camp. Another he knew, but couldn't place immediately—a monotone. A voice with the accent of home.

Images, almost constant. Something about the reporter.

Doctors, medical droids. The humming sounds of equipment, the smell of a medcenter.

Which, it turned out, was *not* a nightmare after all.

"Stang," Admiral Nek Bwau'tu said in a raspy, faint voice.

"Welcome back to the land of the living, nephew," came a familiar drawl. With an effort, Bwua'tu turned his head and smiled faintly.

Eramuth Bwua'tu, Esquire, sat in a chair beside Nek. His cane, black and simple with the handle carved to resemble a beast out of Bothan folklore, was propped against a table. His favorite jaunty hat was perched beside it. Nestled under the table was a small, old-fashioned black bag. His long coat was neatly folded on another chair, and he wore only vest, trousers, and a shirt with the sleeves rolled up. He did not even wear gloves. In other words, for him, he was dressed extremely casually.

"Hello, Uncle Eramuth," Nek rasped. "Don't . . . you have a trial to be attending?"

Eramuth's eyes grew solemn. "Alas," he said in his resonant voice, pitched softly now, "the trial ended with a conviction for my client. And I was shocked . . . *shocked!* . . . to discover that soon after the jury reached its decision, the little nexu escaped. I have utterly no idea where she is."

But his eyes crinkled as he spoke. Bwua'tu chuckled.

"Dear Uncle Eramuth, what do you have up your sleeve?"

"Why, nothing, they are rolled up, as you can plainly see." He leaned forward. "You look a great deal better than you have for the last several weeks. How are you feeling?"

Weeks?

"I would feel better if I knew what I have missed."

"Well, that's quite a lot. Do you—" Eramuth paused in midsentence. One ear swiveled and he jerked his gray-muzzled head up, peering at the door for a moment before he relaxed. "Here's someone who will be almost as glad to see you awake as I am."

The door eased open and Rynog Asokaji entered, bearing two cups of caf.

"Is one of those for me?" rasped Nek. The Bith started, moving deftly in order to not spill the hot liquid, and blinked his large eyes rapidly as he set them down. Eramuth smiled at them both. As the admiral and his aide-de-camp talked, the lawyer fished out a comlink and spoke quietly into it.

"Admiral!" Asokaji's voice was a gasp of happiness. "I would gladly get you an entire pot of caf if the doctors would let me. It is so good to see you back with us."

Nek was becoming more aware of his surroundings with each minute. He glanced up at the vidscreen hanging above his bed, currently displaying a news show. Some things the report was covering seemed familiar, yet he did not remember them before his attack.

"Let me guess," he said to Asokaji. "You've been with me the whole time—at least as much as the doctors would let you. And you've been playing these on the odd chance that something might get through to me in my comatose state."

Asokaji nodded. "Well, sir, the FX medical droid did suggest that exposure to visual stimuli might help you awaken sooner. As soon as I heard that, I obtained permission from the doctors to have it playing constantly. It seemed to help."

Nek nodded. "I . . . think there were some things that did get through. Well done." He was still weak, and it was an effort to turn his head to look at Eramuth. "How is Natasi holding up?"

His uncle's eyes grew sad. "That's . . . one of the things you need to know. But if I'm right, and I often am, your doctors should be here momentarily. They'll have been alerted to your new state." He leaned forward, peering intently at his nephew. "Now, Nek, I want you to trust your old uncle. You're awake, but you're mighty incoherent. Groggy. There might even be brain damage."

He was using his lawyer-to-client voice, and Nek knew better than to argue.

A golden-furred Bothan and a Duros entered. They both beamed at Nek.

"Admiral," said the Bothan. "I'm Dr. Ysa'i, and this is Dr. Javir. We came as soon as we were alerted to your condition. Welcome back."

Nek peered at them, then cast a helpless glance over at Eramuth, who looked somber. "He's been awake for a few minutes, but . . . I'm not sure how *back* he is."

Ysa'i and Javir exchanged glances and frowned. "Our instruments indicate that his brainwave function has returned to normal," Javir said, examining the holographic brain-activity image hovering above the head of the bed. Nek fought back a sigh at how quickly doctors started referring to their patients in the third person; instead he concentrated on looking about confusedly.

"Could there be brain damage?" asked Eramuth, giving an admirable impression of someone deeply worried.

"It's unlikely, given what we're seeing here," Javir replied, frowning at the readings.

"Now, I'm no doctor," said Eramuth, "but I do know one thing from all my years practicing law. And that is while you may know a great deal about the *brain*, the *mind* remains largely a mystery."

Nek almost wanted to smile at the glare Dr. Javir shot his uncle. The Duros turned her attention to her patient. "Do you know these people, Admiral Bwua'tu?"

Nek blinked solemnly at her, but didn't reply.

"How about yourself? Do you remember who you are?"

He frowned, trying to look puzzled and agitated, but not too much so. The last thing any of them needed was for him to be sedated.

"This doesn't make sense," Javir muttered. "He should be recovered, if exhausted, according to the data."

"We'll stay and keep trying to reach him," Eramuth said. "Friendly faces and all. I've got some old stories to tell that might jog his memory."

Dr. Ysa'i tried and failed to hide a sour look at the thought of listening to Eramuth's "old stories." He covered quickly. "We'll continue to monitor him. If there's no change in an hour or so, we'll run some tests. For now, I must tell you, all signs are positive. I'm sure Admiral Bwua'tu will soon be fully recovered."

"Please alert one of the medical droids if the situation changes," Javir said.

"At once," Asokaji assured them. The doctors again checked the stats, then left together, talking quietly. Once the door had closed, the Bith turned back to Bwua'tu.

"Because of your extremely sensitive position in the government, sir, the former Chief of State and I both insisted that there be no monitoring or recording devices in this room, other than those deemed medically necessary. We can speak freely."

"You're certain?"

Eramuth nodded. "Otherwise, with some of the things I've said to young Rynog, I'm certain I'd have been hauled out for questioning." His eyes twinkled briefly, then grew somber.

"I did notice the words *former Chief of State* to describe Admiral Daala," Bwua'tu said quietly. "Tell me what's happened."

He listened, only interrupting occasionally to request clarification, as Asokaji and Eramuth spoke, his heart sinking with every stunning new fact.

Nek had already known that Daala was bent on demonstrating an increasing intolerance in her management of the various uprisings that seemed to be sprouting up like weeds. On the morning when he had been attacked, he'd been prepared to contact Kenth Hamner and move forward with their joint plan. He had a vague memory of the Devaronian journalist Madhi Vaandt reporting on the escalating violence.

"Natasi came to see me," he said, and it was not a question. "She and Wynn Dorvan. I remember. There was a report on . . ." Nek frowned, struggling to recall. "Blaudu Sextus. The Octusi . . . and Mandalorians. Called in to suppress them."

"I remember that visit," Asokaji said. "It was the first time your brain activity had seemed targeted. The Chief—er, former Chief of State—thought that Vaandt had a connection with the attempt on your life." He hesitated. "Vaandt was killed covering that story."

"I am sorry to hear that," Nek said honestly. "She was passionate about what she did. But no, she was not the reason I was interested in the vidcast. I will tell you all I remember about that when you've caught me up. I . . . was concerned about the uprisings and Madhi Vaandt's theory that the Mandos were hired to protect the interests of . . ." He frowned. Some specific pieces of information, it would seem, were still proving elusive.

"The Sextuna Mining Corporation," Asokaji provided helpfully. "Yes—Vaandt seemed to think that that wasn't really the case."

Eramuth had been listening without interrupting, but now his black ears pricked forward. "Really? I wonder who she thought *was* behind it."

Nek closed his eyes. "Vaandt cited the events at the Temple. It's obvious what she thought."

"Was what she thought true, Nek?" asked Eramuth, gently.

"I don't know for certain. But I believe so."

"The Jedi were thinking along similar lines," Eramuth said.

Nek turned his head. "I assume this part is where Daala became former Chief of State?"

Eramuth nodded. "I hate that you need to know this, but you do." Quickly, efficiently, and with compassion, he described the recovery of the "mad Jedi," the bloodless coup, and Daala's subsequent imprisonment. The triumvirate comprising Dorvan, Senator Treen, and Saba Sebatyne worked to continue keeping things from completely falling apart.

"I want to see her," Nek said.

"Well, that's what a lot of folks are saying," said Eramuth. "Someone spirited her away before she could have a fair trial. It was during the chaos of her prison break that my client also escaped."

Nek's eyes widened at that. "I think perhaps I am still in my coma and watching a holodrama," he said, his voice both wry and bitter. "Do we know who came to her aid?"

"We know who it was intended to look like," said Asokaji. "One Boba Fett, in what looked like distinctive Mandalorian armor."

"You think it wasn't?"

"It was someone wearing a very good imitation of his armor."

"In other words, someone wanted us to *think* it was Fett," mused Nek.

"Precisely, sir. No leads yet as to who it really was."

"Fett makes sense," Nek said. He felt a profound sorrow. None of this had needed to happen. He had known Natasi Daala for years. Most of the time they saw eye-to-eye, but this . . .

"Whoever helped her escape, she must be found and brought to trial. A *fair* trial," he said quietly. "I have sworn an oath of *krevi* to protect the Galactic Alliance, and I will do so with my last breath."

"Which," said Asokaji, "you almost experienced." He exchanged glances with Eramuth. "For what it's worth . . . neither of us thinks Daala had a hand in it." His cheek folds darkened a little.

"He knows this because he called her on it," said Eramuth. Nek gazed with renewed respect at his aide-de-camp.

"Her reaction convinced me she had nothing to do with it," Asokaji continued, but he volunteered nothing more.

Nek nodded his understanding. "How is Dorvan holding up?"

"Quite well, all things considered. The man doesn't have a lot of enemies. He might not be the most fascinating conversationalist in the world, but he gets things done and nearly everyone's amenable to working with him. The Jedi aren't out to ruin the GA, Nek."

"I know," Nek said. "That was one thing that Daala never understood." He sighed, growing fatigued by the conversation. "I suppose I'd better fill you in on what I remember of the attack before I drift off again," he said.

"Before you do that, I think we need to bring another participant to the meeting," said Eramuth. He reached into his old-fashioned black bag and withdrew a decidedly modern miniature holographic receiver. He pressed a button, and a very small figure of Wynn Dorvan appeared.

"Admiral," said Dorvan's tiny image.

"Dorvan," said Nek, pleased. "Good to see you, even looking so tiny."

"Not all of us can be tall and intimidating," said Dorvan in his usual bland but pleasant tones. "I am delighted to hear that you are awake and alert. Your uncle has informed me, however, that very few know about your change in condition. I think that's wise, and we should keep it that way for as long as we can. A sort of private club, as it were."

Nek glanced at his uncle, his aide, and the acting Chief of State. It was a good and trustworthy group . . . and just as important, small. He nodded.

"I agree. I remember everything about the attack. Let me tell you about it."

As he spoke, Nek realized that he would be confirming the rumors that he and Daala had been involved personally, but it could not be helped. Everyone needed to know the stark, simple truth if they were to accomplish the goals of shoring up the GA, bringing Daala back to trial, and catching those who were responsible for his attack.

He wasn't surprised that they all accepted the "revelation" without surprise. They asked who knew he was at Daala's residence the night of the attack.

"I don't think anyone did. Not even you, Asokaji. Did you get my signal?"

Bwua'tu had pressed an emergency signal button when he first realized—well, he amended, first *thought* he realized—who was attacking him. He was not and never would be a match for two Jedi Knights. Fortunately for him, but deepening the mystery, was the revelation that they could not possibly have been Jedi—simply because he was alive to tell the tale.

"I did, sir, and help came within moments. Otherwise, you wouldn't have made it. I did, however, assume you might have gone to visit the admiral, considering we found you such a short distance from her apartments."

Nek nodded. He continued with his narrative, describing the two attacking male humans in great detail. "I know I killed one," he said. "The one in Jedi robes. I think the other was injured in a fall earlier on. I'm sure you didn't find him."

"No, we didn't," said the miniature Dorvan. "Though not for lack of trying. We weren't even able to identify the false Jedi you killed. He simply didn't exist."

Nek felt his fur rippling even under the cast as the words sank in.

"We know they weren't real Jedi," he said, "and we know that someone wanted to make sure he wasn't identified. Someone went to a very great deal of effort and paid a large number of credits to ensure that."

"Indeed," said Dorvan. "Sir, you must keep pretending that you remember nothing. Esquire Bwua'tu, Asokaji—one of you, or someone that I personally appoint, is to be with the admiral at all times." He frowned, thinking. "We might even get a Jedi sentry, now that they're all cured. Given the current climate, it will soothe possible fears—and give you added protection. It will have to be someone we can trust completely, though, and that might be challenging."

"Sir? Are you comfortable with that?" asked Asokaji.

"No," Nek said. "Their first loyalty is to the Order. They will think they will have to tell—who is in charge?"

"Master Sebatyne."

Nek grimaced a little at the thought of that fierce warrior leading the Jedi. "Any Jedi will tell her. And if we try to lie, they will sense it. I might be able to fool the doctors, but I'm not a good enough actor to fool a Jedi."

Dorvan sighed. "You raise a good point, sir. I'd like to inform the Jedi at some point, however."

"Agreed, but not just yet. Forgive me, but I am extremely weary. Can we speak again later?"

In truth, blackness was already nudging in around the corners of his vision.

"Of course, sir," said Dorvan. "This all smacks of something far deeper than a simple personal vendetta. I have a great deal on my plate, but I will begin following the threads and . . ."

As he drifted into a weary but true sleep, Nek Bwua'tu thought with a pang of Natasi Daala. He then absently wondered if the fact that Wynn Dorvan's droning voice was letting him drift off swiftly into dreamland was a good or bad thing.

"I mean no insult," Padnel Ovin said, digging into a thick nerf steak in one of the better restaurants in the Senate District, "but Wynn Dorvan's voice put half the Senate to sleep today. I am sure what he said was important, but most of it was drowned out by snoring on my right and left."

Padnel Ovin, former leader of Ovin's Sand Panthers, looked woefully out of place in the refined, subdued atmosphere of the restaurant. Even though he no longer bristled with weapons or wore sand-saturated robes, he looked what he was—a rough-hewn warrior, more used to using a knife to kill an enemy than to simply cut up a nerf steak.

Han and Leia exchanged amused glances. "You're not the only one to have commented on that," Leia said. "And don't worry. He's the first to acknowledge it."

"He would not have made a good Sand Panther."

Han made a noise that fell somewhere between laughter and choking. Leia patted him on the back, hard-pressed not to smile herself. "I do not think Wynn Dorvan would have joined such an organization."

Always alert for criticism, even from friends, Ovin looked at her sharply. "Because he thinks I am a terrorist?"

"Goals can be reached in different ways," Leia said, "and his strengths lie in different areas. Perhaps if one such as Dorvan had been a Klatooinian elder, for instance, the Treaty of Vontor might have been abolished legally. Surely even your brother would have admitted that would be preferable to violence. I know you feel so."

He nodded, and said gruffly, "As I said . . . I believe Acting Chief of State Dorvan has things worth listening to. But a leader needs more. A leader needs charisma and the power of his conviction."

Leia thought of watching Dorvan racing up the steps in an effort to save Raynar Thul from being killed. "Give him a bit more time. He might surprise you. Still waters run deep."

"All waters run deep where I am from," Padnel said. His jowls shook lightly. It took Leia and Han a moment to realize he was making a joke, and then they all laughed.

"It's good to see you, Padnel," Han said. "I'm glad they let you in. I think the Klatooinians have a lot to offer. You'll get in there, shake things up, and the galaxy will be the better for it." The compliment was genuine. The Senate, as it had recently proved, was a staid and conservative gathering of beings for the most part. There were a few exceptions, such as Han and Leia's friend Luewet Wuul. Word of the new Senator from B'nish, Kameron Suldar, was positive, as well.

"That means a great deal coming from you two," Padnel said. "I will do what I can. Perhaps . . ." He hesitated.

"Go on," Leia encouraged.

"Perhaps . . . I am where I should be. Grunel was the founder and the real leader of the Sand Panthers, and will always be remembered as such. But if I can help this way, then perhaps I will honor his legacy while creating my own."

"I think, my friend," she said, "you are well on your way."

# Chapter Twelve

KORRIBAN

THE AIR ITSELF FELT THICK, AS IF IT WERE TRYING TO CHOKE BEN. IT was like . . . inhaling malice. Ben struggled not to cough, or shake off what seemed like a cloak of invisible cobwebs in the Force.

It was worse here than on Ziost. He wasn't sure why; perhaps because this was home to the original Sith, and origins of things had power. He let calm ripple through him in the Force. His breathing became easier and some of the apprehension was chased away into the back of his mind.

Luke showed no sign of distress, though he was clearly on the alert. Jaina was somewhere in between the Skywalkers; she was calmer than Ben, but not as focused as Luke.

Vestara was a conundrum of conflicting emotions.

Concern mixed with—Ben could only describe it as giddiness. She wanted to shrink away from such potent dark-side energy, but at the same time yearned to approach it. He caught her eye and gave her a reassuring nod and smile, and she gave him one of her own—albeit a slightly shaky one.

"Check in," Luke said. "Anyone sense anything?"

"Other than a desire to put on my cloak from Nam Chorios in the middle of a dry, hot world just to have *something* between me and the creepiness of this place, no," Ben replied.

"I don't sense Abeloth, or any of the Sith," Jaina replied. "Just . . . smaller energies. Dark, though."

"I sense them, as well," Vestara said. "It's . . . stronger than I anticipated."

"You come from a world of Sith," Ben said, not cruelly, but just curious. "This should be old hat for you."

"We made our world," Vestara said. "I'm used to it. Used to the eddies and flows. This . . . this is not my world."

Her voice dropped to a hush on the last few words, and Ben understood. Her people were different—they'd had five thousand years to evolve into something that, while definitely Sith, was neither the true old or new Sith. They were unique.

"Those smaller energies are animals, not human or Keshiri," Luke said. "But they're there. Our arrival has not gone unnoticed." He activated his lightsaber, and the rest did likewise. The familiar sound calmed Ben further until he felt . . . almost normal. He had been able to deal with Ziost alone at fourteen. He could handle Korriban with his father and cousin at sixteen.

"Let's start with the citadel," Luke said, and strode across the hard-baked sand toward it. Ben supposed he preferred a place that was intended for the living to dwell rather than a place for the dead, but truth be told, it was all unpleasant.

The complex, an ancient cloister, was encased by a high stone wall. The domes of the towers within were visible over the enclosure. The wall had seen better days. Once, it had been covered in blue tiles, a sort of mosaic. The few tiles that remained depicted unsettling images—fangs, eyes, claws.

Detritus that looked to be decades old was propped up beside the wall, and these pieces of odds and ends—depleted power core casings, portable deflector shields—had also seen better days. All of it was covered in a thick layer of sand, and none of it looked like it had been touched for years.

"I usually don't think of the Sith as being messy," Ben said.

"Our homes are meticulous," said Vestara absently, frowning in concentration. She reached out a foot and nudged a rusted piece of something that once might have come out a landspeeder. A forty-year-old landspeeder.

"It certainly doesn't look like anyone has been here for a while," Luke said. "But looks can be deceiving."

He followed the wall down to the gate, a four-meter slab of durasteel. This, too, showed red flakes of corrosion.

"What are we going to do, ring the doorbell?" Jaina asked.

"Let ourselves in," Luke said. He lifted his hands slightly and concentrated; the others imitated him. At first the massive door resisted, then slowly, centimeter by centimeter, it began to rise.

Ben felt sweat bead on his forehead, and his muscles were quivering with the mental strain. Even Luke's brow was deeply furrowed. They were able to lift the door only about six centimeters before it dropped down again with a definitive thud on the hard sand.

Ben dragged a hand over his forehead. "That shouldn't have been that hard," he said.

"No," Luke said. "It's been altered somehow. Perhaps in its creation the Sith used some of their alchemies. It can resist Force manipulation."

"What about a good old-fashioned lightsaber?" suggested Jaina. "Durasteel is durasteel, isn't it?"

Luke chuckled. Ben stared at him. Here in this forsaken, and—Ben had to be realistic—evil world, his father had chuckled.

"Let's give it a shot," Luke said.

All of them reactivated their lightsabers and began working together to cut a square hole, each taking one line. To Ben's surprise, though it was slow going, it worked. Sometimes, it would seem, the more pragmatic solution was the simplest.

They put their shoulders to the square and pushed. Groaning in protest, it eventually, sullenly yielded, and there was a loud, echoing *bang* as it fell inward.

"And that's definitely rung the doorbell," Jaina murmured.

They moved inside quickly, their lightsabers providing more than enough illumination. Ben extended his senses, but found nothing more sinister than vermin lurking inside. They moved slowly through an archway; a few cautious steps forward brought them into a central courtyard. Balconies glowered down at them, and doorways, any doors long since gone, seemed like empty staring eyes. The sand beneath their feet had changed to black cobblestones. Their backs to one another, their lightsabers at the ready, they slowly looked around. It didn't take much imagination to envision the balconies filled with dark-cloaked, hooded figures, or the yawning doorways opening onto terrors within.

But the reek of the dark side was old here. Not ancient, but certainly not fresh.

"There's no one here," Jaina said. The echoing effect of this place distorted her voice.

Vestara slowly nodded agreement. "It's deserted."

But could they really be sure? Ben wondered. "Do . . . should we search it?" This was a large place. Searching would take hours. And every minute they lingered here, the dark side had a chance to work its will upon them.

Luke focused a little longer, then shook his head. "No. We walked right into what could have been a perfect trap, and we'd be easy prey if anyone was here."

"If . . . they wanted to harm us," Vestara offered. Ben looked at her. Vestara sometimes told the truth when asked a direct question, but it was unlike her to volunteer information.

"What do you mean?" asked Jaina.

"Well," Vestara continued, "if the whole plan is to hide, they wouldn't come out even if we were easy prey."

"A good point," Luke said, "but this close? Your people are good, Vestara, but I don't think so many of them could hide so completely from three Jedi." To illustrate how confident he was, he extinguished his lightsaber.

Nothing happened.

"They may still be here on this world, but not at this site," he said. "Let's go. Daylight's burning, and I don't think we want to be out here at night."

Ben couldn't suppress a shudder.

* * *

The walk down the Valley of the Dark Lords was little better. The statues were enormous and loomed over them, casting long shadows literally now as the beings they represented did metaphorically in life. In those shadows, Ben felt cold.

"Why does this feel . . . wrong?" he wondered aloud. "I mean—I really thought we'd find them here."

"It did seem like our best bet," Jaina agreed glumly.

"We've only just started to look," Luke pointed out. "And if Vestara's guess is right—that any Sith that might be here are hiding—they could have sensed us approaching with enough time to flee the citadel, if not the planet."

"And make it look like no one had been there for years?" Ben asked skeptically.

"Don't underestimate the Sith," Vestara said. "But Master Skywalker is right. They might have left the citadel and be hiding among the ruins in small groups hoping we wouldn't bother to check. It's the sort of thing my—my father would do."

Ben looked at her searchingly. It certainly did sound as though she was doing her best to be of help. Or maybe she was just setting them up, encouraging them to walk into places steeped in the dark side for some kind of ambush? Stang, how he hated this . . . if he could only know one way or the other where she stood. He still hoped that one day, that would come to pass . . . and that she would stand with him, with the light side.

"So," he said, to take his mind off that line of thought, "we just . . . pick a tomb and start poking around?"

"If you have a better idea, I'm open to suggestions," Luke said with a touch of wryness.

Ben didn't.

These were worse, much worse, than the citadel. Ben could feel the chill of the dark side increase almost with every step they took. He extended his senses in the Force, bracing himself for the more intimate brush with the dark side energies lurking here like stagnant pools of ice water. They ascended the steep, long stairs up to the first tomb, craning their necks to look up into the hooded face that scowled down upon them.

There was no face carved on the statue, and that unsettled Ben more than any horrific snarl he might have encountered.

They reached the final step and paused, waiting for Luke's instructions. Ben's father stood looking as calm and unruffled as if he were comfortably in the Jedi Temple, but Ben could sense his alertness. There was a knot in his own stomach, and his brain was telling him, *Flee, flee while you can,* but he ignored it. He knew it for what it was—simple fear, not a true warning. The certainty produced a peacefulness, and the talons digging into him loosened their grip on his mind.

Luke stepped forward and placed a hand on the tomb, his brow furrowing in concentration. He stepped back and shook his head.

"The ancient masons did their work well. This tomb is completely sealed. There's no ventilation, and I sensed nothing living inside. Let's move on to the next one."

The sensation of apprehension, of cold malice, didn't lessen, even as they continued to find nothing in tomb after tomb. One or two of them had been broken into, but robbers—incredibly stupid or incredibly brave, Ben thought—had been there long before. All that remained were scattered coins, utensils, and the bones of the hapless beings that had been condemned to death simply to honor the dead Dark Lord. The tombs themselves were empty and covered with cobwebs.

Ben stepped gladly out of the shadows into the sunlight, feeble as it was, as they moved on to the next tomb.

"Dad," he ventured, "I'm starting to think we're going to come up empty-handed."

"I think Ben's right," Jaina said. "So far, we've found zilch. This is starting to feel like one big waste of time."

"Korriban is but one of many places with Sith history," Luke reminded them. "It was a good idea to start looking here, but I agree that it's looking more and more like we're hunting in the wrong place." He glanced meaningfully over at Vestara, who by either accident or design missed the look. "If we—"

The sudden surge in dark-side energy crashed on them like an unexpected wave. Anger, outrage, hatred, and murderous intent buffeted them. The feeling in the Force was echoed by a hair-raising howling sound that seemed to come from all directions at once.

The shadows cast by the looming figures of beings long dead seemed to come to life, but Ben realized almost immediately what the dark, uncannily fast creatures with glowing red eyes, three rows of teeth from which droplets of slaver fell, and strange wing-like extensions, had to be.

They had disturbed the guardians of the tombs, who were now descending, more than a dozen of them, with a single, driving thought: *Kill the intruders.*

And the Sith hounds would. Ben realized that almost at once. There were simply too many of them, and they were too strong with the dark side of the Force.

Ben had faced death before, and a peculiar calmness descended on him. He lifted his lightsaber, fixed his gaze with that of the leader, and prepared to slay as many of them as he could before the inevitable. The sudden, absurd thought came to him that they were much, much bigger than he had expected them to be.

What happened next stunned him.

Instead of lifting her lightsaber to do battle, Vestara extinguished the red blade. To Ben's shock, she began to run.

Toward the dark blue and black wave of tuk'ata.

Her brown hair flying, Vestara lifted her hand and cried out a single word, sharply.

*"Ur-kaa!"*

The creatures skidded to a halt almost as if physically struck by the word, one of them falling gracelessly over its own feet as it tried to stop too quickly.

"Vestara, what—?" began Ben. She shot him a sharp look of warning, and he fell silent, glancing over at his dad and Jaina. They, too, had paused, like the tuk'ata, but were ready to spring into action in a heartbeat.

Slowly, their glowing red eyes fixed on Vestara, the Sith hounds sat, obedient, but only for this moment. Their tongues lolled, dripping, and their pseudo-wings flexed and strained.

Vestara continued to speak to them in the strange language. *"Haa, neyo la yud masur kee, tah uhnah kahru lur shu."* They listened, ears pricked forward even as their baleful eyes flickered from her to fasten hungrily and hatefully upon the Jedi. When she had finished saying . . . whatever it was she was saying . . . they grew highly agitated. Then, to Ben's astonishment, the tuk'ata pack cringed back, as if expecting a blow.

Vestara again spoke, still more firmly, more challengingly, projecting her strength in the Force.

*"Na-hah ur su ka-haat. Su ka haru aat."* The dogs, for such they looked like now, if huge and impossibly dangerous, positively prostrated themselves, whimpering and shaking. Vestara paused for a moment, and then said something in a calmer, kinder voice.

*"Eyah seh maat, shu kor huaan."* The tuk'ata leapt up and pranced around her, fawning on her, and then turned as one and raced off. Vestara lowered her hand, and Ben saw that despite her assertive stance, that hand was trembling slightly.

"What did you *do*?" he asked, stunned.

"I talked to them," she said. With a barely visible effort, she calmed herself and her hand ceased to shake. "Jaina said earlier that the tuk'ata understood the Sith language. They exist to serve and protect the Sith, so . . . I told them to lead them to us if there were any here." She met his gaze. "There are no Sith on Korriban."

"And we're supposed to believe that." Jaina snorted. "And how very convenient that you just happen to speak the ancient Sith language."

"The ship that brought my ancestors to Kesh is more than five thousand years old," Vestara said. "The Old Tongue was preserved and passed down. Not everyone on Kesh knows it, but those who are apprentices and higher do. It's part of our training."

Jaina looked a bit nonplussed. "Well . . . you could have told us this before."

Vestara smiled, a cold little smile that Ben didn't like. "Why should I?" was all she said.

Anxious to avoid an argument, Ben said, "How do you know there aren't any Sith here? They didn't . . . talk back to you, did they?"

Vestara turned to him, the coldness dissolving as she spoke. "No, not with words. But you saw their reactions. I told them to find the Sith that were on this world, and they cowered. They were upset because they couldn't please me, because there is no one for them to lead me to."

It seemed believable. Hideous and alarming and violent as they were, the tuk'ata were, in the end, canines of a sort, and canine body language seemed to be universal. They had indeed cowered, seeming to beg forgiveness—a proper display for disappointing their "master."

Jaina seemed about to retort, but Luke said, unexpectedly, "I agree."

Ben looked at his dad, astonished. Even Vestara seemed surprised. "You do? Why?"

"Their presences in the Force reflected their obsequious body language. Whatever it was you asked them, they couldn't do it or give it to you." Ben's pleasure faded a little. So his dad was implying that Vestara was lying about what she had told the tuk'ata. He supposed he should have known.

"It also corroborates the evidence—or lack thereof—that we've seen so far. There's nothing here to indicate that anyone's been here for years. Too, I believe that I could distinguish human and Keshiri Force essences from the general miasma of dark-side energy." He shook his head. "No, they're not here."

"So it's another dead end," Ben muttered.

"Oh, cheer up, Ben," Vestara said, her eyes twinkling. "Think of all the other places we're going to get to explore."

Ben gave her an extremely dirty look.

"Fortunately we're not the only ones searching," Luke said. "Once we're away from here I'll contact the other vessels and see if they've discovered anything."

"Then let's go," said Jaina. "I'm anxious to be on to the next one. I'm tired of playing hide-and-seek."

The news was disappointing, to say the least. "Nothing at all?" Luke asked the fourth group they had spoken with.

"No, Master Skywalker," said the calm, almost flat voice of Raynar Thul. "We would most certainly have told you if we found even a clue. No Sith, no Abeloth, no sign that anyone has been here for centuries."

They had received the same response from all of the search parties, including that led by Master Kyle Katarn. No one saw anything to suspect that either Abeloth or the Lost Sith Tribe had ever visited these worlds. Luke thanked them, doing his best to keep the sharpness of his disappointment—and growing concern—out of his voice.

He leaned back in the pilot's chair and closed his eyes, rubbing them with the heel of his hand.

"Maybe they just . . . went home," Jaina suggested. "They seem to keep getting the worse end of the deal."

"You think they slunk back to Kesh to lick their wounds?" Luke said. He shook his head. "No. That doesn't sound like the Lost Tribe to me. For one thing, I don't think they'd survive very long if they came home empty-handed. Would they, Vestara?"

"There are severe penalties for failure," admitted Vestara. "To have lost both you and Ben *and* Abeloth as prizes would not reflect well on the strike force. Better to stay away until they could come home with something to show for it, even if it took years."

Was she simply trying to protect her homeworld still, or was she telling the truth? What she said was exactly what Luke had just stated that he himself believed. It could be—probably was—the truth.

"But you have no idea where they would go," he said. It was a statement, not a question.

"No." He sensed she wasn't lying, but he also knew that one could easily get around detection with the proper mental gymnastics.

Luke sighed. "Then we simply have to keep searching for them. The Lost Tribe and Abeloth both."

"There are an awful lot of old Sith sites in this galaxy," Jaina warned. "Even for several ships of Jedi to be exploring."

"Then we've got to be better hunters," Luke said. "Talk to Natua tomorrow. Let's see if we can narrow the search."

Jaina nodded, looking glum, and bid them good night.

Vestara rose, as well. "If you'll excuse me," she said. "It was . . . kind of a difficult day and I'm extremely tired. I'm going to turn in."

Ben smiled at her. "Thanks for the help with the tuk'ata," he said.

She returned the smile. "Of course," she said, glancing at Luke. He said nothing other than "Good night, Vestara," and he felt a brush of disappointment from her.

Luke more than anyone understood the deep wanting Ben was experiencing. No one ever wanted to believe that someone he cared for was irredeemable. But Ben should know better. Not everyone could be saved.

Particularly if they didn't want to be. And Luke was still deeply mistrustful, despite the girl's apparent effort to help them.

When they had found Abeloth and the Lost Tribe, and Vestara came firmly down on the side of the Jedi in all interactions with them, then he would believe she stood a chance. And not a second before.

The door hissed shut behind Vestara and she leaned against it, closing her eyes. She hadn't lied to the Skywalkers. It had indeed been a difficult day, and she was exhausted.

So much dark-side energy, swirling around her—it had been almost impossible to not joyfully yield to its seductive song. But she couldn't. Not yet . . . and, she thought as she sat down and unbraided her hair, maybe not ever. It had been sweet and alluring, but for the first time she had a glimmer of insight into what the Jedi must feel when encountering it.

The dark side had ice to it. She had never noticed that; it was all she had known. But traveling with Ben and Luke had granted her a different perspective, and that made her feel uneasy.

She knew they were too far for Korriban's Force energies to be reaching her, but like the memory of standing shivering in the cold even after one had come into a warm room, in her mind she could still feel them. Vestara slipped out of her clothes and into a sanisteam, then wrapped herself in the bed's blankets. Tired though she was, she lay awake in the darkness for some time.

She hadn't lied to Luke, but she hadn't told him everything, either. She had indeed spoken to the so-called Sith hounds, telling them not to harm her or anyone she was with, and to find any Sith present on this dark world. And they had cringed and whimpered, because there were no Sith to be found.

What Vestara hadn't told Luke was the third instruction she had given the tuk'ata.

*Harm no one who stands with me, on pain of death. Seek out any of my brethren who might come to our ancient home.*

*And warn them to stay hidden.*

# Chapter Thirteen

SOLO SAFE HOUSE, CORUSCANT

"I'M NOT TIRED." ALLANA SOLO, KNOWN TO NEARLY EVERYONE BUT her closest family as Amelia, scowled fiercely at her grandfather.

"You know, honey, you only use that tone of voice when you're exhausted," Han Solo replied as he tucked her in and knelt beside the bed, searching for the girl's latest favorite stuffed animal, a fuzzy eopie that had seen better days. It had become Anji's favorite toy, too, and had gone downhill rapidly since the day the Solos had brought the nexu cub home as a pet for Allana. "So in effect, when you protest that much, I know it's a dead certainty that you *are* tired." His hand closed on something soft and slightly soggy and he grimaced as he pulled out the beloved toy.

"Oh, you mean I have a tell."

Han, who was tucking the toy beside her, did a double take. "What?"

"A tell," said the eight-year-old. "Like when you're gambling, and you do something that lets someone know if you have a good hand or—"

"I know what a tell is, young lady," said Han, trying to decide if he was amused, proud, or shocked. He thought about it for a moment, then stroked her short, dyed-black hair. "And yes, that's one of them."

She smiled up at him, her eyelids already beginning to droop slightly. "What are my others?"

"Hey, I'm not laying all my cards on the table, missy," he said, planting a loud smooch on her forehead. Beside the girl, Anji gave him a feline smile, eyes half closed as she lazily started gnawing the eopie. "Sleep tight, kiddo."

"I will, Grandpa. Is Grandma coming in, too?"

"She's got something she needs to take care of, but she'll be in soon."

"But I'll be asleep by then!"

"This from the girl who was so adamant that she wasn't tired?"

"Well . . . maybe I am. A little," Allana admitted.

"Well, a grandma's kiss is just as good whether you're awake or asleep," Han promised her.

"I guess you're right. Good night, Grandpa."

" 'Night, sweetheart," Han said softly. He activated the pale blue hologram of a moon, stars, and clouds that always seemed to give Allana such peaceful dreams, then pressed a button and the door hissed shut. He walked down the hall to what served as their office in the safe house and poked his head in.

"What is so fascinating that you have to miss kissing our granddaughter good night?" he asked. He wasn't angry, just curious; Leia hardly ever missed tucking Allana in.

Leia glanced up, and there was worry in her brown eyes. "This." She pointed to a message flashing on the screen.

INFORMATION YOU WILL WANT TO HAVE.
SAFETY FOR YOUR FAMILY GUARANTEED.
REPLY FOR MORE.

"Short and completely mysterious," Han mused, frowning a little. "It came in on my private channel."

"The one only about six people and two droids have access to?"

"That would be the one."

Han's frown became a full-fledged scowl. "So unless Artoo-Detoo has been reprogrammed or Ben is playing a prank, you've been hacked."

Leia nodded. "I'm afraid so. The question now is, do we want to reply or have Artoo start a trace for the hacker?"

"Oh come on, where's your sense of adventure?" Han said. "Look at it this way—if they contacted you legitimately, everything's fine. If they hacked in, they've already got what they came for."

Leia made a sour face. "That's not at all reassuring." But her own curiosity got the better of her.

She leaned forward and typed in, *Replying. Tell me more.*

A few seconds later, more blue letters crawled across the screen.

OLD FRIENDS MAKE THE BEST BARGAINS.

Han felt a chill. Whoever it was, they claimed to know Leia, at least. "So this old friend wants to sell us information."

"Han . . . does something about this ring a bell for you?"

"Someone trying to sell information?" He shook his head. "Everybody wants something. Some people are just honest about the fact that they want credits." He grinned suddenly. "Like me."

She gave him a mock shove, then sobered. "I know, but there's . . . this seems very familiar. I can't put my finger on it."

"Maybe they are old friends."

"No," Leia said with certainty. "Old friends would say who they were at the outset. And we have more old enemies than old friends." She tapped in another message: *What is the nature of this information?*

There was a long pause, and she wondered if perhaps she had scared them off. Then:

OLD FRIENDS KNOW WHERE DAALA HAS GONE. WILL MAKE PARTNERS A FINE OFFER.

And then she knew. "Just when I thought things were looking up," Leia murmured.

"What am I missing? You know who this—oh no," Han said, as realization crashed over him. "You've got to be kidding me," he said. "Not—"

"You bet," said Leia drily.

OFFICES OF THE CHIEF OF STATE, CORUSCANT

"Jedi Solo," came Dorvan's bland voice. "This is an unexpected surprise. I hope it's a pleasant one."

She turned toward him, smiling. "Possibly not, but I promise it's not a disaster, either."

"That is more assurance than I get most mornings," he said. He removed Pocket from his coat and placed her in her small nest on his desk. Leia reached out a finger and patted the little creature, who sniffed at her and then closed her eyes to enjoy the caress. "Caf?"

"Please," Leia said. "I hope it was all right for Desha to show me into your office."

"Perfectly," Dorvan said, pouring a cup for each of them. "My door is always open to you. In fact, my position is open to you, if you'd take it." He lifted an eyebrow in mock hopefulness as he gave her the cup.

Leia smiled, accepting the caf and giving Pocket one last pat. "No, no, I've had my stint. That's . . . actually what I came to discuss with you. I hope that I've been of some help with the transition of government. I might be of more . . . but in a different capacity."

Dorvan sat and sipped his caf, eyes regarding her thoughtfully. "Go on."

"As I know you know, Han and I have . . . connections . . . in various places," she began.

Dorvan raised a hand. "Please," he said, "remember plausible deniability."

She smiled a little at that. "Of course," she said. "But because of those connections, we now have a lead on where Daala might be."

His eyebrows lifted slightly—an indication of great surprise. "Is that lead something you can share?"

"Not until it's verified," Leia said.

"Ah. So you're trying to decide where you could help the most," Dorvan said.

Leia nodded. "This political jumble that you're having to deal with now—I understand it. I'm in a unique position, and I can help you through it. I can help all of us through it."

"You can, and you *are* unique," he agreed. "You're a Jedi, so they trust you to represent them fairly. But we both know that beneath those brown and cream robes beats the heart of a born diplomat. Even Daala knew that."

She gave a small, self-deprecating smile. "Guilty as charged," she said. "Which is what makes this so difficult."

"Do you trust these sources? I'm sure there are plenty of beings out there who would love to lead you both on a wild caranak chase."

"I do," Leia replied. "They're sound."

He was silent for a moment, then spoke thoughtfully. "To be able to put Daala on trial, fairly and publicly, would eliminate any lingering doubt as to the legitimacy of the current administration. I can't think of any other single action that would do more to heal the GA and get things back on track so that it could become an effective institution. No offense to your skills, Jedi Solo, but even the best you could bring to the table would pale in comparison."

"None taken, which is why this is something I feel I need to do," Leia said.

"Then do so." He smiled slightly, and it reached his eyes, turning them warm for a moment. "And I say this as earnestly as is possible . . . may the Force be with you."

Leia thought about whom they were trusting to deliver the "information" on Daala's whereabouts and gave him a wry smile.

"Believe me," she said, "We're going to need it."

MOFF DRIKL LECERSEN'S ESTATE, CORUSCANT

"Sir, there is someone outside who wishes to meet with you." Eethree's voice sounded offended on behalf of his master. Clearly, beings of good manners who understood protocol and etiquette did not show up unannounced on the doorsteps of important personages without appointments, as far as Eethree was concerned. That unspoken but vocally implied censure was also, Lecersen was certain, directed in large part at him. After all, he was the one who instructed the protocol droid to keep an eye out for such things.

"What species?" he asked, setting aside the datapad he had been perusing. The hour was late, and the Moff was alone in his sitting room. Busts of various late heroes of the Empire occupied positions of honor in the room, as did antiques and souvenirs Lecersen had collected over the years. Save for these objets d'art, the room was spare and austere, lacking the enveloping quality of the dining room with its heavy furnishings and thick fur rugs. Surrounded by evidence of the glories of the Empire—the Empire he was now moving steadily toward ruling—this was Lecersen's favorite place to retire, think, plot, and plan. The only concessions to comfort were the artificial fireplace and two large chairs, so that he might pursue such endeavors more easily.

"A Minyavish," replied Eethree.

That, Lecersen had not expected. A member of a species that had formerly been slave owners on Qaras, but who now were removed from such positions of power over others. Who, in fact, were themselves facing exile. Why would such a being come to him? And why in so clandestine a fashion? The little mystery that had started with the piece of low-tech flimsi was becoming more and more intriguing . . . and potentially dangerous. He thought for a moment.

"Show him in, and then leave us alone until I summon you."

"Are you quite certain, sir? The fellow has a rather shifty look about him. I don't know that I'd give him the time of day, let alone—"

"You are qualified to comment on his manners, Eethree, not his personality," Lecersen said sharply. The E-3POs, which had been developed for Imperial use many years earlier, had a reputation for arrogance and haughtiness due to their proprietary TechSpan I module. This allowed them to interface with various Imperial networks denied to other protocol droids, and the cursed things thought themselves superior. Eethree had served Lecersen well for many years, and he often found the droid's snooty attitude amusing. However, tonight it irritated him.

"Very good, sir," said Eethree promptly, though not without the droid equivalent of a "*hmmph!*" of injured pride. He turned around and left the sitting room.

Lecersen continued to sit in his chair, sipping a glass of Hapan gold wine, his mind racing a thousand kilometers a minute. He did not bother to rise when Eethree returned, escorting the first Minyavish whom Lecersen had ever seen in the flesh. Of the two sentient species that lived on Qaras, Lecersen had to admit that the Minyavish were by far the less attractive.

They were bipedal, feathered, and squat; humanoid, but only just. A large head sat atop rounded shoulders and a chunky torso, but that head sported some of the largest, most intense golden eyes Lecersen had ever seen, with darker gold, slitted pupils. The being wore little in the way of clothing; the bright green, purple, and gold feathers were more than sufficient for modesty. His barrel chest was, however, crisscrossed with two pieces of fabric as colorful as his feathers, and he sported an armband inlaid with four large, winking blue gems. Lecersen had found it was often difficult to read the expressions of members of an alien species unless he was familiar with their mannerisms. This one looked irritated and pugnacious, but for all he knew, he—she?—could be wearing the Minyavish version of a large smile.

"Moff Drikl Lecersen," said the droid, "may I present Tiyuu'cha Mahlor."

"Charmed, I'm sure," said Lecersen. He still did not rise. "Have a seat. May Eethree offer you something to drink?" Whatever the Minyavish's poison might be, Lecersen was confident he had it. He had one of the largest exotic liquor collections on Coruscant, having found early on in his career that any credits expended thus were sound investments when it came to dealing with other beings.

"No, thank you." The voice was gruff, hollow sounding. The Minyavish—Mahlor—sounded as irritated as he looked. He trundled to one of the larger overstuffed chairs by the holographic fireplace and eased himself down gingerly until he was certain the chair would hold his weight.

"That will be all, Eethree. I'll call for you if I need you."

"Of course, sir." With a whir of servos, the droid left the room, and the door automatically closed shut behind him.

"To what," drawled Lecersen, sipping his wine, "do I owe this rather peculiar visit?"

Mahlor chuckled. At least, that's what the raspy noise sounded like to Lecersen. "I think you will be grateful that I chose to be so . . . peculiar . . . when you hear."

"Please, I am all ears."

The Minyavish blinked, three times. "For more than seven thousand years, my people have quite happily managed Qaras, with the Jessar serving us."

"If by *managed* you mean 'dominated' and if by *serving* you mean 'enslaved to,' then I am already well aware of this."

The feathered brows, a startling purple over the yellow eyes, drew together. "Wordplay doesn't serve you well, Moff Lecersen."

"On the contrary, it has served me well many times in the past. If my wit is too sharp for your liking, then pray tell me what you are getting at, Mahlor. The hour is late, and I rise early on the morrow. I am an extremely busy man."

"Yes, of course you are." A sneer, it would seem, was recognizable in any species. "Very busy indeed, as I understand it."

Lecersen had already been deeply suspicious, but now his inner alarms were going off like klaxons. He smiled slightly, keeping his expression and body language calm. "So why don't you get right to the point?"

"We were the masters of our world, until the Jessar got it into their heads to overthrow us."

Ah, a complaint. As if he hadn't heard something similar from every former master of every overthrown government of every world that had had a revolution recently. It was growing rather tiresome.

"Your government has already lodged its request through the proper channels. You'll have to take it up with them. Dorvan's a difficult man to make an appointment with, but his assistant might be able to get you on the schedule. The offices of the galactic acting Chief of State are open—"

"I have no desire to contact Wynn Dorvan," said Mahlor. "I came to see you."

Deliberately, Lecersen set his now-empty glass on the small table by his chair, folded his hands in his lap, and regarded Mahlor steadily.

"I tire of this conversation, and I have finished my nightcap," he said. "You have thirty seconds to get to the point before Eethree escorts you out."

The great eyes narrowed, and the being's feathers ruffled. With an effort, he settled them. "I blame the Freedom Flight for stirring up the rebels."

"Of course you do. Everyone always does. It can never be possible that the system was antiquated and dysfunctional." His voice dripped with sarcasm. Despite his words to the Minyavish, he was privately enjoying this; it had been a long time since he had been able to be so free with his tongue.

"And I blame *you,*" Mahlor said, leaning forward intently, his huge eyes wide and unblinking, "for the Freedom Flight."

Lecersen's stomach, warm from the gold wine he had been drinking, suddenly turned into a cold, hard knot. He recovered almost at once.

"I would say you had been drinking too much, but as you haven't touched a drop, I must simply conclude that you are either insane or in desperate need of attention. This conversation is over." He lifted his finger, about to stab it down on the small button that would summon Eethree.

"Don't."

If Lecersen had had any doubt as to the fact that Mahlor had come from a species of beings used to being obeyed, it would have vanished at the tone of that single word. He lifted an eyebrow and stared coldly back.

"What . . . did you just say to me?"

"Don't press that button until you have heard me out," said the Minyavish.

Lecersen debated for a moment, then concluded that it would probably behoove him to listen. "Fair enough."

"I have information and evidence that links you to the Freedom Flight," Mahlor continued. "I know that you created it initially, and continue to fund it."

"I'll play along. What sort of evidence are we talking about?"

The slit that passed for a mouth among the Minyavish curved in what was meant to be a grin. "Data. Witnesses. Recordings of conversations. Repair bills for vessels."

"All of which could be falsified," replied Lecersen, waving a dismissive hand.

"Each on its own? Certainly. Taken together, it's a rather condemning picture."

"I presume you have a point."

"I do, indeed. I do not think you would appreciate the galaxy knowing about your connection to this organization, Moff Lecersen. But if you would assist us, this information could quietly vanish. And so could the witnesses."

"And with what endeavor do you require assistance?"

The Minyavish suddenly quivered, all over, rather violently, and when he spoke it was with a deep intensity. "Justice, Moff Lecersen! Because of the Freedom Flight—your organization—my people have toppled from positions of power, wealth, and influence to beings with barely any credits and no home. We are being exiled from our own world by that—that—*Roki Kem*." He spat the word, his body still shaking with his outrage. "This would never have happened if the Flight had not come and stirred up trouble."

"Now, now, you don't know that," said Lecersen mildly. "Freedom is a deep-seated need for many beings. It's possible that—"

"No. Unrest has been fomenting only in the last few years. Never before had the Jessar experienced this so-called 'deep-seated need.'" His voice dripped contempt. He was wrong, of course. Lecersen had done his homework. He had heard about the Silence oath, and was well aware that it was an old, old tradition among the Jessar. Slaves who were planning to escape, or who had managed to do so only to be recaptured, submitted to being beaten—sometimes to death—rather than reveal anything that would harm future escape attempts for others. The Minyavish, like most beings who fancied themselves decent, had lied to themselves about the true nature of the institution.

Nonetheless, he continued to humor the fuming Minyavish. "What form would this . . . justice take? An army, to slaughter your enemies and take back your world?"

The feathers rose along every inch of Mahlor's body, reminding Lecersen of the way a Bothan's fur would ripple in irritation.

"You are already believing Rokari Kem's propaganda," he snarled.

"We are not brutes! We could win back our world, yes, but at what cost? Your kind might not shrink from having so much blood on your hands, but no species on Qaras would willingly embark on so violent a course. No. We have been exiled, and so we will go. But we have no place *to* go. We are a large populace—three billion. There is no world that has offered to shelter us, and we do not have the means or funds to tame a new one. That is what I want from you. You are directly responsible for the Minyavish being forced to leave Qaras. You will find us a new home."

Lecersen was not pleased. He had not expected such a pacifistic response by the seemingly belligerent Minyavish. Covertly funding another revolt would be more cost-effective, and he might have been willing to consider it. Such a debt from the Minyavish could prove useful if—no, *when*—they won. Lecersen didn't support losers.

But relocate three billion beings?

"That is absurd," he said. "What you ask is a massive undertaking, and there's nothing in it for me."

"You have connections."

"Oh, indeed I do, but there's nothing in it for *them,* either."

"Then you leave me no choice. I will expose your connection to the Freedom Flight."

Lecersen laughed. "Oh, dear," he said mockingly. "Reveal the fact that mean old Moff Lecersen actually wanted to do a little good in this galaxy. How awful it will be to be exposed as someone who wants to help free enslaved populations. Go right ahead, Mahlor. I dread the fact that the galaxy will know my deepest, darkest secret—that I am a decent being."

"You are not," growled Mahlor. "Your reasons for founding the Freedom Flight were not in the least altruistic. Nor were those of your cohorts."

Lecersen had been relaxing the more the Minyavish spoke. Even if the evidence of which he spoke was real, exposure of his role wouldn't harm him. It might even boost his popularity in certain quarters, which meant expanding his influence. That stiff-necked Jagged Fel would certainly approve. But now he tensed, ever so slightly.

"Do go on," he urged.

"You didn't do it to free slaves. You did it because you knew it would cause upheaval at a time when the Galactic Alliance—particularly the Chief of State—was in no real position to handle it properly. You knew how Admiral Daala would react, and you knew what that kind of reaction would do to her popularity rating."

It was as if the Minyavish had had a prime seat at the table the other day.

"You spoke of cohorts."

The ugly smile grew. "Senators Fost Bramsin of Coruscant and Haydnat Treen of Kuat. I am certain there are others, but I think that's enough to prove my point. I'm sure that they might be willing to listen to me if you are not."

This was bad. This was quite bad.

"Did your government send you?"

"No," he said. "They would never stoop to begging. But if I presented them with a deal already worked out, they would take it. They would have to." Again the chuckle. "And I would be the savior of my people."

Lecersen gave him a slow, dark smile. "So you are acting alone. What's to stop me from killing you right now?"

"I have cohorts of my own," Mahlor replied. "If I do not meet them within an hour, they have orders to approach Bramsin and Treen with the same deal I am making you—and they, too, will tell others. So you'll cooperate."

"You know," said Lecersen languidly, tilting his head to the side and frowning as if in consideration, "I don't think I will."

He pushed a button on the arm of the chair.

A droid entered immediately, but it wasn't the amiable E-3PO. This was a gray skeleton, glowing red eyes staring out of its metallic skull, its mouth yawning open as it lifted its right arm. Integrated into the limb was a blaster cannon, and it was pointed straight at Mahlor's midsection—a broad target indeed.

The Minyavish's horrified reaction was quite gratifying. He shrank back against the chair, his eyes enormous as he stared at the sinister-looking YVH and the even more sinister weapon.

"No! You wouldn't kill me!"

Lecersen nodded to the YVH.

The droid fired, and the Minyavish sprawled in the chair, limbs akimbo, head lolling.

Lecersen rose, lifting a hand to instruct the droid to lower its weapon, and stood staring down at the limp form.

“No,” he said, “I wouldn’t. Not yet, at least. Not until I know everything that you do.”

# Chapter Fourteen

INDIGO TOWER RESTAURANT, CORUSCANT

"I've never heard of this place," said the fledgling Senator from B'nish, Kameron Suldar.

"That's because I daresay you haven't had the opportunity to travel much beyond your lodgings and the Senate Building," said Senator Haydnat Treen. She beamed at him and patted his hand. "You know what they say about all work and no play."

"It makes you successful?" He gave her a sly smile. Gracious, but he was a handsome fellow. Several years younger than she, of course, but with the gray hair and facial lines that told the world he was no callow youth. *Much* more appealing than Drikl Lecersen. And Treen did like surrounding herself with pretty things, and pretty people. But useful as she hoped he would be, Suldar was nowhere near becoming Emperor, and thus she would be nowhere near becoming Empress if she changed direction at this late point. She didn't even know for certain if he would be amenable to joining their cause.

But Treen had not become a Senator from a planet of politically astute—some might say cutthroat—humans without being a superb judge of character. She was fairly confident that by the time they reached dessert and caf, he would be joining their merry little band bound for glory.

"No, dear boy, it makes you dull and hollow-eyed and unable to properly seize opportunities when they come your way."

He gave her a smile, but his gaze sharpened, ever so slightly. "And tonight will present me with such an opportunity?" he asked, his voice light.

"There will certainly be an opportunity to have an exquisite dessert called Vagnerian canapés. There is often a debate as to what pairs best with them, but let me assure you, only plebeians drink Cassandran brandy with them. The two flavors do *not* complement each other, and the brandy should never be drunk simply to wash down a dessert. I would recommend simple black caf."

He chuckled. "I yield the floor to your expertise, ma'am."

"Then you are certain to go far. Oh . . . I do hope you like the color blue."

The air limo pulled up to one of Coruscant's most exclusive restaurants, the Indigo Tower. Modeled after the famous Skysitter Restaurant, it enjoyed fame based at least partially on the novelty of being a revolving dining room on a tower high above the Coruscanti skyline. Its exterior was made of shining, blue-black durasteel.

The chauffeur opened the doors for them, and Suldar shivered a little. "I understand why you suggested the overcoat and scarf now," he said.

"Yes, it's rather chilly at this altitude, but the temperature is always perfect inside."

The doors slid open to reveal a world of blue. Thick, soft blue carpeting, blue-black chairs and tables, midnight-blue ceiling with softly winking lights simulating stars. The light, also a soothing blue, made everything look cool and mysterious. "Ah," Suldar said, looking around. "Fortunately, Senator, I do like blue."

"Excellent."

A young female Ortolan, her skin matching the décor, greeted them cheerfully by name. "Good evening, Senator Treen, Senator Suldar. I understand, sir, that this is your first time dining with us?"

"Indeed," said Suldar, glancing with mild surprise at Treen.

"Please let us know if there is anything we can do to make your experience a memorable one. Senator Bramsin arrived just a few minutes ago. Please follow me."

She led them through the main dining room, past a trio of another Ortolan and two Bith. A Pa'lowick stepped up to the mike and was met with applause; clearly the performers were well known in the establishment.

Treen saw something ugly and mean-spirited flash across Kameron Suldar's face for an instant, then it was gone. The Ortolan hostess opened the door to one of the private dining rooms.

It was cozy rather than intimidating, the blue theme slightly more subdued by a white tablecloth and a multicolored bouquet of flowers. Fost Bramsin looked up from his drink and extended a hand.

"Hope you don't mind if I don't get up, young man. It's a bit more challenging these days than when I was your age."

"Of course not, sir," Suldar said, quickly stepping over to shake the elder statesman's frail, liver-spotted hand. "It's an honor to be dining with you tonight. Thank you both for the invitation."

"The food here is superb," said Bramsin. "And they serve some very rare and very fine beverages. It makes up for the staff."

Again, Treen noticed something flit across Suldar's face. Treen thought she knew what it was.

"Fost and I don't much care for nonhumans," she said. It was the first card. If he took umbrage, they could simply all have a pleasant evening and she would move on to another potential ally.

To her pleasure, Suldar looked relieved. "I'm . . . rather glad to hear you say that," he said. "I admit I don't, either. There are only humans on B'nish, and while one likes to be open-minded, I haven't really liked any of the nonhumans I've met. They're so . . ." He sighed. "Well . . . inferior."

Bramsin and Treen exchanged pleased glances. "We always arrange to have human waitstaff, so you will be spared further unpleasantries."

"Well, as you assure me the food is excellent and I can certainly say the company could not be better, we are sure to have a wonderful dinner," Kameron said.

"Oh, I'm absolutely *positive* of it," said Treen, smiling like a sand panther.

## MOFF DRIKL LECERSEN'S ESTATE

Minyavish, mused Lecersen, were much tougher than they looked.

Mahlor had not broken for several hours, even when subjected to the tender loving care of an IT-O interrogator. The decades-old droid was part of Lecersen's collection of antiques. Few knew it was still quite functional and had been employed more than once in recent years.

Still, in the end, Tiyuu'cha Mahlor was no Princess Leia Organa, and Lecersen was interrupted in his study by Eethree bearing the pleasant news that Mahlor was "willing to talk now, and, fortunately, is still sufficiently coherent to do so."

There was a room deep in the bowels of the estate where this unfortunate but necessary duty was performed. It was cold, spare, and slightly damp. There was a single chair, a table with a pitcher and a glass, a few glow rods, and the hovering interrogator, always fashionable in basic black.

The Minyavish was a sorry sight. Much of his beautiful plumage had been plucked out and lay strewn about the floor, the purple, green, and gold providing vivid color in sharp contrast to the stark gray of the room. The revealed skin was pale blue and bore evidence of acid burns, puncture wounds from the interrogation drug syringe, and the unmistakable gouges of shears and scalpel. His species' blood, Lecersen noted with mild surprise, was the golden color of honey.

Both of his large, lovely eyes with their slitted, dark gold pupils had been utterly ruined.

He sat, tightly bound, no longer proud and boastful and arrogant, but sobbing, producing a soft, cooing sound of deep agony.

"Well," said Lecersen, "not so cocky now, are you?"

Another soft sob. Lecersen eyed the hovering ball.

"Eethree said he was willing to talk. I trust the interrogation ceased the moment he said so?"

"Such is my programming," said the IT-O in a deep, chilling monotone. "I am ready to recommence if you so order."

"Let me hear what he has to say first."

"His tongue is intact," the interrogator confirmed.

"Well now, Mahlor," Lecersen said, "I'm all ears."

"You . . . were right," rasped the Minyavish, his huge head drooping over his plucked, barrel chest.

"I often am. About which part?"

A clacking sound. "W-water?"

"Later. About which part?"

"No . . . cohorts." Each word was clearly costing the Minyavish dearly.

Lecersen smiled slowly. "I see. I rather gathered that when, within the allotted hour, absolutely no one contacted me at all. Senators Treen and Bramsin are, I believe, quite happily at dinner at the moment. So, you've no fellow conspirators. Who else knows about this evidence?"

Again, the cooing sob. "No one."

"Come now, all that evidence . . . or were you lying about that, too? Do I need to order the IT-O to—"

"No!" The word was a shriek ripped from the being's very core. "Please, please, no! The evidence does exist! I wasn't making it up!"

It would have been in Mahlor's benefit to lie, to say that there never was and never had been any hard evidence, just a rumor that he had gambled was true. Instead, he was confirming his earlier threat. Proof enough to Lecersen that the IT-O, once again, was working as intended.

"If you could just write down—oh," he said. Writing would be rather hard for a blind being. "Tell me what exactly you have, and where I might find it."

"I told you . . . p-please, water . . ."

Lecersen waved a hand. Emitting its unique throbbing, humming sound, the IT-O maneuvered on its repulsors over to the table. Its grasping claw extended, gripped the pitcher, and poured water into the glass. It bore the glass over to Mahlor and pressed it against his mouth.

At once the Minyavish opened wide, gulping and coughing as the droid interrogator poured water into his mouth and down what little plumage remained on his mostly plucked chest.

"Careful," admonished Lecersen, "we don't want him to choke."

At once the droid withdrew, replaced the now-empty glass on the table, and hovered, awaiting its next instructions.

"Tell me what the evidence is and where I can find it," Lecersen repeated.

Mahlor did. Words spilled out like the water that had spilled down his chest. Lecersen grew a little pale at the litany of names of witnesses, the nature of the recordings, and what exactly was contained on the datachips. And fortuitously enough, all this precious and quite damning evidence was located in a safe-deposit box on Minyavish. Mahlor told him the name of the institution and the box number.

"Astonishing," Lecersen said, not without a trace of admiration. "That must have been difficult to acquire. Your people might have a fine future ahead of them as spies, once you learn not to go blundering arrogantly into the rancor's pit."

"I . . . can even get it for you," Mahlor said.

"How?" Lecersen demanded. He dearly hoped that the security didn't require a retinal scan.

" . . . code," he said. "Memorized."

"You'll tell me," Lecersen said.

And it was then that the poor creature realized that he wasn't going to get out of this room alive. "No, please," he begged. "I'll give you everything, then go away . . ."

"Yes," Lecersen said affably, "you will." He turned to the IT-O. "Continue until he reveals the code. Then I'll dispose of him."

"Affirmative," replied the interrogator droid. It thrummed over to bob gently up and down in front of the blind Minyavish, who began to shriek before the door had slid shut behind Lecersen.

A few hours later, E-3 came in to deliver several messages as Lecersen was finishing his nightcap.

"I am delighted to report that the IT-O was successful in extracting the code from your guest, sir," he said. "Termination was immediate once the interrogator determined that the fellow was telling the truth."

"Excellent news." While the Moff fully recognized the necessity for torture if information could not be extracted in a more restrained and less messy manner, he did not particularly care for it. Once he had what he needed, the torture had ceased and the subject had been eliminated quickly and painlessly. That was how civilized beings operated. "Tell the YVH to dispose of the body in the usual manner."

"Certainly, sir. Also, Senator Treen is standing by on the comm to report on her meeting with Senator Suldar."

Lecersen, buoyed by the first bit of news, was hopeful that the evening would bear yet more fruit. He accepted the comm the droid handed to him and then waved E-3PO out.

"Senator Treen," he purred, taking a sip of the delicious chak-root liquor. "I trust your evening was productive and entertaining both."

"Indeed it was, Drikl," she said. "We all had the most splendid time. The nerf steak was impeccably grilled, and I am delighted to report that the Vagnerian canapés were as delicate and flavorful as ever."

"Glad to know the Indigo Tower has not suffered a decline in quality." He didn't mind the banter. Treen got right to the point if things were bad. When she went on a tangent about immaterial things, it was a reassuring sign.

"Indeed, we must go there again sometime soon."

"How was the company?"

"Charming, attractive, and every bit as ruthless and power-hungry as the rest of us," Treen said chirpily. "And very willing to be molded, it would seem."

"Appearances can be deceiving," warned Lecersen. He took another sip, the liquid burning his throat in a most pleasant manner.

"Don't I know it!" She chuckled. "However, Fost and I have been at this game almost as long as he has been alive, and I highly doubt he'll squirm away. Besides, he has far too much to gain."

"What does he offer?"

"Well, as I said, he is quite charming, and is making a superb impression on some of the other Senators. Especially the ones who are fledglings, and who are a bit more timid and less ambitious than he."

That piqued Lecersen's interest. "Go on."

"He apparently has quite the following. It's rather endearing, really. There's one in particular he's been working closely with. You'll never guess who."

"I probably won't," Lecersen agreed readily, "so please enlighten me."

"Padnel Ovin, the new, rather scruffy Senator from Klatooine."

"Really?" Lecersen was surprised. "They seem like an odd pair. I'd be surprised to learn that Padnel Ovin even remembers to take a sani-steam once a day."

"Well, it seems as though Kameron is grooming—oh my, I didn't even mean to make the pun—" Treen giggled. "—Senator Ovin for something rather key later on down the line. And he has intimated that others of his little gaggle of admirers are in positions where they could give us a great deal of support."

"What positions are those, and who are we talking about?" Lecersen drained his drink and put it on the table.

"He was rather coy about that, but I don't think he's fibbing."

"You're hardly a Jedi, my dear, to be able to tell such things."

"Ah, but I am a most *excellent* judge of character, and you cannot argue that, Drikl."

He supposed he couldn't. "Well, for now, that's a very promising start. I will leave him in your extremely capable hands. There is something I'd like to bring to your attention, and you had best pass it along to the others."

Quickly, he told her about the nighttime visit from Mahlor, from the unfortunate Minyavish's arrival to his end.

"How unpleasant," said Treen. He could imagine her wrinkling her nose in distaste and smiled a little. "And he mentioned Fost and myself specifically by name?"

"He did. He did not seem particularly experienced in how to handle such negotiations. I believe if he had known about the rest of us, he'd have said so."

"Well, how honored we are to be singled out," she said archly. "This does not make me particularly happy, Drikl. And I was having such a pleasant evening."

"Well, the good news is, he gave me the location of the evidence and the code to locate and destroy it. While he resisted torture rather well, I do think in the end I retrieved everything he had to tell me."

"So you do believe he was acting alone?"

"My dear, hardly anyone *truly* acts alone, whether they realize it or not," Lecersen replied. "If one being was able to acquire this type of information, we'd do well to be on the alert for more insects crawling out of the woodwork."

"I'm afraid you're right."

"I'd best be turning in. Tomorrow is going to be a busy day. I'll dispatch someone to take care of the evidence on Minyavish and by nineteen hundred hours I'll be en route for Imperial Space. It sounds like you all have things well in hand."

"If you refer to Senator Suldar, I would say *eating out of* would not be inaccurate."

"I don't doubt it for a minute, my dear." His voice was warm with affection. He'd grown rather fond of his co-conspirator, as long as he didn't have to have too much interaction with her. She, Bramsin, Jaxton, Parova, and Thaal were right where they should be, and he was about to go where he should be.

Into Imperial Space, where human Moffs—*male* human Moffs, which were the only right and proper kind—were treated with the respect they were due.

Where he would eventually launch his bid to become Emperor.

# Chapter Fifteen

OUTER RIM TERRITORIES

ADMIRAL NATASI DAALA, STILL IN HER OWN MIND THE RIGHTFUL—AND greatly wronged—Chief of State of the Galactic Alliance, sipped at the cup of poor-quality caf Boba Fett had provided and stared out at the stars streaking past.

An hour after they were safely away on the actual *Slave I*—after escaping on an extremely fake *Slave I* and then transitioning to an ordinary shuttle—Daala had been on the comm. Fett had agreed to take her wherever she needed to go, and there was no doubt in her mind where that was. She had been busy, calling in old favors, talking to old friends—and old enemies—and new friends. She had much, much more to do, but for now it was a good start. She would have appreciated the chance to have a sanisteam and new, proper clothing instead of her prison garb, but Fett's generosity didn't stretch that far. Even so, she was grateful to be free. She could handle prison clothing for a while longer, just so long as her wrists and ankles were no longer "decorated."

The initial round of contact over, she and Fett had broken out some rations, and now were sipping caf. He'd had only a few questions for her, and had been silent for a while, but then, so had she.

"You've been quiet," Daala said.

He shrugged. The audacity and simple brilliance of the plan still astonished her. Boba Fett had broken her out of her Galactic Alliance prison cell by pretending to be . . . Boba Fett. It was a deception within a twist that her own complicated mind could most definitely appreciate—would have even found amusing, if she had any energy to spare for such lighter things. He was leading the uncertain and wobbly "triumvirate" on a wild caranak chase, because, according to all logic, if it was the infamous Boba Fett, legendary bounty hunter, he would never attempt a rescue as himself. No, for a while at least, what passed for the GA would be wasting time and resources looking for a Boba Fett impersonator, not the genuine article, sitting right in front of her clad once more in his actual armor and helmet.

"Long flight. Plenty of time to talk when you're ready."

"Genius, by the way, and such a nice little jab at the Jedi. The disguise, I mean."

He turned his head toward her as she sat beside him in the copilot's seat. "Oh—you mean the mad Jedi and their imposters. Thought that was a good touch myself."

Until very recently, Jedi Knights had been snapping—believing that everyone they met, including those they loved, had been replaced by an evil doppelgänger. "You are your own evil twin."

"Then wouldn't I be good?" he shot back.

Daala did allow herself to smile at that. It faded almost at once as she thought about what her own "doppelgänger" would be like. She'd lived that life for too brief a time. Happy, whole, in love with Liegeus Vorn, a good man who had been ripped away from her far, far too soon.

Daala had been chasing a hopeless ideal, trying to be a good, decent, fair leader of all the beings who made up the Galactic Alliance. All her attempts to restore order had failed. She was not the "Empress Palpatina" that some would paint her as. She was happy to work with any gender, any species, as long as they were willing to obey orders and uphold the law. She did not endorse slavery. Once she had brought the

Jedi to heel and had them serving in their proper capacity, she would have been free to turn her attention to these burgeoning new governments. Would have employed due process of law.

But no one, it seemed, wanted that. Not the Jedi, not Dorvan—to whom she had given more trust than she really should have—and certainly not the Solos.

No, she realized, her resentment more bitter than the bad caf she sipped. She'd been fooling herself to think that. Had been fooling herself, too, in thinking that she just might, finally, be able to love someone who wouldn't be ripped away from her by murder. First Wilhuff Tarkin, then Liegeus, then Nek Bwua'tu. Oh, Nek wasn't dead, but she wasn't sure he would call the lost, befuddled state in which he currently existed "living." She certainly didn't.

No happy doppelgänger Daala for her. And it was just as well.

She drained the cup and made a face. Turning to her rescuer, she said, "One of the first things I'm going to do when I come to power again is make sure you Mandos have the ability to make a decent cup of caf."

Fett snorted slightly. "As long as it keeps me sharp, it can taste like poodoo for all I care. We've got a more pressing problem you can help with."

*Here it comes,* thought Daala. She had known there would be a fee, she just hadn't known what it was. "I owe you a great deal," she admitted freely.

Again the helmet turned toward her. She couldn't see his eyes, but she could feel the intensity of his gaze.

"That you do. But before I name my price, I'm going to make it a bit sweeter for you to pay it. I've learned a few things you might be interested in hearing."

She was intrigued. Her brooding and soul-searching was growing tiresome; she was ready to move forward. "Go on."

"Moff Drikl Lecersen is not your friend."

Now it was her turn to snort. "And Luke Skywalker is a Jedi. Are we through with the obvious?"

"Not yet." He didn't rise to the bait. Fett never did. "He's been operating behind the scenes plotting your downfall for some time.

Even gone to some pretty extraordinary measures and very complicated, long-simmering plans."

"Sounds like a recipe for brogy stew."

"It does at that. Maybe I'm hungry." He shrugged. "He's no friend of mine, either, but I'll get to that in a minute. I've learned something very interesting about the Moff. He's behind the Freedom Flight."

Daala was glad she'd finished the bitter brew earlier; she was afraid if she'd been drinking, she'd have choked. Her brows drew together.

"That's a poor joke, Fett," she said in an icy voice. "That sleemo would rather have his hand cut off than do anything noble."

"I think that was an unfortunate side effect as far as Lecersen is concerned," Fett continued, completely unruffled by her reaction. "He didn't set it up—or rather, hijack it—in order to help poor downtrodden species obtain their rights. He did it so there'd be too many situations you'd have to respond to, quickly, without thinking it through. Think of it as arson. He was lighting fires all over the galaxy."

"And I rushed to put them out," Daala said slowly. Comprehension dawned sickly over her, causing her stomach to clench hard. "That whole organization . . . it's just a front?"

Fett shook his head. "Not at all. Most of the poor fools who are the 'pilots' are as idealistic as you'd imagine. Think they're doing good, and they are. They're just being moved about by Lecersen, like pieces on a hologame table. We Mandos had the opportunity to . . . shall we say, learn more about the Flight when you sent us in to put out the fires."

"Crush the uprisings," Daala said harshly. "Call it what it is." She was done with the kind of metaphors and justifications she had used when speaking to Wynn and Nek.

"Fine by me. I like plain talk," Fett said. "We've gotten some information from some of the slaves. But they can't tell us what they don't know. And most of them don't know much."

"It was underground before it became so high-profile," Daala said. "Three beings can keep a secret if two of them are dead." It was an old quote that many worlds claimed as theirs, and it was still brutally true.

"Or if they only know a little," Fett continued. "It's like a link in a chain. Each being could only implicate a handful of others, and none of those was anybody worth going after. Except one. A Minyavish had apparently discovered some things that linked Lecersen and a few other highly placed individuals to the Flight. We weren't able to recover the actual physical evidence, or any other names, but he certainly sounded convincing about Lecersen."

"Should I ask how you got this information?"

Fett shrugged. "You didn't hire us to calm tempers with jeru tea and sweetcakes."

"No, I didn't," Daala replied. "This is most enlightening. Things that made no sense whatsoever before suddenly have become quite plain."

"Such as the attack on Admiral Bwua'tu."

She gazed levelly at where his eyes would be, if she could see them. "Such as that, yes."

Someone had gone to great lengths to implicate the Jedi in the assassination attempt on Nek, but had botched the job. "It also explains the attack on the Solos and Fel at the Pangalactus Restaurant."

"You had no part in that?"

Her green eyes, thoughtful a second before, turned to jade ice. "Even if I wanted them dead, I wouldn't put a child in the line of fire. There are other ways."

Fett nodded, as if satisfied. "It all fits."

Yes. It did all fit. Another troupe of players had come onstage, after lurking in the wings unobserved for so long.

"And so," Fett said, "we have a common enemy, you and I, and we get to the issue of my payment."

"I knew we'd get to that eventually. Proceed."

"I've overheard some of your plans," he said, "which you clearly didn't mind or else you'd have declined when I offered you the use of my communications array. Sounds like you've got some pretty powerful contacts and a solid base of operations. I'm prepared to give you still more. Continued, if covert, use of my people and our technology. I want you safe and solid."

"I'm touched, old friend," she said, and there was actually a hint of sincerity in the words.

"Friendship is a part of it, I don't deny that," he said. "But once you're safe and solid and the head of the Empire, you'll be in a position to say thanks. And you can do that by finding a cure for this *but'u-unla* nanovirus."

One hand curled into a fist as he spoke. Slowly, he unclenched it and returned it to the controls.

Daala understood, and sympathized. No one, it appeared, was untouched by Darth Caedus's treachery. Toward the end of the Second Galactic Civil War, the Moffs had created an airborne nanovirus that could be specifically tailored to a certain genetic code. It was first used in the Battle of Roche, where it targeted and killed only the Verpine soldier caste. Later, it was used to attack the Hapan royal house, causing the death of the young Chume'da, Allana, and ensuring Tenel Ka's enduring hatred for the Moffs.

Another family would share that sentiment. Caedus had obtained a sample of the blood of Fett's granddaughter, Mirta Gev. From that, the Moffs had attacked their next target—the Fett line. Fortunately for grandfather and granddaughter, neither had been on Mandalore at the time of the nanovirus's release, but because of the nature and lengthy life of the concoction, Boba Fett would never be able to return to his homeworld.

Unless a cure was found.

*Home*, thought Daala. *We all want it, and so few of us really seem to find it, be it a physical place, or with someone we love.*

"I understand," she said, and she did. "You want to go home. I'm sure you know, however, that finding a cure for this nanovirus cannot be a top priority, at least not right away. I've got to claim all this power and make sure my position is, as you put it, safe and solid, before I'll have the funds and talent pool to turn toward that."

"I know. Not right away," he agreed, "but soon. Very soon." The helmeted head turned toward her. "I trust we understand each other."

She nodded. As favors went, this one wasn't unappealing. She might have even done it had he simply asked, without his having to have gone to the effort of rescuing her.

But she was glad he had.

"And it's more than a wish to go home," Fett continued. "It's about revenge. I imagine you've got an inkling of how I must feel."

She smiled, a smile as frosty as his voice had been. "I do indeed, Fett. I do indeed."

"Good. On occasion it's nice to mix business with pleasure."

"Yes, it is," Daala mused. "I need your comm again, I'm afraid. There's an old enemy-turned-friend who would appreciate an update on this situation as much as I do."

WATERFRONT DISTRICT, VARLO, ROONADAN

If she allowed herself, Leia could almost believe that they were indeed just a family on vacation.

The day was sunny, the sky a lovely blue. The artificial river that wound its way through this part of the capital city of Varlo was clean and made pleasant burbling sounds. Trees in sturdy duracrete pots provided just enough shade at the small café table where she, Han, and Allana sat perusing the menu.

They'd already ordered drinks. Allana was happily sipping a creamy concoction made from frozen blue milk. Han had ordered a Corellian ale, and Leia was drinking iced tea. The breeze was cooling and so were the beverages.

Several tables away sat Zekk and Taryn Zel. Zekk wore protective sun visors that, very conveniently, covered much of his face. Taryn, her distinctive red hair dyed a subtler auburn, wore one of the large floppy hats considered fashionable outerwear by the females on this world. Both seemingly had their noses buried in their own menus, but Leia knew that their eyes were on the Solo family. They were here, close but unobtrusive, to guard Allana should anything go wrong. The Solos had wanted to give their granddaughter as much of a normal life as possible, but in the end this button-nosed little girl would become ruler of her world, and perhaps much more. So they had struck a compromise that pleased all involved. Well, except Allana, but as she knew nothing of the arrangement, she couldn't protest it. Zekk, a Jedi Knight, and Taryn Zel, cousin to Tenel Ka, were the best possible bodyguards Leia could imagine for a Chume'da thought dead.

The waitdroid hummed over and hovered. Many droids designed to serve in such a capacity were humanoid. This squat droid more resembled R2-D2 than C-3PO. Barely a meter tall and rather narrow, with a head that opened to extend a serving tray, it was clearly designed for the sole task of waiting tables, and Leia doubted it was terribly expensive.

"May I take your orders?" it inquired in a pleasant, if droning, voice.

"We're still looking." Leia offered a smile, more for the benefit of any onlookers than for the droid itself. "A few more minutes."

"Of course, ma'am." It buzzed off and repeated the inquiry at another table.

"I think we should order something," Han said. "I'm starving."

"Me, too," Allana said. She took another gulp of her blue milk shake and her straw made a loud sucking sound. She looked embarrassed. "Excuse me."

"You just drank that whole thing?" Leia shook her head. "That concoction has enough calories to feed a Hutt for two days. We should drop you somewhere and you should live off it for a while."

Allana giggled. Leia turned back to Han. "I don't want to order anything and then just leave when they comm us," she said.

"Which they were supposed to do half an hour ago, once we arrived. If that droid was a living being he'd be getting suspicious. Or at the very least worried about his tip."

"Well, fortunately for us, he's not," Leia said. She, too, was hungry, and they hadn't had time to stock the *Millennium Falcon* with anything other than the standard rations. Both Han and Allana turned their noses up at said rations unless they were hungry enough to eat parts of the *Falcon* itself. Which, Han had mused, might just be tastier.

There were times when Leia felt that she had *two* grandchildren.

Still . . . imported Roba steak with Xixor salad and a dessert of Vagnerian canapés was sounding very tempting. "Let's order a basket of hubba chips," Leia suggested as a compromise.

"I like hubba chips," came a high-pitched voice.

"Me, too," came another.

"Gamorrean snack crackers are *my* favorite, but you'll need an Anoat malted to dunk them in," chirped a third.

Three small, blue, rodent-like heads with large ears and bright eyes peered over the edge of the table.

The Squibs had arrived.

# Chapter Sixteen

A SECOND LATER THE THREE SQUIBS WERE DRAGGING SPARE CHAIRS from other tables and scrambling atop them. Han stared at them.

"You were supposed to comm us," he said.

One of them, a female slightly smaller and more delicately built than the other two, waved a hand airily. "But that's so impersonal. Nothing's nicer than sharing a meal with one's partners while the deal is discussed."

"Who's the fuzzling?" another one said.

Leia sighed. "Amelia," she said, "these beings are Grees, Sligh, and Emala. Amelia is our adopted daughter."

"*Amelia* sounds too much like *Emala,*" Sligh said at once. "That's going to make for some confusion, since we'll be traveling together awhile. She'll need another name. Hey!" He waved over a serving droid. "Some hubba chips, Gamorrean crackers, and an Anoat malted."

"Wait, what?" said Han, nearly choking on his ale. Allana was watching all this with bright, interested eyes, but saying nothing. "Who said anything about traveling together?"

"Sligh just did," said Grees. "Something wrong with your ears?"

"I think something may be wrong with yours," Han shot back. "They're enormous. Bigger than I remember them."

"We're not traveling with you," Leia said, trying to get the conversation back on something vaguely reminiscent of a topic. Although now that Han had said something, the Squibs' ears—always long and tufted—*did* seem a bit larger in proportion to their small bodies. "You said you had information for us. We're willing to pay for it. That was the deal."

The waitdroid arrived. Its tray accessory was extended, and perched atop the square sheet of metal were their appetizers. Allana's eyes were fastened on the Squibs and, contrary to her earlier statement, she didn't seem at all interested in the snacks. Sligh picked up a Gamorrean cracker and dunked it in the malted as he spoke.

"I don't believe we negotiated the finer points at all, actually," he said, crunching the cracker with sharp white teeth.

"Sitting here with three Squibs is hardly inconspicuous," Leia said, glancing at Allana quickly and then around at the neighboring tables. A few heads were turned their way.

"Hey, *you're* the one who brought a fuzzling into this," said Grees. "She's your problem."

"Amelia is not a *problem,*" Han said through gritted teeth.

"Whatever," Grees said, shrugging his narrow shoulders. He reached for a hubba chip and rubbed it on his cheek, the Squib equivalent of taking a good long whiff. Leia realized for the first time that they had more clothing on than usual. Squibs wore clothing more for decoration and storage purposes than to protect themselves from the elements, covered as they were with fur. Too, their fur was used as an olfactory organ, and so most Squibs went uncovered. Yet both the males were wearing tunics, pants, and boots, and Emala had a long-sleeved, floor-length dress. They must have been stifling; Leia, in a light dress and sandals, was warm. "Still changes the deal, though."

"What?" Han was turning red, and it wasn't from the weather. "That's it. We're done. No information is worth this."

"Han," Leia said, gently but firmly. "The information is about the Chief."

Han looked unhappy, but he sat down. Emala reached for a hubba chip and, annoyed, Han snatched the basket away, plopping it down in front of Allana.

"Hey!" Emala protested.

"Food wasn't part of the deal, either," Han growled.

Allana picked up a chip and ate it, still observing silently. She had the same rapt expression she wore when watching a favorite holoshow.

Leia sighed inwardly. "Let's finish our chips and crackers and drinks, then take a walk along the river. We can talk then."

Sligh's ears—they were definitely larger than Leia remembered them—drooped slightly. "But we've come in a hurry, and we're awfully hungry."

"A hurry?" Han leaned forward. "Why? What's timely about the information you have? And what kind of payment do you want?"

The Squibs had been deliberately vague about payment, among other things. Which was not out of the ordinary. All Han and Leia knew was they claimed to know where Daala was, they wanted to meet at the Riverview Café in Varlo, and they were confident that Han and Leia could meet their price.

"Well, lunch is a start," Emala said. She beamed at Allana. "You're a pretty little fuzzling, for a human. We can't call you Amelia, so what would you like us to call you?"

"It's her *name*," Han said, exasperated.

Grees had a look of long-suffering patience. "We told you, it's too close to Emala. And Emala's had her name longer."

Something clicked in Leia's head about the statement, but she pushed it aside, anxious to get to the heart of the matter. "It won't be a problem."

"I'd like a Squib name," Allana said unexpectedly.

The Squibs beamed and exchanged self-satisfied looks. "See? The fuzzling sees the potential for disaster," said Emala. "How about Pika?"

"I'm partial to Veeshu," said Grees.

"Nah, she's more of a Muatisi," put in Sligh, reaching for another cracker and dunking it vigorously. "*Definitely* a Muatisi."

"Her name," said Han, his voice unsettlingly calm, "is Amelia. You have information about the Chief. We want that information. We will pay and even buy you lunch if that's what it takes to shake you vermin off."

*"Vermin!"* gasped Sligh, his hand to his small chest, his eyes wide with hurt that might have been real but probably wasn't. "How rude!"

Leia buried her face in her hands. She had, mercifully, forgotten just how irritating the Squibs could be. They seemed to have even more enthusiasm and energy than they had the last time she and Han had encountered them, although they were elderly for their species. In fact, they looked even better than she recalled. Some species had all the luck, it seemed.

"Let's order lunch," she said. "Perhaps this will go more smoothly when we've all had something to eat."

Grees was glaring at Han, and Sligh's whiskers were quivering while Emala patted him on the back gently. They all perked up when food was mentioned. The waitdroid returned and they placed their orders, along with a request for a second basket of hubba chips.

"You shouldn't have called them vermin," Allana said to her grandfather. "That wasn't polite."

"No," Han said, taking an overly long pull at his ale. "It wasn't." Leia knew the apology was sincere, but Han's voice was still gruff with annoyance.

"We knew you didn't mean it," Emala said kindly. "Partners sometimes get a little testy with one another."

"I'm sure all *your* partners do," Han said. Leia put a hand on his arm and squeezed.

"So," she said. "Tell us about the Chief."

"Oh, you'll like this," enthused Emala.

"But first, our terms," said Grees. "We want you to take us back to Coruscant with you. Second, we'll want enough credits to buy a ship and be comfortably supplied. Third, you let Jagged Fel know who helped him out, 'cause friends of good partners often make good partners themselves. And finally—lunch and all other meals are on you."

It was not an inexpensive deal, and Leia fancied that they'd end up getting the worst of it. She wasn't sure that what she and Han thought was important about Daala and what the Squibs thought was important were one and the same. Still . . . she knew in her heart that she wouldn't have come if she didn't think they knew something worth hearing. And any lead was a good lead at this point.

"And in exchange," Han said, "we get this information, which you have indicated is very important."

"Oh yes," Sligh said. "Very important."

Han and Leia exchanged glances. Leia gently touched the Force, to ascertain if the Squibs themselves were comfortable with their end of the bargain. If they were bluffing, she'd sense smug satisfaction; Squibs always wanted to come out the winner in haggling. If Han and Leia were getting the better part of the deal, they'd be feeling resigned.

What she sensed surprised her.

"You're . . . afraid," she said softly, stunned.

"Afraid? Us?" scoffed Grees. "You know, you keep doing that Force thing, we might just walk with our information. I'm sure others would find it just as valuable as you would."

But they wouldn't. Leia knew it, and she was suddenly very worried. Squibs usually erred on the side of overconfidence, particularly *this* family unit. She'd seen them cheerfully backtalk armed beings and launch themselves at Imperial stormtroopers without a second thought.

She caught and held Sligh's gaze. He blinked at her with large, soft brown eyes, then his gaze slid away.

"Sligh," she said, keeping her voice calm, "what have you gotten yourselves involved—"

Blasterfire interrupted her.

Han turned the table over, sweeping Allana into his arms and racing for one of the large duracrete pots that held the shade trees. Leia and the Squibs were right behind them, all four drawing and firing their own weapons as they ran. Two blasts later, the table and chairs where they had been sitting were nothing but twisted piles of metal. Other diners dived for cover, and the patio of the Riverview Café, so peaceful just an instant before, was now filled with the sounds of blasters and screaming.

Leia and the Squibs dropped down beside Han and Allana. The duracrete pot was holding up better than the table and chairs, but that wasn't saying a lot. Leia met Han's eyes and nodded. At a signal from Han, they poked their heads around the container, each on one side, and fired. The quick glace didn't tell them much, only that their attackers wore vaguely Imperial-styled armor, they had blasters, and the blasters were firing at them.

"This pot isn't going to hold for much longer," Han muttered. He caught Leia's eye. Decades spent fighting beside this man had given Leia an insight into how he thought that few others possessed. She knew what he wanted to do and, worse, realized with a sinking feeling that he was right. The pot wouldn't hold, and then—

It was the safest of two very unsafe options. Leia gave Han the briefest of nods.

"Amelia," Han said, "you're going to have to make a run for it. Head back toward the *Falcon*. We'll cover you and meet you there as soon as possible. It's not far and you know where to go. Can you do that, sweetheart?"

Eyes wide, breathing accelerated, Allana nodded. With a brief pang, Leia realized that her granddaughter was getting used to having pleasant moments interrupted by blasterfire. Allana was heir to a throne. It was not the first time, nor would it be the last, that the girl's life would be disrupted by danger.

Leia firmly set aside her worries and returned her attention to distracting their attackers long enough so they wouldn't notice one little girl fleeing to safety.

Allana was thinking furiously. She glanced around, trying to figure out the best way back to the spaceport. Dive into the river? Run behind other tables? She looked over at the restaurant—and there was her escape route. She braced herself to race for safety, then turned her head to regard the Squibs. They were jumping up and down, firing around the pot and shouting insults, but she could sense the fear rolling off them.

Allana made her decision. She grabbed Emala by the arm and pointed. Emala's eyes widened in understanding and she alerted her mates.

"One, two, three!" cried Allana, and bolted for the meter-high, narrow door that admitted the waitdroids into the kitchen. The Squibs were hard on her heels.

"Amelia!" It was Han's voice, full of fear and anger. Allana's heart lurched but she ignored him, running full speed. Sligh squeaked once as blasterfire burned the duracrete a few centimeters from his feet. Allana didn't slow to see if she had miscalculated the height and width of the entrance, merely kept running until she was halfway inside the tiny corridor, then stopped, catching her breath. One of the Squibs charged into her, nearly knocking her down.

"Why are we stopping?" Emala demanded.

"Quiet," hissed Allana. "I want to hear if they're inside the restaurant, too!"

Grasping the potentially lifesaving logic of the comment, the Squibs fell silent at once. All of them strained to listen. There was shouting and fear in the kitchen, the banging of pots as they fell to the floor, and the whining whir of alarmed droids. But there was no sound of blasterfire. Then the voices grew distant.

"There's a door to outside," Allana said. "Come on!"

They hurried through the rest of the corridor. Allana nearly fell when she slipped on a puddle of spilled sauce, but Emala caught her. Straight ahead, through the kitchen and past the dropped crockery, was the outline of a door.

Allana didn't need to point. The Squibs saw it, too, and as one, three blue rodents and one little human girl raced for freedom.

"What in blazes did that girl do?" bellowed Han to his wife, leaning out and firing, then ducking back as a retaliatory bolt scorched the duracrete pot.

Leia started to answer when she was interrupted by the barely audible chirp of her comm.

"Grandma?"

"Honey, where are you?"

"I'm at the spaceport."

A chunk of duracrete blew off and Leia ducked. "The Squibs still with you?"

"We're all here. I'm on Zekk's ship."

Leia and Han stared at each other for a full second until another round of attacks got Han's attention.

"It's okay," Allana assured her. "I've noticed Zekk and Taryn hanging around before. And this time, the hat didn't disguise her at all. I know what his ship looks like and I used the Force to unlock it. We're here and safe and waiting for you."

"Well, that makes things easier," Leia said, both to Han and to Allana. "Sit tight, honey. We're on our way." She clicked off the comlink.

"I can't believe she figured it out," Han said.

"I can," Leia said. "She's a Solo."

Han gave her a crooked grin before he leaned out to fire again. Leia clicked the com. "Zekk? Allana made you and Taryn and she's in your ship."

"What?" came Zekk's voice, astonished. She knew where he was—a few dozen meters away, he and Taryn holding off some of the . . . soldiers? Hired thugs? Leia had no idea, but knew who would.

"Draw off the ones firing on you, then double back to the spaceport. We'll do the same."

"Okay."

Leia glanced over at the restaurant. She'd seen Allana go through the waitdroid-and-child-and-Squib-sized doorway, but she was willing to bet her granddaughter had found a more normal-sized back door. It was their best shot.

Leia heard some of the blasterfire moving away. Zekk and Taryn were luring them off. It was time. She and Han had been in so many situations like this she didn't even need to tell him what she planned.

"Ready?" she asked.

"Always, sweetheart."

She gave him her blaster pistol. Han rose, a pistol in each hand, and began firing in earnest. At that same instant, Leia shoved her left hand forward. Two of their attackers went flying. She raised her right hand, and the melted metal table rose. As hard as she could, Leia Force-hurled the table toward the center cluster of those firing upon them.

The table crashed down and the rain of blasterfire paused. Leia turned and raced for the restaurant entrance, with Han right behind her.

"Why can we never just sit down and have a decent meal anywhere in the galaxy?" Han complained as he caught up to her.

Leia glanced around at the spilled food, broken plates, and damaged cookware as she headed for the back door.

"Maybe you should tip better," she said.

# Chapter Seventeen

ABOARD THE *JADE SHADOW*

"DAD," SAID BEN, WITH THE SORT OF EXAGGERATED PATIENCE THAT one might use when speaking to a child, "we took her to Korriban. You know, Sith homeworld? And far from turning on us, she defended us."

"I know," Luke said. He was listening to his son, but his eyes were on a slowly turning blue-green sphere. The planet he was regarding with such intensity was either ocean or marsh, with very little dry land. It was a marked contrast with Korriban, which had been their last stop. But it was, to Luke's mind, every bit as dangerous.

Maybe more.

"I mean—those tuk'ata were pretty vicious, and she got them obeying her and leaving us alone."

"I know, Ben, I was there."

There was a long pause. Ben fidgeted.

"And there was a whole *pack* of them and—"

"Ben!" Luke's voice was not angry, but it was sharp and laced with irritation.

"Quit while you're ahead," Jaina advised.

Ben shot her a skeptical look. "Like *you* do?" he retorted.

Luke tuned them out, focusing on the deceptively calm-looking world before him. Watery a planet as it was, simply finding a safe place to land would be a challenge. It got harder from there. He would not be the first Jedi to land here. Kyle Katarn had been here before.

So had Mara.

Both had been lucky to escape alive.

The world was so dangerous that Luke had not felt the Jedi were ready to explore its mysteries; it had been allowed to remain a myth, the subject of cautionary tales to make sure wide-eyed young apprentices stayed on the path of the light side.

But Dromund Kaas was real. Darkly, frighteningly, dangerously real, and they were about to land on it.

The discussion—*argument* was too strong a word—he had been having with Ben was about whether Vestara should be permitted to join them on its soggy surface. The young Jedi Knight had raised a point—a good one, one Luke could find no argument with. Vestara indeed could have set the hounds on them, buying at least enough time to flee back to the *Shadow* and escape with it. Instead she had protected them all, possibly putting herself in danger to do so.

It wasn't a very Sith-like thing to do.

It was more of a Jedi thing to do. And she had done it spontaneously, swiftly, with no hesitation.

Luke didn't like it.

He leaned back, stretching a little in his chair. Vestara emerged from the refresher, where she'd taken a quick sanisteam. She looked around at the three pairs of eyes on her and said, "Okay, what now?"

"Noth—" Ben started to say, but Luke interrupted him.

"I was considering whether it would be wise to take you with us when we visit Dromund Kaas."

Vestara cocked her head. "Oh? I thought it was acceptable for me to accompany you. What made you change your mind?" She didn't seem offended, merely curious.

"I didn't say I had changed it. I was simply reconsidering." Luke nodded at the image of the planet. "That's an extremely dangerous place. And very, very strong with the dark side."

Vestara folded her slender arms and leaned against the bulkhead. She kept her gaze locked with Luke's as she quirked an eyebrow.

"I fail to see how it's different from Korriban, or any of the other places on Jaina and Natua's list."

"There are some interesting historical aspects to this world," Luke said. "Things that perhaps only you and I know, depending on what you've learned from Ship. Such as the fact that this world was a colony of the Sith Empire, but faded into obscurity until after the Great Hyperspace War. It was rediscovered by a Sith armada wandering for two decades. Sound familiar?"

A muscle in Vestara's jaw clenched, but she remained silent. Ben's agitation in the Force increased.

Luke continued. "They rebuilt this world. It became the capital of the next Sith Empire. Until that fell. Its next round of rediscovery came by someone who rejected the Rule of Two, who thought that there was more than enough of the dark side to go around."

"Dad—" Ben started to say.

Luke held up a hand. "He founded a religion that would become known as the Dark Force. There's an ancient temple there still. It was serviced for centuries by the Dark Prophets. It's so steeped in the dark side that it formed its own nexus—one so powerful it interferes with all weaponry and technology except for lightsabers."

"Well," drawled Vestara, "it's good that everyone here can handle one then, isn't it?"

"I think you see my point."

"That there are similarities between the origins of this culture and my own? Beings are beings, Master Skywalker. The galaxy is old, and there are only so many stories in it."

"And Sith are Sith."

"Meaning that I'll be irrevocably drawn to this dark-side nexus."

"Master Kyle Katarn succumbed to it," Luke said, and he felt Jaina and Ben's shock. "He was brought back to the light side of the Force only by his pupil. Ben's mother."

"Ironic," said Vestara, "that a Jedi Master was saved from the dark side by a woman who used to be the Emperor's Hand."

"Mara was never a Sith," Luke replied.

"So what's your solution?" Coldness emanated from her. But mixed in with the anger, which Luke had expected, was something else. Hurt. "Here are your options as I see them. One: kill me. End of problem. Two: leave either Ben or Jaina behind to watch me, reducing your group to two Jedi instead of three Jedi and me. Three: take me with you. It's your ship, your mission, and your call. But if you honestly believe I'm going to be tempted to turn on all of you by simply being on a Sith planet after all you've seen from me, you should start thinking about Option Number One. Because anything else is going to either hamper you or distract you. And frankly, I'm tired of it."

Luke was surprised. So was Jaina. Ben wasn't, and Luke felt his pride and pleasure like a sun in the Force.

For a moment, no one spoke. Finally Luke said, "The similarities between the history of Dromund Kaas and the Lost Tribe's own might make it appealing to them. They might see those commonalities as destiny. Fortunately for us, there are a very few places on this planet with solid ground, so it will narrow our search. Unfortunately, that works both ways—if the Tribe *is* hiding out here, we'll be fairly easy to spot. We need to watch one another closely. If Master Katarn could be swayed, then any of us could. Not just Vestara."

"Probably not you, Dad," Ben said. His voice was still sullen, but mitigated by Luke's decision.

"Probably not. I've been there and back. I like it here better. Let's go, and remember . . . it's going to be soggy down there."

It was an understatement. It seemed to Ben that it took forever simply to find a place to land, as his father had warned. There were two places that Luke was interested in investigating: the mighty Kaas City itself, which from the air looked as urban as much of Coruscant, and the dark temple.

There had been no sign of any vessels in orbit, neither ChaseMaster frigates nor Ship. Vestara had said that it was likely that either the ships had landed and been hidden, or else the Sith had clustered their ships elsewhere.

They dipped below the cloud cover. They emerged to see, even in daylight, a world of dismal gray, blue, and green. Below them stretched Kaas City: dark, as a Sith city should be, with no sign of any lights that would indicate current habitation. It was a well-designed, if sinister, skyline of mostly squares and rectangles jutting skyward, with a few spires here and there to indicate that the Sith of long ago shared another interest with the Lost Tribe—an appreciation of aesthetics.

Although the place looked deserted, Luke veered away from it quickly. "We'll start with the temple, a bit more to the west," Luke said as he skillfully brought the fifty-five-meter-long *Jade Shadow* in for a landing on what seemed like approximately fifty meters of solid ground in the midst of a steaming, stagnant marsh. "It's a more controlled and much smaller environment than the city."

"I'd just as soon not have to explore an entire Sith city on foot if I can help it," Jaina said. "There's a lot of places they could hide. It would be an ideal spot for an ambush, and in that space we'd have no chance against their numbers."

"Besides," Vestara offered, "if the Lost Tribe is there, they may live in the city, but they will definitely have visited the temple first. The nexus would call to them, just as the Fountain of Knowledge called to Taalon. There would be indications that someone had been there recently."

Ben gave her a grateful smile. What his father had revealed about Dromund Kaas's history had shaken him. He, like everyone else, had believed that it was nothing more than a myth. And the parallels Luke had drawn *were* uncomfortable. But he had faith in Vestara. Faith that wasn't just built on hope, but on what he had seen from her. How she had grown. On what he felt *from* her, not *for* her. And she'd gotten in a good riposte with her comment about his mother's having saved Kyle Katarn.

Even so, he knew that Vestara was the one most at risk. Luke, as he had said, had been to the dark side and returned. He, Ben, had danced perilously close to that edge—close enough to take a good look and turn his back on it. Jaina, too, had had her life irrevocably altered by it. But Vestara—he knew that in many ways, for her it would feel like coming home.

But so had Korriban, and they had all seen how she behaved there.

The noisome smell of fetid water and decay was borne to them on the still, warm breeze as they walked down the ramp, boots squelching in the muck. Ben thought that if the dark side had a smell, it would be this reek—almost sweet in the way that rot could be, stifling, and impossible to avoid. Dark-side energy, as Luke had warned, was extremely strong here, as strong in its own way as it had felt on Korriban. There it had been intense and almost arrogant, power-hungry. Here those dark energies felt more insidious, more purely evil for evil's sake than fuel for a lust for power. Despite the warmth, the moist air felt clammy, like wet skin slapping against his own. Nausea, both physical and spiritual, rippled through him.

Their destination lay straight ahead. Home to the Dark Prophets, site of an extremely powerful Dark Force nexus, the Sith temple loomed upward, a black, somber silhouette against the gray daylight sky, rendered mysterious and unclear by the mist that occasionally thickened to drizzle. No lights punctured its cold darkness.

"Uncle Luke, you take us to the nicest places," Jaina said.

"I'll take you and Jag out to dinner at the Indigo Tower when we get back," Luke replied. "You weren't able to actually eat the last time you were there, if I recall correctly."

"Please—don't talk about eating," Ben said. "My stomach's already reconsidering lunch."

Vestara alone appeared to be unaffected by the stench. She smirked a little and said, "You can block it with the Force."

Ben was about to chide Vestara on her too-casual use of the Force when he realized he'd done the same thing more than once on this strange odyssey on which he and his father had embarked. His stomach heaved again, and he took her advice. Sometimes "casual usage of the Force" was more a necessity than a whim. He'd do none of them any good if he got sick.

Luke stood for a moment, his eyes and other senses searching the landscape. "Anyone sense anything?"

Ben extended himself in the Force, both opening himself to the vile sensation of the dark side and utilizing his senses—even smell, temporarily at least—to gather what information he could.

"Other than the obvious, which is a metric ton of dark-side energy, I can't sense anything," Jaina said.

Vestara, too, shook her head. "I can't feel the presence of anyone familiar here."

Luke's gaze fell on Ben. "Nope," Ben replied.

"All right. Be aware that this world hosts ysalamiri. It's possible if the Sith are here, they've figured that out and will be making use of them to hide themselves."

"It's also possible we might fall flat on our faces if we Force-leap near a tree," Ben said.

"That too," Luke agreed, "which is even more likely. Let's go." The four of them Force-leapt from dry spot to dry spot, mindful of trees cradling ysalamiri and their Force-blocking bubbles, heading southwest of where they had landed the *Jade Shadow*. It was easy not to lose their way with such a prominent landmark to guide them.

Sometimes they miscalculated in their negotiation of the treacherous terrain, either thinking land was solid where it wasn't or surprised by an ysalamiri bubble, and sank into the reedy marsh water instead. Where there was no mud or water, there were tangles of vines, roots, and weeds that needed to be cleared with lightsaber slashes. After a very short while, all of them were in dire need of sanisteams.

"I think I liked Korriban better," Jaina said. Strands of her brown hair were plastered to her forehead, both from sweat and from the moisture in the air.

"Yeah," Ben said, scratching his head. "At least it was a dry heat."

"And it had puppies," Vestara added, using the Force to leap free from the marshy grip that had both of her feet. "Who doesn't like puppies?"

The banter was a grim sort, a way to keep their spirits up and prevent the ubiquitous, lurking presence of the dark side from unsettling them completely. Luke lifted a hand, and they fell silent at once, turning to him attentively.

"We're about two kilometers away," Luke said. "I'm sure we're all feeling it. It's just going to get more intense. We should be very careful."

They nodded, even the most halfhearted attempt at humor extinguished by the warning, and moved forward without speaking. Ben found his attention wandering toward Vestara, and not in the usual pleasantly distracting manner. He watched her out of the corner of his eye, hoping—and mostly believing—she would not suddenly turn on them, but knowing it was still a possibility.

Drenched by the falls into filthy water and the varied precipitation, Ben grew colder the closer they drew. He knew it had nothing to do with his body, and everything to do with his very essence—and the Force. The dark temple ceased to be a sullen unnerving shape on the horizon and instead became a looming threat. He extended himself in the Force, hyperalert for anything as he had been on Korriban. There they had been attacked by the tuk'ata. Here Ben could feel there were worse things lurking, just on the periphery of his Force sensing.

Luke came to a stop some twenty meters from the temple. He drew his lightsaber but did not light it, not yet. Ben emulated him, feeling his father's own heightened attention in the Force. For a moment, they all stood, subconsciously forming a row, and regarded the temple.

It was solid stone, gray and massive, and heavy with banked threat. The darkness emanating from it was almost like a sound so deep that one could not hear it, but could feel it in one's bones or blood. Ben could well believe that in its presence blasters and other mundane energy weapons and technology would be rendered useless. The lightsabers were both simpler and more complex; the technology was simpler, but because of their deep heritage with the Force, they were far more complicated than a blaster.

In the murky light, the four couldn't possibly miss the pair of giant, golden statues of hooded figures, hands folded across the pommels of swords. The figures were more disquieting in this dark, dank place than the ones Ben had seen in Korriban's desert. Painted vines with ominous blossoms and probably deadly thorns twined about the base of the temple.

"What do you sense?" Luke asked quietly, his head turning as he looked around.

"That nexus," Jaina said promptly.

"Yeah," Ben said. "And . . . some Dark Force manifestations, but not close. Not yet, anyway."

"It's . . . so *strong*," Vestara breathed. Ben glanced over at her. Her brown eyes were wide, and her voice was a mixture of horror and attraction.

"Vestara," Luke said, sharply but not angrily, and she blinked as if coming out of a daze. "Do you sense any signs of the Sith or Abeloth?"

She shook her head, looking more like her usual alert self. "No. That nexus pretty much drowns out anything else."

"Agreed," Luke said. "Let's look for more ordinary clues. Stay in the courtyard, where we can all see one another. If anyone finds anything, comm me. Stay away from the direct entrance to the temple, though. When we go in there, I want us to do so together."

Ben found the instructions a relief. They moved forward, the ground beneath them giving way to carved, inlaid flagstones as they entered the courtyard proper. As on Korriban, these were etched with disconcerting images: eyes, five-fingered hands, claws. They had been created with ritual and infused with dark-side energy, and Ben felt as though he were stepping on ice with bare feet.

Luke and Jaina wandered off to the left exterior side of the temple, each taking a different corner. Ben and Vestara found themselves on the right. Vestara went a little ahead to examine some ancient braziers, and Ben lowered his gaze to the sinister flagstones. He was not looking at their art; he was looking for footprints, fresh mud, or stones that jutted upward as if they had been stepped on recently.

"These braziers haven't seen fire in a long time." Vestara's voice came to Ben over his comlink, even though she was only a couple of meters away. Ben realized that since they had drawn near the temple, they had spoken in quiet tones. Of course, part of his brain reasoned; if Abeloth or any Sith were lurking nearby, none of the Jedi—nor, apparently, Vestara—would want to announce their presences by shouting. But he knew there was another reason.

The dark side was here.

"Yeah, I'm not seeing any signs here that anything has been recently disturbed. No markings other than our own."

A few more minutes passed. Ben felt irritation and frustration begin to chase away his alert apprehension. He clicked his comlink again, this time speaking to his father.

"Nothing here, Dad."

"Nor here," came Luke's reply. Ben caught Vestara's eye and nodded, and they walked back toward the center of the courtyard. Jaina and Luke, Jaina looking like she'd like to punch something and Luke looking disappointed, met them.

"I don't like this," Luke said without preamble. "More than half a dozen places searched and no one's found anything. Nothing at all."

"Well," Ben offered, finding himself in the unusual position of wanting to reassure his dad, "the galaxy is a fairly large place."

"Of course," Luke said, "but we should still be finding something. If nothing else, I'm surprised Abeloth hasn't . . . taunted us in some way. She needs an audience. This absolute inability to find anything at all, about either her and Ship or the Lost Tribe—" He shook his head. "It's not adding up. She's not hiding from us because she's afraid. She's hiding because she's planning something. Combine that with the same inexplicable disappearance of the Lost Tribe—I'm willing to bet that they're working together. They're planning something. And when Abeloth and the Lost Tribe drop out of sight to plan something—it's going to be very big, and very bad."

Everyone, even Vestara, looked unhappy at his words. Ben sighed. "Well, I don't think we're going to find them here."

"I think," came a rich, deep voice, "you already have."

# Chapter Eighteen

THERE WERE TEN OF THEM, SITH SABERS ALL, MOVING DOWN THE STEPS of the temple. Their lit lightsabers bathed their smirking faces in a sinister red glow. At their head was a man whom Luke had hoped never to see again.

Gavar Khai.

Ben whirled on Vestara, activating his own lightsaber in the same movement. He didn't know how she had done it, but somehow she must have gotten word to her father. He should never—

Her own lightsaber was lit, as were Luke's and Jaina's. But Gavar Khai's beautiful and treacherous daughter wasn't facing Ben, or even Luke. She was facing her father, her eyes wide and face pale with shock and . . . fear?

And Gavar Khai's gaze, his eyes narrowed and angry, was on her.

"You're so predictable," Luke said. "You should try varying treachery with actual trustworthiness on your future infiltration missions."

Luke's eyes were on the Sith. He hadn't seen Vestara's reaction, perhaps hadn't even felt it.

"Dad—" Ben began.

"I didn't," said Vestara. Now Luke apparently did sense her terror, for he spared her a quick glance, still poised for an attack. Beside him, Jaina, dark brows drawn together in concentration, trembled like a leashed creature, more than ready to decorate the temple with pieces of Sith.

"My embarrassingly malleable daughter does not lie," Khai said. "Such promise. And such disappointment. Your mother is dead, Vestara."

Truth, undeniable and powerful, slammed into Ben. Vestara gasped. "What?" Then, with dawning horror, "Did—did you kill her?"

"No. But I did not stop her from being killed," Khai said. "I will start fresh. A new wife, a new child. Both are easily replaced." Vestara, usually a master of her emotions, jerked slightly as if slapped. "Take them." Before Ben could even register this, Khai Force-leapt down the stairs and charged.

At Vestara.

Ben moved toward Khai, but sensed that he himself was under attack. At the last minute he Force-leapt straight up, turned a somersault, and kicked out with both feet. One boot impacted a Sith's face with a satisfying crunch. The other Sith ducked in time. Ben heard the sizzle of a lightsaber moving and jerked his foot up just in time to avoid having it sliced off, but the move forced him to land awkwardly. He hit the flagstones with his body half turned and tried to roll out of the way as the lightsaber slashed down. He was half a heartbeat too slow, and he hissed as the red blade seared his shoulder.

Ignoring the pain, Ben leapt upward, back on both feet and in a crouch as three Sabers turned on him. Their Force auras blazed with confidence. Ben smiled to himself. He parried the two blades with his lightsaber clutched in one hand, whipping back and forth between the two foes. With the other hand, he Force-hurled the third into the air. Alert and attentive, he unerringly directed the Sith's flight toward Gavar Khai, who was bearing down on his offspring so forcefully their blades were a blur.

Ben was rewarded with a grunt from Khai before he had to return his full attention to the remaining two Sabers. His gaze flickered rapidly back and forth between one and the other, keeping their eyes on him as he used the Force to dislodge a flagstone and bring it down with a terrible final smash on the left one's skull. The Sith dropped, his head a bloody mess, and Ben felt the first stirrings of apprehension as he turned on the last one.

Luke and Jaina were fighting back-to-back. The Sith attacking them had two advantages. One was the fact that they outnumbered the two Jedi. The second was that they were being reinforced by the emanations of the dark-side nexus within the temple. It surged forth like psychic sewage, clogging the Jedi's reflexes as it fueled their enemies.

But Luke had fought the Lost Tribe before, and he knew their style. He knew, too, that because until very recently they had only sparred and perhaps dueled among themselves, they had a lot to learn. But even Luke Skywalker would be foolish not to completely focus on a battle against six Sith.

He felt Jaina in the Force, strong and calm, her back to him but not quite touching his. Bonded by blood and the Force itself, they performed a duet of death to the half dozen Sith pressing in for the attack. They leapt and swung, ducked and kicked in such swift, perfect harmony that an observer might have thought their moves had been choreographed. More than once, an overly confident Saber charged, only to end up slashing at his fellow Sith. In short order two were on the ground, and the odds were now a mere two to one.

Luke could hear the sizzle of lightsabers clashing behind him, only centimeters away, and then the acrid stench of burned flesh as Jaina's blade struck home. Calm, focused, Luke feinted and then came up under one of his adversaries, slicing off both legs in an almost serene manner. The Sith crumpled, but did not cry out. Luke looked at the single remaining Sith who had targeted him, gazing without anger into the Keshiri's narrowed eyes, and felt the first brush of real fear from his opponent.

"I will be as swift and sure as I may," Luke assured her, almost compassionately, and bore down intently.

* * *

For a precious instant Vestara was so stunned at her father's actions, she hesitated as he sprang at her.

Surely it was a ploy, to distract the Jedi so that the Sith could destroy them. Once they had been dispatched or captured, she would explain everything to her father. He would be in good spirits with such a victory and—

*This is not "Papa."*

*This is Father. And Father has come to kill me.*

With the barest fraction of an instant to spare, Vestara brought her lightsaber up and blocked what would surely have been a single, killing blow. He stared at her with loathing, his dark eyes piercing her mere centimeters from her face, and spat on her.

"You have disgraced my name!" he shouted. "Perhaps you are not even my get!"

Vestara's mind flashed back to the theoretical discussion she'd had with Ben—what she would do if her mother had ever had an affair. Anger rushed through her at his implication. Her mother *loved* her father. She would never betray him.

But Vestara would.

Hadn't she already? Was betrayal in actions, or in thoughts? Were her "letters" to a fictitious Jedi parent betrayal?

She shoved the distracting thought aside, focusing on the hot anger, channeling it and using it—as he had taught her to do. He sensed the change in her and smiled contemptuously.

"*Now* you listen to my lessons," he snarled, "but it is too late for you to save yourself."

He sprang up and leapt over her head, turning as he went to slash out with the lightsaber, attempting to carve through her skull. Vestara ducked and struck upward with her own glowing red weapon, shoving it aside so that Khai had to twist to avoid striking himself. She was surprised at how easy it was. Was she really that much better a fighter after her time with the Skywalkers?

"Very good," he said. "Your skills have improved. But not your loyalties."

And suddenly Vestara understood what was going on. Why he

seemed so out of control; he, Saber Gavar Khai, who had prided himself on using his emotions as he saw fit, who would never surrender to them. Her own sense of outraged betrayal surged through her at the realization.

"Where does *your* loyalty lie, Father? Not with the Lost Tribe, I think!"

Shocked, he dropped his guard for a moment. She took advantage of the opening and charged, feinting left and then sweeping right with the glowing red blade. Lithely he dodged, recovering quickly. Their blades clashed and he twisted hard, using both the torque of the blade and the Force to nearly snap her wrist. She dropped her lightsaber and he closed in for the kill.

Her heart shaking her with its pounding, Vestara shoved one splayed hand out in Khai's direction and extended her other hand. Her lightsaber flew toward her as her father, Force-shoved, stumbled back. He looked—surprised. A fierce grin twisted her mouth and she sprang on him, raining blows and shouting wordlessly. More surprise came from him as he was forced to use all his years of expertise to block her.

Vestara was a mixture of surging emotions. Rage, hatred, hurt, love—she gathered them to her and used them all. Her father had loved her, but still had used her for his own ends. And when she had stumbled, he had not forgiven. He had not forgiven, because he was Sith, and Sith do not make mistakes and live. She had turned her back on the Tribe, letting her heart wander to Ben, and yet she had been a dutiful daughter. All the contradictions, all the logic and illogic—she used them as fuel to the fire of her intense desire to survive.

Khai recovered quickly. "So be it," he said, acknowledging her renewed, laser-keen intensity, volatile and violent. "I am done with you."

No. *She* was done with him.

Vestara's world constricted to this, and nothing but this: the blending of body, will, and passion, and the centimeters of space between two living beings . . . one of whom would be dead soon.

Ben drew more and more heavily on the Force—it was difficult here, so close to a dark-side nexus, and it took more out of him. Two of his foes were down. One was dead. The other, having nearly been cut in two, was lying thrashing on the flagstones, her face twisted in a silent scream.

His senses were sharp, extended, focusing not just on battling the Sith but also on observing how his father, Jaina, and Vestara fared in the fight. As he had expected, the uncle–niece team of Skywalker and Solo were doing just fine. He could see the corpses strewn about, and with a flash of black humor thought the Sith, now potential tripping hazards, were more of a threat dead than alive.

Vestara's voice rang out over the sound of battle. "Where does *your* loyalty lie, Father? Not with the Lost Tribe, I think!"

Gavar Khai's reaction was strong. So strong that the Sith fighting Ben paused as if buffeted by it. It was only an instant of inattention—but when Saber and Jedi Knight battled, an instant was all that was needed. Ben didn't hesitate, but plunged the blade forward into the Keshiri Sith's chest. She died with a look of surprise on her face.

Ben whirled, glancing first at his father and Jaina. They were more than holding their own, so Ben turned to Vestara. He had just spun around when he realized he needn't have bothered.

Vestara had never looked more beautiful, nor more deadly. Her long brown hair was flying with the speed of her movement, her lightsaber a blur as she pushed the attack. Gavar Khai took one step back, then another and another, even with a state-of-the-art prosthetic arm clearly having difficulty countering his daughter's savage attack.

Vestara cried out, sharply, wordlessly, her voice raw as she swung with all her skill and speed.

Her red blade sliced through robes and flesh, cutting through him from right shoulder to left hip. He collapsed, dead before he hit the ground.

Vestara reached out a hand. His still-lit lightsaber, sizzling on the flagstones, sprang to her. Panting slightly, her skin gleaming with sweat and the moist air, she clutched a lightsaber in each hand. Her eyes met Ben's and their gazes locked.

Lost in that piercing gaze, Ben heard, as if from a great distance, the sound of lightsabers being extinguished and knew that his father and Jaina had won their fights. He turned to them as they approached.

"You okay?" Luke asked.

"Yeah," Ben said. "A burn on the shoulder, but should be all right. You?"

"We'll need the bacta salve, but otherwise fine." Luke regarded Vestara with an expression that was both cautious and kind. "I don't think your father agreed to die just to convince me you'd betray him," he said, and his voice was gentler than Ben had ever heard it when speaking to Vestara.

She blinked, as if coming out of a daze. "I—I had to kill him," she said. Her voice was thick. "I had to kill my father . . ."

Ben stepped up to her, wanting to comfort her, not knowing how. All the phrases he could say fell far short. *Sorry about your father. You did the right thing. It'll be all right.* They were all hollow in comparison to the vastness of pain and shock Vestara was feeling.

The right words came from an unexpected source. "I had to kill my own brother," Jaina said quietly.

Vestara looked over at the Jedi, listening, her eyes bright with unshed tears.

"I knew it was the right thing to do," Jaina continued. "I did it to save my own life and the lives of many others. I still miss him. You'll miss your father, too."

"I . . . I had no choice."

"No. You didn't. Other than be cut down yourself," Jaina continued. "It was the right thing for you to do, too. But you'll still miss him . . . and wish there had been some other way."

Vestara nodded, looking at Jaina gratefully. She took a deep breath and Ben felt her aura in the Force steady. He reached out and touched her arm gently. She gave him a shaky, broken smile.

"There were only ten," Luke said. "They figured out where we were going somehow."

"I didn't—" Vestara began.

"I don't think you did," Luke replied. "They probably assumed we'd do exactly what we have been doing—investigating planets traditionally associated with Sith history. Khai probably chose this place because of the nexus. They could send a smaller team and still be stronger."

"Or so they thought," Jaina said.

"That means that their main flotilla is somewhere else," Luke said.

"They're with Abeloth," Vestara blurted.

"What?" Ben said.

"I sensed it in my father. He—he questioned my loyalties, so I questioned his. And I was right." She lifted her gaze and met Luke's blue eyes evenly. "He no longer identifies with the Lost Tribe. He's with Abeloth now—and I bet the rest of the flotilla is, too."

"You're sure?" Luke pressed.

She nodded. "I think . . . she was doing something to him."

"Like with Taalon?" Luke recalled the metamorphosis of High Lord Taalon after he had drunk from the Fountain of Knowledge. He had started to become like Abeloth.

"Not that dramatic," she said. "But . . . mentally. His mind—he wasn't the way he used to be. I think that's why I was able to win against him at all—because he wasn't as focused. He was so proud of being Sith, so proud of what the Lost Tribe had accomplished. Now he's—he was—blindly following Abeloth. And if my father succumbed, then I am certain the others did." She looked away again, swallowing hard. "He was a strong man."

Ben let out a slow whistle. "So now the Sith have gone from wanting to capture Abeloth to wanting to serve her," he said. "And we've still got no clue as to where to start looking for her—or them."

"The trail's gone cold," Luke said. "I think our best bet, for now, is to regroup and head back to Coruscant. We'll talk to the historians, share with them everything we've learned. Maybe we've overlooked something. There are many brilliant minds at the Temple. It's time we availed ourselves of them. Maybe they can see something we can't." He sighed.

Ben smiled. "It'll be nice to get back," he admitted. "Kinda tired of attending the Mobile Chapter of the Academy."

"It won't be for good," Luke warned.

"Oh, I know. But it'll still be nice."

Ben also knew, though his father would not say so in front of Vestara, that Luke was concerned about the situation with the Jedi and the GA. Everything seemed to indicate that things were going smoothly with the triumvirate system that had been put into place. But it was clearly time for Grand Master Luke Skywalker to return, at least temporarily. All signs pointed to it; it seemed to be the will of the Force.

He looked back over at Vestara. She was doing her best to recover from the shock and horror of being forced to kill her own father, whom Ben knew she had loved. And, tough girl that she was, she was doing a good job. But he still knew she was shattered.

"Come on, stinky," he said. "You need a sanisteam."

She gave him a ghost of her old smirk. "All I have to say to that is that it's a good thing I can block out how bad *you* smell."

It was feeble jesting, but Ben was heartened by it anyway. He felt for Vestara, but believed with all his heart that what she had done here today, anguishing though it was, was a good thing. She had freed herself from Gavar Khai and his dark influence forever, and Ben had hope that she had taken a big step along the path that would eventually bring her out of the Sith shadow, into the light.

He hesitated, then held out his hand to her. She took it. Hand in hand, they moved out of the cold shadow of the dark side temple.

"Khai has failed."

Abeloth's voice came through loud and clear on the bridge of the *Black Wave*. These were not the dulcet female tones that Tola Annax was used to hearing; the voice was . . . liquid sounding, garbled, deep, and raised the hairs on the back of Annax's neck. Both the sound of the voice and the words shot a thrill of apprehension through her. Ship was visible on the viewscreen, an orange-red eye with wings, seeming to glare balefully at her, and Annax shuddered inwardly. *At least,* she mused grimly, *I don't have to be the one actually delivering the bad news.*

Abeloth still might destroy them, though, and she knew it.

"I very much regret so, yes." Annax used the Force to keep her voice sounding calm and confident. "We lost all ten of them, some of our best Sabers."

"A pity," said the strange, gurgling voice. "I wish we had not. But it is no matter, is it, Captain Tola Annax?"

Relief flooded through her, leaving Annax feeling slightly weak. "No, not at all, no."

"Then all is well. I have others to serve me—and other plans to execute." And that quickly, Abeloth's transmission ended. Annax leaned back in the chair she had occupied since Khai's departure, and a slow smile spread across her lovely features.

*Captain Tola Annax* had such a nice ring to it.

Had Abeloth permitted a holographic transmission instead of a simple verbal one, Tola Annax would have seen something that might well have haunted her for the rest of her days, if it had not snapped her mind permanently.

On the "floor" of Ship's interior was a collection of pulsing, half-formed body parts, attached in a way that no student of any kind of anatomy would recognize. It shifted and writhed, a human foot popping out here, a tentacle there, then subsiding back to a no-shape *thing* that undulated for a moment, before a face formed with gray eyes to see. It was a human face, peering out from the otherwise formless, undulating mass that was Abeloth.

The gray eyes were fixed on the wall, which was transmitting images from dozens of different holonews channels. Beings of all species were reporting—on uprisings, on the latest word from the interim government of the GA, on the Jedi, on the Imperial Remnant, on the influx of new Senators. Abeloth saw the jowly face of Padnel Ovin of Klatooine, the beaming, charming smile of Rokari Kem of Qaras, the reptilian visage of Jedi Master Saba Sebatyne glaring at holocams being shoved in her face, and the elegant Senator Haydnat Treen courting those same holocams, protestors marching. She saw funeral pyres for the slain Octusi, the grave face of Perre Needmo announcing a scholarship in the name of the late journalist Madhi Vaandt.

The human mouth smiled, widening slowly, stretching across the face as the gray eyes grew black with tiny pinpricks of light.

Oh, yes. Other plans to execute, indeed.

# Chapter Nineteen

ABOARD THE *JADE SHADOW*

DEAD. GAVAR KHAI, SITH SABER, WAS DEAD. IN THE BIZARRE PATH THAT had taken him from the Lost Tribe to Abeloth's side, he had forsaken his people, permitted his wife to die, and attempted to slay his daughter. Vestara Khai was an orphan. And try as she might, she just couldn't seem to wrap her mind around the cold, brutal fact.

She lay in her cabin aboard the *Jade Shadow,* sleepless, staring at the ceiling, going over the battle in her mind's eye, hearing again the heart-lacerating words that cut deeper than any lightsaber.

*I will start fresh. A new wife, a new child. Both are easily replaced.*

No. They weren't. Nor was a father.

She saw again the contempt in his dark eyes, felt again the warm wetness of his spittle. The realization of the abandonment—not just of her, but of the Tribe; the out-of-control nature of his fighting; the feeling of savage rightness when she harnessed her own emotions, both the dark and the light, in order to defeat him: these things played over and over again in her mind's eye, like a holovid on endless repeat.

There was a sickening inevitability about it all. Each mental path she went down led her to the same conclusion. If she had gone with him—he would have killed her. If she had not fought as hard as she could—he would have killed her. The galaxy, so vast and complicated, had suddenly become very small, and very clear. A Khai had needed to die, and when it came down to it, Vestara had been unwilling to be a sacrifice.

Growling softly in her frustration at being unable to sleep, she rose and went to the small computer built into the bulkhead. It had been a while since she had read the two letters, but now she wanted to revisit them. To feel the comfort of the happy and utterly fictitious relationship she had created, now that there was no chance of ever restoring even what they'd once had. Once, she had been loved, in a way, and she knew it.

She hesitated, then dived into the file she had created. She had known it would have been safer to leave the letters in her head, that she was tempting fate to write them down. But seeing the words on the screen had helped. It had given them a reality that had comforted her, and now, she hoped, would comfort her again.

Up they came. She looked down at her folded hands for a moment, then lifted her face and began to read.

Only two. They would soon have one more to keep them company. One final letter, an orphan girl's wishful memories of a father who had never really lived.

Swallowing hard, she raised fingers that trembled, ever so slightly, and began to type.

> Dear Papa,
>
> I know you are gone, and I will never be able to laugh with you, or hug you, or listen to your wisdom ever again. I know that you have become one with the Force, and that in a way you will always be with me. But that gives me very little comfort now, when I am missing you so much.

> Master Skywalker spoke with me about how he had felt when he lost his mentor, Obi-Wan Kenobi. Even though Obi-Wan had been with him for a very short time, Master Skywalker speaks eloquently of the pain of the loss, and the comfort that he found when "Ben," for whom my own dear Ben is named, found a way to return to him.
>
> Dearest Papa, you have always guided and supported me, gently steering me through the myriad challenges that have come my way as a Jedi. No daughter could have asked for a better father. No apprentice could have asked for a wiser master. I cannot tell you how much I miss

The door slid open, and Ben stood there, bleary with sleep, concern on his face. "Vestara, I—*what are you doing*?"

Frantically she rushed to delete the file, then turned, startled and angry at his intrusion.

"What are *you* doing, Ben? Walking into my room at this hour?"

But she couldn't distract him. He had suddenly become very, very awake, and he sprang for the computer. She shoved at him, and he whirled on her.

*"What were you doing?"*

"It's none of your business," she said heatedly. "Why are you even here?"

"I heard you crying, and you didn't answer when I knocked. I got worried, so I overrode the lock," he said, his voice hard and angry and cold and sharply at odds with the tenderness of the words. She was taken aback, and as she blinked, she realized that there were indeed tears clinging to her dark lashes.

"Apparently I didn't need to be concerned," Ben continued. His hands shot out and gripped her wrists. "Move."

Embarrassment, hurt, and anger rushed through her. Her eyes narrowed and she Force-shoved him back. Not expecting it, although he should have, Ben barely reacted in time to keep from slamming against the bulkhead. He turned in midair, landed, albeit imperfectly, on his feet, and lifted a hand sharply. To her complete shock, Vestara felt an invisible hand crack across her cheek. He had used the Force not to defend himself, or to restrain her, but to strike her in anger.

Her face stinging from the invisible blow, she flicked a finger and her lightsaber sprang to her hand. Ben had gathered himself to leap at her and had to twist his body sharply as she swung, the glowing red blade singing its unique and unmistakable song as it sliced through air. Vestara pursued, forcing her body to calm, even though she was trembling with outrage.

A whirling kick that she should have seen coming a kilometer away knocked the lightsaber out of her hands. Ben extended a hand and it flew to him, and Vestara had the unique sight of Ben Skywalker, Jedi Knight, standing in a dark room with his angry features lit by the red glow of a Sith lightsaber.

She sprang toward him, but he lifted his left hand and the pillows rose to attack her with soft, harmless vigor that nonetheless blocked her vision and pressed in close to her face, smothering her. The precious second she struggled against them gave Ben all the time he needed to pin her against the bed and use the Force to swathe her in the bedsheets.

She struggled against him for a long moment, then suddenly sagged. He stood, catching his breath, his face still eerily illuminated by the scarlet glow, then extinguished the lightsaber.

"Now," he said, "I'll let you up if you tell me what the stang you were up to."

"Just go away, Ben, it's got nothing to do with you. It's personal."

"Everything and nothing is personal with Sith," Ben growled. He moved over to the computer and frowned. "Where is it? What you were working on?"

"I deleted it."

"Now it's my business."

"Blast it, Ben!" Her voice cracked and he regarded her with surprise. She looked away, fearful that he would see the traitorous tears still glinting in her eyes. "I give you my word, it wasn't anything against you. Please, just go, okay?"

"I wish I could believe you," he said. "But if it wasn't anything important, you wouldn't be so determined to hide it from me. Do I have to truss you up? I will if I have to. Or I can comm Dad to watch you while I go digging for this stuff."

Fear and defeat both fluttered through Vestara, and suddenly her body, tense and tight, sagged against the blankets tightly wrapped around her. Ben would do it, too. Then both Skywalkers would see the letters. She could either fight until she killed him, or her secret would be revealed.

And she found, not a little bit to her surprise, that she didn't want to kill Ben Skywalker. She didn't want to see him harmed in any way, least of all by her hand. But for him to see this . . .

She tried one more time, turning her head to look him full in the face. "Ben," she said quietly, though her voice trembled slightly, "I give you my word. Any word you want, any promise or vow you would believe. What I was doing had nothing at all to do with you, or Luke, or the Jedi, or anything. It was personal and private. That's all."

Something flickered across his face for a moment, then his expression grew hard again. "There's no assurance you could possibly give me that I'd believe. I'm getting awfully tired of being played by you, Vestara. And I'm getting more insulted with each day that you seem to think I'm stupid."

*You're not stupid,* she wanted to say. *You're just . . . trusting.* Which, she supposed, *was* stupid, when one was dealing with the Sith. She recalled his words some time earlier, when he had asked if she didn't tire of always mistrusting, of always having her guard up. What he didn't know was how right he was. She had not understood, until she had come across people for whom this was not second nature, how . . . exhausting . . . mistrust was. How complicated it was to spin lies. She felt as though she had suddenly realized that since the day she could talk, she had been carrying a burden that had been draining her life energy.

What would happen if she let that burden go? If she decided not to lie anymore, to open her heart and mind to trusting someone?

*You trusted your father, and look what happened. If your own blood could try to kill you, what would a stranger do?*

But her father had been a Sith. Ben wasn't.

Quietly, she said, "Look if you feel you have to, Ben. And you'll see that I'm telling you the truth."

"I *am* going to look. And if you are telling the truth, it would be a first," Ben muttered. That wasn't entirely accurate, and both of them knew it. Vestara hadn't always lied. Sometimes the best deceptions had the most truth in them.

The thought hurt, in an odd way.

She turned her face to her wall and braced herself for the shame and ridicule that were certain to come.

Vestara hadn't had a lot of time to cover her tracks, which was fortunate. Even though she was relatively new to the technology he'd grown up with, and they hadn't given her much chance to explore the *Jade Shadow* unsupervised, the young Sith woman was highly intelligent and keenly observant. If she'd had more than a moment or two, Ben was certain that Vestara would have figured out a way to permanently delete the files or corrupt them so that whatever she'd been doing would never be discovered.

He fumed as he worked, digging deeper into the levels of security to recover the data. He had wanted so badly to trust her. He knew that his dad was at least partially right: Ben was attracted to—okay, maybe even smitten with; just a bit, though, not enough to impair his judgment—Vestara Khai. He *wanted* her to be redeemable. But maybe Luke was right. Maybe Ben saw in that lovely face with the odd, endearing little scar at the mouth what he wanted to see. Maybe it really was just a mask covering something hideous and horrible.

He stabbed angrily at the keyboard. What had she been doing? Sending—

Letters.

Stang.

He got as far as *Dear Papa,* before he whirled on Vestara. "I should kill you right here," he snarled. "This was dated weeks ago! You've been spying on us this whole time, just like my dad said!"

She turned to face him. She'd been crying, even though she was trying to pretend she hadn't, and she wasn't even bothering to hide her presence in the Force. That presence was usually uniquely sharp, bright, and strong. Now it felt . . . dull. Muffled. Not frightened, or angry, as it might have been expected to feel to him had she been plotting the treachery he had just uncovered. His brow furrowed in confusion.

"You shouldn't jump to conclusions," she said without rancor. "You've found them. You're reading them, even though I practically begged you not to. Read them all, Ben. Go ahead."

Uncertainty washed over him. Still frowning, Ben turned back to the screen.

> Dear Papa:
>
> I hope you are feeling better, and that the hurts you have recently suffered have been well tended.
>
> The other night, seeing Ben blindsided by reminders of his mother, seeing how her loss still affected him, and seeing how his father instinctively reached out for him, to comfort him, I was of course reminded of you.

He felt his jaw drop open and closed it immediately, slamming walls down over his own presence in the Force. Vestara was reminded of her father watching Luke comfort Ben? What was going on? What in—

And then he understood.

Ben remembered thinking that Vestara walked on a knife blade in dealing with Gavar Khai. It made his own clashes with Luke years earlier seem like unimportant spats. Even at their worst moments, Ben had never experienced the sort of fear Vestara had to face every waking moment—knowing that if you disappointed your dad, you wouldn't get a lecture and a sigh, but a lightsaber to your gut.

She had created a fantasy relationship with the parent who would indeed later try to kill her—whom she would have to slay in order to survive.

"I've seen enough," Ben said, and started to delete the letters.

"No." Vestara was angry at him again now, and he didn't blame her one bit. He felt . . . embarrassed. Ashamed, at intruding into this deeply personal moment. Vestara's wistful yearnings for the sort of thing Ben had taken for granted all his life shamed him. He shouldn't have pried—but how could he have known?

"You wanted to read them? Then read them. All of them."

"I . . . shouldn't. I don't want to make you feel uncomfortable."

She laughed, harshly. "Too late," she said. "Read them."

So he did.

> And I wonder sometimes what I would be like if I had grown up with a father who was cold and indifferent, or determined to drive me toward a hard destiny in a more cold and ruthless world. I'm not sure I would like myself, and I'm so happy that you have always been kind and supportive.

There was a second letter, in which Vestara expressed her gratitude for her "Papa's" protective nature. The final letter, the one he had surprised Vestara writing, was the most astounding of all. Gavar Khai, a Jedi Knight? Vestara, his loving daughter and dedicated apprentice? In the letters depicting a completely false reality was a warmth and ease he had never seen between father and daughter in real life. Quietly, he turned off the computer, rose, and turned to face her.

He had released the wrapped blankets and now she lay uncovered, curled up, facing away from him. Words crowded his throat, too many to speak all at once. Ben stood for a while, until it became awkward, then muttered, "Ah, to hell with it," and lay down beside her. Knowing he'd get an elbow to the stomach or worse if this was the wrong thing to do, he wrapped an arm around her slender waist and curled his body protectively around hers.

She lay still, stiff in his embrace, and then he felt her shaking with silent sobs. His heart aching for her, he leaned his cheek on her hair.

"I'm so sorry, Ves. I didn't know. I *couldn't* know . . ."

Vestara nodded, still silent, still shaking. Ben reached and gently stroked her hair, as if this fierce and proud young woman were a child in need of comforting, and she accepted it. Ben closed his eyes, melting against her. They lay like that for a long time. Ben was almost asleep when she turned in his embrace.

"Ben?" She lifted her face up to his. "Do . . . you think I could?"

"Could what?"

A long, long silence. She had completely dropped her guard. He could sense her in a way he never had before, and knew that whatever she was about to ask meant everything to her. That she was full of hope and fear so strong it almost overpowered her, and that she knew she was opening completely to him. He waited, patiently. In this moment that seemed to stretch out forever, Ben realized that when it came to Vestara, he had all the patience in the universe.

Then, softly, in a voice that quivered, she said the words that made Ben's heart leap. The words he had been wanting to hear for so long.

" . . . become a Jedi."

For a moment he couldn't speak. He felt her fear grow—fear of rejection, fear of the trust she was offering, and while he struggled for the words he concentrated on sending her reassurance, comfort . . . yes, and love . . . in the Force.

"Vestara Khai," he said, his voice as soft as hers had been, "I know you can do anything you want. Yes. Oh, yes. You can become a Jedi. And it would be the greatest honor of my life to help you. I'll be there every step of the way. I promise."

Relief and joy and hope emanated from her, chasing away the tense, cold, disabling fear, and she smiled radiantly. Following an impulse, Ben reached and brushed the little scar at the corner of her mouth gently with his thumb. She didn't pull away, instead closed her eyes. His lips followed his touch, pressing a kiss on what he knew she despised most about herself, letting her know he found it beautiful, found *her,* all of her, beautiful. She understood at once, and he tasted the salt of sudden tears as she turned her head slightly to complete the kiss. He held her tightly, both of them trembling, caught up in the overwhelming release of at last laying down the weapons of suspicion and hatred.

She would become a Jedi—a great Jedi. Finally, she would walk in the light, and feel its warmth, and open her heart to the joy of giving and receiving complete and utter trust.

Trust . . . and love.

And Ben would be with her.

Every step of the way.

"I'm glad to hear you're finally coming back to Coruscant," Leia was saying. Her hologram stood before Luke, and he couldn't help but think about the first time he had seen her—just like this, a small hologram. Forty years had come and gone since that time, and they had been through so much together. But at her core, she was still the Leia he had seen then, determined and beautiful, the brave and amazing woman he was proud to call "sister." Jaina sat beside him, letting him do most of the talking.

"We should, I hope, be arriving at the same time," Leia continued.

"I thought you were working with Dorvan and Treen," Luke said. "And you said you wanted to help Padnel ease into his role."

"I was working with Treen and Dorvan, and we were at least able to have dinner with Padnel. From what I've heard, he's doing fine on his own. We . . . left for a while to chase a lead on Daala's location."

Luke and Jaina exchanged glances. "Any luck?"

Leia glanced over at something or someone Luke couldn't see and made a slight face. "I'll let you know. We ran into some . . . old friends. It's been . . . interesting."

Luke couldn't help but chuckle. "Sounds like nothing's changed much then. We'll see you soon."

" 'Bye, Mom. Give Dad a hug for me."

When Leia's image had disappeared, Jaina turned to Luke. "When we get back, I need to talk to Natua," she said. "She thinks she may have a lead on Ship. I didn't want to say anything to Mom until Natua told me about it."

"That would be the first good news we've had in a while," Luke said.

Jaina nodded. "At least Gavar Khai isn't going to be a problem anymore."

"True." It was not the outcome Luke would have wished, but it was a threat that was now eliminated. He had been sensing some very intense emotions from both Ben and Vestara after the fight on Dromund Kaas, but had chosen not to interfere. He trusted his son not to do anything foolish, and who knew but that this tragic and brutal event might make Vestara take a hard look at her future.

And also—she deserved someone to be kind to her. Her father certainly never had been.

Still . . . "Don't tell Ben or Vestara about this possible lead, either, not just yet," he said. "It might be a dead end. And even if it isn't, we have things to take care of on Coruscant first. There'll be time for this once we know more."

Jaina nodded. "They've got enough to deal with."

"Choices between dark and light," Luke mused. "Coming to grips with killing a parent. Knowing hopes might get raised only to be dashed."

"Hormones."

Luke shuddered. "And hormones," he agreed. "I take it back. They've got *more* than enough to deal with."

# Chapter Twenty

THIRD MOON OF VEXAR, CORPORATE SECTOR

"NOW," HAN SAID, SMILING WITH FALSE CHEER AT THE THREE SQUIBS, "you are going to tell me what that was all about. And you are going to give me the information we agreed to pay for. And if I don't like any of what I hear, *this* is going to be your new home. Got it?"

It had been two hours and forty-three minutes since the attack at the café. Zekk and Taryn had made it to Zekk's ship and departed Roonadan with Allana and the Squibs aboard. Han and Leia had had a slightly more extensive adventure, their vessel being more recognizable, or perhaps simply more infamous, than Zekk's nondescript shuttle. Eventually, though, they had shaken pursuit long enough to make an escape and had rendezvoused on an out-of-the-way rocky moon orbiting a gas giant. The gas giant, obviously, could not support human life; the rocky moon, just barely.

All of them had disembarked onto the moon's surface. Currently Han, Leia, Zekk, and Taryn had subtly formed a circle around the three Squibs. Allana stood next to her grandmother, although she was frowning slightly.

"Is this any way to treat your partners?" Grees protested, gesticulating emphatically.

"Partners generally let someone know if they're going to come under fire," said Han.

"We didn't know! Honest!" Emala protested.

Han and Leia exchanged glances that communicated without words how much they believed *that.*

"Oh come on," said Grees. "You think we would have lingered for lunch if we'd known someone was after us?"

Han hesitated; they'd raised a good point. Squibs weren't stupid, though they sometimes appeared to other species to be cheerfully reckless; nor were they Hutt-like gluttons.

"All right. Let's say you didn't know you were going to be attacked," Leia said. "Do you know who was firing?"

"That's got nothing to do with our deal," said Emala earnestly. "That's something else *entirely.*"

"That's half truthful," Leia said.

"You don't have to be a Jedi to know when someone's hiding something from you," Taryn put in, folding her arms and looking archly at the Squibs.

"But it helps," Zekk said.

"I seem to recall something in your first message along the lines of *safety for your family guaranteed,*" Han said. "Someone was taking shots at my daughter. That is not keeping with your deal."

For the first time since the whole escapade began, the family of Squibs exchanged glances. "We didn't know there would be a fuzzling coming along," Sligh said. "And we *did* keep to the bargain. That comment was referring to the bounty on your heads. Which, by the way, was lifted when you agreed to meet us. Not that you've thanked us for it yet."

"Aren't you glad you don't have to worry about that anymore?" asked Emala brightly.

Han rolled his eyes. "I haven't worried about that for some time," he said. "What I *worry* about is what happened in that café happening again."

"You had something important to tell us," said a small voice. "I made sure you got to safety. Don't you think it's time you told us something? That seems like a fair next step to me and in keeping with the deal."

*Girl takes after her mother—and her grandmother,* Han thought. *Natural-born diplomat.*

"For a fuzzling, she's pretty sharp," Grees said.

"Yeah, especially for a *human* fuzzling," Sligh said.

"You gotta agree to take us with you and help us get to safety," Emala said. She, like the others, was no longer looking at any of the adults, but at Allana. "You promise that, we'll tell you what we know."

"We must ensure our own safety, too, and that of Amelia," said Leia. "If we take you with us, we're going keep an eye on you until we're sure it's safe for all of us. Agreed?"

The Squibs leaned in to one another, whispering in Squibbal. Emala poked her head up and regarded Allana with large, soft, doe-like eyes for an instant before rejoining the blue huddle. Finally they seemed to reach an agreement and stepped back.

"You got a deal," Grees said.

"Finally," muttered Han.

"You know where Daala is?" pressed Leia.

"We know where she's heading. She's not quite there yet, or she might be, we don't know," Sligh said. "She's heading for the Meridian Sector. Pedducis Chorios, specifically."

"Why there?" asked Zekk. "I thought for sure she'd be heading for Imperial Space."

"She wanted to go back to familiar ground," Emala said. "She's got a history with that place."

"Yes, she most certainly does," Leia said. She looked meaningfully at Han. "That was where she went when she found Liegeus again. I think she was there until his murder."

"There's a Moff there she's got it in for," Grees said. "Except he's got a bantha-sized head and thinks she wants to ally with him instead. Name of Tol Getelles. We were doing some, um . . . research on him for the Imperial Remnant."

"Also half true," said Zekk. "By some mathematical reckoning that might add up to a single entire truth."

"Not by mine," said Han. "Keep going."

"I'm not lying!" Grees protested, scowling and showing teeth that were startlingly sharp and white for a Squib his age. "That's how we were able to intercept the communication. From there, we were able to back-trace it and tap into some other messages. She talked to several people. We have them recorded, verbatim."

"We'll want to listen to those, but give us the short version first," Han said. Leia stepped away for a moment, clicking her comlink and speaking softly.

"Moff Vansyn and Moff Getelles," said Emala promptly.

"What about them?"

"You said you wanted the short—" began Sligh, but as Han took a step toward him, he put up his small hands. "Okay, okay, hold your dewbacks. She contacted Moff Vansyn first. There's apparently some *other* Moff she doesn't like—"

"She doesn't seem to like very many of them," Emala said.

"—named Lecersen," said Grees, picking up where Sligh left off. The transition was handled with ease and familiarity. "Seems Vansyn used to be friends with Lecersen, but he's been feeling ignored recently. Daala promised Vansyn that if he supported her claim to become Head of State of the Empire, eliminating first Jag and then Getelles, she'd see to it that he would get Moff Getelles's territories."

"A tempting offer," Leia said, returning to the group. "I just contacted Ashik." Ashik was Jag's devoted Chiss assistant. Han nodded. If anyone could shed some light on the Squibs' claim, it would be him. "Their story checks out. In a very convoluted manner, they actually *were* working for Jag."

"See? And to think you doubted us," said Sligh.

"I still do. Keep going," said Han.

"Isn't that enough?" asked Sligh in an injured tone. "What more do you want from us? We've told you where she's going, who she's working with, and who she's setting up."

"How many recordings do you have?"

"More than enough," Grees said quickly as Emala opened her mouth to answer. "We've told you everything we said we would. Now you need to take us to safety."

Han held up an index finger. "One moment," he said. He patted Allana on the head and motioned to Leia. The two of them stepped aside and spoke quietly.

"What do you think?" Leia asked.

"I think we ought to leave them here with some supplies and take off before whoever came after them comes after us and Allana," Han said.

"You wouldn't."

Han scowled. "I miss being the bad guy."

"Softie."

"Those oversized pack rats will see just how soft I am if any of those guys gets near our granddaughter again."

"That reminds me," Leia said, glancing back over to the Squibs. Taryn and Zekk still stood nearby, but Allana had gone right up and was talking to them. She was, Leia noted with a pang familiar from three decades earlier, already taller than Emala. *How quickly they grow . . .*

Again something flitted across her mind, but she dismissed it. "When I was talking to Ashik, I described the uniforms to him and he was able to ID them for me. Guess who our attackers work for?"

" . . . Moff Getelles."

"You get a prize."

"That's the same guy the Squibs were spying on. What the heck did they do to get him so ticked off at them? Some gloriously complicated scheme no doubt."

"Or something as simple as getting caught," Leia said. "Every covert operative runs that risk, Han. You should know that."

"Then why are they acting so mysterious?" Han wanted to know. "Something's going on they're not telling us about."

"I agree they're hiding something, but . . . they're Squibs. Think about their culture. It's quite likely that they're *always* hiding something," Leia pointed out. "They've delivered on their end of the bargain. We need to do the same. Not just because it's the right thing to do, but because they put their lives at risk in order to get this information to us. Knowing where Daala is and what her plans are is going to help both the GA and Jag."

Han sighed. "I suppose you're right. Do I have to like it?"

"No."

"Good."

ABOARD THE *JADE SHADOW,* EN ROUTE TO CORUSCANT

Luke supposed he should have been prepared for this. He wasn't.

"A Jedi," he repeated, dumbfounded. The two teenagers exchanged glances, then Vestara nodded.

"You've got to know I don't believe you," Luke said.

"Dad—"

Vestara laid a gentle hand on Ben's arm as he spoke. The gesture looked . . . comfortable. Luke didn't like it.

"Master Skywalker, I would be surprised if I received any other reaction from you," she said. "There was a time when such a statement would indeed be a lie—a trick, a trap. But . . . you have exposed me to thoughts and ideals that I had never seen before. And if I *had* run across them before I met you, they would have been presented as vices. But I know how I feel about them. I . . . like them. It feels good to help someone, just because they need it. It feels good to—to be cared for"—she looked shyly at Ben—"and know there's no hidden motive. Even as a child, I never had that."

"So, a few months of exposure to a new way of thinking has completely contradicted everything else you knew since the time you were born." Luke tried hard not to sound sarcastic, but he thought he wasn't doing a good job.

"It's more complicated than that," Vestara continued. "I saw what the beliefs of my people really are. I saw a lot of them in Abeloth. And I saw who—what sort of man my father really was." Her voice broke at this last and she cleared her throat. "I don't expect you to believe me right away. But I hope that with time I will be able to prove myself to you. All I'm asking for is that chance."

Luke leaned back in his chair, arms clasped behind his head, and regarded her intently. "All right. Drop your guard. I know you're extremely strong in the Force, and I know that you've had walls around you probably since you could crawl. Drop them."

She looked uncomfortable, but not surprised. Ben reached for her hand and pressed it briefly.

"It's just Dad," he said.

"Just the Jedi Grand Master," she replied wryly.

"If you're sincere, then you should have nothing to hide," Luke said.

"If—if I do, then you'll believe me?"

"It would be a good start, yes."

She nodded and took a deep breath. He saw her visibly relax her jaw and shoulders. Then Vestara met Luke's eyes and nodded.

He could have been harsh, rough. But that wasn't the Jedi way. He reached for her in the Force gently, in an exploratory fashion, as one might reach a hand out to a timid animal. There was ugliness there; there would have to be, given her history. But there was nothing ugly and dark that was new. Instead, to his surprise, Luke found a small, timid gleam of hope and a desire for and fear of joy. He sent reassurance to her, and that small spot suddenly expanded, and did not contract to its former weak strength. He focused on what it meant to be a Jedi: to protect those who were victimized and could not defend themselves. To trust, to love, to be willing to give of oneself. To fight and risk one's life for those ideals.

And the little place in Vestara's Force aura drank it all in. As gently as he had approached her, he disconnected.

"Well?" Ben asked impatiently.

"When we return, I will undertake your training myself, if you wish," Luke said. At the expression of delight on both young faces he cautioned, "But you've got a long way to go."

"You're nervous," Ben said. He and Vestara sat together on the edge of her bed. Ben had his arm around her, and she leaned on his shoulder. Her hair was soft against his cheek, and he breathed in the scent of it with closed eyes. He was glad Vestara couldn't see him right now, as he knew he had the most idiotic smile on his face. He was okay with that.

"No, I'm not," Vestara said, far too quickly.

He squeezed her arm. "Yeah, you are. I would be, too. You're about to meet a whole bunch of people who not long ago were your sworn enemies and say, *Hi there, I used to be Sith but not anymore. It's okay because I'm dating the most amazing, best-looking, smartest Jedi in the*—ow!"

She'd used the Force to smack his head. The blow was clearly playful, but it stung, and Ben used his free hand to rub his ear.

"Don't get cocky," Vestara said. Her voice was teasing, warm with affection, and Ben was discovering he loved to hear that tone. "All right. I am nervous. Who wouldn't be? No one is going to believe I've really had a change of heart. And I don't blame them."

"The Jedi believe in second chances," Ben told her, growing serious. She needed to trust in that, or else she would be in danger of backsliding. "I know it's hard for you to be open, but you've got nothing to hide anymore. Let everyone see what I see, and they'll believe you."

"I hope so," Vestara said. A slight quaver had entered her voice. "Master Luke . . . *seems* to."

Luke's response had heartened both Ben and Vestara, but Ben knew that facing so many Jedi, who had very recently been attacking Sith ships, had to be an unsettling concept for a Sith born and raised.

"It'll be all right," he reassured her. "You might sense a little doubt and some hostility. Okay, maybe a lot. But you'll win them over."

Vestara pulled away from him slightly, her brown eyes shining with mischief. "Will I?" she said in a mock-sultry tone.

"Yeah, but you don't kiss anyone but me, okay?"

Her teasing smirk melted into a smile—full, genuine, warm. "Okay," she said.

"How did your parents handle it?" Luke asked Jaina. She was serving as his copilot during the last few hours before they arrived at Coruscant.

"Handle what?" Jaina asked. "They've handled a lot of things. Especially me."

"That's what I'm referring to," Luke said. "And Jacen, and Anakin. How did they feel when you . . . well . . . when you noticed boys as more than people to spar with?"

She chuckled. "Mom and Dad were pretty okay with the boys. Dad was a bit overprotective of me, as you can imagine. I think honestly any problems they might have had with me and Jag . . . and Zekk . . . stemmed from the fact that they weren't around to share a lot of our younger years. We seemed to grow up too fast for them. They weren't ready for me to be an adult, to be forced to think about me having a relationship. I think they realized how much they missed, and that's why now they're focusing on spending so much time with Amelia."

There was no bitterness in her voice, just a statement of fact. Luke thought, *Even if a parent is able to be around for all the special moments—it still goes by too fast.*

"I was thinking about what you said a while ago. Before we let Vestara accompany us to Korriban."

She looked at him, confused. "What did I say?"

"You told me not to underestimate the power of love. And that maybe if Ben believes Vestara is redeemable, it's because she is."

"Oh that, right."

"I . . . can't help but wonder if you're right. Vestara seems completely sincere. I've always been able to sense when she's hiding things, at least to some degree. But . . . I don't think she's lying this time."

"She's only sixteen, Uncle Luke. She's had her father try to make her a head shorter with a lightsaber and is effectively cut off from her whole culture now. She's had a chance to see far beyond what she's been taught, and to make up her own mind about what she wants to do. And she's obviously in love with Ben and he with her, even if they won't admit it, and he's a good influence."

He eyed her. "They're awfully young for that. Infatuation, yes. But love?"

Jaina turned to look him squarely in the eye. "Tahiri was fifteen and Anakin seventeen when he died. Don't you think those two were really in love?"

Luke felt slightly chastened. "Because of all he's been through, I understand that Ben is more of an adult than most people twice his age. I guess I just never thought about him having that level of maturity with regard to relationships."

"Some people never become mature with regard to relationships," Jaina said, returning her attention to the console. "Some people's hearts settle early, and for good." She smiled a little. "Even when they don't realize it."

Luke sighed. "Maybe I'm the one who needs to change," he said. "Maybe I'm too set in my ways to believe that someone who was born Sith, raised Sith, and grew up surrounded by Sith can set that aside enough to become a Jedi."

"Well, I would have used the word *crotchety* myself, but yes, that's what I'm thinking."

"That's what's wrong with younglings today," Luke said, grinning. "No respect for your elders."

She grinned back and they fell silent again. Finally Luke said, "All right. My son is dating a former Sith who wants to become a Jedi. I should at least give her a chance. I don't want her forbidding me to see my grandchildren, after all."

"Whoa, whoa, don't go *too* far on the other side here, Uncle Luke."

"Good point," Luke quipped, rubbing his chin. "Don't want to look as weathered as your father quite yet."

"I'm going to tell him you said that."

"I look forward to telling him myself."

# Chapter Twenty-one

JEDI TEMPLE, CORUSCANT

LUKE KNEW THAT THE MASTERS WOULD WANT TO WELCOME HIM BACK with a celebration. It had been a tremendously painful and challenging time for all of them, and they would be relieved to again see the founder of their Order.

He also knew that with so much going on, there was no time for ceremony or fanfare; nor would it be appropriate. Not yet. So he had requested a quiet arrival, and a few moments alone in the Masters' Chamber before undertaking his first task as returning Grand Master.

It had been a long time since he had stood here, and he admitted to himself now he had indeed thought that perhaps it would take several years instead of only one before this moment came at last. While this pause—alone in so familiar a space, a room that had seen so much conversation, so much cooperation, and, yes, so many clashes—was precious and he was savoring it, he also deeply regretted the necessity that had led to his return.

Daala had wanted answers as to why Jacen Solo had become Darth Caedus. Luke and Ben had wanted answers, too. They had embarked in search of them, thinking to revisit places Jacen had gone in an effort to discover, piecemeal if they had to, how a good man had strayed so far into the shadows. They had learned much of what Jacen learned; skills that no other Jedi had known for centuries, if ever. And they had learned that his fall had been inevitable.

Standing here, his mind and heart open, Luke realized they should have known that part of the mystery long before they had even set foot onto *Jade Shadow*. It seemed obvious now. Vergere's torment, in essence a new, if brutal, morality, had molded Jacen and set him on the path. He had been taught his specialness, but had misunderstood it. While every being was unique and had a gift to offer the galaxy, Jacen had seen his uniqueness as a destiny—one that gave him the right, perhaps even the *duty,* to trample whatever stood in his path in order to do what he felt was best. He had started the Swarm War in an attempt to prevent a dark future, had convinced himself that the means justified the ends, and by the time of his death at his twin's hand had been willing to sacrifice trust, love, family—everyone and everything except Allana, who seemed to be his last tie to his humanity. All this, to stop the vision he had seen of the dark man on the throne.

The true tragedy of Jacen Solo lay not in what he had done, but in *why* he had done it.

Luke sensed her at the door, waiting for permission to enter. He turned, projecting welcome and warmth into the Force, and the door slid open.

Master Saba Sebatyne entered, stopping a few paces away from Luke and dipping her head in acknowledgment. He was surprised at her physical appearance and her presence in the Force. Saba had always been a warrior Jedi, fierce, strong, proud of her heritage, with a passion for doing what was right unclouded by the personal doubts and second-guessing that often plagued humans. He could both see and feel the toll her tenure as acting Grand Master had taken. She seemed slightly . . . smaller in stature, as if she had been diminished, and her presence in the Force reeked of self-doubt and uncertainty. Quickly Luke hid his surprise, lest she misinterpret it as censure.

"This one is gratified by your safe return to your proper role, Grand Master Skywalker," she said. Even her voice was subdued.

"And I am glad to be back, Master Sebatyne," Luke replied.

"This one presentz herself for the judgment of the Grand Master. This one is filled with regret at the repercussionz of her actionz in your absence," Saba continued. "The death of Master Hamner was in no manner the desired outcome."

Had she been a human, Luke would have gone to her and placed a reassuring hand on her shoulder. Instead he merely smiled, again sending out calmness and comfort in the Force.

"I would have known that without knowing any of the details, Master Sebatyne. I read your report, and those of others. And I am ready to render my judgment."

She straightened, her tail twitching slightly, regarding him steadily.

"Master Hamner was my friend," he said. "He was yours, as well. I believe that everything he did, he did thinking only of what was best for the Jedi Order. Do you believe that also?"

The tail-lashing increased. "This one did not think his judgment the right one. But this one would never have accused Master Hamner of knowingly doing something to harm the Jedi."

"Yet in your opinion—and the opinion of all the other Masters—he was doing precisely that."

She hesitated, then nodded. "Yes."

"Master Hamner could not relinquish the responsibility he was given," Luke said. "As a military man, he could not do something he saw as abandoning his post. He did everything in his power to stop you from doing what he felt in his heart was wrong."

He sensed Saba's confusion and increasing worry in the Force. He disliked drawing out the ordeal, but felt strongly that she needed to comprehend everything. He could forgive her, but Saba also needed to be able to forgive herself. And that kind of forgiveness could only come with true understanding.

"You were faced with a terrible decision," Luke continued. "Let Master Hamner die and permit the fleet to launch, or ground the fleet—probably for a long time—and spare him. Did it occur to you that Master Hamner expected you to make the choice that you did? Was even *relying* on it?"

She lifted her head sharply in surprise. Clearly such a thing had not occurred to her.

"His duty would be to escape—by any and all means necessary. To win back the seat that, in his mind, he was not at liberty to abandon, not even by force. He entered into conflict with you knowing he would most likely die. And sooner or later, it would have happened. He would not have stopped until he had won—or was dead."

Now Luke closed the gap between him and the Barabel, although he still did not touch her. "He died performing his duty, Saba. He fought what he believed with all his heart was the good fight. There could have been no other outcome."

"You would have found one," Saba said quietly.

Luke considered that. In a way, the statement could be true. Perhaps he could have intercepted Kenth earlier, or won the fight sooner, or thought to post double guards around the deposed Grand Master.

"There have been hundreds—probably thousands—of times in my life when I thought, *If only.* And there will probably be more. But I know them for what they are—useless exercises. Jedi can't allow themselves to overindulge in *if-only*s. Regret, reflection on a situation in order to learn from it—that is what *if-only*s are for. Would I have found a different path? Perhaps. But I wasn't there. You were. Could you have done otherwise and still have been true to yourself?"

Saba's eyes lit with understanding, and she considered a long moment. "No," she said at last. The single word was hard for her to utter, but he sensed a lifting of her spirit in the Force. "This one . . . could have done nothing else."

"Then be content," Luke said. "Saba Sebatyne. You have been judged by the Grand Master. I find no fault here—not with you, not with any of your decisions, nor with the other Masters for following your orders. Jedi are *supposed* to protect the weak and helpless. You were right to support those trying to win basic rights for their people. To stop the abuse of sentient beings. To send the fleet to Pydyr to fight the Sith. Even to topple Daala. Those were the acts of a Jedi, and they were necessary. But you know that the Jedi Order's place is not to rule."

She had straightened more with each passing word, and now she seemed almost her old self again. Saba Sebatyne was nothing if not strong and great of heart. Luke knew that a huge burden had been eased, and that with time, she would come to know as he did—know, not just believe—that she had led the Jedi well during a time of extreme duress.

"Grand Master Skywalker speakz truly, as alwayz," Saba said.

"There is much I need to tell everyone," said Luke.

A hint of humor gleamed in Saba's eyes. "This one thinkz that Master Skywalker'z wordz are an understatement," she said.

"This one thinks you're right." Luke grinned. "Now—let's get this meeting started. I sense there are several people outside eager to come in."

Saba sissed, her Force presence easing by the moment. "You did not need to use the Force to know that, Grand Master."

"Who says I did?" Luke said. He turned his attention to those gathered outside and sent them a warm, heartfelt welcome. The door slid open and many voices spoke at once.

"Master Skywalker!" exclaimed Cilghal, her rasping voice as pleased as he had ever heard it.

"Luke!" This from Kyp Durron, never one for formalities. The younger Master rushed forward to clasp Luke's arms. Kyle Katarn clapped him warmly on the back. Corran Horn stood off to the side, grinning and looking like his old self again despite the new crow's-feet framing his eyes. Octa Ramis and the newest member, Barratk'l, inducted during Luke's absence by Kenth Hamner, were also present and beaming at him.

Luke was poignantly reminded of his departure from the Temple; of the crowd of beings who had lined up to bid him a sorrowful farewell. He thought of Kenth Hamner's arm around his shoulders as he viewed those assembled, and that man's words: *Forty years ago, there was one practicing Jedi in the galaxy, and the Order and the Temple were just ill-formed notions taken from suppressed rumors. Today, what you see before you—this is your doing, Master Skywalker.* And even as he permitted himself to miss and remember Kenth and that moment, the heaviness in the room lightened. There was much that awaited them all, and the danger posed by both the Sith and Abeloth had not decreased in the slightest. Yet Luke felt buoyed, refreshed simply by being here, in his old position, surrounded by friends who both respected and loved him, and for whom he would do anything.

At last the ebullience subsided slightly, and Luke motioned for everyone to take their seats. "Thank you for your welcome," he said. "You've no idea how good it is to be home, at least for a while. I've missed you, and this Temple, so very much. I told Master Sebatyne, and I want to tell you all, that I commend you for your actions during my absence, hard and personally painful though some of those choices had to be. And I must warn you, there are difficult times ahead. But I know we will triumph.

"I believe you have all been caught up on what has transpired while Ben and I were traveling, thanks to Ben and Cilghal's correspondence." He smiled at the Mon Calamari, who inclined her head. "When my sentence was lifted, there was nothing stopping me from sending you all I knew about Abeloth, the Sith, and what we've learned about them during our travels."

Luke hesitated, wondering how much he should say about one thing in particular. He didn't want to discuss it in so formal a setting, but it was better to address it now than to have rumors, accurate or not, flying.

"We are bringing home a guest with us. You know about Vestara Khai, daughter of Sith Saber Gavar Khai. She has worked with Ben and me for a while now, initially reluctantly, but recently wholeheartedly. She has expressed interest in becoming a Jedi."

Murmurs rippled through the room. "No disrespect intended, Master Luke, but are you certain her . . . conversion is genuine?" asked Katarn.

"She was attacked by her own father, who clearly intended to kill her," Luke said. "She killed him defending herself. There's nothing for her on her homeworld now. And," he added, "she seems devoted to Ben, and he to her. She allowed herself to be open in the Force, and her desire is sincere. "

"How open?" asked Octa Ramis.

"Open enough so I sensed she was hiding nothing."

"That's good enough for me."

The others nodded their agreement. Their trust in his abilities was humbling.

"So unless there are any questions," continued Luke, "there are two matters of great import I'd like to address. Both involve how the

Jedi Order is going to move forward, given the circumstances. Since Daala's deposition, I have given a great deal of thought as to what our role should be, and I have come to a decision."

Disciplined Masters that they were, everyone had settled down to listen intently once Luke had started speaking. All eyes were on him. Luke hoped that they would understand and agree with his decision, but he was prepared to make it an order if they didn't.

"I firmly believe the Jedi should not be in charge of the Galactic Alliance. What you have done so far was necessary to keep order. But it's time we move, and move quickly, to transition out of the government. And once we have done so—"

Luke took a deep breath, bracing himself for the inevitable protest.

"We leave Coruscant. Completely."

"What?" The word came from so many throats at once that it was hard to pinpoint exactly who was talking.

"To what end?" asked Kyle Katarn.

"Leave the Temple? For good, you mean?" Kyp asked.

"This one will not leave!" Saba lashed her tail. Luke was surprised—earlier she had been almost dejected in her attitude. Now he did not need to use the Force to sense her determination and resentment.

He held up his hands and exuded calmness. "I will answer all your questions. This is not a decision I came to lightly."

Luke knew that by opening with such a controversial subject, he had startled the Masters. Some of them were likely wondering if his recent confrontations with the Sith and with Abeloth had addled his wits.

Those who had stood resumed their seats, even Saba, and Luke continued. "There are several reasons for this. One—and this will soon be made public, not just to the Jedi Order but to everyone—is that we need to make it clear beyond the shadow of a doubt that the Jedi Order is not interested in politics. The coup was necessary, and you all handled it well. But from what I am hearing, things are piling up, and very little progress has been made. To mix metaphors, poor Wynn Dorvan's hands are tied when they are already too full. He—or whomever is chosen to become not just acting Chief of State but the true, legitimate Chief of State of the Galactic Alliance—needs the ability to function without the Jedi or the Senate approving what he or she puts in their caf every morning. The new Chief needs to learn how to be not just part of a triumvirate, but a solitary leader who works cooperatively with separate branches of the government. And we—the Jedi—are not *branches of the government.* We are our own Order. And we need to demonstrate that we are."

"But surely we can do so without leaving Coruscant," said Octa.

"I don't believe we can," Luke said. "Not anymore. Remember how Daala focused on the Jedi. She respected us and our abilities, but she wanted to be able to direct them at her will. Saba—you decided to act against her, and against Kenth, who also tried to act within that kind of mind-set. You did the sort of thing Jedi need to do. We can't risk being trapped in our own Temple again, held hostage by a government that wants to make us a tool in their arsenal. We need to be separate, so that the only conscience and mandates that dictate our actions are our own. And that can best be achieved by putting physical distance between us and the seat of government, at least for some time."

"Even if it means leaving the Temple?" asked Kyp.

"No," said Saba forcefully before Luke could even reply. "This one will *not* leave. Nor will the other Barabelz in the Temple."

So that was why she had reacted so strongly. Luke had heard about the strange mystery involving the Barabel Jedi, who had sequestered themselves in the Temple. He knew better than to probe further. He trusted Saba to do nothing harmful to the Order or other Jedi, and besides, he would probably only anger her.

Luke considered for a moment. "The Barabels currently in the Temple will be permitted to remain for . . . as long as is necessary. But I must have your word, Master Sebatyne, that they will not interfere with the fledging government, and as soon as they can, they will join the other Jedi."

Saba sissed. "Trust me, Master Skywalker. They have no wish to set foot outside the Temple—nor to let anyone in—for quite some time yet."

"Also, they can serve even so," he said. "They can be watchful of the Temple, and make sure that it is not violated. It is our home, even if we can no longer live here. For now, to emphasize our unity, the Jedi should leave together, but I would not deny any Jedi entrance to our own Temple. Infact, Tesar and Wilyem and any others staying behind could do me two favors, if they wouldn't mind."

Saba cocked her head. "That dependz on the nature of the favorz."

"One—remove the guard-grates from the water supply mains." He gave her a quick smile. "Every slicer knows you need to leave a backdoor."

Saba sassed. "This is truth," she said. "And the second?"

Luke sobered. "Ask them to undertake guardianship of the Temple. Protect it."

Saba considered for a moment. "Yes," she said finally. "That would not interfere with their . . . other activities. And if they are permitted to be undisturbed, this one will accompany the other Jedi."

"Please give them my thanks," he said. "Are we in agreement with all that I have presented?"

They considered, then all nodded. Luke could sense that they were grateful to again feel part of a group being *led,* rather than dictated to. "Good. We'll return to some of the details of those decisions in a moment. They are, of necessity, to be made public. What I have to say next—will be for your ears only."

Vestara was silent, following Ben and Jaina through the Temple as they approached the library. Most of what she had seen so far was turbolifts and corridors. Jaina had wanted to see Natua first thing, to thank her for her hard work, and had told Ben that he and Vestara were free to explore the Temple on their own after that.

After a few moments, Ben broke the uncomfortable silence. "So what do you think?"

She turned to him. "It's . . . quite large."

"Jedi have been on Coruscant for a very long time," Ben reminded her.

"Sith have been on Kesh for a very long time as well, and yet our Temple is much smaller."

Ben filed that away for further inquiry later. "Well, once we're done in the library, we can go anywhere you'd like. You had a chance to study the plans. What sounds interesting?"

Vestara, who had been closed and somewhat shy toward him since their arrival, suddenly melted. “Everything!” she said, sounding almost more like Allana than her normal cool, controlled self. He gave her an answering grin and squeezed her hand.

It was hand in hand that they entered the library. Ben braced himself for beings coming up to him and welcoming him back, but the library was hardly a hubbub of socializing, and what few beings were here seemed engrossed in their research.

Even, it seemed, Natua Wan, whom they finally found as Jaina peered behind several stacks of datapads.

“I commed you about seventeen times,” Jaina greeted her.

Natua glanced up and did a double take. “Jaina!” she exclaimed. “Ben! Welcome back. I’m sorry . . . I had it turned off. I was completely lost in some research I’ve been doing.”

“So I see.” Jaina grinned.

Natua had risen to greet them, and now turned to Vestara. “You must be Vestara Khai,” she said. Ben winced inwardly at the caution she was exuding, both in the Force and through her species’ natural release of pheromones. “Master Luke tells me you wish to become a Jedi.”

Vestara nodded. “I do.” Her unguarded sincerity seemed to reassure Natua.

“I look forward to talking with you,” Natua said. “I didn’t know much about the Sith culture before I started doing research for you all. Now I find it fascinating.”

“I think I will like learning about Jedi,” Vestara offered. “Of course, I’ll tell you what I can to help.”

Jaina carefully moved a pile of ’pads from a chair and sat next to Natua. Ben and Vestara emulated her. “I wanted to come and thank you for all you’ve done,” Jaina said. “You’ve been extremely helpful.”

Natua grimaced a little. “Even if all you reached was a bunch of dead ends?”

“Even so. It’s hardly your fault the Sith have a lot of hidey-holes we need to investigate one by one.”

“Well,” she said, “the wild caranak chase just might be done. I was going to comm you myself shortly. I wanted to do a bit more research first, but since you’re here, you might as well know.”

"What have you found?" Jaina, Ben, and Vestara leaned forward eagerly.

"I'm not certain," said Natua, "but . . . I might have found Ship."

"What?" Jaina's yelp was so loud that a few heads turned her way. Natua laughed. Ben, too, felt happy and excited, and didn't care that the feeling largely flowed from the pheromones that Natua was emitting. He'd feel the same way regardless—if they really could find Ship.

"I know that we wanted to focus on known Sith worlds, going on the idea that if we knew about it, the Lost Tribe would as well," Natua said. Ben could sense that despite her pleasure and enthusiasm, Natua was going to present things in an orderly fashion. "But one night, I decided to just randomly start reading about worlds we knew very little about, or that didn't really play a significant role. One of these worlds is called Upekzar."

She touched a datapad, and a display of a rather nondescript planet appeared. Ben, Jaina, and Vestara rose, peering over Natua's shoulder.

"Upekzar has been mostly forgotten," Natua continued. "By and large, this seems to be a pleasant and temperate planet. There are polar ice caps, rain forests, oceans, plains, mountains, forested areas—most climates are represented here. Unfortunately, but unsurprisingly, the unpleasant spots are where we need to target our investigation."

She pointed at the image on the datapad. There was a chain of islands and coastlines clustered in one part of the world. "See this ring here?" Natua drew a finger along the chain, starting near Upekzar's south pole, going up through its equator, toward the north pole, and then down again. "The ancient Sith called this Circle of Visions. The rest of the planet went undeveloped while they focused all their attention on five specific sites along this circle."

"Why was that area so special?" Vestara asked.

"The abundance of volcanoes," Natua replied promptly.

"Yeah, that sounds about right for the Sith, jumping into volcanoes," said Ben softly to Vestara, his voice playful. She shoved him, but she was smothering a smile.

"More specifically," Natua continued, "they valued what the volcanoes left behind. Volcanic caves, caverns, tubes—all formed when lava continued to flow beneath a top layer that cooled faster, forming a crust. The Sith thought these caves significant, and when they ventured to explore them, many Sith suffered hallucinations."

"From various fumes contained in the caves?" asked Jaina.

"No." Natua shook her head, her fingers tapping on the console to call up another holographic image. It was a sort of insect, with six legs, a multisectioned body, antennae, and what looked like a two-pronged tail extension.

Ben's eyes widened. "I know what that is," he said solemnly.

Vestara glanced at him. "You do?"

He nodded. "It's . . . a *bug*!"

"Your sense of humor is almost as bad as Jacen's was," muttered Jaina. Ben smiled a little. He realized that he was starting to let Jacen Solo replace Darth Caedus in his mind—and in his heart. And he was glad of it. Of course, ever since Vestara had told him she wanted to become a Jedi and they had begun exploring what "relationship" meant, he'd felt happier and more confident than he had in a long, long time.

"What *type* of bug, Natua?" Jaina asked.

"It's a variety of diplura. A type of hexapod, which is a . . ." Natua looked at the blank expressions around her and smiled a little. " . . . a bug. Variations of diplurans are found on almost all habitable worlds. It's this particular species that is interesting. During various parts of its life cycle, it excretes a certain fluid rich with pheromones. These pheromones happen to be a powerful hallucinogen for some mammalian species. From what records survive, the hallucinations were terrifying."

"And of course, the Sith believed it was the work of the dark side," said Vestara.

"Was it? In part?" asked Ben.

Natua nodded. "Yes to both. At first, the Sith had no idea what was going on. Later, once they understood, they deemed the volcanic caves special places, and conducted initiations and other rites of passage without protection from the pheromones. The caves were, if not a dark-side nexus precisely, definitely a site in which the dark side flourished. Centuries of rituals imbued with the power of fear and anguish induced by the pheromones only strengthened that. Also—while the Sith did not live in the lava tubes, their interactions with the bugs became the foundation of their culture. They dwelled close to the five major places where they performed their Mysteries. Each settlement was located near an elaborate lava cave system that had a specific focus."

She indicated various areas on the image as she spoke. "The one located here, near its south pole, was for Cold Rites—presumably focusing on tempering emotions, hardening hearts, and so on. The one on the equator, for Rites of Fire. This might be where the Sith focused on their anger and passions, how to use them to serve the dark side. However, I believe that this one here, in a very temperate zone—the one that hosted what was called the High Rites—might be the most significant area to explore. Only the highest-ranking Sith—the ones strongest in the Force—conducted rituals here. And correspondingly, the most powerful Sith on Upekzar lived only a few kilometers away from this cave system, in a city that lies in the shadow of a dormant volcano."

She touched the screen, and a map of the area replaced the image of the planet.

"Ben, you first found Ship on Ziost," Natua said. "He was . . . docked, for a better word, below an abandoned citadel, in the ground. What remaining documents there are indicate that this site was 'the nest of the future Sith.' I thought it was a nursery or a school . . . until I saw this."

She touched the 'pad again. The map disappeared, replaced by the image of an orange, pebbly-surfaced, too-familiar Ship. And even though everyone knew exactly why they were here, there was still a flicker of apprehension in the Force at the sight.

"While it's highly doubtful this is the same Ship we seek, considering how long he seemed to have been on Ziost," Natua continued, "it is definitely a Sith training vessel. It's not too much of a stretch to believe that Ship might decide to return to a known 'nest' to 'roost.'"

"So, it sounds like we'll have two goals," Jaina mused, thinking aloud. "We'll explore the city to see if we can find a trace of Ship in its, uh, hangar, and we'll investigate the nearby volcanic caves to search for other information that could help us if he's not there. Natua, what do we know about the rites that were conducted in the lava tubes?"

"Unfortunately, nothing," said Natua. "They were secret—only for the initiated. Once the Sith started using the diplurans, or rather the pheromones they produced, the records go silent on what actually transpired." She sounded a bit frustrated that she could not provide answers. Ben realized that, like most of the formerly "mad Jedi," Natua was trying to atone for the harm she had caused while under Abeloth's influence. Jaina, too, obviously saw what was going on and squeezed Natua's arm in a friendly fashion.

"Upekzar is a small and not very well-known bastion of the Sith to begin with," Jaina said. "Add to that these . . . bugs . . . and secret rituals, and nobody's going to find much information on them."

"*Rhak-skuri,*" Natua said. "The Sith called them *rhak-skuri.*"

"Dream Singers," Vestara translated.

"That's an awfully nice name for bugs," Ben said.

Vestara turned to him. "To the Sith, nightmares are really no different from ordinary dreams. They offer opportunities for growth. To be able to control the direction of your nightmare—to defeat it—means you are strong. So creatures that caused visions would be valued and respected for the challenges they brought."

"Yeah, but they don't sing," Ben pointed out. He glanced at Natua. "Do they?"

The Falleen smiled. "Not as far as I have been able to determine."

"It's a metaphor," Vestara said. "They could have been called dream makers, or weavers, or creators, or—"

"I get your point," Ben said, holding up his hands in a mock-surrender gesture. "Are the rhak-skuri dangerous in any other way, Natua?"

"No," Natua replied. "The secretion is nontoxic and they are otherwise harmless. Even their mandibles are too small to pierce skin."

"You're going to make the Grand Master of the Jedi very happy," Jaina said. "And if you'd like—I'd love it if you'd come with us. Seems to me you've more than earned your right to participate in the hunt, and I'm going to tell Luke so."

Natua's eyes widened. "I . . . I would of course be honored to help the Grand Master, if he wishes me to come. Thank you, Jaina."

Not so long before, Ben knew, the two women had been locked in a lightsaber battle. But Natua was now healed, and determined to make up for the illness Abeloth had forced upon her. He was glad of it. He was just plain glad right now.

"I'm going to leave a message for Uncle Luke, and then I'm off to see my fiancé."

"Don't do anything I wouldn't do," Ben quipped.

"Hey—I certainly hope I *do,* and you better not," Jaina shot back. She was already striding off at a brisk pace, speaking quietly into her comlink.

"So," Ben said, "time for me to play tour guide. Where would you like to go first?"

"It's your Temple," Vestara answered. "I want to see everything, so where would you like to go first?"

"Honestly?" Ben said, giving her a rueful grin. "The cafeteria."

Vestara rolled her eyes.

# Chapter Twenty-two

ABOARD THE *MILLENNIUM FALCON*

"I WISH SHE'D STOP CARRYING ON WITH THE SQUIBS," HAN MUTTERED. His jaw was set, his eyes narrowed as he sat in the pilot's chair of the *Falcon*, staring outward with grim determination to get home as fast as possible.

"You were the one who suggested she learn how to play sabacc," Leia mused.

"I *thought* it would teach her something about human nature," Han replied. "I didn't expect her to actually sit down and play it with three little—"

"They're not using actual credits," Leia reminded him.

"Doesn't matter."

"And she's winning."

Han brightened slightly as they slowed and emerged from hyperspace, the stars slowing and finally becoming stationary. The yellow-brown orb of Coruscant, glittering with lights that never went out, appeared before them.

"Home, and none too soon," Han said.

Leia leaned over to touch the communications array, using her proximity to her husband to steal a quick kiss. "Not quite yet," she said. "There are a few people we need to talk to first."

Han sighed. From behind them he heard, "No, no, Mistress Amelia, you don't want to put that card down!" in a distinctively fussy voice, and Han grimaced.

"Threepio, what have I told you about commenting on someone's hand?" Han called. R2-D2 tweedled something that sounded like *I told you so.*

"Well, Captain Solo, I know *you* don't wish my advice or calculations when you indulge in games of chance," came 3PO's voice. "But as one of my duties is assisting with Mistress Amelia's education, I thought it incumbent upon me to—"

"Well, it's not, so don't."

"Oh. As you wish, Captain. Mistress Amelia, you may indeed play the Star if you wish."

Han winced at the comment. Leia grinned. Much as Han feigned annoyance with the golden droid—okay, sometimes it was genuine annoyance—she knew he was as fond of C-3PO as anyone. And when 3PO was fussing, all was right with the world.

Jag's voice crackled over the comm system. "Jagged Fel."

"Jag," Leia said warmly, "it's Leia and Han."

"Oh, hey, Mom and Dad," came their daughter's voice.

Han and Leia exchanged surprised smiles. "Hi, honey," Leia said. "When did you all arrive?"

"Just a couple of hours ago. Uncle Luke's talking with the Masters, and Ben and Vestara are wandering around the Temple. Seems she wants to become a Jedi."

"A Sith wants to become a Jedi?" Han echoed. "What's Luke think about this?"

"Both he and I think she's sincere," Jaina said. "You should talk to him yourself, though." Translation: *Keep it short. I'm enjoying time alone with my fiancé.*

"I will, just as soon as I'm done with your future husband. Jag, Han and I have just returned from a rather informative expedition. We've got some news to share with you as soon as possible."

"I'll be in my office first thing tomorrow morning," Jag said. Translation: *Don't interrupt right now.*

Leia couldn't help but smile. She knew how they both felt. It was one reason she and Han, in recent years, had tried to avoid getting embroiled in adventures without each other as much as possible. "I'll contact you then and we'll set something up. Jaina, welcome home."

"Thanks, Mom." From anyone else at any other time, the sudden *click* would have been rude. Hearing it now from Jaina only made Leia happy.

"Home now?" asked Han.

"Luke now," Leia said. Because Jaina had said he was in a meeting, she expected simply to leave a message, and so was surprised and pleased to hear her brother's voice. "Luke! Jaina said you'd returned."

"It's good to hear from you!" Luke said. "I thought you and Han would be here when I arrived."

"We left before you sent word and, well, we've been a bit busy. We're getting ready to land shortly. When can we meet and catch up?"

"The sooner the better, and it's all work unfortunately," Luke said. Han scowled. "I've just finished up with a meeting of the Masters, and I'd like to share some of the decisions we reached. One is that the Jedi will be withdrawing from any official involvement in the government, and I'd like you to be present when Saba and I inform Treen and Dorvan. The Jedi would like Dorvan to officially become the new Chief of State of the Galactic Alliance."

"Poor Wynn," Leia said at once. "He's not going to like that."

"He won't have to like it, he just has to accept it," Luke said.

"He will," Han said. "Underneath that perfectly groomed and boring exterior beats the heart of a good man."

"I think we all agree on that. Maybe even the part about the boring exterior," Luke said. His voice was warm with humor, although he sounded tired. "The second thing is, the Jedi are leaving Coruscant. As soon as possible. When the transition is stabilized, I'd like you to join us."

Leia was so stunned she couldn't speak for a moment. Even Han looked surprised.

"Luke—I don't know if—" she started.

"I know, I know," Luke said. "But this needs to happen, Leia. I'll explain my reasoning when we get together, and I know you'll understand. Meet me at the Temple. We'll grab a cup of caf, work up a game plan, and then head over to the Senate chamber."

"All right, we'll be there shortly. By the way, my nephew is apparently wandering around the Jedi Temple in the company of a Sith girl. I'm going to want to hear about that, too."

Luke chuckled. "I promise. See you soon."

OFFICES OF THE CHIEF OF STATE, CORUSCANT

"Grand Master Skywalker," Wynn Dorvan said, rising as Luke, Leia, and Saba entered the meeting room at the offices of the Chief of State. He extended a hand. Luke took it, smiling. "Welcome home."

"Thank you," Luke said. "It's good to *be* home." *Even if it is only for a short while,* Luke thought.

"Jedi Solo, also good to have you back," Dorvan said, turning to Leia. "I hope your trip went well."

Leia gave him a smile. "Indeed it did."

"Master Sebatyne. Welcome. Grand Master, I don't know that you've met Senator Haydnat Treen, of Kuat."

The elderly woman rose with fluid grace, smiling warmly at Luke. "Master Skywalker," she said. "What a pleasure to finally meet you. We are so very glad you have returned."

Luke was used to dealing with politicians. He was not as familiar with them as Leia was, but he did not much care for the rather unctuous Senator. He sensed a coolness behind her effusiveness, a calculation, and secrets that were well kept.

Of course, he mused, that could be said of most politicians. And all beings had secrets. Nonetheless, her presence in the Force was not one that endeared her to him. He smiled pleasantly.

"Thank you. And of course I know of you, Senator Treen. Master Sebatyne informs me that you have helped things move along quite smoothly during your tenure as acting joint Chief of State."

Nothing changed physically, but he felt her put up her guard. Treen was not Force-sensitive, but the effect was very similar. She knew how to keep things buried. Quite deep.

Further pleasantries were exchanged, then the five of them sat around the table.

"I'll get right to the point," Luke said. "Senator Treen, Dorvan—I believe you know that the Jedi never intended to rule the Galactic Alliance. The coup was performed for the sole purpose of eliminating a leader who had become a threat to the very government she was attempting to run, nothing more. And this triumvirate the three of you have managed was meant only as an interim measure."

"It's been working rather well," Treen said. "All things considered."

"And the galaxy is fortunate that three cool heads prevailed," Luke said. "But I must inform you now that one of those beings will no longer be able to perform in that role any longer. I intend to withdraw the Jedi from any position of power or authority in the Galactic Alliance. The Jedi will become an order responsible only to itself and to those beings it serves."

That took both Treen and Dorvan aback. Luke went on to tell them what he had told the Masters—that the Jedi needed to become autonomous. That the Sith and Abeloth still needed to be hunted, as the threat they posed was not just to the Galactic Alliance, but to the entire galaxy. And that while Luke trusted that no one in this room was on their way to becoming a second Daala, he believed that the Jedi needed to be able to act on their own, freely and immediately, with no one to forbid or direct them.

As he expected, he sensed both dismay and relief from Treen and Dorvan. "Daala's desire to make the Jedi perform like an extension of her own will was ill advised from the start," Dorvan said. "Her first mistake was in exiling you, and she continued to compound that mistake. I can appreciate your Order wanting to be able to act independently. But what does that mean for the Galactic Alliance?"

"Friendship," Luke said at once, sending Dorvan sincere reassurance. "We're not abandoning you. If you have need of us, we will be there. The only real difference is we're not confined to helping only those beings the GA wants us to help."

"I think it's a splendid idea," Treen said. "You're not droids or hired thugs, Master Skywalker. You should not be treated as such. While I commend Master Sebatyne on the civilized nature of the coup, I think it high time that the Jedi and GA politics disentangled themselves." She paused and cocked her head. "Except . . . how do we actually go about that?"

"The triumvirate you formed was an emergency measure," Leia said. "Legally, once the emergency is past, you need to hold a formal election as soon as possible."

"Leaving aside the difficulty of arranging a parade," Dorvan said drily, "that will still take some time."

"We're all just making this up as we go along. The GA has been fortunate that it's worked so far, but I think with the withdrawal of the Jedi, we should look to precedent. And while I wish none of you ill, the closest type of precedent would be how we would determine another Chief of State if the present one were to die."

Dorvan consulted his datapad. "Current law would stipulate that the Senate elect a leader to serve for no more than two standard months until such time as a proper election can be duly held," he said. "That being the case, I would suggest that Senator Treen, as she has already been serving in that capacity, would take over Daala's position." He seemed heartened by his conclusion.

"Oh, dear me, no!" exclaimed Treen. "The little taste I've had of this so far has convinced me that I want no part of it. Kuat is starting to think I've forgotten about them and their specific interests. It's far too complicated, and there is no time for proper caf breaks. I would refuse such a position if the Senate were to offer it to me. I rather think that the Senate would wish to continue with you at its head, Wynn."

Leia smiled at him. "Wynn," she said, "we've known each other a long time. You're in a unique position."

Dorvan sighed. "I didn't even want to manage an *assistant,* let alone an entire government."

"Better you than someone hungry for power," Luke said. "It doesn't have to be forever. At least let the Senate put you in charge until there's a chance for a fair and legal election. No one says you have to run for office then. But for now, it sounds like putting you in the role of Chief of State won't cause upheaval and chaos at a time when the GA needs stability."

"Very well," Dorvan said, in a hollow tone of voice.

"Oh, come come, Wynn," Treen said brightly. "You sound like you're being led off to execution!"

"I rather think I am," said Dorvan. "But I suppose there's no help for it."

The five eased quickly into the details of how the departure of the Jedi would be handled. And there were a great many. Even so, it seemed like all of them were in harmony. By the time the meeting was over, they had a date, an itinerary, had gathered copies of the necessary documents, and had decided when, how, and by whom the various revelations would be made. It had been a highly successful morning, but Luke could tell Leia was not as comfortable as she had appeared to Treen and Dorvan.

As he, Leia, and Saba walked together back to the Temple, he asked her about it.

"I agree with your reasons for the Jedi leaving," she said. "But . . . I don't trust Senator Treen. She's hiding something."

"I noticed that as well," Luke said.

"Even this one did," Saba said. "This one had hoped it was simply unfamiliarity with the nature of human politicz. Otherz in the cabinet, too—something seemz unquiet. But this one is confused. If Treen hungerz for power, why did she refuse it when it was all but handed to her?"

"I don't know, but I don't like it," Leia said. "I don't like any of this. And we're not having a private meeting with Dorvan about that because . . . ?"

"Oh, we'll have a private meeting with Dorvan," Luke assured her. "For one thing, I'd like you to brief him on who in the Senate you think he'll be able to work with. Beings like Lando's friend Senator Wuul. I also have a favor I'd like to ask him."

Leia glanced at Saba, who seemed more amused than anything else. "But we don't want to warn him about Treen?"

"Not yet." Luke leaned over and said in an exaggerated whisper, "Trust me."

Leia rolled her eyes.

* * *

It was *The Perre Needmo Newshour* that got the scoop. Luke, along with Leia and Han, had always been impressed with the format Needmo had chosen to keep the public informed. Except where a segment was clearly identified as an editorial, as was the case with the late, greatly missed Madhi Vaandt's segments, the news was presented in a clear and unbiased manner. There was no mudslinging, no vicious scrambling for ratings—and Luke suspected that the fact that *The Perre Needmo Newshour* eschewed such things was why it actually landed in the top five week after week.

Needmo himself had volunteered to conduct the interview, and Luke was looking forward to it. He now settled in the interviewee's chair, having endured the unusual activity of having makeup put on his face and his hair styled, and made himself comfortable.

"I've been interviewed before, of course," he told his host as he sipped a cup of water, "but usually it's on site and right in the middle of the action. I haven't been in a studio before."

"I am proud that we are the first, then," Needmo replied, his small eyes crinkling in pleasure. "I have a top-notch team, Master Skywalker. They're consummate professionals."

Luke nodded. "I saw the interview you did with Rokari Kem, of Qaras," he said. "I'm glad she'll be coming to Coruscant. We need beings who can combine compassion with levelheaded leadership."

"Indeed we do. She has granted me another exclusive once she settles in as Senator. I'm looking forward to it."

The studio was a hive of activity. He'd met the director, Jorm Alvic, and the producer, Sima Shadar. Now tech specialists checked lighting and sound quality, and droids hummed and whirred on various errands. Jorm, a human in his early middle years, leaned forward into a mike and announced, "We'll be live in one minute, gentlebeings."

"We're ready, Jorm!" said Needmo cheerily. A slender Twi'lek adjusted both their personal mikes, brushed a stray lock of hair off Luke's forehead, and scampered off the set. The energetic music of the opening credits began to play, and the cam operator counted down. Three, two, one—

*And go,* he mouthed.

"Good evening, gentlebeings, and welcome to tonight's edition of *The Perre Needmo Newshour,*" said Needmo. "We open our show tonight with an exclusive: a one-on-one interview with the Grand Master of the Jedi Order, Luke Skywalker. Welcome, Master Skywalker."

Luke smiled. "Thank you. And you're welcome to call me Luke. Before we continue, while I'll be happy to answer your questions shortly, I need to tell you that I have chosen your show as a platform to make a very important announcement."

Luke sensed through the Force that Perre was taken off-guard, but the elderly Chevin was such a professional that neither his body language nor his voice betrayed his surprise. "Why, I'm honored, Luke. I'm sure that with all that's going on throughout the galaxy, you'll have a lot of important things to share with us. By all means, please continue."

Luke turned so he was facing the cam. "Over the last forty years, I have endeavored to build and manage the Jedi Order in accordance with our highest ideals: cooperation, peace, freedom, decent treatment for all beings. Recently, in my absence, the Jedi were faced with a terrible choice—disobey the Chief of State and risk having our very Temple attacked, or answer cries for help from beings struggling to free themselves from slavery. They chose to overthrow Daala's government, and since that time the Jedi, including my sister, Leia Organa Solo—who was once Chief of State herself—have been working closely with Acting Chief of State Wynn Dorvan and the Senate. Our goal is to completely transition the Jedi out of the government of the GA. After much deep thought and meditation on the subject, I have come to a decision. I have reached the conclusion that the Jedi can best serve the beings of this galaxy by becoming an Order that is independent of any and all political ties—by going even further than removing ourselves from the direct act of governance. While we support the Galactic Alliance, we will no longer be an official branch of it. And to that end, the Jedi will be departing Couruscant as soon as the transition of power is complete."

Perre Needmo had been right about the professionalism of his staff.

There was a huge spike of surprise from them and from Needmo himself, but though there were several open jaws and wide eyes, no one uttered a sound.

Needmo leaned forward slightly. "Luke, it's my understanding that the public never did think that the coup's purpose was for the Jedi to gain power. Daala's policies were becoming increasingly harsh and militaristic, and it's safe to say that she won no friends by bringing in the Mandalorians to enforce those policies. Polls indicate that the populace is content with the Jedi's current level of participation. Are you sure this isn't an overreaction? It's possible that beings will feel the Jedi have abandoned them."

"Not abandoned *them,*" Luke emphasized. "Abandoned constrictions and restraints on our ability to help as we are called. Once the Jedi are autonomous, our ability to help those truly in need will actually be increased, not decreased."

"Can you give me an example?"

"A perfect one is the recent slave revolts," Luke said. "Daala met those uprisings with force. The Jedi have gone to help with negotiations—my sister Leia, for instance, has only recently returned from Klatooine. When the extremely peaceful Octusi were being ruthlessly suppressed, the Jedi stepped in to stop it."

"Don't you think that makes you a vigilante organization?" pressed Needmo. "Some would say, without constraints the Jedi would run amok."

Luke smiled gently. "I think those who would say that are those who, like Daala, wanted the Jedi safely under their thumbs. The Order has been around for a long, long time. I think this new move is going to benefit everyone. Initial meetings with Wynn Dorvan and Senator Haydnat Treen are progressing very well. The Senate will move to elect an interim Chief of State, and I think we all know who that's going to be."

"If it is Wynn Dorvan, then certainly no one could ask for a more meticulous Chief of State," said Needmo. "Though there was an incident not too long ago that showed a different side of the onetime chief of staff. Let's take a look."

The vidcams began to display the image, now engraved upon the mind of every Coruscanti citizen—and probably the vast majority of citizens of the entire Galactic Alliance—of Wynn Dorvan racing up the steps of the Temple.

And with that segue, Luke Skywalker knew that all would be well.

"Are you watching, my dear?" said Treen into her comlink. She was propped up in bed on nearly a dozen perfectly fluffed pillows. The heavy draping of the bed's canopy was parted on the end to reveal a large vidscreen displaying Luke Skywalker's lined yet still somehow boyish face several times larger than life. On the bed beside her was a tray of small, delicate pastries and a cup of hot cocoa.

"Indeed I am," came Kameron Suldar's pleasant voice. "I usually don't like *The Perre Needmo Newshour*. Staring at a Chevin is not my idea of a pleasant way to get information."

"Nor mine, but Master Skywalker's news is nothing but good for all of us. The boy is sometimes wretchedly naïve."

"You're sure he doesn't suspect?"

Treen took another sip of cocoa. "Suspect what? Dorvan would have loved it if I had relieved him of his burden, but that wasn't what we wanted. I was quite serious when I said being Chief of State was too complicated, and I have far grander ambitions."

"Let us hope Moff Lecersen can deliver as promised."

"My dear boy, don't you worry about Drikl Lecersen. I know how to handle *my* ride to power. Do you know how to handle yours?"

"Indeed I do, Senator. Indeed I do."

# Chapter Twenty-three

CORUSCANT

"I WOULD HAVE THOUGHT YOUR FAMILY WOULD HAVE MOVED BACK into a regular apartment by now," Jag said as they approached the safe house where Han, Leia, and Allana had been forced to live over the last few months.

"Are you kidding? When would we have had time to move? Even with droids to take care of most of it, moving is a pain. And we've been a bit busy, you know," Jaina replied.

Jag smiled a little. "I suppose you're right. I guess I just never liked the idea of the Solos having to live in a safe house at all."

It still was technically a "safe house." Jag and Jaina, having had a lot of experience recently with just this sort of thing, had swapped vehicles a few times and were fairly certain they had eluded detection. With the coup, or "transition of government," depending on which term one preferred, there seemed to be no real risk anymore to Jaina's famous—some would say infamous—family. Still, they were the Solos, and the current situation could change at any moment. One day, no doubt, they would find better and more public accommodations, but now, their home base needed to remain secret. It was just safer that way.

Jaina and Jag had had "the discussion" earlier—the one that, in months past, might have blown up into a real fight: the discussion about what each of them had to do to move forward. Now, however, although it was not what they ideally wanted, Jaina and Jag had found they could discuss the situation calmly.

"I'll be departing with the Jedi—temporarily, at least," Jaina had said. "With all the controversy around the coup and the Jedi's new direction, the Jedi need to be seen as completely united behind Uncle Luke's decision. I'm . . . Jag, I'm not sure how long we'll be gone, nor what's going to happen to the Jedi in the end."

He had nodded. "I expected you would go with them," he had said. "And I completely agree with your choice."

"You do?"

"Absolutely. You're needed there for now. Luke has made a bold move. It would undermine his authority if his niece chose to stay behind, no matter *who* she might be engaged to."

She nodded. "I knew you would understand duty."

"Oh, I do. I also know that it's what you want."

"Jag, don't think for a minute I—"

He had taken her hand and pressed it to his heart, smiling at her. "I know you want to be with me. I want that, too. And we'll have that eventually . . . or we won't. You don't just feel obligated to travel with the Jedi—you *want* to, just as much as you want to be with me. And all of that is okay."

She regarded him searchingly as he continued. "And frankly, after your parents' cryptic message, I am getting the distinct feeling I won't be lingering around Coruscant much longer, either. After this meeting, I suspect I'll be heading straight for Imperial Space. And I don't know what's waiting there for me any more than you know what's waiting for you."

"About that meeting," Jaina said, tension leaving her posture. "I was told that you're to join us for dinner tonight. They wanted to have sort of a going-away celebration for me. And it sounds like for you, too."

"Leia's staying behind then?"

"Just for a while. Dorvan asked her to and Luke agreed. Not so much because she's a Jedi, but because there are few people in the galaxy who have the kind of diplomatic and governmental experience she has."

"Dorvan is a wise man. I'm glad she's staying, for however long. He and the GA can only benefit. And I'll be there for dinner," Jag assured her. "Wherever . . . *there* is. I never have learned where your family's safe house is."

"They won't be using it after tonight, so I guess they figured it didn't matter if you knew the location." Jaina grinned.

"I feel *so* honored," Jag said sarcastically, mitigating his tone with an answering smile.

"Either that," she said, draping her arms around his neck, "or they wanted to officially welcome you to the family. Maybe you finally got Dad's approval."

"Now, now," he chided, "don't shake my universe up too much."

The door was opened, not unexpectedly, by C-3PO. "Goodness gracious, how pleasant to see you again, Head of State Fel!" the droid enthused. "If only Master Luke and Master Ben were here, the entire family would be gathered together. It's been some time since that last occurred. I rather miss it."

"Good to see you again, too, Threepio," Jag said. R2-D2 toodled a happy-sounding welcome, as well. Jag started to reply when he was suddenly simultaneously charged by a madly purring young nexu and a beaming eight-year-old girl.

"Anji is happy to see you and so am I!" the little girl said. He mussed her black hair affectionately, then extended his hand to his future father-in-law.

"Glad you could join us tonight, kid," Han said. "Family's going to be going off in all kinds of directions tomorrow."

Jag was surprised at how good it felt to be included in the Solos' definition of *family*. "Indeed," he said, "and about that . . . ?" He let the question trail off and merely lifted his eyebrows in inquiry.

Han pressed a Corellian ale into Jag's hand and went to pour a glass of red wine for Jaina. "After dinner," he said. "In the meantime, I can't take all of this with me, so drink up."

"I don't think I've ever seen a safe house with such a well-stocked liquor cabinet," Jag commented. He sipped the ale and nodded appreciatively.

Han shot him the familiar lopsided grin that had, forty years earlier, won the heart of a Princess. "There are some things you just don't skimp on. For me, that means good alcohol, and good blasters."

"Which go together *so* well," said Jaina, rolling her eyes at her dad.

Leia came out of the kitchen and, with a smile and a quick kiss, accepted the glass of wine that Han had poured for her. "Dinner should be ready shortly. In the meantime," she said, sobering, "there's something very important you need to see."

Jag was instantly alert and focused. "What?" he asked.

With great seriousness, Leia said, "Amelia has taught Anji four new commands."

An hour later, after Anji had successfully stayed, savaged a stuffed eopie and then dropped it at a single word, and blocked Jag from getting up—all at a few hand signals from Allana—a pleasant visit ensued until it was the girl's bedtime. She was clearly disappointed at having to leave, but obeyed cheerfully, giving Jag a hug and heading for her room with the devoted nexu at her heels.

Jag eyed the table, a little confused. It was set for five. "I thought Amelia would be eating with us," he said.

"At this hour?" said Leia. "Oh, no. She'd be far too cranky in the morning. No"—she smiled a little—"someone else will be joining us."

Three dark heads turned to the hallway expectantly, and Jag followed their gaze.

A young woman, slender and golden-haired, stepped into the living room and smiled a bit uncertainly. "Hello, Head of State Fel," said Tahiri Veila.

Blinking at her, Jag wordlessly turned to the Solos for an explanation.

"Sorry to spring this on you, but we thought this was the best way for all involved," Leia apologized. "She came to us for help."

Tahiri remained standing. "I had a chance to escape," she said. "Just disappear in the chaos of Daala's breakout. For a while, I did just that. I thought about going to Eramuth, but I realized I would put him in a terrible position if I did."

"So you went to the Solos," Jag said, a touch of anger in his voice.

"I know what you're thinking," Tahiri continued quietly. "I was found guilty in a court of law. I was sentenced to execution. And I'm running away from it. And viewed in a certain light, that's completely accurate. But . . . I want to make things *right,* Jag. My death won't help anyone. It won't bring Gilad Pellaeon back, it won't repair any damage I've caused. It's legal . . . but it's not just. I have many debts to repay, many errors to correct. And I want to do that."

"When she came to us with this, I had an idea," Leia said. "Technically, the crime was against a former Imperial admiral. Justice would best be served by having Tahiri tried in an Imperial court. And until such a time as that can be arranged, Tahiri has offered to begin making reparations by assisting the Empire."

"And these days," Jaina said, "that's you, honey."

Jag stared at all of them, then back at Tahiri. She gazed levelly back at him.

"I'll abide by whatever decision you make, Jag," Tahiri said quietly. "If you want me to turn myself in, I will. I'll sit in prison, and I'll have factions using me to advance their own agendas, and it will be a holojournalist's field day until the GA gets around to executing me. Or I can come with you, and serve you with my life. And when the dust settles, I'll get a fair Imperial trial for what I've done."

Despite the tension in the room, Han snorted. "Times sure have changed when Imperial trials are certain to be fairer than Galactic Alliance trials."

Leia shushed him with a gentle hand on his arm, her brown eyes watching Jag.

"This isn't a setup, Jag," Jaina said. "We've all agreed to abide by whatever you choose to do."

Jag leaned back against the sofa, thinking. There was a time when he'd have disbelieved Jaina, but he didn't. The situation—the safe house, Tahiri on the run—all of this necessitated the secrecy.

"I think now would be a good time for you to tell me where you and Han went for a few days," he said to Leia. "And elaborate just a tiny bit on the whole I'm-in-danger thing."

"I don't know about the rest of you, but I'm starving," said Han. "Can we talk while we eat?"

"Just not with our mouths full," said Jaina.

Over a delicious, though slightly cool, meal of fried endwa, the orange gravy congealing slightly, chaka noodles, and steamed Ferroan spinach, the story unfolded.

Leia filled Jag, Jaina, and Tahiri in on everything that happened, from the initial strange message to the discovery of the Squibs, to the attack and, finally, the revelations. Jag's eating slowed and finally stopped altogether as he sat, food cooling and forgotten fork in hand, and listened.

"Squibs," he said.

"Squibs," Han confirmed.

"Who were working for me and the Imperial Remnant?"

"Ashik confirmed it," Leia said. "We didn't fill him in on the details. We wanted to tell you first."

"Do we know why Getelles's people were after him?" Jag asked. He seemed to notice the food for the first time in several minutes, and ate the bite on his fork. He didn't taste it.

"Unfortunately not," Leia said. "They're staying with us. Well, with some . . . friends. You can talk to them if you'd like."

Jag raised an eyebrow, but Leia said nothing further. "Let me make certain I understand everything," he said calmly, putting the fork down. "Some Squibs you met years ago contacted you out of the blue. They just happen to be working for me, although I was unaware of it. They have information on where Daala is going, what she plans—which is targeting my job—and who she's working with and who she's planning on betraying. Said Squibs have done something to warrant Getelles's people trying to kill them, but we don't know for sure what that is. Have I gotten it all correct?"

"That sounds right." Han did not suffer from the lack of appetite that now plagued Jag. Beside Jag, Jaina ate steadily, staying silent.

"You've been back for a few days," Jag said. "Assuming this is true—and I confess, I'm dubious—why didn't you tell me sooner?"

"Because we needed to make sure it was true before coming to you with rumors or misinformation," Jaina said, unable to keep quiet any longer. "Mom and Dad wanted to check out their story. All parts of it. They needed to make sure the recording the Squibs gave them was genuine."

"And it is," Leia said.

"Don't feel bad," Han said. "I was surprised, too."

Jag leaned back in his chair, thinking.

"So," Jaina said, exchanging glances with Tahiri. "What are you going to do?"

"Have you told anyone else about this?" Jag asked Leia and Han.

"Not yet," Leia said. "We wanted you to know first. Dorvan does know that I've been following up leads on Daala's whereabouts, however."

"Thank you," Jag said. "Do you think he'll act on the knowledge?"

Leia hesitated. "He might," she said. "But frankly, it's chaos there right now. Dorvan's a cautious man. I think he would wait until there's more stability with this current government before he did anything. He'd certainly want to know more before committing GA resources toward extracting her. Though she's an escaped prisoner, she's under the protection of Moffs. Which makes it your business more than his."

"Ashik's confirmation of the Squibs' involvement on behalf of the Imperial Remnant goes a long way toward convincing me," Jag said. "Dorvan doesn't have anything comparable to go on. I agree with you—it should be his decision whether or not to act, not ours."

"So," said Jaina, "like I asked earlier . . . what are you going to do?"

"I'm going to talk with your parents' little blue friends first," Jag said. "Depending on what I learn, I'm going after Daala. I have an escaped prisoner hiding in Imperial territory, protected by a Moff who is supposed to be loyal to me. It's my right to seek her out."

He didn't miss that Tahiri was very studiously not looking at him after the words *escaped prisoner* had been used twice in in as many minutes.

"I had a feeling I wouldn't be sticking around Coruscant after I got your message," Jag said to Leia and Han. He turned his head to regard

Tahiri, gazing at her until she felt it and lifted her head. "You do know I have a very fine security detail, headed by Ashik."

"Ashik," said Tahiri, "isn't a Jedi."

"And you are?"

She hesitated.

"Well, that's the million-credit question, isn't it?" Jag said. "Are you a Jedi, Tahiri Veila?"

"I—would like to be again, yes. And I will serve you in that capacity, if you will take me with you."

"I tried my best to bring the Imperial Remnant formally into the GA. But it never happened. And because that never came to fruition, the Empire is a completely separate entity, not bound by the laws of the Galactic Alliance. And therefore, as Head of State, until such time as a lawful court trial can be held—and I must say, it's looking like that won't be anytime soon, considering Daala is attempting to wrest control of the Empire—I hereby agree to take custody of you, Tahiri Veila. You will obey my orders to the letter, and not go haring off as if your last name were Solo."

"Hey," said two voices. Leia just chuckled.

"Basically, you're on parole," Jag continued as if he hadn't noticed. "Don't violate it."

Tahiri's eyes were suspiciously shiny. "I won't, sir."

"And don't call me sir. I'm Jag. And I'm also hungry. I've ignored this delicious meal for too long. Tomorrow, I want to meet your friends. But for tonight"—he squeezed Jaina's hands—"let's enjoy the rest of the evening as a family."

# Chapter Twenty-four

It was, Luke mused, no doubt a security nightmare. All three members of the soon-to-be-dissolved triumvirate, the Jedi Grand Master, and a former Chief of State all gathered together in one place. Someone in a position of arranging this would be sweating profusely today. Luke thought that that unknown being should count him- or herself fortunate that Dorvan, like himself and Saba Sebatyne, was someone who did not particularly relish the spotlight. The ceremony would go relatively quickly.

"This one is relieved that this is the final duty she will be asked to perform as part of the triumvirate," Saba Sebatyne said. "This one is eager to be about more useful pursuitz."

Saba, Luke, and Leia stood together near the main entrance, awaiting their cue to process forward. Saba and Luke were clad in traditional Master's robes. Leia, knowing what the public expected of her after more than forty years of participating in politics, wore a formal, full-length overdress with slashed sleeves to show the dark brown underdress. Her hair, though much grayer than that of the youthful Princess she had once been, was meticulously styled and threaded through with gold. She wore little makeup—she did not need much, and she was proud of the wrinkles she had accumulated over the years. Each had been bought at the cost of pain, or given as the gift of laughter.

"I wish I could go with you," she said to them. Normally Jaina and Han would be standing with them, but Jaina was in the hangar preparing her ship for departure, and her father, fiancé, and niece were keeping her company.

"I would enjoy running around the galaxy chasing down Abeloth with you," Luke said, smiling at her. "But we both know you will help more here. This fledgling government is going to need you."

Mindful of the listening ears of their Jedi escorts, they said nothing more. Luke knew Leia's comments were merely wistful longings, and that she more than agreed with his decision to ask her to stay behind. She, too, had a job to do.

Luke, Leia, and Saba would walk from the Temple to the platform specially erected in Fellowship Plaza for the occasion. Dorvan and Treen would approach from the Justice Center. Jedi Seha Dorvald had a small device in her ear and was monitoring the activity. She turned and gestured to them.

"It's time," Luke said. He offered Leia his arm, and she took it, gliding forward as smoothly as if she were not wearing heels to give her a few extra centimeters of height. Saba followed.

Together the three Jedi made their way across a plaza crowded with well-wishers. Luke had expected some hecklers, but he was pleasantly startled to see mostly happy faces in the throng. Either the populace of Coruscant was largely content with the direction their government was going, or else the GAS had managed to corral all those who approved of the situation and steer them up front.

Dorvan was clad as he was every day, in a muted business tunic, though perhaps this one was just a shade more formal. Behind him, waving and smiling at the crowd, was Senator Haydnat Treen. She managed to wear what Luke would ordinarily consider garish colors and make them look stylish. As the three Jedi and the two politicians greeted one another, Luke couldn't think how much nicer Leia looked, in the more subdued tones and classic style. Fortunately, he was not here to render a verdict on the latest fashion.

There was a brief flurry of handshaking and smiles were exchanged, and then Dorvan, Saba, and Treen stepped forward. Since Treen was the most comfortable with public speaking, it had been decided that she would deliver the speech.

"Beings of the Galactic Alliance," she began. "Today is an extremely significant day for all of us. Today, we say a fond farewell to the Jedi. Grand Master Luke Skywalker"—she turned to nod at him—"Master Saba Sebatyne, Wynn Dorvan, and I all believe that this step is for the best—for both organizations. They have served the Galactic Alliance well, their final duty as an official branch of the GA being to relieve us of a difficult and frankly inappropriate leader, and to work with former Chief of Staff Wynn Dorvan and me to steer us through a most challenging time. With their departure, the unusual but effective triumvirate must perforce be dissolved."

She smiled brightly. "Impressive a body as the GA is, even it cannot have a triumvirate with only two members!" There was some mild chuckling from the crowd, and Treen continued. "Within the next few days, as the law requires, the Senate will be holding an emergency session to elect an interim Chief of State until such time as we can arrange to have a proper and legally binding election.

"And now, I turn the podium over to our dear friend, Jedi Grand Master Luke Skywalker."

Luke smiled at her and stepped up to the podium, looking out over the crowd for a moment before beginning to speak.

"For millennia, Coruscant has been the home to the Jedi," Luke said. "The decision to leave it, and our beloved Temple, was not an easy one. Jedi exist to help, to serve, but that help and service cannot be confined to any single species, creed, or political association. By formally allying with the Galactic Alliance, with the best of intentions, we found ourselves overly bound to it. So—we are now separate entities, but we remain the best of friends. I am completely confident in the GA's ability to handle any crisis that comes its way. I am sure the Senate will give you a fine interim Chief of State."

And now, the moment had come. He looked out at the thronged Fellowship Plaza, back at the Temple, and smiled softly.

"I will miss you, and Coruscant, but my heart is easy with this choice. Farewell—and may the Force be with you."

* * *

The good-byes, Jag thought, were getting easier. Not because he and Jaina missed each other any less when they were apart, but the new bond that had been forged between them connected them even when they were separated by distance. They did not live in hope that all would be well between them; they lived in certainty of it.

But neither had to actually *like* saying good-bye.

They had had a more intimate farewell in Jag's quarters an hour earlier. Now Jag stood with Jaina and her parents in the Temple hangar. The place was alive with calm, controlled activity, but even Jag—utterly non-Force-sensitive—could feel the excitement in the air, the mingled joy and regret that the Jedi felt upon their imminent departure.

Jaina hugged her mother tightly. "You'll come join us soon?"

"As soon as we can, I promise," Leia reassured her. "Dorvan has asked me to stay, and I can't deny him what help and advice I can."

"I know. But I think you'll be the last Jedi on the planet."

Leia chuckled. "There's still the Barabels. But I probably will be the last to leave."

Han held out his arms and his daughter went into them, snuggling up to him. Han squeezed her so hard Jag feared Jaina would have difficulty breathing. "Save a little bit of Abeloth for your mother," Han said. "You know how grumpy she gets when she misses the action."

"That's you, Dad."

"So it is." He grinned and planted a kiss on her forehead.

Allana clung tightly to her aunt. "I want to go, too," she said.

"From what I understand, you've had plenty of adventure already, young lady," Jaina said, tweaking her nose.

"Dealing with Squibs isn't an adventure," Allana protested.

"Oh, yes it is," said Han.

"An adventure I will shortly undertake," Jag said. "Amelia has offered to introduce me."

"Lucky you," said Jaina, slipping into his arms for a final, sweet kiss. For his ears only, she whispered, "Don't you dare let Daala get the jump on you."

"I won't," he whispered back. "I have you to come home to, don't I?"

"Darn right you do," she said, pulling back. "Well, time to go. I'll be in touch."

With a final wave and a grin, Jaina strode off to her StealthX. She didn't look back.

They watched the hatch close on the StealthX. Jag felt a small hand steal into his. He looked down to see Amelia looking up at him earnestly and tugging on him.

"They're waiting in the *Falcon,*" she said.

"Is that safe?" asked Jag.

"As safe as I could make it," Han said. "Don't have anywhere else to put them. Threepio and Artoo stayed aboard to see that they don't get into too much trouble. Personally I'd have drop-kicked them into the next solar system, but you said you wanted to see them."

"Your patience is commendable," Jag said. "By all means, lead on, Amelia."

Smiling happily, she did. They strode up the ramp, and a golden form hastened into view as fast as its servos could carry it.

"Mistress Leia, Master Han—thank goodness you've come to liberate us!" exclaimed 3PO. R2 rolled into view, and even his normally cheerful toodles and tweets had an anxious edge to them.

"See?" said Han.

Three blue heads poked out from the side, and six long, tufted ears swiveled forward. Their eyes were bright with curiosity.

"So this is our boss?" said one.

"About time," said another.

"How exciting to meet the Head of State!" said the third.

Jag strode up the ramp, putting on his best diplomatic demeanor. "So these are the Squibs who have been so helpful to me and the Empire. You must be Emala," he said to the smallest one, bending over and extending his hand. Emala closed long fingers about it and rubbed it on her cheek. Jag took no offense; he was familiar with the habits of this species.

"I'm Grees," said one of the males, emulating Emala.

"And I'm Sligh," said the third.

"I understand you've known the Solo family for quite some time," Jag continued.

"We're old friends," said Sligh. Behind him, Jag heard what might have been a muffled snort from Han.

"Old friends who put bounties on their heads?" Jag continued in the same mild tone of voice.

"Well," said Grees, "there *were* reasons behind it. Very *good* reasons, actually."

"And now there aren't," said Emala. "So now we're partners again. And in a way, partners with you, too."

"So it would seem," Jag said. "It looks as if the life of adventure suits you all, considering how long you've known the Solos."

Grees's whiskers bristled, but Emala said, "Well, some beings just age better than others."

"That's it!" said Leia. "You're too young!"

"Flatterer," said Emala.

But Leia shook her head. "It's not about flattery, Emala. It's about the simple fact that all three of you *are younger than you were when we first met you.*"

Beside Leia, Han was nodding. "You're right. There was something—wrong. I couldn't put my finger on it."

"Clean living," said Sligh.

"Yep!" said Emala. "Helping out partners and doing the right thing."

"That's poodoo," Han said, growling. "Your ears!"

"What about them?" said Emala, looking impossibly innocent.

"They're way too big. And Sligh—take off that coat. Now."

Sligh looked offended and clutched the coat tighter around his frame. "Why should I do that?"

"Sligh, please. Humor Captain Solo. I'd be very appreciative if you would." Jag smiled.

The three exchanged glances, and the overly large ears drooped. "Okay," muttered Sligh.

He removed the coat and stood before them with his blue-furred torso exposed. "See? Nothing wrong with—"

"Turn around, please," said Jag.

Muttering in Squibbal, Sligh turned around. His fur—thick, silky, and shiny with good health—sported small spots of lighter blue all along his back.

Allana said in a delighted tone of voice, "You're like a nexu! One color when you're a baby, another when you're grown up!"

"We're not fuzzlings, Fuzzling," Grees said. "We just . . . got younger."

"You don't just *get younger.*" Jag wondered if he heard a trace of resentment in Han's voice.

"Getelles," said Leia. "Oh no . . . You didn't . . ." She looked at Han, her eyes wide.

"The drochs," Han said. "Did that sleemo manage to smuggle drochs out?"

Jag felt a punch of cold apprehension in his gut. Of course he knew about the Death Seed plague, carried by the insects of Nam Chorios known as the drochs. He imagined that nearly everyone in the galaxy knew about the horrific creatures. They drained the life energy of their victims, causing necrosis and finally death. Ever since this discovery there had been a strictly enforced policy that under no circumstances were drochs permitted to leave Nam Chorios.

Several years ago, Getelles had been working with a company on Antemeridias to take over the Meridian sector. Part of the plan involved releasing the drochs on anyone who wasn't on his side. He'd been sitting quietly for many years, rebuked, fined, and penalized, but still keeping his seat.

But Jag didn't understand how Leia had made the jump from the Death Seed plague to eternal youth.

"From my understanding," said Jag, "the drochs siphoned life energy. They didn't give it back."

"They did if you ate them," Han said.

The Squibs were doing their best to put on sabacc faces throughout this conversation, but apparently they weren't fooling the Jedi Knight present. Leia glowered at the rodents, who unconsciously pressed in closer to one another.

Han closed the distance between himself and Grees in two strides, grabbed the Squib by his coat lapels, and lifted him up. "Does Getelles have drochs?"

"Dad! Put him down, please!"

The voice was young and earnest. Han paused, glanced down at his adopted daughter, then put Grees down. He didn't let go of the collar, though, and he repeated his question in a deceptively calm and measured voice.

"Does Getelles have drochs?"

"Well, not in the way that you're thinking," said Emala, casting a quick glance at Allana. "He isn't breeding them."

"So he's got dead ones?" Allana asked.

Sligh sighed and scratched one of his overly large ears, which, presumably, he would grow into, as Anji was starting to do with her enormous paws. "Sort of."

"Genetic material?" Jag pressed.

Grees eyed him. "I'm not saying any more until I get paid for the information. You want it, it's worth something to you, so we make a deal."

"Not on your—"

Jag held up a hand, and Han fell silent. "I believe you were working for the Imperial Remnant. Which means me. Is that correct?"

They looked at one another and nodded.

"And did you officially terminate your employment? Or were you otherwise formally released from that contract?"

He knew he had them when they looked up, down, at something in some distant part of the ship, anywhere but at him.

"I see. So then you're still working for me, and as part of that already-arranged deal, you need to tell me what you know. Because if you don't, then I might have to do something very unpleasant to you. All simply as part of honoring the deal, of course."

Sligh let out a pained sigh. Emala patted him. "All right," Grees said. "Getelles has a few scientists working for him who also worked on that nanovirus that killed the little Hapan Chume'da—Allana, I think her name was."

Jag heard the Solos gasp softly. Allana had gone very still.

"Go on," Han said in a cold voice.

"Getelles is apparently all kinds of excited about the thought of doing something with drochs to prolong life."

"And rejuvenate older beings," said Emala.

"And rejuvenate older beings," Grees added. "So we volunteered to be test subjects." Seeing Han's glower, he said, "Hey, don't look at me like that. It was an excellent opportunity to gather information to give to the Head of State. Once we got the information, we escaped. To tell him everything we knew via our good former partners, like we're doing right now."

"That's not all," pressed Jag. "You wouldn't want to renege on your deal, now, would you?"

Grees scowled.

Emala sighed. "Better tell him, Grees," she said.

Grees's scowl deepened, and he fished in the pockets of his jacket. He pulled out a small, tightly sealed vial approximately as long as his finger. "As you can tell, the experiments were a rousing success. We've gotten the chance to live our lives all over again. We wanted the same for our people."

"For the right fee," said Han.

"Well of course," said Sligh, puzzled at Han's tone. "We'll be able to spend our lives all over again in a very comfortable fashion."

"And we want to do the same for our children," said Grees. "They're getting on in years, as well. We didn't want to outlive them. Who wants that?"

It was uttered in a very nonchalant tone, and Jag was certain that Grees didn't realize the impact those words had on Han and Leia. He couldn't feel them in the Force, but he didn't need to. The slight tensing of Leia's slender frame, the sudden softness in Han's eyes as he looked off to the right—these gestures told him that the Squibs' words, spoken offhandedly, had struck deep.

The Solos had outlived two of their three children. And they would never have the chance to watch Anakin or Jacen live their too-brief lives over again.

Jag cleared his throat and extended his hand. The three Squibs stared at it as if it were an appendage they had never seen before. "The serum," he said. "Give it to me, please."

Grees clutched it to his chest. "Why? It's ours! We went through a great deal to bring you that information, and this has nothing to do with you!"

"The Empire greatly appreciates your efforts, and you will be amply compensated. But that serum was developed in an Imperial laboratory, by Imperial citizens, for use of the Empire. I'm afraid it's stolen property."

"You can't have it," Emala said bluntly. "It's for the children. This wasn't part of the deal."

"Neither, I am quite certain, was stealing Imperial property. I would prefer not to arrest you, but I will if I must."

"What do you need it for? You have plenty of years ahead of you. Are you planning on giving it to Captain Solo?"

"Now wait just a—" began Han.

"No," Jag said. "I have another use for it. A very important use that could help the galaxy. It doesn't belong to you."

When Grees didn't move, Jag sighed and spoke into his comlink. "Ashik? I'm afraid that I need to have someone arrest—"

"Okay!" snapped Grees. He bared his very healthy, very white teeth and almost flung the vial at Jag. "But we have rights, too! We feel this was taken from us without due compensation, as the deal *we* negotiated originally did not include obtaining and delivering—at tremendous personal risk—a sample of an extremely valuable serum."

"You've got to be kidding me," Han said.

"Sounds to me like they were supposed to listen and bring back what they learned," Allana said. "If they brought back more, shouldn't they get paid extra?"

Emala beamed at her. "You sure you're not half Squib, Fuzzling?"

"Quite sure," Leia said. "Jag—"

"Leia, I'm sorry. This has given me some unique leverage, and I need to put it to use right away."

"See?" said Sligh gleefully. "Unique leverage. Procured by us."

"You're a pretty poor haggler, Head of State Fel. Sorry to say so but it's the truth," said Grees.

"Look," said Jag. He was holding the small, precious vial very tightly. "We'll discuss recompense when I return. Because if you don't let me go now, you'll be negotiating with Daala."

Their ears drooped slightly, and they murmured unhappily.

"Excellent," Jag said. "I see we understand each other. Han, Leia—I'll leave them in your care until I return."

Han paled, and even Leia looked flustered. "Oh, no!" gasped C-3PO.

Allana, however, looked extraordinarily pleased.

# Chapter Twenty-five

MOFF VANSYN'S ESTATE, IMPERIAL SPACE

"IT'S SUCH A PLEASURE TO FINALLY BE ABLE TO HOST YOU FOR A change," said Moff Porak Vansyn. He selected a cigarra from the humidor proffered by the serving droid and snipped the end off. The droid moved to Lecersen, who declined but lifted his glass in a silent request for a refill of the delicious gold wine.

"It's good to see you, Porak," said Lecersen, and to his surprise he actually meant it. He'd always been rather fond of the slightly younger, debonair Moff, with his droll manner of speaking and unfashionably thin mustache. "I regret that the tides of politics have separated us these past few months. You appear to be doing very well for yourself."

Vansyn leaned forward and allowed the droid to light his cigarra. Blue-gray smoke trickled up to form a wreath around his head as he replied. "Well enough, though I would say that you are poised to do still better."

Lecersen raised an eyebrow in feigned perplexity. How much did Vansyn know? "What makes you say that, Porak?"

Vansyn grinned around his cigarra. "You're here in Imperial Space, for one thing."

"Isn't a Moff allowed home now and then when things become unpleasant at the seat of government?"

"Come now, Drikl," said Vansyn. "We've known each other too long. You are like a spider in the center of its web. You feel the vibrations from elsewhere, but you stay in the center and let opportunities come to you. It's magnificent, all the strings you manage to keep track of. Quite an inspiration."

"What a nice compliment," said Lecersen, honestly flattered. "It's true I do believe in maximum results with minimal effort."

"So therefore, when you stomped your foot and made much to-do about returning to Imperial Space, I knew that the action was no longer truly on Coruscant, seat of government notwithstanding. You're plotting something." Vansyn's eyes were bright. "Do be a good fellow and let your old friend in on it, hmm?"

Lecersen considered how much he should tell Vansyn. While he had indeed approached the other Moff in the hope of acquiring his assistance, he was actually taken by surprise at Vansyn's perception. The logic held, of course, and for a moment Lecersen wondered if he was that transparent to all his friends—and enemies. But Vansyn had known him for a long time. Maybe it was time Lecersen brought him into the thick of things.

"You've got a lovely home here, Porak," Lecersen said. "A good, solid reputation. I'm not sure I can in good conscience ask you to risk it."

Vansyn waved a hand dismissively, sending loops of smoke leaping about. "Come now, Drikl, you know I'm a high-stakes player."

"In sabacc, yes, and you've lost to me more than once, if I recall correctly."

Vansyn chuckled. "Guilty as charged. But you said it yourself—I've got a good, solid reputation. I think you could use my aid—if your thoughts bend in the same direction mine do."

*Let him say it first,* thought Lecersen. *Call the bluff.* "And what might that direction be?"

Vansyn tapped the ash off his cigarra and took another thoughtful puff. “Neither of us is overly fond of one Jagged Fel. He’s utterly botched his leadership of the Empire. Daala’s been run off like a scared eopie. Seems to me that leaves a rather large hole that needs filling. And, a touch too coincidentally, here you are, back in Imperial Space.”

“And what am I doing here, do you suppose?”

“Planning to take over the Empire. You’d make a jolly fine Emperor, you know. I’d follow you.”

There it was. Lecersen relaxed back in the comfortable chair and sipped his wine.

“I see” was all he said. “I think I’d make a jolly fine Emperor myself.”

“I assume things are already in the works?”

Lecersen made his decision. “They are,” he said. “And permit me to apologize right now for keeping you ignorant of it. I wanted you to have plausible deniability if things fell apart before we reached this stage.”

“That’s very kind of you, Drikl,” said Vansyn. “And I’m just as pleased you’re choosing to include me now.”

“I definitely have plans for you, my old friend,” Lecersen said warmly. Plans that included utilizing the other Moff’s dominion as a base and, eventually, rewarding Vansyn for his cooperation. “There are quite a few of us who are rather unhappy with both Daala and Fel right now. And we’re in very high places.”

“Oh?” Vansyn looked keenly interested, leaning forward. He was, Lecersen realized, very excited at being included in something so ambitious and simultaneously clandestine. As he should be. When this was all over, every single one of the conspirators would get exactly what he or she wanted. “Who?”

“Haydnat Treen was the one who approached me first,” said Lecersen. “She’d already been hard at work behind the scenes, and was able to bring in several other key players. For example, when Bwua’tu was attacked, we found his temporary replacement highly ambitious and willing to participate.”

Vansyn’s brown eyes had widened. “Astounding,” he said. “How did you all manage to meet without being observed?”

Lecersen chuckled. "We only had one simple dinner at my estate," he said. "The rest of the time, we were in disguise."

"Disguise?"

"You're familiar with the costume nights at the Gleaming Fortunes Casino? And the willingness of Obrigadar's Simulator Palace to indulge customers in military garb as long as it's either decommissioned or twenty years out of date?"

A sharp bark of laughter escaped Vansyn. "So you could meet right out in the open and no one would know it was you! Delightful!" he exclaimed. "Ingenious! You, sir, are indeed a master at this game! I am distressed I couldn't have picked a costume and attended myself."

"When this is all over and the goal achieved, I promise I'll host a masquerade, and you may come as anyone you'd like."

"I am already planning my costume. Please continue—this is absolutely fascinating."

Lecersen knew when his ego was being stroked. Vansyn was rather obvious about it. Filled with good food and good liquor, he opted to relax and enjoy it.

"Daala zigged when she should have zagged, which made our job easy for us. She acted like an Imperial Admiral when she should have acted like a Chief of State. An understandable mistake, but a mistake nonetheless. I wonder if Tarkin would have approved or disapproved, and if he saw it coming, what he would have done."

"He probably wouldn't have noticed. Men are sometimes blind when dazzled by the charms of a lovely woman." Vansyn said. He grinned. "And of course, Daala's half blind already herself."

It was a cheap shot, but Lecersen found himself laughing. "True," he said. "Poor Daala. I actually feel a bit sorry for her. If she'd only embraced the uprisings and sent in teams to discuss terms rather than quash them, I wouldn't be sitting here at this table having this chat with you, Porak."

"Well then, lucky us," Vansyn said. "Fel isn't winning many popularity contests, either. One might wish they'd just go at each other and save us the trouble of overthrowing one or both of them."

Lecersen tensed. "Why would they go at each other?" He kept his voice calm, languid, and sipped his gold wine with a hand that trembled not at all. Inwardly, he was on high alert. It might have been an offhand comment.

Might.

Vansyn coughed. He waved at the smoke from his cigarra too vigorously. "Apologies, Drikl. I don't smoke these very often. Don't usually have something worth celebrating."

"And you do now?"

He was certain that if Vansyn hadn't been filling the room with the cigarra smoke, he could have smelled the other man's fear.

"But of course! My old friend is back, and he's going to be Emperor." Vansyn was too cheery, too quick to respond. "What's not to celebrate?"

And that was when Lecersen knew he had walked into a trap. He sprang to his feet, but he heard a door hiss open behind him and realized he was too late—the trap had already been sprung.

Without turning around, he said, "Hello, Admiral Daala."

"Moff Drikl Lecersen," Daala said. "Please be seated. Porak, could you pour me a glass of whatever he's having? He certainly seemed to be enjoying it."

Lecersen had seldom tasted true despair. He did now, bitter and acrid at the back of his throat, and no fine vintage gold wine would take that taste away. His opponent had seen all his cards, but he was still determined to keep playing to the last minute.

To the last breath.

Vansyn at least had the grace to look uncomfortable as he poured Daala a drink. The admiral and former Chief of State slid into a chair next to Lecersen and lifted her glass in a toast.

"To the Empire," she said. Lecersen did not touch his. She frowned. "Oh for pity's sake, at least enjoy the wine. You've provided me with both information and entertainment in one brief conversation, Drikl. You've earned a drink."

"Do I get a last meal, too?" Lecersen said drily.

"You don't necessarily have to," Daala said. Vansyn was staring very intently at the smoke coming up from his cigarra. "And please, Porak, put that disgusting thing out."

"Of course, Admiral." Vansyn ground out the cigarra at once. *Syco-*

*phant,* thought Lecersen. Why he had ever liked the man was now quite beyond him.

"Just to satisfy my curiosity, when exactly did you decide to betray me, Porak? And what was your price?" asked Lecersen. He couldn't keep a biting tone from his voice.

"Um," said Vansyn. "I wouldn't . . . exactly say *betray.*"

"You shouldn't abandon your friends just because they are not immediately useful to you, Drikl," Daala said. "You hurt poor Vansyn's feelings. So when I happened along and offered him my support, he was more than happy to give it."

"In other words, worms should be squashed once they cease to pass fertile soil," said Lecersen. "A valuable lesson, Admiral. I assure you I won't forget it."

She smiled, icily. "I know you detest me. And Vansyn—I didn't appreciate your attempt at wit at the expense of my eye, either."

Vansyn had the grace to look embarrassed.

"He was right about one thing. Fel and I are, indeed, going to be *going at each other* quite soon. The question is—are you with me, Lecersen, or are you dead?"

"I presume this is the part where you tell me you were recording everything, and that you'll blackmail me and my cohorts if I don't throw my lot in with you," Lecersen said.

"No," Daala said. "This is the part where I tell you that not only was I recording everything, but I also know about the Freedom Flight, and the involvement of not just Senator Treen, but Senator Bramsin as well. You yourself kindly mentioned others in positions of power—it won't be that hard to figure out who they are. It's also the part where I tell you that the reason you never heard back from the agent you sent to Qaras was that we intercepted him and acquired all the evidence in that safe-deposit box." She smiled. "Your agent told us everything before he died. It seems like your little Minyavish was wrong. He did have cohorts—they simply didn't let him know of their existence."

Lecersen had been concerned before, but now he fully understood just how badly he had messed up—and how much Daala held the reins. He had underestimated her. Badly. She saw the blood drain from his face, and smiled the grin of the sand panther.

"I am happy to leave the GA in the hands of your little conspiracy," she said, "though my sources are telling me that Treen is running the show in your absence. You should have stayed put, Drikl. The Jedi are leaving Coruscant, and while I am not one to discount Wynn Dorvan, I don't know how well he'd do in an ambush one dark night against—oh, let's see—*two fake Jedi*?"

The gloves were off, and she was showing terribly, terribly sharp claws. Lecersen swallowed hard. Had the blasted woman figured *everything* out?

"Bwua'tu's still alive" was all that Lecersen could manage to say.

Her face hardened even more. "Alive and, from what I hear, still incoherent. I'd rather he died than live with a damaged brain, never to remember, or think, or—" She caught herself. "But he is not what I wish to discuss. I'm keeping you alive because I can use you, if you're willing to be used. But don't you dare mistake this bargain for anything else. You will work with me, and serve me as I retake the Empire. And in return, you'll get to live. Serve well, maybe you'll get a little more."

The word escaped him before he could call it back. *"How?"*

She knew what he meant. "You haven't heard a single rumor of my whereabouts because until today, I haven't been in Imperial Space. I have another base of operations. I have many beings who have been loyal to me for a long, long time. With your penchant for using, abusing, and discarding beings, loyalty and devotion aren't things I expect you to readily understand. Not everyone in this galaxy is out for himself. I've got old friends willing to break me out of jail, old comrades-in-arms willing to give their weapons, artillery, ships, and lives if necessary to me and my goal. I've got teams supporting those species who have been displaced or overthrown due to the slave uprisings, and who are eager for a benevolent Empire to give them back what was once theirs. And as you've no doubt rather ruefully begun to realize, my spies are everywhere.

"So, what's it to be?" She leaned forward, green eyes blazing with intensity. "I have an opening on my team—and I have a blaster. It's up to you."

# Chapter Twenty-six

SOLO SAFE HOUSE, CORUSCANT

"GRANDPA, ARE YOU SURE WE CAN'T INVITE THE SQUIBS TO LIVE HERE?"

Leia grinned at Han, who was tucking their granddaughter into bed. "The Squibs would hate it here," Han said confidently.

"Why? It's small, but it's nice."

"Trust me, they would."

"I miss Threepio and Artoo," the little girl grumbled. Anji jumped onto the bed and Leia observed that the animal was growing almost as large as Allana, and that perhaps it was time to suggest that Anji start sleeping on the floor. She debated the bed's ability to fit them both when Anji reached adulthood.

"We do, too," Leia reassured her. "But we can't ask Zekk and Taryn to spend all their time watching the Squibs. They've got to get some sleep sometime."

Allana made a face and cuddled her eopie. "I know. But . . . does someone even have to be watching them? I mean, it's clear they want to stay and get their deal."

"Honey . . . with Squibs, you just never know," Han said. "Now get some sleep, kiddo." He leaned over and kissed her forehead. Leia did likewise, patting Anji, as well.

They closed the door and looked at each other. Han opened his mouth. Leia raised a finger to her lips, nodded at the door, and they went into the kitchen. Han poked about for something to eat while Leia prepared some tea.

"That meeting was supposed to be just a formality," Han said.

"I know," said Leia. "I'm worried, too. I don't know what can be taking this long. Treen was quite sincere that she didn't want the job, but there was . . . I don't like or trust her."

"From what you told me," said Han, getting some snack items ready, "she, you, Saba, and Luke all agreed that Dorvan was the right guy for the job."

"That's exactly what happened," Leia said, spooning some sweet syrup into her tea. She turned around and noted that Han had prepared a plate of fruit, cheese, and crackers. "I thought you didn't like those things."

"I thought I didn't, either," Han said. "I hate to be beholden to the Squibs for anything, but those crackers are pretty good."

Without either one needing to say a word, they both headed for their small office. Han perched on the desk while Leia sat in the chair. Both of them pointedly avoided staring at the comm unit. Steam wafted up from their cups.

Han popped a cracker in his mouth and crunched on it for a moment. "So Dorvan's election should have taken all of about five minutes."

"Should have," Leia agreed.

"And they met today at two, and they're still in the meeting seven hours later," Han said.

"Sure are," Leia said.

"I'll say it," Han growled. "Something's wrong."

Leia nodded wordlessly and picked up her tea, trying to let the hot beverage calm her. But of course, Han was right. With every hour that passed, her anxiety had grown. This should have been the easiest vote the Senate had ever had. Dorvan knew his job, had no real long-term ambitions, and seemingly had no enemies.

Seemingly.

"I wonder if we were just a little too smug," she said quietly.

"What do you mean?" Han asked. He frowned a little as he ate another cracker. "The Squibs were right. These are better when you dunk them in a malted."

"We know Dorvan is the best one for the job," she said. "We know he's sincere, honest, and wants to do what is best for the GA. Moreover, he doesn't have his own agenda."

"Exactly," Han said. "Even Treen seems to know that."

"She didn't want the job," Leia said slowly, "but that doesn't mean someone else didn't."

Han stared at her. "You think she set this whole thing up to get someone else elected Chief of State?"

Leia lifted solemn brown eyes. "I can't think of any other reason for the Senate to still be in session."

Han swore and thumped his mug down so hard some tea splashed onto the desk. Leia reached for his hand and covered it with her own.

"We shouldn't give up all hope," she said. "At least whoever it is, is getting some opposition. Otherwise, if it were a done deal, the session would have wrapped up quickly. There are some good, decent beings in the Senate, Han."

"Some," Han admitted. "Too few for my liking. Let's hope they're strong enough to not let themselves be bribed, bullied, or outvoted."

The call came at two in the morning.

Leia awoke, instantly alert after years of dealing with late-night emergencies. "Leia," she said into her comm. She heard the bedsheets rustle, knew Han was awake and listening.

"Leia, I'm sorry to disturb you at this hour," came the voice of Sullustan senator Luewet Wuul. "But—I thought you should know."

"Wynn Dorvan was not elected as interim Chief of State," said Leia. It was a statement, not a question.

"Is there anything you Jedi don't know?" Wuul said, attempting to sound bluff and hearty.

"Plenty of things, Luew," Leia said. Her heart felt heavy in her chest. "What happened?"

"I'm not sure *I* even know," Wuul said. He sounded tired, angry, and frustrated. "It had been my opinion that Dorvan was the logical candidate. In fact, he was the *only* candidate. But when his name was put forward, really almost as a formality, that new Senator from B'nish, Kameron Suldar, started speaking. He said that Dorvan was too closely affiliated in the public mind with Daala's administration to perform effectively, and that the GA needed a fresh new face to represent it. Someone who could never possibly be accused of consorting with Daala."

"That's nonsense! Wynn was just doing the best he could as Daala's chief of staff! In fact, he did a lot to mitigate some of her more egregious policies! Besides, he'd only be governing for two months. The stability of the galaxy should come before putting in a *fresh new face*."

Behind her, Han groaned slightly.

"Further, Suldar said the GA needed someone who did not side so openly with the Jedi, and he indicated that he thought Luke's decision was a good one. There is more anti-Jedi sentiment in the Senate than I thought, Leia, I'm extremely sorry to say. It was honestly a bit alarming."

Leia thought about the now-famous image of Wynn Dorvan racing up the Temple steps, and her heart sank further. "They can't have it both ways," she said, her voice harsh in her worry. "He can't be both too pro-Daala *and* too pro-Jedi."

"You know that, and I know that," Wuul continued wearily, "but apparently many of the other Senators thought this was a perfectly valid argument. So there we sat for the next twelve hours, debating whether to put an experienced, trustworthy diplomat or a former terrorist in charge of the Galactic Alliance. And in the end, the terrorist won. Leia, I must tell you, I don't know what things are coming to. Makes me want to take my burtalle and retire to Sullust."

A sudden chill seized Leia. Behind her, Han, frustrated with only hearing one end of the conversation, kept whispering, "What? What?" She waved him to silence and took a deep breath, calming herself in the Force.

"Terrorist? Who would that be?"

She knew before he even said the name.

"It's that new representative from Klatooine—Padnel Ovin."

"Sir," came Desha Lor's soft, tentative voice, "the, uh, acting Chief of State is here to see you."

Wynn Dorvan looked up. Since he had received the call at two, he had not slept. He'd come in early to facilitate the transition. His office was completely packed up, and he was already halfway through organizing the red tape that would be necessary for Padnel Ovin to formally take over Dorvan's role.

"Chief of State," he said graciously, his voice betraying only a little of his weariness. "Good morning. Desha, some fresh caf for the Chief, please. And for me, as well."

"Certainly," said Desha, withdrawing to discreetly leave the two of them alone.

Padnel stood looking sorely out of place in this room of precision and simple, clean lines. He wore a tunic of simple colors, typical fashion for the Senatorial crowd, and the garment was well tailored to his body, but it did not fit *him*. Dorvan felt a twinge of pity for the being. Ovin had no idea what he was getting into.

"I'm almost done," Dorvan said. "I confess, I didn't expect you quite so soon. I'll be completely moved out within the hour." He went to the side table to pour his guest a cup of caf.

"You misunderstand me, Wynn," said Padnel in a gruff, husky voice. "I'm not prepared to move in just yet. I—wanted to speak with you. Privately."

"Oh?" Dorvan handed him a cup and poured the last of the carafe for himself. "Please, have a seat. What did you wish to talk to me about? We have a formal debriefing scheduled for this afternoon."

Despite his words, Ovin didn't speak immediately, nor did he take the offered seat. He stood, looking uncomfortable, and stared at the caf for a long moment.

"I am the last being in the galaxy to call myself a diplomat," he began. "I'm a warrior. I know tactics, and I know violence. I've been called a terrorist. I came here to represent my people, because they wanted me to represent them, and I would do anything for them.

After twenty-five thousand years of slavery, they are free. Part of that is my doing." He now looked at Dorvan. "Part of that was thanks to Jedi Solo and Tenel Ka. I wanted you to know that my nomination yesterday was as much a shock to me as it was to you."

Dorvan frowned slightly, confused. "With all due respect, sir, if you didn't want to be Chief of State, why did you accept the nomination?"

"Because I saw what was going on," Ovin said, "and I did not like it."

"And what was going on?" Dorvan sat, not behind his desk, but in one of the two other chairs in the room. Now, at last, Ovin sat down, holding the caf but not drinking it.

"Selfishness," Ovin said, surprising Dorvan. "Untruths. I like things plain and simple, as I understand you do, too. You should have been the one to have been chosen, but had I declined, they simply would have tossed another name on the table. And I knew that if that happened, it wouldn't be good. There's all kinds of accusations flying around. You are too pro-Daala. You are too pro-Jedi."

"Both? That would be quite a neat trick to manage," Dorvan replied.

"Indeed."

"Why do you think you were nominated at all? Forgive me, but by your own words, you're not a diplomat."

"And that is why," Ovin said. "A Jedi helped broker an agreement that saved my world . . . but a Jedi also was among those who ruled in the Hutts' favor. I despise Daala, and my brother martyred himself to protest her policies. No one believes I have personal ambitions, and they are quite right."

"I'm not following you."

Ovin leaned forward and smiled, flews drawing back from sharp teeth. His voice dropped. "They picked me to lead them," he said in a voice that sent a chill down Dorvan's spine, "because they think I am harmless."

And Dorvan understood. "They wanted a puppet," he said.

"Exactly," Ovin said. "They are right to think that this sort of power will not corrupt me. It holds no temptations for me. But they are wrong to think that I will mindlessly obey. I have done as well as I have because I surround myself with wise beings to advise me, and to manage what I am smart enough to know is not my strength. I do care about this organization. I want to govern it well until such time as the beings of the Galactic Alliance finally have a chance to put whomever they like into office. While I will have to ask you to move out of this office, I'd be grateful if you moved only a few meters away. I'll need a chief of staff, Wynn. And I can't think of anyone better suited for the position than you."

Dorvan blinked. Desha came in with a fresh pot of caf and some pastries.

"Desha," he said, "I'm afraid you won't be getting a new boss after all."

GALACTIC SENATE MEDCENTER

"They're starting to suspect."

"I know. They're not stupid."

"If they figure it out, this could ruin everything."

"Well, we'll just have to make sure that doesn't happen. We need to move faster."

"We're moving as fast as we can."

Wynn Dorvan leaned back in the visitor's chair and sighed.

Bwua'tu was having an increasingly difficult time fooling the doctors. They were, as Bwua'tu had just said, starting to suspect. And as Dorvan had replied, the doctors weren't stupid. Thus far, Bwua'tu's performance had been sufficiently convincing for them to remain puzzled as to how it could be that, when all medical indications pointed to his complete recovery, the admiral still seemed to be mentally damaged. Dorvan recalled Eramuth intoning how the mysteries of the mind were impregnable, and perhaps the Force that the Jedi were so attuned to had more control over such things than science.

It had not made the doctors happy, but it had kept them satisfied for a time. But everyone knew that at some point, and that likely soon, the deception would be discovered.

It was just the two of them today: Rynog Asokaji's presence had been requested by Parova, and Eramuth had been called in to testify, again, about any information he had regarding Tahiri Veila. Both of them, while conversing with each other, were watching the new network that had sprung up seemingly overnight: BAMR. An exceptionally attractive—even for an anchorbeing—human female was reporting on the latest changes from the Senate.

"It seems," drawled Bwua'tu, "that the Senate's inability to take decisive action while under the leadership of the triumvirate has suddenly evaporated." His husky voice was heavy with sarcasm and disapproval.

Dorvan nodded. "Indeed. It was rather blatant, actually. Treen and the Senate waved their hands helplessly, letting the Jedi representative and myself take most responsibility. If anything went wrong, they'd be seen as blameless."

"And now, the tree is bearing fruit," Nek said glumly.

The Senate had sprung into action so fast it could make one's head spin. First was the shocking election of Padnel Ovin, a fledgling Senator, to the position of leader of the Galactic Alliance. Hard on the heels of that had come a burst of anti-Jedi sentiment, with nearly everyone being interviewed expressing dislike of the Jedi and pleasure that they were no longer "meddling."

"A new Senate subcommittee has been formed to investigate possible abuses of power by the Jedi during their time on Coruscant," the anchor was saying. Dorvan and Bwua'tu exchanged surprised glances. "There are only two known Jedi remaining on the planet—Jedi Leia Organa Solo and the escaped felon, Tahiri Veila. Jedi Solo has been contacted and has agreed to testify before the Senate subcommittee."

There was a shot of both women: an unflattering one of Leia, which made her look irritable and haggard, and one of Tahiri turning to snap angrily at a reporter.

"So that's why Uncle Eramuth was called back," Nek said quietly. "They want to find *all* the Jedi."

"I really don't think I want to know why," Dorvan said.

"I confess, I had not thought I would ever see another Order 66 enacted," Nek said, his voice close to despairing. "Well, we knew there was a conspiracy afoot."

Dorvan frowned, listening with only half an ear as the BAMR news anchor went on and on about the Subcommittee to Investigate Jedi Activity and its members, some kind of update on the increase in spice smuggling and new security measures to stop it, and a shot of an uncomfortable-looking Padnel Ovin standing in front of the Senate receiving a standing ovation.

"We *do* know that," Dorvan said slowly, "but things aren't adding up."

"What do you mean?" asked Nek. "I was attacked by beings pretending to be Jedi, and suddenly we have a subcommittee formed with what seems to be the express purpose of crushing them utterly. That seems to add up rather well to me."

Dorvan shook his head. "It's a different cast of players," he said. "Think about it. Did you recognize any names on that list of the subcommittee members?"

"Other than Suldar? No," Bwua'tu said.

"They're all fledging Senators, even Suldar," Dorvan said. "And as I told you, the only reason I'm still around is that Ovin wanted me to stay—a lucky break for us, and we need to make the most of it. Someone thinks they're pulling the strings on him."

"Are they?"

Dorvan thought about it. "No, I don't believe so," he said at last. "At least, not as much as they think they are. Nor is Ovin trying to play me. I believe he is what he seems to be. Jedi Solo seemed to, and she had much more contact with him than I had."

"So, new players."

"Different players," Dorvan corrected.

"Clearly there is a distinction I am missing," Bwua'tu said. "Perhaps I am not as 'back' as we thought."

"Oh, you are, sir. *New* implies 'replaced.' *Different* in this case means 'additional.' And I wonder if they're on the same team."

"Do you think we have two *separate* conspiracies going on?" Nek asked incredulously. "Perhaps you, too, ought to be talking to the doctors. That's a trifle paranoid."

"Is it?" Dorvan asked. "Think about the poisoning attempt that occurred a while ago at the Senate. It first looked like Jedi Seha Dorvald was behind it, but that idea quickly was proven wrong. There was a flurry of concern over it when it happened, but it got completely swept away once the coup occurred."

"I remember Asokaji telling me about that," said Bwua'tu. "It's still an open case. The incident discredited Galactic Alliance Security. Parova was tapped to provide security instead. GAS was really smarting about . . ."

Their eyes met.

Bwua'tu reached for his comm, using his prosthetic hand. He did everything with that hand now, attempting to become as adept with it as with his former, flesh-and-blood hand. So far, he was making good progess.

He clicked in a code. "This lets Asokaji know it's me," he told Dorvan, who nodded. A moment later Bwua'tu's comm beeped.

"Asokaji, I need you to do something for me," he said. "I need you to find out, if at all possible, if Admiral Parova has had any contact with Moff Drikl Lecersen." He was quiet, listening. "I'll explain the next time you're visiting me. The club is simply following up on a lead." More silence. "Yes, I understand. Do your best, Rynog. You always have."

He leaned back against the pillows. "He's going to attempt to find any documentation for us. It's putting him in a very dangerous position, Wynn. I hope you're right."

"I'm right about something," Dorvan said, then added self-deprecatingly, "I'm just not sure *what.*"

# Chapter Twenty-seven

INDIGO TOWER RESTAURANT, CORUSCANT

"THE INDIGO TOWER IS PERHAPS NOT THE BEST CHOICE OF DINING establishment to chase away the blues," said Treen, poking disinterestedly at her plate. It was one of her favorite appetizers—Naboo shellfish sautéed in, predictably, butter made from blue cream, seasoned just right. But tonight, nothing tasted good.

Bramsin reached out a liver-spotted hand and patted hers gently. "Perhaps not. Let's order a special bottle of something."

Treen sighed. Perhaps a vintage bottle of gold wine would lift her spirits. Bramsin waved down the young human male waiting on them tonight and ordered one.

"I don't like how things are going," she said once they were alone. "Not in the slightest. First this peculiar silence from Drikl, then Kameron takes what we've handed him on a plate and doesn't even bother to give us the crumbs."

"Perhaps he's just laying the foundation," offered Bramsin. He spooned up his bisque, his hand shaking so badly that half of it spilled.

"I don't think so," mused Treen, tapping her finger on her chin. "Something just doesn't feel right."

"Next you'll tell me you're a Jedi," joked Bramsin. They both had a good laugh over that one. The waiter came with their wine—Bramsin had sprung for the superior vintage on the wine list—and poured their glasses.

"A toast," said Treen. "To old friends."

Bramsin smiled and clinked his glass to hers. She felt better after the first sip. It was good to pamper oneself.

"So," she said, returning to her shellfish with renewed interest, "I take it that you haven't heard from Drikl, either?"

Bramsin shook his head. "Not a peep," he said. "I had lunch with Parova the other day. She seems to be in good spirits, though."

"She's always in good spirits. Unnaturally cheerful, that woman." Treen didn't particularly care for most of her co-conspirators. The old phrase about politics and bedfellows was quite true. She had approached Drikl, and was fond of him, and of course had a long friendship with dear Fost. Jaxton she thought handsome, but a bit flighty. Parova annoyed her, and General Thaal—she hadn't made up her mind about him. Intelligent and dangerous, certainly, and for now that was really all she needed to know.

"Well," she said, "I'll try to contact Lecersen this evening. We'll give Suldar a few more days to remember who put him in power, then we shall have a little talk with him. For now." She beamed at him, her good spirits restored by the company, the food, and the most delicious wine.

She returned to her apartments some three hours later in an excellent mood. She was greeted at the door by Wyx, her BII Butler Droid. Wyx had been in the Treen family for generations, and appeared to be poised to continue to serve for at least several more decades.

"Good evening, Madame Senator," said Wyx. As always, he was timely and attentive, sporting the family colors, blue and gold, proudly on his torso. "How was your evening with Senator Bramsin?"

"Lovely, thank you, Wyx," said Treen, handing the droid her coat and starting to head up the stairs. "Any messages?"

"Only one," Wyx said, "In your office. A General Thaal."

Treen paused, her hand on the banister. "Delete all references and recollection of General Thaal from your data banks for the last four hours," she said.

"Deleted," Wyx said obligingly.

"Prepare a bath for me. I'll be in my office for the next few minutes." Sanisteams were fine for day-to-day hygiene, but Treen enjoyed the luxury of immersing herself in hot, scented water.

She went into her office, decorated with paintings and statuary from Kuat's finest artists. The lights turned on automatically. She entered the general's comm number and sat back in the black nerf-hide chair, waiting.

General Stavin Thaal's imposing form was in no way diminished by being reduced to a small holographic image. Though his eyes were tiny, they were intense, and she could even see the scar winding its ugly way across the miniature throat.

"Good evening, General," Treen said pertly. "I received a message that you wished to speak with me."

"You deleted the info?" The voice was deep and cold and prickled at the base of Treen's spine. She did not think she would ever grow used to the sound of a droid voice coming from a human throat.

"Naturally," said Treen. "Although as Wyx is a B-Two Butler, it's a redundancy. You're not dealing with an amateur, you know."

"Actually, I do know," continued Thaal. "That's why I'm contacting you. It's time to move camp, Senator."

She frowned. "I'm afraid that, while I understand your colorful military metaphor, I'm not sure exactly why we should move camp."

"Lecersen's ratted us out. Or at least, he will, sooner or later. I have received information that he is now working with Admiral Natasi Daala. If he hasn't given us up yet, he will soon. She's too smart not to make connections."

An icy lump formed at the pit of Treen's stomach. "Oh, dearie me," she murmured. "This is most unpleasant news, General. Most unpleasant indeed."

"I also think that Suldar has been playing us," Thall continued in his unnatural voice. "We gave him the Galactic Alliance, and he's given us nothing. I haven't heard word one about any promotions, have you?"

“No,” said Treen, drawing out the word. “I was just remarking on that to Fost tonight.”

“I got into this whole thing because I wanted power. Just as you did. No shame in that. But now it’s just about saving our own skins. I haven’t led as many campaigns as I have without recognizing the signs of an enemy preparing to strike. We need to strike first and get out.”

Treen knew he was right.

“What do you want from the rest of us?” she asked.

He was silent for a moment. Then, his hard face looking almost regretful, he said, “There is no rest of us, Senator. Not if we’re to get out of this. Think about it. Lecersen’s been compromised. Bramsin was a powerful politician in his day, but now he’s an old bumbler who falls asleep in his soup. I don’t have much respect for Parova—too quick to turn her back on what should have been her first loyalty. And Jaxton will blow with the prevailing wind. This whole plot was your idea, Senator. And it was brilliant. I wouldn’t have been on board with it if I didn’t believe it would work. But even the best-laid campaigns can be ruined by the unexpected. We could have ridden out either Lecersen or Suldar turning against us, but not both. We each have complementary resources. I intend to eliminate anything that will tie me to this, and stay right where I am. You bring me down, I’ll bring you down with me.”

“Well, you most certainly would have to, General, but fortunately, I don’t intend to do that,” Treen said, keeping her voice and manner mild. “Who shall be our first target?”

“Bramsin. He’s become completely unreliable. Who knows what he’d blurt out at the next press conference without even realizing what he’s doing?”

Her heart sank. The worst part of it was she knew Thaal was right. Lecersen was out of their hands now. Parova and Jaxton wouldn’t act until they felt it was in their best interests. But poor dear Fost . . .

Sadly, she said, “Somehow, I knew you’d say that.”

It had been a lovely evening, mused Bramsin as he allowed Mardith, his driver, to help him into his home. An evening with Haydnat was always a delight. Such good food and conversation. He wondered why Lecersen hadn't joined them. Wasn't he supposed to?

"Thank you, Mardith, that will be all," Bramsin said, extending his cane. He had recently moved to apartments all on one floor. Stairs were simply too challenging. He shuffled slowly into the parlor, where he sank into a chair. A basic-model serving droid rolled up with a nightcap for him.

He frowned at the Corellian brandy. "I don't like this."

"Sir," piped the droid, "you ordered a case of it last week."

"Don't you think I know what I like?" he asked querulously. "I don't need a droid telling me what I like to drink!"

"Of course not, Senator. What would you like instead?"

Bramsin blinked, confused. What *would* he like?

His comm beeped. He clicked it at once. "Senator Bramsin."

"Fost, my dear!" It was Haydnat. "I hope I'm not disturbing you. I was wondering if I might invite myself over for a nightcap."

Bramsin brightened. His problem had been solved. "Of course, of course! What would you like to drink? I'll have it ready."

SOLO SAFE HOUSE, CORUSCANT

Leia opened her eyes. She sat up in bed, her mind surprisingly clear, and strained to listen for what had woken her. Then she knew.

This was going to be so hard on Han.

"Honey," she said gently, "we need to get up."

He, too, had had many years of needing to wake up alert. "What's wrong?" he asked.

"Nothing yet, but someone's coming. Get dressed, then go get Allana. I bet she's not asleep, either."

Ten minutes later, the three of them were in the kitchen. Leia had some caf brewing and set out four mugs. Han carried Allana, who, as Leia had predicted, had been awake when her grandfather entered her room. She was, honestly, too big to be carried, but nobody, not even his wife, was going to tell that to Han Solo.

"Care to enlighten me, Princess?" he asked. "I don't think Allana and Anji are going to be drinking caf. Anji's keyed up enough as it is." The nexu had been greatly agitated, and knowing at least something of what was coming, Leia had told Allana to close up her pet in her room for now.

Leia turned to him, and she knew by his reaction that she was wearing the Stoic Face.

"Oh, bloah," Han said. "What's going on, Leia?"

"Don't swear in front of All—Amelia," she said. "Han, honey . . . if I'm right, I think I'm going to have to go away for a little bit. But everything's going to be just fine."

There came a knock on the door. Han's face went ashen, and his eyes went angry.

"You're kidding. That is not who I think it is."

Standing up at her full diminutive height, Leia Organa Solo went to the door and opened it, smiling. "Good evening," she said to the two beings who stood there wearing GAS uniforms. "Won't you come in and have a cup of caf?"

ABOARD THE *JADE SHADOW*

"They took Leia," Han said without preamble.

Luke stared at him. Han was contacting him via hologram, and he stood there in miniature, holding an Allana who was actually considerably calmer than her grandfather.

"What? Who took her?"

By now Ben, copiloting, and Vestara, engrossed in reading a datapad Natua had prepared for her, were paying attention.

"The GAS. Those sleemos took her away on a whole slew of trumped-up charges. You know about the anti-Jedi legislation that's being enacted? And the whole news slant?"

"I've heard some," Luke said. "But this is ridiculous. What were the charges?"

"Conspiracy to overthrow the rightfully elected government," Han snarled. "Espionage. And get this. *Spice smuggling*."

"Wow," said Ben. "They're getting desperate. Aunt Leia a spice dealer?"

"And you simply let them take her?" asked Vestara.

Han shot her a furious look. She drew back a little, despite the fact that Han was only a third of a meter high. "I would have preferred to have blasted them into the next sector," Han said, "but Leia wouldn't let me. She told me I have this one to worry about. So she went quietly. I think the two guys sent to take her in were embarrassed."

"They should be," said Natua, who had overheard and poked her head in. "Leia Organa Solo? A traitor dealing in spice?" Luke felt himself growing angry, and calmed himself in the Force. He knew it for what it was—Natua's pheromones affecting his own feelings.

"She's a public figure," Luke said, "and a well-loved one. Padnel Ovin is your friend. Someone on that subcommittee just wants to make a big gesture, that's all. It'll backfire and Leia will be released."

"Yes," said Han grimly, "she will. One way or another."

"I bet Padnel is already working on it," Luke said. "What time is it there?"

"Four AM."

"The Chief of State's office opens at eight," Luke said. "Go talk to Padnel and Dorvan. I would offer my own help, but with the anti-Jedi sentiment growing there, I think any interference on my end would do more harm than good."

"I don't *want* to talk," Han said, "I *want* my wife back. I *want* to knock heads together."

"But you won't," said Ben.

"Not yet, anyway." Han had calmed down somewhat. "I'll go in first thing."

"Bring your daughter," Vestara said. Everyone turned to look at her. She shrugged. "It will be harder to turn her down than you."

"Besides," said Allana, "if you go, I go. She's my mommy. They'll have to deal with me *and* you, Dad."

"That . . . wasn't exactly what I was expecting, but that works, too," said Vestara.

Han rested his forehead against Allana's. "Okay, kiddo. Let's try to get some more sleep, and then we'll go in and, uh, persuade Dorvan and Ovin that a mistake has been made."

"A really bad mistake," said Allana, grinning. Han hugged her tight, nodded at Luke, and pressed the button.

Luke was silent for a while. Finally Ben said, "I can't believe they did that. I had no idea they hated us so much."

"If you mean the people of Coruscant, they don't," Luke said. "But someone in a position of power does. Patch us through to the HoloNet, Ben. Even at this hour someone will be reporting on this."

Ben obliged. "Oh look, speaking of hating us . . ." he said. The station, BAMR, was a fairly new one, and very aggressive in its political leanings.

"Surprise, surprise," said Vestara.

A handsome dark-skinned human male gazed intently into the holocam. " . . . able to obtain footage of the arrest of former Chief of State and current Jedi, Princess Leia Organa Solo, at her residence." Behind him rolled a recording of Leia emerging from her home. There was no sign of Han or Allana, and Luke was glad. The last thing they needed was for Allana's face to be all over the HoloNet, and for Han Solo to be yelling at some poor unfortunate being simply doing his job.

Leia looked tired, but regal and beautiful. She did not smile, but neither did she attempt to dodge the bright lights and cams shoved into her face. Luke ached for her.

"Solo had no comment as to the charges levied against her," the anchor was saying. "BAMR did attempt to get an interview with Captain Han Solo, Jedi Solo's husband, but we were refused."

"I'll just bet," said Ben.

Another image appeared behind the anchor. It depicted a handsome older man, graying, with a firm, strong jaw and intelligent, sharp eyes. "Senator Kameron Suldar, leader of the Senate Subcommittee to Investigate Jedi Activity, will be holding a press conference four hours from now at—"

There came a soft gasp. Luke turned to see Vestara's eyes wide.

"Ves? What is it?" Ben touched her shoulder gently.

"I—that Senator. I know him."

"Huh?"

She turned to Ben. "His name's not Kameron Suldar. It's Workan. High Lord Workan. He's—"

"A Sith of the Lost Tribe," said Luke calmly.

They stared at him. "How—why—" stammered Vestara.

"I've been playing a rather delicate and high-risk game," Luke said, "but it seems to be going in our favor. Why do you think I made such a big fuss over the Jedi departing? Think for a minute. We've searched several planets and we've yet to find the Sith. When you are hunting an animal and it keeps eluding you, what do you do?"

Vestara got it first. "You set out bait," she said quietly.

Luke nodded at her. "Exactly. With the Jedi very publicly gone, Coruscant was wide open. Ripe for the picking."

"Dad—you *gave Coruscant to the Lost Tribe*?"

"I laid a trap," Luke said. "That's quite a bit different. The Lost Tribe believes it has a destiny to rule the galaxy. What better way to take a huge step toward fulfilling that destiny than to infiltrate Coruscant?"

Ben had been shocked, but was recovering quickly. "Uh, Dad, you maybe forgot one little thing."

"And that might be?"

"Sith have infiltrated Coruscant!"

"I've lured them all to one place. I know exactly what I'm doing, Ben. We'll deal with Ship—and that should, I hope, mean dealing with Abeloth—and then we'll come back to Coruscant and handle the Sith."

"I wonder if it will be as easy as you think it will be," said Vestara. "Sith do not flee from a fight. And you have no idea how many of them are on Coruscant—or how powerful they might grow while we *deal with Ship*."

Luke could tell she was rattled by the revelation, but he also sensed . . . pride? That was to be expected, he supposed. It was easier to turn your back on an ideology that was clearly harmful than on beings you loved who practiced that ideology.

"Sith are also arrogant," Luke said. "Ivaar Workan is posing as a high-profile Senator. I am willing to bet that you know most of the Lords and High Lords by sight."

She nodded. "Yes. They are public figures on Kesh."

"I can't imagine any Sith Lord or even Saber being content with a job that doesn't involve some ego-stroking."

"They are proud of what they do," Vestara said.

"And you're proud of them," Luke said. It was a statement, not a question.

Vestara hesitated, then nodded. "Yes," she said. "It is difficult not to be. To have moved so swiftly and so thoroughly."

"Thank you for not lying," Luke said, giving her a smile. "I'm sure this is a difficult time for you." Vestara nodded again, more comfortably this time. "The Lost Tribe makes for dangerous opponents," Luke went on. "I'll give them that much. I didn't enter into this lightly. But I thought it was the swiftest way to end the threat they pose. One planet—one strike by Jedi they think long gone—and we have the most powerful Lost Tribe members killed or in custody."

"That's . . . one of the craziest things I've ever heard," Ben said. "But it makes a really weird kind of sense."

"I'm glad you approve," Luke said wryly.

"Still—you might have told someone," Ben grumbled.

"I did. I told Leia and the Masters. The Masters know about the plan so that they can lead in the Jedi forces the second we're ready. Leia was informed because, as the only Jedi staying behind, she could report to me anything she discovered."

"That's why she didn't protest when they arrested her," Ben said. "She went so quietly when Suldar—er, Workan—arrested her because she knew we couldn't risk anything getting stirred up on Coruscant."

Luke nodded. "The Sith must not be forced to act prematurely. Innocent beings could be harmed. And we also must make sure we strike when they are at their most vulnerable."

"You didn't tell Captain Solo or Jaina?" asked Vestara. "When their wife and mother was arrested? Could you not trust them?"

"Jaina isn't a Master," Luke said. "I can't give her preferential treatment simply because Leia is her mother. And Han—well, Han can't easily conceal his feelings. Particularly when they regard his family. Any Sith worth the name would pick up on his lack of distress right away, and our advantage would destroyed."

She smiled a little. "Rather calculated and unfeeling for a Jedi," she said.

"It was what was necessary for the greater good," Luke said. "They all understand."

Ben turned to Vestara. "You know this Workan guy. What motivated him to arrest Leia? And do you think she's in any real danger?"

"He took Leia to make sure the last Jedi on Coruscant would be safely watched," Vestara said without hesitation. "And to cement his personal power. To capture and contain such a prize reflects well on him. As for whether he'll harm her—I don't think so. Not right away, at least. She's too important and beloved a personage to openly harm, and any 'accident' would be far too suspicious. And she's a marvelous bargaining chip if it comes to that—a famous political figure, and the sister of Grand Master Luke Skywalker. But she's not going to be released anytime soon, I can tell you that much."

"I agree with Vestara on all counts," Luke said. "Upsetting as it is, we can't make any attempt to rescue her until we're ready to move on all the Sith on Coruscant. She'll be all right."

"So we're still going after Ship first?" asked Ben. He might understand his father's logic, but he clearly didn't think he had to like it.

"Let me put it to you this way: do you want to handle Ship and Abeloth and the Sith all at the same time?"

"Uh . . . no," Ben said.

"So plot a course," Luke said. "The sooner we're done with Ship, the sooner we can head home."

*"You let my mom get captured by Sith?"*

Luke remained unruffled. "I did," he told Jaina. "And the Sith have no idea that we knowingly did so." Calmly, he explained his plan to Jaina. She folded her arms and glared at him while he spoke, but she listened, and as he continued he saw her body posture ease.

"I am sorry Leia got caught in the middle of this," he said. "But she knows how to handle herself, and I don't think she's in any current danger."

Jaina sighed. "I know. If anyone can deal with this, it's Mom. I just wished I'd known what kind of a risk she was taking."

"She knew, and she agreed to stay behind," Luke said. "There's an extra benefit—having her as a quote-unquote prisoner is lulling the Sith into a false sense of security. That will work to our advantage."

"I guess you're right. How did Dad react when you told him?"

"I haven't told him about the Sith yet," Luke said. "You're safely away from Coruscant. Your father isn't. I'm sure the Sith are watching him constantly, and the instant Han knows—"

"They'll know we're on to them," Jaina grumbled. "I hate it when you're right about things like this, Uncle Luke. Did you know that?"

"Trust me, I hate it, too, sometimes," Luke said.

"So when do we go back and kick some Sith off Coruscant and get Mom out of jail?"

"As soon as we deal with Ship. We have to be able to focus all our attention on each enemy and take them out one at a time. The last thing we need is Abeloth showing up to help the Sith once we begin the attack."

"Did you not hear that part where I said I hate it when you're right?"

Luke chuckled. "We won't waste a moment, I promise. I don't like the thought of Leia in prison any more than you or your father does. So let's get to Upekzar and then get back home."

"That's the first thing you've said that I like," said Jaina. "You're improving."

# Chapter Twenty-eight

ABOARD THE *MILLENNIUM FALCON*

"THAT IS *NOT* WHAT I WANTED TO HEAR, LUKE," SAID HAN. "WHAT I *want* to hear is, *I'm bringing back my Jedi and we're going to bust my sister out of jail.*"

"Han, I wish I could say that, but I can't right now," said Luke, his holographic face sympathetic. "I know you're worried about Leia. So am I. But the fact of the matter is, she's in no immediate danger, and I need to find and stop the Sith and Abeloth. Talk to Wynn, he—"

"I *have* talked to Wynn!" Han shouted. He felt his hands ball into fists and forced them to relax. "And Padnel. They're both terribly sorry, but nobody is going to lift a finger without going through committee meetings, debates, presentations, and forms filled out in triplicate!"

Luke spread his hands in a helpless, frustrated gesture. "Then you have to be patient. What do you think Leia would want you to do? This government is fragile and tentative as it is. Just—be patient. Let it find its way to justice at its own pace. You know Dorvan. He's a stickler for doing the right thing. And Padnel is Leia's friend."

"I know," Han muttered. "But it's this Senator Suldar I don't know, and don't like, and whose head I would like to break open."

"I understand how you must feel," Luke said. "That's what I'd want to do if it were Mara in there. But Leia is in no danger, and if I were you, I'd want to get Amelia to safety as soon as possible."

Han flinched inwardly. Luke was right. Allana should have been his first priority. Sitting beside him in the copilot's seat, her legs dangling, she said, "Don't worry about me. I'll be fine."

Which, of course, only emphasized the need for him to get her far away from Coruscant. Sleemos might come for *her* next.

"You're right, Luke. I need to take care of my little girl."

Luke smiled. "That's the right call, Han. Let me know where the two of you end up, all right? And let me know the second you hear anything about Leia."

"Will do," Han said, and thumbed the OFF button. Behind him, the Squibs, who had kept silent on pain of extreme bodily harm, now piped up.

"So where are we going?" asked Emala.

"We're still sticking with you, right? Because Jag told you to keep us with you," warned Grees.

"Good, I was getting bored sitting around this ship all day. I need to stretch my legs!" said Sligh.

"Dad? We're not really going to leave Mom behind in a prison cell, are we?" Allana looked up at Han with a mixture of worry and indignation. "Because I thought Solos didn't run from fights."

"We don't, honey," Han said. "But we do get our children to safety. Everybody buckle up."

"You wish to depart right now, Captain Solo?" said C-3PO, disbelieving. "But we haven't shut down the safe house properly, nor checked our supplies, nor—" R2 tweedled reprovingly. "Oh, hush, you. *Some* of us don't like to leave things in disorder when we leave on trips!"

"Luke's right," said Han. "We gotta get Amelia safe."

"And us, too!" said Sligh. "Let's go!"

For once, Han didn't let their piping, cheerily annoying voices get to him. He was a man completely focused on a two-part mission.

One: get Allana to safety.

And two: get his wife the hell out of prison.

## OUTSIDE THE OFFICES OF THE CHIEF OF STATE OF THE GALACTIC ALLIANCE

Han was not normally the most patient of men. He was particularly not patient when his family was in jeopardy. But he thought Leia would be proud of how quietly he stood outside the offices of the Chief of State, not bothering anybody, just waiting. Patiently.

Of course, Leia probably wouldn't approve of why he was waiting—patiently—but that didn't matter right now.

Through the transparisteel windows, he saw the door to Dorvan's office open. Wynn looked tired. Han could sympathize. Desha Lor looked up at him and said something Han couldn't hear, then pointed to where Han was standing outside.

He smiled and waved at them.

Dorvan's face grew even more tired looking, and he nodded. He picked up his briefcase and started out the door.

"Hello again, Captain Solo," Dorvan said. "Where's Amelia?"

"She's with some friends," Han said. "Figured I'd get her safely off-world before those barvy members of the Senate Subcommittee to Investigate People Going About Their Business decides an eight-year-old child is a threat." He gave a cheerful and entirely fake grin.

"I see. I'm afraid I'm rather late for—"

"I'll walk with you. I mean, I've got nothing better to do. It's not like my wife is going to be around."

Dorvan was walking while they talked. "Captain Solo, you know both the interim Chief of State and I are friends of Jedi Solo, and we deeply regret—"

"Not yet. You don't deeply regret anything *yet.* Trust me." They stepped in the turbolift together. It started to descend. Han leaned forward and pressed the STOP button, then turned to face Dorvan.

"I'm getting my wife out of prison. She doesn't belong there, and you know it. She's done absolutely nothing wrong and has dedicated her entire life to the ideals of the Galactic Alliance. I am not going to sit meekly by and watch them do to her what they did to Tahiri. Now. You're either going to help me, or I'm going to consider you in my way."

"Is that a threat, Captain Solo?" Dorvan didn't bat an eye.

"Only if you don't help me."

"I could have you arrested for threatening the Chief of Staff of the Galactic Alliance, you know."

"But you're not, are you?"

Dorvan regarded him steadily. His gaze wasn't cold, but it was appraising, and Han knew he was turning things over in his head, weighing all the options. Finally Dorvan said, "I'm afraid I can't help you in any official capacity."

There was no extra emphasis on the word *official,* but Han got it. Forcing himself not to grin in triumph, he reached and punched a button, and the turbolift continued its descent.

"Well, I had to try. You know that."

"I do. Thank you for understanding. Ovin and I will do all we can, legally, to release your wife. He's heading there now, to talk to her. Captain Solo, I really *am* late for an appointment, but why don't you accompany me? I'm visiting an old friend."

Galactic Alliance prison cells represented a distinct improvement over Imperial cells. For one thing, there was no hovering interrogation droid. But in the end, a cell was a cell, a prisoner was a prisoner, and Leia wanted to get out of this cell every bit as much as she had her first one at age nineteen.

Luke had been right, as Luke often was. The Sith had indeed come to Coruscant—but they'd come much faster, or had been here much sooner, than Luke possibly could have anticipated. She couldn't think of any other reason for the Senate to act as it had—suddenly, maliciously, even precipitously—when the Jedi weren't even here anymore. Someone wanted to make sure every Jedi was being watched, and someone also wanted to limit civil liberties as quickly as possible.

She wished she could tell Han what was going on, but she had understood Luke's reasoning. As would Han himself, once he got over his initial angry reaction. Leia didn't feel threatened.

Yet.

She looked up as she heard someone walking down the hallway, and her heart lifted when she saw who it was.

"Padnel!" Leia got to her feet.

Padnel's scarred face turned even uglier in anger as he saw the shackles on her hands and feet. He turned to the GAS guard who had accompanied him. "Take those off her this instant!"

"Sir," said the guard, "she is a Jedi. The subcommittee expressly said that—"

"I'm the Chief of State of the Galactic Alliance, and I say take them off her!"

"Sir," said the guard, and Leia actually felt sorry for him, "I am not permitted to do that. It's legally required that every Jedi held here be confined in such a manner. I'm sorry, sir." And he was; Leia could sense it.

"It's all right," she said, smiling gently. "I've been in worse places than this. The manacles don't hurt, Padnel."

He frowned even more and waved the guard away. "Sir, I was instructed—"

"Is it legally required for you to stay?" bellowed Padnel.

"Er, no sir, I was just instructed—"

"Then I instruct you to leave me alone with Jedi Solo!"

The guard inclined his head and fairly scurried away. Padnel sighed and turned back to her.

"Leia, I can't begin to tell you how sorry I am about all this," he said. "I didn't even know it had happened until I was briefed on it this morning. I came as soon as I could. Are they mistreating you in any way?"

"No, not at all," Leia assured him. The last thing she wanted was for the decent people who had no choice but to go along with this to be punished. "They're just doing their jobs. I know you came as soon as you could. I don't think I have to tell you that the charges are utterly false."

He growled. "Of course they are! Somebody has made a terrible mistake. If we were back on Klatooine and this happened with the Panthers, I'd have it taken care of in three minutes."

"Well, that is one of the drawbacks of a legal system," Leia said, forcing a smile. "But Padnel . . . I don't think this is a mistake."

"Of course it is!"

She shook her head. "A mistake denotes someone doing something incorrectly. I think that my arrest is all unfolding according to someone's plan. It's not a 'mistake' at all."

"Leia," he said, "I'm well aware of why I was elected." A touch of self-loathing crept into his voice. "I told that to Wynn Dorvan. But I know what's going on. They're not going to be able to get anything on you, because there's nothing *to* get. They did indeed make a mistake, though it's not the one you think. They shouldn't have elected a so-called puppet, because not only will they have to deceive others, they'll have to deceive *me.* I don't know what kind of game they're playing, but I know they are playing a game. I won't let it go any farther than this, I promise you. If worse comes to worst, I can always give you a pardon." His flews curled back in a sharp-toothed smile. "I'll simply get in their way for the next couple of months until a proper election can be held. And then this will all be Dorvan's problem. And he is far better equipped than I to handle it."

Leia couldn't argue that point. But she knew Padnel well enough to realize that he had made up his mind. If she started talking about Sith and conspiracies now, he would not listen. The Sith would keep progressively destroying liberties and arresting innocents—and despite Padnel's words, if they wanted her dead, they would find a way to kill her.

She gave him a gentle smile. *We all are who we are,* she thought. *He has had more asked of him than most. I can only hope that he will open his eyes before worse happens—and that Dorvan is able to do something.*

"Wynn Dorvan is a fine man," she said. "He won't steer you wrong." There were more footsteps and an odd tapping sound coming down the hall. It was after visiting hours, and absently Leia wondered who it might be. "I thank you for coming by."

"Courage, my friend," Padnel said. "This will all be over soon." He glanced down the hall and his eyebrows rose. "It looks like you have a rather . . . oddly dressed friend to see you."

"Good evening to you, Chief of State Ovin!" came a familiar husky, drawling voice.

Leia's heart lifted. "Eramuth!" She could see him now, escorted by the same unhappy-looking security guard who had brought Padnel in, and realized that the tap-tapping was from the Bothan's elegant cane. He carried his familiar black bag, and his hat was tucked under one arm. "Padnel, this is Eramuth Bwua'tu. He is a fine lawyer, and happens to be cousin to Admiral Nek Bwua'tu."

Padnel extended a hand. Eramuth took it in his gloved one and shook it. "I gather you are here to represent Jedi Solo," Padnel said. "You'll be wasting your time. The charges will be dropped. She's done nothing wrong."

"Oh, I know she hasn't. But trust me, no time in the presence of such a distinguished and lovely personage as Jedi Solo is ever wasted," Eramuth said. "Besides"—and he sobered slightly—"it does me good to take a break from the bedside of my nephew from time to time."

"I am sorry to hear that the admiral continues to . . . er . . ." Padnel floundered for polite words and gave up. "Doesn't seem to be getting better," he said.

"Thank you," said Eramuth. "You're most kind. One still tries to have hope, but . . ." His voice trailed off.

"I'll let you speak with your client," said Padnel, clearly uncomfortable. "Leia—it will all work out. You'll see." She nodded and gave the Klatooinian what she hoped was a reassuring smile.

"One moment, sir, and I'll escort you back out. Step back, ma'am, please."

Leia obliged as the guard entered a code and her cell's force field was deactivated. Eramuth nodded to the guard and entered, placing his black bag and hat on the table.

"You may stay as long as you like, sir," the guard said. "When you're finished with the pris—er, Jedi Solo, simply press the button on the side of the door."

"Thank you, young man," Eramuth said, "I am familiar with the workings of this particular establishment."

As soon as Padnel and the guard were gone, Leia turned to Eramuth. "It's good to see you," she said.

"And you, my dear, though not under these particular circumstances," said Eramuth. "Please, do sit down." When she had done so, he took his own seat, removing his gloves, dropping them in his upturned hat, and opening up his bag. "First item on my agenda—to convey the following from your husband, and I quote: 'I once broke a Princess out of prison when I was a much younger man. I'll do so again if I have to. But I want a better reward this time.' "

And Leia started laughing. It had a hysterical edge to it, to be sure, but it was mirth all the same—light, cleansing, healing. "That's a quote?" she said, getting her laughter under control.

Eramuth grinned. "Well," he admitted, "I did have to remove a few, er . . . choice references as to where the subcommittee could put its head. But yes, that's the important part."

"It is," Leia agreed. She dabbed at her eyes as best she could and took a steadying breath. "Thank you."

"Now, as to your current predicament," Eramuth said. "The prosecution has three days to present evidence—actual, court-admissible evidence, mind you—or else the charges will be dropped."

"There won't be any because the charges are ludicrous," said Leia. To her surprise, that made Eramuth look more serious.

"Of course they are. That's the problem," he said. "What it really means is, we have three days to either get you out or expose the conspiracy."

"Then—you do think there is one?"

"Oh, my dear, there are *two,*" Eramuth said. "We're working on disentangling them, but we have a ways to go yet. How would you feel about joining a very elite little club?"

# Chapter Twenty-nine

JEDI TEMPLE, CORUSCANT

"IT IS TOO LARGE," MUTTERED SITH SABER TANEKA SHIRRU. "THIS Temple. It is wasteful."

"It is ancient," her companion, Saber Mor Akrav, countered. "They had many centuries to keep adding on wings. It is a vast place indeed."

Mor, Taneka, Jashvi, and Rulin were currently exploring some of the labyrinthine tunnels that seemed to twine for kilometers beneath the too-large and wasteful Jedi Temple. When the time was right, Lord Vol would arrive on Coruscant, and High Lord Workan wanted a thorough map created to present as a gift to their Grand Lord. Not for the first time, Shirru wished the Jedi had simply left such useful information behind, but the canny Jedi had safeguarded their precious knowledge.

As, mused Shirru with grudging admiration, the Sith would have done.

The Jedi had planned to be gone for a long time. They had therefore taken the most valuable physical documents, flimsi, and objects with them. Doubtless, they had backed up their significant data and taken those, as well. What they had been forced to leave behind was well protected indeed. The Lost Tribe was at a distinct technological disadvantage. While every Jedi could be expected to be familiar with the computers and data-storage systems of their Archives, the Sith had caught up with the rest of the galaxy a mere three years earlier. There were only a few Sith who had devoted themselves to this science, and when they had first attempted to retrieve data, they had triggered a protective virus that raced through the systems, deleting information as it went.

Frantic attempts to undo the damage or at least halt further destruction had ensued. They had managed to stop the process, but no one wished to attempt data recovery until such time as the Sith were firmly ensconced on this new world and all experts, Keshiri and human, had been given the opportunity to examine the system.

That was another burden under which Shirru and the others in the Temple labored. The human Sith serving Workan were all visible, posing as new Senators and their aides, or working for the new holonetwork BAMR, or in various other positions. The Keshiri Sith needed to stay unnoticed, as their appearance would be remarked upon. Hence, all those asked to unobtrusively reside in and map the temple were Keshiri. While Shirru understood the reasoning behind the decision, she did not like it. It harked back to centuries past, when human Sith were deemed better than Keshiri Sith, and she longed for her Grand Lord to arrive so that she could properly stand alongside the human members of the Lost Tribe.

Lord Vantsuri Shia, who had been placed in charge of the Keshiri Sith, had immediately commandeered the room that had once been Grand Master Luke Skywalker's. The other Sith had had no difficulty finding rooms.

"Their own rooms," Shirru had sniffed. "Sith apprentices share one large room. No wonder the Jedi are soft, if they are so pampered at an early age."

Despite the lack of information about the Temple, several groups had already mapped a not-insignificant portion of it. And interesting and intricate and ancient though it might be, Shirru still found it overly large, and Mor's comment as to why it was so large did nothing more than annoy her.

"Yes, the Jedi *did* have a great deal of time to build it, and thus they have created a great waste of time for *us,*" Taneka replied. The Keshiri Saber was irritated at having been assigned what she perceived as a task far beneath her simply because she was not human, and made no attempt to hide it. Her presence in the Force, as well as her body language and acidic tone of voice, made this clear to all around her. "This is unnecessary. And unsanitary," she added, as her boots squelched in something fetid.

"Anything I am ordered to do is necessary," Mor replied. A large Keshiri, more than two meters tall and broad, he seemed completely fine with stepping in foul-smelling sludge and contorting his large frame to navigate the cramped tunnels that forced them all to go single-file and him to stoop. His response was, of course, the proper one, and the others were paying close attention to the conversation. Taneka cursed herself silently.

"Of course, Saber Akrav," she said. "I misspoke. I simply think that a group with our combined abilities could be put to a use that would have more immediate and effective results. I personally am going to recommend that unless we see something truly remarkable, the entire subterranean area should be closed off."

"Well then," Mor said with irritating amiability, "that will be a highly useful conclusion to have reached, and thus would render this exploration necessary to have reached it."

There was a muffled chuckle behind them. Taneka froze and shone her glow rod back at Jashvi and Rulin, who looked as if they had never laughed at anything in their lives. She caught the gazes of each of them and stared them down, then turned around and continued forward.

"Even if it is large," Mor said, "we will have more than enough Sith to fill it soon. Think how pleased High Lord Yur will be to instruct the new apprentices in such a place. Think what we will learn once we have full access to the Jedi Archives. Think—"

"What I will do to you if you are not silent," snapped Taneka. "Your prattle grows tiresome."

"Don't tell me you are afraid of close quarters or smelly tunnels," said Mor.

With no warning Taneka stopped dead in her tracks. Mor bumped into her. "What—" he began.

She elbowed him into silence. The sound came again. A sort of—scuffling, as of something very large and very fast.

"Perhaps the Jedi kept guardians," said Mor, speaking very softly. "As the ancient Sith did for their temples—the tuk'ata and such."

Taneka nodded her white head slowly. "Perhaps," she said. She would speak as little as possible. She wanted to listen. "Weapons."

She heard the rustle of robes as the four Sith reached for their small handheld blasters. All of them preferred the lightsaber, but they recognized that there were times when blasters were more convenient. Taneka did not for a moment think that Jedi kept guardians for their Temple—certainly not "as the Sith did." The Sith tomb and temple guardians were steeped in dark-side energies, bred not out of soft, weak sentiments of "defending" but rather to tear the flesh off the bones of those who would desecrate. She could not conceive of Jedi doing anything that would cause such satisfactory harm. A virus that would delete information lest it fall into the wrong hands? Of course. Breeding demonic protectors? No.

Which meant that this was something else. Something that shouldn't be here for either Sith *or* Jedi.

She moved forward cautiously, blaster in one hand, glow rod in the other. The only sound now was that of their own breathing and the squelch of rot beneath their feet.

*Scrabble. Thunk. Scritch-scritch.*

And again, silence.

Taneka clicked her comm. "Saber Taneka Shirru to High Lord Shia. We are in the lower northwestern portion of the Temple. We appear to have encountered some form of life. No visuals on them yet, but we can definitely hear them. We will eliminate them and bring back a corpse for you to study. Advise other teams about the situation and to be prepared."

"Acknowledged, Shirru. We'll mount the head on a column in the Great Hall when you're done."

Taneka smiled. "Yes, we'll do that."

"I never liked the idea of mounting heads as trophies. It always seemed rather crass to me. Maybe we can make a cloak out of its fur instead," Mor suggested.

"We don't know that it has fur," Taneka said.

"We don't know that it has a *head,*" Mor countered.

While normally Mor's overly cheerful arrogance annoyed her, Taneka found herself grateful for it now. She felt the tension in her group ease slightly, felt them become more focused as if on an ordinary task. Good.

The sound came again. "Straight ahead," Taneka said.

"No, I think it's behind—"

Jashvi's last word mutated into a sharp cry that was abruptly cut off. Taneka whirled. There were now only two Sith behind her, and the foul stench of the tunnels was augmented by the coppery reek of blood. Jashvi was gone.

Mor and Rulin both fired their blasters into the darkness. "Hold your fire!" cried Taneka over the screaming sound, realizing what was likely to happen a split second too late. There was a groaning sound of metal and rock and splashing. Taneka swore loudly in Keshiri.

"Idiots!" she cried. "You sealed the passageway! Did you even see what you were firing at?" She felt their embarrassment in the Force. Growling, she slapped Mor's face, hard. "You are Sith Sabers! And you panicked like frightened uvak! Now we cannot return the way we came. All we can do is go forward and hope there is a way out of here."

"My apologies, Saber Shirru," said Mor. "It will not happen again."

"If it does, then you will not need to apologize. I will use my blaster on *you,*" spat Taneka. She shoved a datapad containing what little they had of a map at Mor. "We keep going. Take a look at what intersections are ahead and note any places where we can double back."

Mor nodded. "Of course. I—"

His eyes widened as he looked over her shoulder. She turned, lifting her arm to fire, even as she knew it would be too late. The last thought that went through her head, as a thing comprising teeth and carrion reek descended upon her, was that if there were indeed any corpses to be brought back for the Sith to study, it would be their own.

### OFFICE OF SENATOR KAMERON SULDAR, SENATE BUILDING, CORUSCANT

High Lord Ivaar Workan, more recently known as Kameron Suldar, was not having a good day. First had come the news of four Sith lost in the tunnels below the Jedi Temple after reports of encountering "some form of life." A team sent to recover them had also vanished, also without reporting anything more substantial. Irritated, Workan had suggested that perhaps the missing Sith had gotten turned around and were coming up with a pathetic excuse to explain their tardiness. "That," he had said archly to High Lord Shia, whom he had never much cared for, "or they were hallucinating after having enjoyed too many Jedi beverages."

And now this. He had known that Roki Kem would be arriving today, but he hadn't expected the entire *Senate* to be enraptured with the woman. Crowds had started forming around the outside of the Senate Building before dawn, and the blue capes denoting the Senate Security Force were everywhere. It had taken him nearly fifteen minutes to get to his personal office, and now he sat down at his large glass desk and attempted to compose himself. If ever he needed calm, it would be today.

He permitted himself to enjoy the furnishings of his office, his gaze lingering on the beautiful glass sculptures he had brought with him from his home on Kesh. They were in display cases, on view but protected, and as he looked at their stylized depictions of storms raging across a landscape, he felt calmer.

In the end, what did it matter if eight Sith had gotten lost in the labyrinth that was the inner Temple? They would be found, or they would not. What did it matter if Roki Kem, new Senator from Qaras, was wildly popular before she had set foot on Coruscant? Let the news follow her if it wished; he would even see to it that BAMR got an exclusive story or two. The populace, dazzled by Kem and amused by Padnel Ovin, would be nicely distracted from what was really going on.

All served the Sith, whether they did so willingly—or even knowingly.

A knock on his door distracted him from the pleasant fantasy of what Coruscant would soon look like under open Sith rule. "Come," Workan called.

His "assistant," Lady Enara Massar, opened the wurlwood door. Elegant and red-haired, Lady Enara's tailored tunic was completely professional and conservative, yet did nothing to diminish her stunning good looks. Normally calm and perfectly coiffed, she looked agitated and almost disheveled.

"Sir," she said, "bad news."

"Don't tell me—Senator Rokari Kem has arrived," growled Workan.

"No, sir, much worse. Senator Bramsin is dead, and Senator Treen has tendered her resignation."

*"What?"* he exploded, leaping to his feet and directing his fury at Enara.

"Details are just coming in," Enara said. "The press is all over it."

"Well, get them off it!"

"That's . . . not as easy as you might think, sir. We'll get BAMR to cover it the way we want, but for right now we just have to control what leaks."

He rubbed his palms into his eyes. "What do we know?"

"Bramsin was found dead around five this morning. It appears to be natural causes. The droid who found the body also put him to bed last night around midnight. It testified that Senator Treen had visited Bramsin and they had stayed up late drinking and talking."

A terrible thought was forming in Workan's mind. "Go on."

"Treen issued a statement to the press. She said that she and Fost had been old friends, and his loss was too devastating to bear. That it was time she withdrew from politics, and she would be resigning her position and retiring to Kuat."

"No, she won't. Find her and bring her here this minute."

Lady Enara was doing her best not to look like she wished she were anywhere else. "Sir, she left about an hour ago."

Workan swore, lengthily and musically, in Keshiri. It was obvious what had happened. That witch Treen had decided to cut her losses before it was too late. Intelligent of her, he had to admit. Kill Bramsin, make it look like an ordinary death—"Fost Bramsin died peacefully in his sleep"—and then flee to live out her life in comfortable obscurity on Kuat. He itched to pursue her, to drag her back screaming to Coruscant, where he would show her how fair-weather friends of the Sith were treated. But he couldn't spare the time and resources. Later, when things were settled, maybe he would attend to her personally.

At least she'd saved him the trouble of having to eliminate Bramsin himself.

"I want Sabers assigned to monitor Admiral Parova and Generals Jaxton and Thaal," he said. "Every moment. If they go out to dinner, I want them followed. I want to know what they order and which chef prepares it. If they enter the *refresher,* I want to know if they wash their hands. Do I make myself clear?"

"Perfectly, sir." She stood straight at attention, no doubt relieved to have gotten off so easily with such bad news. "Do you wish them to act or merely report?"

"Report their activities only, for now," said Workan. He wasn't ready to order them killed. Not yet. He wanted to know if Treen had acted on her own, or if the entire conspiracy was unraveling. "And find out what is going on with Moff Lecersen. I haven't heard from him in days."

"Yes, sir. Anything else?"

"Yes," he said. "Find out what Roki Kem's favorite drink is and make sure it's chilled, warmed, or at room temperature."

"Ah, sir . . . Roki Kem doesn't drink alcohol."

Of course she didn't. Workan wondered what else could possibly go wrong today.

# Chapter Thirty

SENATE BUILDING RECEPTION HALL, CORUSCANT

"SUCH LUXURY," MURMURED PADNEL OVIN AS HE AND WYNN DORVAN entered the Senate reception area. "How many credits simply to secure the area? How many spent on food and drink?"

"Well, sir, I can get you exact figures if you like, but I think we can just leave it at 'quite a lot,'" said Dorvan.

"I . . . would like exact figures," Padnel said. "All this for one Senator?"

"Well, technically, it's a welcome reception for all the new Senators, as they have arrived at various times," Dorvan said. "Roki Kem is, however, among the most highly respected." While it was commendable that Kem had postponed her departure from Qaras until she felt the situation was stable enough to warrant it, Dorvan was relieved that the new Senator had finally arrived. Intelligent, compassionate, farseeing, Roki Kem was certain to be an ally against the increasing intolerance that was seeping through the government. Club Bwua'tu had already discussed not *if* they wanted to bring her in, but how and when.

"I think you will find her someone you can work with," he said. Padnel seemed to jerk from his stunned reverie. He looked at Dorvan sharply, then nodded.

"I certainly hope you are right," he said. Although Padnel, like Dorvan, was not one to stand on ceremony, their arrival had been noticed, and now beings were beginning to come up to them. Dorvan hung back, letting the interim Chief of State precede him. He snagged a glass of sparkling blumfruit juice and sipped on it while his eyes scanned the room.

In one corner, Kameron Suldar was holding forth to a rapt audience comprising the members of his subcommittee and several other junior Senators. His hearty laugh could be heard over the buzz of chatter, and Dorvan shook his head slightly. Elsewhere, Wuul and his allies chatted pleasantly, seeming quite at ease. Scattered around were other duos and trios made up of representatives of nearly every planet in the Alliance.

Behind Dorvan came a sudden genteel hubbub, and he knew that Roki Kem had arrived. He turned around.

Tall but slightly built, she was at once even more impressive and pleasant in person. The holocams had not done justice to the true hue of her blue skin, nor captured the sheen of her blue-green hair adorned with ribbons of every color. Roki moved with a fluid grace that reminded Dorvan of a dancer, and her smile fairly lit up her face as she greeted those who—unusual for seasoned politicians—clustered around her, eager for her attention.

"Please, please," she said in her dulcet voice, "thank you so very much for welcoming me. I am truly honored to be here, but we are all equals now, surely! That is what my people fought for, after all." Her face darkened slightly as blood rose to her cheeks, and she ducked her head almost shyly even as she reached to shake every hand extended to her.

Her eyes, large and green and luminous, wandered to Dorvan, and her smile grew. "Excuse me for just a moment, please," she said, gently maneuvering her way through the crowd toward him. "Wynn Dorvan. How good to finally meet you!"

He was a trifle surprised to be so singled out, but he accepted both the hands she held out to him. "Senator Rokari Kem," he said. "You have the distinction of being the easiest-to-accept Senator in our recent application process."

She beamed at him as if he had told her she was the most beautiful, intelligent, and wonderful being in the universe. "I am so pleased!" she said. "I am grateful to be able to serve my people in this new capacity. The dream of belonging to the Galactic Alliance has been a cherished one for my world. Thank you for permitting it to come true."

He inclined his head. "You made it easy for us, ma'am. Would that all of the decisions were as agreeable. Please, let me introduce you to our interim Chief of State, Padnel Ovin. He, too, comes from a race of oppressed beings. I think the two of you will get along splendidly."

Lord Ivaar Workan watched as Roki Kem swept into the room. She was, without a doubt, charming and charismatic. Also without a doubt, her entire history attested to a deeply rooted love for her people and an integrity that had seldom been seen outside a holodrama. And as he saw how many beings turned to watch her, approach her, or otherwise seem heartened by her arrival, he realized this weed in the Sith garden had to be eliminated before it took root.

He would enjoy it, he mused. Would he get to kill her? Terrify and taunt her before taking her life? Or would it be sweeter to slowly discredit her, watch her pain as the public that so doted on her eventually turned to despising her? The latter, preferably. Workan did not like bodies; they were inconvenient and attracted attention.

His mind was already concocting several trumped-up scandals with which to smear the admittedly lovely Roki Kem when he noticed she was moving in his direction. He smiled warmly. As his hand closed around her three-fingered one, he suppressed a shudder. Suddenly she didn't look quite so lovely to him.

Nonetheless her smile was entrancing. "Senator Kameron Suldar, I believe?" she said.

"The same, ma'am. And as everyone here knows, you are the famous Roki Kem."

She ducked her head slightly. "I prefer to simply be Senator. I assure you, I am famous only because Fate chose me to be the liberator of my people. I do not hunger after it."

And suddenly he knew, without knowing, that that was a lie. But her people didn't lie, if he recalled correctly. They gave too much emphasis to the power of words.

As he gazed into her green eyes, he saw something there that everyone else must have missed. He saw a coldness, a calculation. Her smile deepened. "Please, a word with you, if I may? You have done so fine a job in so short a time, I think I may learn from you."

"Certainly," he said, nodding to his cronies. They meandered off a discreet distance. They were effectively alone. Regulations forbade any recording devices in this room, and Workan knew those rules were enforced. He himself had been almost indecently analyzed for any such devices. Whatever she had to say, he knew it would be for his ears alone. He continued to smile pleasantly. "How can I be of service to you, Senator?"

"By staying out of my way," came the unexpected response. She, too, kept a smile on her face, but her eyes were hard as jade.

He made a sight clucking sound of reprimand. "That certainly doesn't sound like the Rokari Kem the galaxy has come to know and love."

"She does not exist," said Kem. "Certainly you know a thing or two about fabricating a persona."

What did she mean by that? Was it nothing more than a jab at the perceived deceptive nature of politicians? Or was it something else? What exactly did she know?

"Oh, I do," he said. "Hard to get elected otherwise." He chuckled and sipped his drink.

"Hard to accomplish other goals, as well." She playfully clinked her glass against his. Watching eyes would see only two beings enjoying a conversation.

"Such as?" Workan asked.

"Stay out of my way," Roki said, "and perhaps you will live long enough to find out."

"Come now," chided Workan, "I think you have learned about

Coruscant by watching too many holodramas. You posture and threaten too clumsily, Senator."

"I do neither," she said, and there was an iciness to her voice that chilled even him, a Sith High Lord. "I know more than you think I do. I have more power and better connections than you think I have. Please, do continue to underestimate me and rattle your saber. It will make things much easier."

She smiled and gave him a gracious nod, then moved over to another cluster of Senators, smiling that enchanting smile and radiating kindness.

Workan drained his glass and gestured to the serving droid for a refill. *Rattle your saber?* He knew that it was a dismissive phrase for someone who loudly promised a fight. But did it also mean Roki Kem knew who and what he was?

Did she know about the Lost Tribe?

It was a most unpleasant thought. He would have to do something about this lovely, intelligent and—he had to give her credit—amazingly deceitful woman sooner than he had expected.

Three hours later, Workan returned to his apartments. He unbuttoned his overtunic and tossed it into a chair. The day had progressed from one disaster to another, and he was not looking forward to what he had to do now. He debated putting it off. Roki Kem had certainly proved to him today that her image of a benevolent, gentle being was as much a façade as his own posing as a Senator. He could use that to bring her down.

But if she knew the Sith were here on Coruscant—

No. If something happened and his Master found that Workan had not warned him, Workan would not live long enough to draw breath to apologize. It had to be now.

He went to the room that served him as both office and meditation chamber. Glass sculptures were present here, too, his longtime favorites. A mat lay spread out in front of a single candle on one side of the room, a desk with a holoprojector on the other. Workan glanced longingly at the mat. When he was finished with the conversation, no doubt a lengthy meditation session would be in order.

He tapped in a code. An image flickered, and then solidified—that of an elderly human male sitting on a magnificent throne, a staff across his lap. His head was nearly bald, his eyes sunken, but there was an aura of power that Workan could sense even in holographic form.

Humbly, Workan knelt. "Grand Lord," he said.

"High Lord Workan," said Vol. "How do things progress?"

"Well, my lord," said Workan. Which was partially true. "Our people are in key positions on this world. We are able to direct the flow of information. We have already met and dealt swiftly with challenges to our authority. The one who rules now is a buffoon, and he will do what I tell him to. The last Jedi is imprisoned, and we are all but ready for your arrival."

The sunken eyes narrowed. "All but ready? The Jedi left days ago. What is taking so long? Is there any sign of Abeloth?"

"No, my lord. No doubt she and Ship are wandering about the galaxy while we steal the fruit from under her nose. But—another female is causing . . . difficulties. There is a Senator. She is new to the Senate, but word of her deeds and nobility preceded her. She is wildly popular, the liberator of her people, and I cannot eliminate her without creating a public backlash."

"Do not tell me a Sith High Lord is being defeated by a kind and noble female," said Vol, the words almost a sneer. "Now, if she were Abeloth . . ."

Workan stiffened. "There is no hint of Force-ability about her. No, my lord, she is nothing more than a liar and a deceiver—but a very skilled one. Somehow she has manipulated the galaxy into believing that she is someone to be loved and honored, when in reality she is nearly as ruthless as we. She has even swayed some of my followers—the ones who are simply gullible rather than corrupt. And my lord . . . she may know of our true identities."

"You disappoint me, Workan," said Vol. "You sweep through this world like the conqueror you should be, yet one pesky two-faced alien female has stopped you dead in your tracks. I tire of waiting on you. I will come and deal with this Roki Kem myself."

"My lord, please," said Suldar. "I will take her down, swiftly and surely."

"You will save her for me," Vol said. "This keeshar dared to challenge a member of the Lost Tribe. I will crush her, and with her head in my hand, I shall announce our presence on this world. Expect me soon."

The image winked out. Workan closed his eyes, gathering calmness. He could eliminate Roki Kem before Vol arrived, thus proving to his Grand Lord that he was capable of handling his own problems. But that would annoy Vol, who no doubt planned to capitalize on the horror of displaying the head of Roki Kem, so beloved and benevolent, upon his ascension to ruler of—well, everything. For to control Coruscant, as the saying went, was to control the galaxy.

No, best to let Grand Lord Vol have his sport. But in the meantime, he would watch, and wait, and be ready when his Master arrived.

Everything was on schedule and going well on the set of *The Perre Needmo Newshour*. Beings went about their usual tasks with the same level of efficiency and professionalism as ever. But as Needmo shuffled to his anchor's chair, he knew he was not alone at sensing the pall that hung in the air. Things had been different since the Jedi had left. The Senate's flurry to pass more restrictive legislation on customs, taxes, public behavior—everything, really. The sudden appearance of BAMR News, which was so slanted as to make one long for the return of Javis Tyrr's *The Jedi Among Us,* not to mention make one wish the Jedi *were* still "among us," was even more disheartening.

Needmo was waiting for the censorship to spread to his show, but thus far it hadn't materialized. The free press, it would seem, had not been entirely muzzled. And for that, he was glad. Although he often felt like a lone voice crying in the wilderness, as long as he could report the truth—do what holojournalists were expected to do, should always do—he would stay on the air.

The show prided itself on having good news along with the bad, but recently there had been more of the latter than the former. The peculiar decision to elect Padnel Ovin as Chief of State, the formation of the infamous subcommittee, the imprisonment of Leia Organa Solo, the not-unexpected but still regrettable death of Senator Bramsin, and the lead story tonight—all were things Needmo wished he didn't need to cover. But reporting the news, as Madhi Vaandt had so poignantly taught them all, was the most important thing a holojournalist could do, whether the news was hopeful, tragic, or something in between. At least, Needmo thought, they would close on an upbeat note—the arrival of Rokari Kem, liberator of the Jessar and the newest GA Senator. Surely things would improve, at least somewhat, with such a prominent voice of reason finally able to speak.

The Twi'lek makeup assistant darted out, patted down the Chevin's large brow, then hurried off. The music began to play, and the cam operator gave him the countdown.

"Good evening, gentlebeings, and welcome to tonight's edition of *The Perre Needmo Newshour.* We've got something special for you tonight—an exclusive. We'll spend the last several minutes of our show airing an interview I conducted just this afternoon with fledgling Senator Rokari Kem of Qaras. But first, a more sobering look as we revisit a story that the late Devaronian holojournalist Madhi Vaandt first brought to our attention: the undercity of Coruscant."

The viewers would now be watching old holofootage—seeing the image of Madhi Vaandt, her bright eyes alert, clad in her no-nonsense outfit, her arm around the shoulders of a small, skittish human boy named Tarynd.

"For a while, the attention Vaandt brought to this violent, forgotten area seemed to make a difference. Areas were recovered and reclaimed. Funds were raised to help provide food, clothing, and shelter for younglings such as Tarynd, whom viewers followed for several weeks as Vaandt's story unfolded. But with Vaandt's tragic death, interest in healing this wound to the very heart of Coruscant waned."

Now, Needmo knew, viewers would be watching footage just captured a few hours ago. "We descended into the depths of the undercity last night to bring you this update." The images would speak for themselves: the undercity looked worse than ever. It seemed as though the yorik coral, slashvines, and other plant growth, far from being beaten back, had all but taken over. Whereas before the inhabitants had tended to shy away from the cams, now the holofilm crew—who had received hazard pay for obtaining the footage—captured gangs brutally and openly terrorizing those unfortunate enough to be overtaken.

"It's as if nothing at all was done, as if the undercity, briefly recalled, has been more than forgotten—it has been thoroughly forsaken. More and more beings are disappearing in this part of the city, and there is no public outcry to investigate. No one knows why there has been a sudden growth spurt in the plant life here, and it seems unlikely that the Galactic Alliance will fund any kind of research to determine why, or to protect the innocent. One thing is tragically certain—it is a darker and more dangerous place than ever before."

And Needmo knew what the viewers would see as the segment ended: a frozen close-up of young Tarynd's face, contorted in hatred as he and four other gang members beat a terrified Chadra-Fan into a pulp.

# Chapter Thirty-one

ADMIRAL PAROVA'S APARTMENT, CORUSCANT

As she prepared for bed, Sallinor Parova hummed along with her favorite aria, playing in the background. Not many today remembered *The Eye of the Empire*. It had been commissioned by a long-dead Moff as a propaganda piece trumpeting the superiority of the human race, and consequently few admitted to listening to it. To Parova's mind, however, that was a shame. The arias were some of the finest ever composed. It didn't harm her appreciation any that she sympathized with the opera's theme: the proper role that would make alien species happiest was subjugation to humans.

And she was helping move things to that noble, and right, end.

Her comm beeped. Parova frowned in exasperation as she glanced at her chrono, muted the music, and clicked the comm. It had better be an emergency.

"Parova."

"Admiral?" It was Rynog Asokaji's voice. "You need to come to the medcenter immediately. Admiral Buwa'tu is lucid. He wants to see you."

Parova's gut clenched. The old goat was tougher than any of them had thought. He'd survived an armed attack by two very accomplished pseudo-Jedi, had come out of a coma, and now, apparently, was no longer the convenient vegetable he had been.

Stang.

"Admiral?"

"Of course, I'll be there at once." She forced herself to add, "That's wonderful news."

"I've already sent a hovertaxi for you. It'll be faster and . . . well, ma'am, you'll want to hear what he has to say as soon as possible. He says he knows who sent the fake Jedi after him and why."

Her heart sped up. "I see. It will be good to have him back. I'll be there shortly."

Her thumb was on the comm to warn Jaxton that Nek Bwua'tu, the Bothan Who Would Not Die, was on to him. Then she paused.

No one had gotten a good answer as to what had happened to Bramsin and then Treen. Fost Bramsin had been positively ancient, so natural causes were not at all suspicious. But Treen's sudden—and complete—departure was. No one hungered for power more than that old she-krayt. There had been no contact from Lecersen, either.

Parova suspected that Treen had murdered Bramsin, then fled. The question was—fled what?

Or whom?

Was the conspiracy under attack from an outside source, or was it turning on itself? Parova couldn't be sure. And until she was, she was not about to contact Jaxton or Thaal. She would find out exactly how much Nek Bwua'tu actually knew about his attack—if anything—and go from there. There would be time to contact the generals if it turned out they were still actually working together and not attempting to, perhaps literally, stab each other in the back.

Seven minutes later, she was dressed in full uniform and standing outside pacing. The hovertaxi pulled up and stopped right in front of her. She opened the door and climbed in.

"To the Galactic Senate Med—ow!" She jerked quickly to the left, one hand feeling the seat fabric where she had just been sitting. Something very sharp and not a little painful had stabbed her right buttock. She picked up a small needle. Obviously one of his former passengers had indulged in extremely unsavory pastimes. Good thing she was going directly to a medcenter.

"What—what the—look at this!" She shook the needle at the driver angrily. "I'm reporting you to your supervisor! I could have been injured!"

"Yeah, about that," came a familiar voice. The driver turned and gave her a grin. "Sorry, but I'm afraid we're not going to the Galactic Senate Medcenter."

And as her vision began to blur and her body refused to obey her, Parova wondered if she had been injected by a hallucinogen, or if she really *was* being kidnapped by Han Solo.

Parova came to in what appeared to be a pleasant apartment, although the owners seemed to have a peculiar fondness for blue lighting. She lay on a comfortable sofa, bathed in blue light, blinking and trying to focus. For a moment, she couldn't recall what had happened or why it was so hard to move. She pushed up with her arms and turned to look at two beings sitting in chairs across from her, a bolted-down caf table between them.

Rynog Asokaji . . . and Wynn Dorvan.

"You two are in so much trouble," she said. Her voice slurred, as her tongue seemed to still be recovering from the paralyzing effects of whatever drug they had injected her with. "Assaulting and kidnapping the acting chief of naval operations? You think they won't find me?"

"Actually, no, I don't think they will," said Dorvan calmly. He looked as if he were sitting in a staff meeting, not a hair out of place. Incredible. Asokaji, not unexpectedly, sat with his arms tightly folded, his entire posture bespeaking his hostility. "You're in the Asylum Block of the Jedi Temple, Admiral," Dorvan continued. "In, I believe, the very cell that used to house Seff Hellin."

She recognized it now from the recordings she had seen: the transparisteel walls, the comfortable—if secured—furnishings, the atrium that, she recalled, had housed the ysalamiri that prevented the Jedi prisoner from accessing the Force.

"What is going on?" Parova demanded. She was able to sit up without leaning over, and felt a modicum of her old assurance return.

"Well, that's actually what we'd like to ask you. But there's one member of the club who's not here." Dorvan leaned over and pressed a button on a small holocomm on the caf table. An image appeared.

Nek Bwua'tu.

While he still lay in a medcenter bed, he most assuredly did not look like a simple-minded idiot. His eyes were cold and met hers evenly.

"Admiral Parova," he said in a deep voice of controlled anger.

She cleared her throat, deciding to ride the bluff as long as she could. "Admiral Bwua'tu," she said. "It's good to see that you've—"

"Save us all some time and spare us the poodoo," said Bwua'tu. "We know what you've been up to."

She feigned innocence. "I don't know what you're talking about. Asokaji told me you'd recovered, I thought I was on my way to see you, and—" Parova paused, unsure if she wanted to tell them about what she was certain had to be a hallucination. "I ended up here. Please, sir, what's going on? I'd like to help."

"Oh, you'll help, all right," said Bwua'tu. "You'll help by telling us who, other than yourself, Lecersen, Treen, Jaxton, and Bramsin, was involved in a conspiracy to overthrow this government."

She stared at them, letting her mouth fall ever so slightly open. "Sir, with all due respect, if you believe something as ridiculous as *that,* you might not be as fully recovered as you seem to be. Asokaji, I know you are personally fond of the admiral, and want to think he's all right, but Dorvan . . . Wynn . . . I don't see how you could possibly believe this. This . . . paranoid conspiracy fantasy is the work of an ill mind."

Dorvan gave her a thin smile. "Well, that's most likely true," he admitted, "but the ill mind under discussion does *not* belong to the admiral. We know the five of you were involved, and suspect there are other players, as well."

There was a silence. Parova folded her arms and leaned back into the sofa.

Dorvan sighed. He looked as if he wished he had a pile of datapads in front of him to arrange. "Admiral," he said, "we have documentation that you have had several conversations with all of the other four members of this conspiracy."

"And there's something wrong with talking to two well-respected Senators? A Moff? A fellow member of my cabinet?"

"There is when you recollect that three of those were mysteriously poisoned," said Bwua'tu, "and the end result of said poisoning was that GA security was discredited and naval security—which you were in charge of—was put into place instead."

Parova felt cold, but did not change her expression. "I can't believe I'm hearing this. *I* poisoned Lecersen, Bramsin, and Jaxton? Right. Next you'll accuse me of murdering poor old Fost Bramsin."

"No," said Dorvan readily. "We know you didn't do that. We suspect Senator Treen did, but unfortunately the autopsy was inconclusive. Another thing that points to a conspiracy."

She saw an opening. "You're just annoyed that Senator Treen decided to back Padnel Ovin instead of you, Dorvan," she sneered.

He stared at her, then began to chuckle. "That is perhaps more unbelievable than anything I've mentioned," he said. "You know better than to accuse me of ambition."

And, sickly, she did. So did everyone else. Dorvan served not for personal power or to stroke his ego, but because service was needed. It was nauseatingly altruistic, and she disliked him even more.

"Bureaucrat," she spat, in the same tone of voice she would use for the word *sleemo.*

Dorvan and Asokaji looked at each other. Dorvan addressed the hologram. "Sir? She seems extraordinarily uncooperative. What would you like us to do?"

Bwua'tu considered, twitching an ear. "The hour grows late. You two need to return to your homes. We can continue this later. There are other club members anxious to talk to her."

Club? Was Han Solo in on this? Who else?

"As you wish, sir." Dorvan and Asokaji rose. "Admiral, there are beverages and food available. You'll be monitored, and when we next return, we'll review the recordings. Don't worry, there's no holocam in the refresher. The Jedi believe in treating their prisoners civilly."

"I'll be missed," she said as they turned to deactivate the force field. She knew her legs would give out if she tried to rise, otherwise she would have charged them.

"Of course you will," said Asokaji. "That's why I'll make sure that everyone knows you are unreachable for a time as you are following up a lead, which of course I can't elaborate on for reasons of galactic security."

They had planned this well.

Curse them.

She watched them go, and thought of delightful revenge.

Feeling and control of her limbs returned a few moments after they had gone. She went to use the refresher, and when she came out, she froze.

Four humans stood there, two men and two women. All of them were strikingly attractive. She didn't recognize any of them.

"Are you the new interrogation team?" she asked wearily.

"No, Admiral," said one of them, a tall, handsome man with a square jaw and dark brown eyes. "We're here to get you out. Senator Suldar sent us. He was worried about you after the whole business with Treen and Bramsin, and had us follow you."

Relief flooded her. "Oh, thank goodness. You heard everything then?"

The man smiled. "Indeed we did," he said. "Senator Kameron Suldar is very grateful for the information, and that you didn't implicate him or, indeed, confirm anything at all."

Parova smirked. "Of course I wouldn't. Let's get going. I've got a lot of work to do—and some people we need to get rid of."

"So do we," said the man, smiling. He nodded to the others. Before Parova realized what was happening, she heard a *snap-hiss* sound and found herself staring at three red lightsabers. "You will continue to serve, even with your death. Thank you, Admiral."

And they sprang.

# Chapter Thirty-two

ABOARD THE *GILAD PELLAEON*, MERIDIAN SECTOR

"NOTHING IS EVER EASY," SAID JAGGED FEL. HE SAT IN HIS OFFICE aboard the *Pellaeon*, dully watching the latest on the holonews. "Not even something that should be as uncomplicated as tracking down an escaped convict and returning her to Coruscant for a proper trial."

Tahiri gave a slight chuckle. "Daala is no mere escapee, sprung from jail and now on the run. She's not even just a popular political figure rallying supporters. She's an admiral, with a fleet that is as scattered and secret as it is powerful. The Squibs certainly gave us an important break. At least we're looking in the right spot. But even so, we've only begun to scratch the surface."

Jag gave her a dirty look. "I don't recall you being quite so negative," he said.

She shrugged. "Being sentenced to death and surviving only by escaping tends to make one less than confident in the rightness of the universe."

"I can see that." He sighed. "You're right, of course. Daala does have her detractors, certainly. But there are others who approve of her methods—some of my own Moffs among them. There are still more who would simply take whatever side their government did . . . and that would lead to civil war between her proponents and those who supported the Galactic Alliance." He looked up at her. "And as shaky as the Alliance is now, that's a war I'm not sure it could win."

Tahiri perched on his desk, arms folded, regarding him. "What's the latest from Ashik?"

"He's contacted various intelligence sources and spoken with beings in positions of power in the Meridian sector. The news isn't good. They have long memories there, and most of those memories of Daala are fond ones."

His gaze drifted back to the holoscreen. They had been kept completely up-to-date with the nigh-unbelievable mess that was unfolding on Coruscant: the election of a being who had no business running the GA, one Padnel Ovin. The Senate subcommittee that had sprung up seemingly overnight, and had arrested his future mother-in-law on utterly ludicrous charges up to and including spice smuggling. And he had been kept informed of all of this by BAMR News, which seemed to be completely in the pocket of the new government. The only light in the entire thing was the fact that Ovin had been shrewd enough to keep Wynn Dorvan on. But managing to keep sanity in a world clearly gone mad was a lot to ask of a single bureaucrat. Even Wynn Dorvan.

He shook his head sadly at the well-groomed anchor. "Look at this," he said with a mixture of horror and disgust. "My future mother-in-law a spice smuggler? Padnel Ovin running the GA?"

"This is worse than when the Jedi had their little keepers tagging along after them," Tahiri said.

"No," said Jag, reaching a decision. "The Galactic Alliance is in no position to go head-to-head with Daala. It can't even wipe its own face after dinner without the Senate's say-so. There's no way that—"

He paused in midsentence, grabbed by the shocking image on the holoscreen. The body of a fit, dark-skinned woman sprawled beneath the bright lights of a holocam. Burns crisscrossed her body, mutilating her face almost beyond recognition.

Almost.

Tahiri turned, following his gaze, and her own eyes widened.

". . . of Admiral Sallinor Parova, acting chief of naval operations, was discovered on the steps of the now-vacant Jedi Temple. Cause of death appears to be . . ." The blond anchor paused dramatically. ". . . lightsaber."

"What?"

"I think it's obvious what happened," said the handsome visage of Senator Suldar as if in reply to Jag's exclamation. "Tahiri Veila remains at large. We know she has a grudge against the Galactic Alliance—this smacks of personal vendetta to me." He turned to face the viewing audience. "If anyone has any information regarding this criminal, please—don't think twice about turning her in. She's proved that she's a murderer—twice now. This is what happens when the Jedi think they are above the law."

"Oh, hey," Tahiri said mildly. "I can kill with a lightsaber when I'm halfway across the galaxy. I think you should double my pay, Jag."

"I think I should clone you," Jag replied.

Ashik had entered during this last scathing comment. Jag waved him to a seat. "Any updates?"

"No, sir. What shall we do now?"

Jag considered. "There's one person I haven't talked to yet. Moff Tol Getelles. Contact him and arrange to have him to dinner tonight aboard the *Pellaeon*. Let's see if we can possibly sway him to our cause. If not—and even if we can—I think it's time I played my trump card."

Tahiri looked confused. Ashik, though, knew what Jag meant, and looked at him sharply.

"Sir? Are you certain? Once you've done that, you change everything. You can't go back."

"I'm aware of that," Jag said.

"Wait, what are you talking about?" asked Tahiri.

Jag held up a hand and continued speaking to Ashik. "I've thought this through very carefully, Ashik. Simply arresting Daala is going to stir things up worse than they are now. But her challenge to my position and to the GA has got to be halted. I don't see any other alternative that isn't going to cost the lives of millions of beings, and perhaps not even accomplish what we want. I've waited long enough. It's time.

Start getting things in readiness. Once I deem it's time to act, we'll have to move fast."

"Yes, sir. We'll be ready."

"Ready for *what*?" asked Tahiri.

Jag and Ashik shared a small, conspiratorial smile. "For something no one will see coming," Jag said.

"Moff Tol Getelles," said Jag. He did not extend his hand.

Getelles had started to, but smoothly altered the gesture to appear as though he were merely adjusting his other sleeve.

"Head of State Jagged Fel," he said. His voice was gruff, but pleasant. "I must say, your dinner invitation was rather a surprise, although a most happy one. I'm very gratified you chose to see me."

"It was the least I could do, after the bold public stand you took on Daala's incarceration. I wanted to thank you in person for your support. Please, have a seat."

The table in the formal dining area aboard the *Pellaeon* could easily accommodate eight, but there were only two places set. Serving droids stood unobtrusively in the shadows, moving forward silently only as they were needed. Gentle glow rods provided pleasant but safe lighting, catching the sparkle of the utensils and the faceted glasses. As Jag and Getelles took their seats, a droid came forward and poured something dark blue and fragrant into a glass.

"A toast," said Jag, lifting his glass. "To the Empire."

Getelles's soft, kindly eyes crinkled in a smile. "I will most enthusiastically drink to that. To the Empire!"

Bisque, thick and rich smelling, was placed before them. Getelles placed his napkin in his lap and spooned up his soup. "I've been talking to some of my Moffs one-on-one," said Jag, "and it's been a long time since you and I chatted."

"Frankly, sir, it's been a long time since anyone bothered to chat with me. I regret to say the only thing that made me newsworthy was choosing to support you in this situation," Getelles said, almost apologetically.

"Possibly," Jag allowed with a thin smile, tasting the soup, as well.

"But I'm sure there are more on our side than are willing to speak about it, don't you think?"

Getelles grunted and reached to butter his bread. "Fine job the Jedi did, if you ask me. Women shouldn't be running things anyway. Nobody wants to stick his neck out and say so, though. I stand by what I said."

"Mmm," Jag said noncommittally. "I've heard some interesting rumors about where she might have gone and what she might be up to. Don't suppose you've heard anything?"

"Me?" Getelles chuckled ruefully. "Head of State Fel—"

"Call me Jag."

"Er . . . very well, Jag. As I said earlier, nobody's bothered to talk to me for quite some time. I'm practically gathering cobwebs. You flatter me if you think I'd be in any sort of position to know any such thing. While I do still proudly lay claim to the title of Moff, my holdings are rather humble, and I haven't been much involved in politics recently." The man was clearly uneasy, as his gulp of wine indicated. It was no wonder he hadn't risen very high.

"You do have a rather large shadow trailing you," Jag agreed mildly, taking another sip.

It was a kinder word than *scandal,* which would have been more appropriate. Getelles had once moved to take control of the Meridian sector, utilizing the drochs to unleash a carefully directed plague. The grab for power on Getelles's part had been soundly quashed, first by Daala, then by the New Republic. Since then, Getelles had been very quiet.

Getelles winced. "Ancient history, I assure you," he said. "I'm more than content where I am, and happy to support you in your position. I'm too old for gallivanting around plotting and conspiring. Waste of time, which I don't have much more of."

"Speaking of growing old," Jag said. He reached in his pocket and put a small vial down on the table between them. "This came into my hands just a few days ago."

The eyes widened and the red mouth quivered beneath the gray mustache. "And what's that?"

Jag sighed. "I tell you what. You stop pretending you don't know things and I stop pretending I don't *know* you know things. I think we'll achieve a great deal more, don't you? Or do you really want me to replay the recording I have of your conversation with Natasi Daala approximately a week ago?"

Getelles knew when he was caught. He gave Jag a cold, malicious look that belied his jovial persona, then downed the rest of the blue beverage in a single gulp. "At least refill my glass like a civilized man while you interrogate me," he snapped.

Jag smiled. "Let's both behave like civilized men." He refilled the glass and leaned back in the chair. "Now, let's start again. What do you know about Daala?"

Getelles took another gulp of wine and followed it with a bite of bread and soup. He was obviously intent on going to what he assumed was an inevitable prison cell drunk and well fed.

"What I said about my holdings was true," he said. "I'm a minor Moff as most plotters and schemers recognize such things. After the debacle of my attempt to wrest control of Meridian, I became persona non grata. My gut feeling is that the only reason I wasn't stripped of my rank and property was it was just easier to let me keep them."

Jag suspected he might be right, but said nothing.

"I languished, largely ignored and forgotten. I really have no idea why Daala singled me out. My forces aren't that considerable or sophisticated, but I suppose she's simply trying to gather as many allies as possible—if only so that there are fewer who support you."

"So she is swapping Chief of State for Head of State as her preferred title?"

"I imagine she'd *prefer* Empress," Getelles said. There was sufficient resignation and bitterness in his words and demeanor that Jag believed him.

"So she added you to her list. I'll want to follow up on that, but right now I'd like to ask about this." He indicated the vial. "I know you know what it is."

Getelles narrowed his eyes and took another swig. "I know," he muttered. "It was the one area we were making progress. Where we weren't in last place—the sciences."

"The sciences of life and death," Jag said. "My source tells me that many of the scientists who created the nanovirus targeting Tenel Ka and the Fett genetics have quietly gravitated to Antemeridias. What's this made of, Tol?"

He didn't answer. Jag shrugged and started to open the vial.

"No!" Getelles moved startlingly swiftly for an elderly man, seizing Jag's wrist. Jag raised his eyebrows and gazed pointedly at Getelles's hand. Slowly, Getelles released him.

"Thank you for confirming the nature of the serum," Jag said. "Obviously it is highly valuable."

"You know what it can do," Getelles said. "Damn rodents. If I had known the scientists were experimenting on Squibs—"

"You harm one hair on their bodies and I will come for you so fast and so hard, you'll wish I were a Mando," Jag promised, his voice calm. Getelles paled visibly, but recovered.

"You sound like Daala. Perhaps there isn't such a difference between you two after all."

The droids hummed to life and the second course was served: blue and purple and white vegetable chunks with a spicy green sauce. It was delicious, but Jag ate without savoring it. Getelles's enjoyment of the meal, too, seemed subdued.

When the droids returned to their corners and shut down again, Jag continued.

"You spoke out against Daala even before she escaped," Jag said. "You obviously *do* think there's a difference between the two of us. What changed your mind?"

Getelles eyed him, and then shrugged. "Her offer, combined with the escape of the Squibs with my serum, changed my mind," he said. "Frankly, Jag, it's one thing to ally with you when Daala's in jail. It's another when she's in your sector, with an old grudge against you, in a position to either wipe the floor with you or elevate you higher than you ever dared dream."

Jag could appreciate the position Getelles was in. "I see your point. I think she actually picked you because you had spoken out against me. Because I wouldn't think of you as someone who would betray me to work with her."

"I'm afraid you're right," Getelles admitted. "I was supposed to get you to trust me, then turn on you at the last moment."

"You do understand that I have you on so many charges, you might not live long enough to stand trial for them all," Jag said, refreshing Getelles's glass. "Treason, illegal drug experimentation, possession of droch material—"

"Oh, I do, believe me."

"How'd you like the charges dropped?"

Getelles raised a gray eyebrow. "If I threw my lot in with you?" Jag nodded. Getelles inclined his head toward the small vial. "What about that vial?"

"This vial?"

Getelles frowned. "Yes, that vial, right there. I want that as part of the bargain."

Jag frowned, then sighed. "All right," he said. "You've got it."

"And Jagged Fel, you foolish innocent," Getelles said, sighing as he pulled out a blaster, "I've got *you*."

He fired.

Jag Fel toppled to the floor.

"Did you get all this, Admiral?" Getelles said, speaking into a small recording device carefully inserted under the rather saggy skin of his throat.

"I did indeed," she said. "You took a few cheap shots, but you made the one that mattered. How do you intend to get out?"

"The droids are in a sleep phase, the room is soundproof, and I'll simply feign an emergency call from Antemeridias," the Moff said. "I'll be safely away before they even know anything is wrong." He reached for the small vial and closed his hand about it tightly.

"Here I thought an assassination would be so difficult, and they welcomed you with open arms," said Daala. "Meet me at the rendezvous base in twelve hours. You will find me most appreciative of your efforts, Moff Getelles. If I don't forget grudges, I also don't forget favors."

"I'll remember that, Admiral," Getelles said, "but for now I must make haste."

"Twelve hours," Daala said.

"Twelve hours," Getelles replied.

# Chapter Thirty-three

EXODO SYSTEM, MERIDIAN SECTOR

FOR THE FIRST TIME SINCE TAKING THE OATH OF OFFICE OF CHIEF OF State of the Galactic Empire, Admiral Natasi Daala stood on the bridge of the *Chimaera* and surveyed the Maw Irregular fleet.

It was smaller than it had been when she had come, too late, to Gilad Pellaeon's aid and turned the fleet loose on Jacen Solo. Gone or dismantled were the vessels that had some of the more . . . unique . . . upgrades that had in the end proved too costly to maintain. Still, there were several vessels left at her disposal. In addition to the *Chimaera,* which was an *Imperial II*–class Star Destroyer, the museum-quality but still powerful and deadly Maw Irregular remnants included another Star Destroyer, a *Venator*-class; an *Acclamator*-I class assault ship; a *Republic*-class cruiser; several frigates; and a handful of corvettes of two classes.

It was a fine start.

Daala had always prided herself on her ability to be ready for the vagaries of changing fate. She did not forget old friends, or old enemies, and so she had been pleased, but not surprised, at the alacrity with which her allies had come to her aid. Of course, there was something in it for them, too. "Everybody's got an angle," Han Solo had said once, and nowhere was the saying more true than in politics.

Daala had not come lightly to the decision to assassinate Jagged Fel. She felt it was a disrespectful way to deal with one's enemies, and she did respect Fel. But it had been necessary. A realist, Daala knew that she was acting as much to protect and promote herself as to support any political agenda. But she also had faith that the path she had followed, crooked and backtracking and strange as it had been, was the right one. She had earned her position as Chief of State, and had done her best to govern wisely and well. The galaxy needed what she had to offer. There were many who agreed with her. She had a power base, and she was not going to give it up. And so, Fel had needed to be eliminated.

Daala had been monitoring communications as best she could, utilizing her network of contacts and spies. Fel's people were keeping the assassination quiet. There was no mention of it anywhere on the Holonews, not even from the new, sensationalist network, BAMR. She had heard no response from the Solo family. Leia was in prison, which brought a spark of admittedly petty pleasure, and Han had apparently dropped out of sight with their adopted daughter. Jaina was with the Jedi, wherever they might be gallivanting off to.

What mention or coverage there was of Fel was brief and was either old or else consisted of grainy footage of someone who looked an awful lot like Fel. Daala knew the man had employed a double on more than one occasion, and she had to admit that whoever Jag had hired would easily fool someone who didn't know him personally.

In other words, all was playing out as she expected. News of Jag's death would rock what was left of the Empire at a time when, in the public eye, everything else was in chaos—a new and woefully inexperienced Chief of State; she, Natasi Daala, vanished; the Jedi gone. Eventually they would be forced to make some kind of an announcement, but not immediately, not until they got something into place. Which played right into her hands.

Exodo II, the rendezvous point, was nothing remarkable. It had been a hot, stormy, and unpleasant world even before the Yuuzhan

Vong had gotten to it, and now it was no doubt even less attractive. Nor was its moon, Boreleo, worth notice. Once a mining colony of little note, it had been abandoned at some time long ago, probably even before the Yuuzhan Vong had terraformed the world it orbited. More recently, it appeared to have been the site of an accident, if the abandoned hulk of a battered transport that a routine scan had discovered was any indication. In short, it was nondescript, little thought of by anyone, and conveniently located in the Meridian sector. Which was perfect for Daala's needs.

"Admiral, several vessels are dropping out of hyperspace," *Chimaera*'s captain, Tors Remal, said. A thin, elegant man with silver hair and a matching goatee, he was an excellent choice to command her flagship. He never batted an eye at the more violent things he occasionally had to do—in fact, he even seemed to get a certain enjoyment out of them.

"That should be Drikl, right on time." She did not betray any of her anxiety. Lecersen had assured her that he would be able to bring up to three-quarters of his available vessels. He did not mention exactly how many that would be.

There were several flashes of light, and any tension she might have had eased considerably. Right in the forefront was Lecersen's flagship, an old *Imperial II* Star Destroyer named the *Empire Maker,* followed by an *Interdictor*-class cruiser. In formation were nearly three dozen vessels—frigates, corvettes, an escort cruiser, and a starfighter carrier.

But how many starfighters? she wondered. "Open a channel," she instructed, and a moment later she was smiling at a small holographic image.

"Drikl. You are more than punctual. And I confess, you bring a better collection to the fray than I had anticipated."

"You'll find that I am an excellent ally, Admiral," he said. He did not seem in the least distressed that she casually referred to him by his first name while he addressed her by rank.

"You know, Drikl," she said, "I think that we might have wasted rather a lot of time attacking each other instead of someone else."

He inclined his head. "We have certainly had our differences in the past, and I have come to that conclusion myself."

She wasn't sure that he had, and she would not make the mistake of assuming him trustworthy, but thus far he was cooperating.

"It has, at least, given you time to assemble a rather decent-sized flotilla," she continued. "How many wings of starfighters?"

"Nine."

"Good. I have twelve," she said. "We're off to a promising start."

"Who will be joining us?"

"Your friend Vansyn, Moff Getelles, and Moff Trevin, for now. We'll be rendezvousing with others shortly, and then we should have a total of eight Moffs, as well as aid from other sources."

"Such as?"

"A girl doesn't tell all her secrets, or else there's no mystery. All you need to know for now is that they are already en route to the rendezvous point."

Lecersen frowned slightly. "If I'm to be of the best aid possible, then I should be told more, Admiral."

"Well, how about some good news then? Jagged Fel is dead."

That rattled his composure. Warring emotions played over his face. *"Really?"*

"Really."

"You've seen the body?"

"Next best thing. I heard the attack." She did not mention that the incident reminded her of being an audio witness to the murder of Pellaeon three years earlier. *What goes around, comes around indeed,* she reflected.

"I find myself torn. On the one hand, Fel has been a terrific thorn in my side, and none of my efforts were successful. On the other, I have armed the *Empire Maker* with several baradium missiles in the hope of dispatching him myself. How *did* you manage it?"

Daala smiled thinly. She was beginning to wonder if there were *anything* this sleemo wasn't behind. Politics did indeed make strange bedfellows.

"Don't worry. I am certain we'll find some suitable targets for your missiles," she said. "As for dispatching Fel, it was ease itself, really. One of my allies was invited to a private dinner aboard the *Pellaeon.* While the droids were inactive, he killed Fel quietly, begged off, and departed in his own ship. He was long gone by the time the death was discovered."

"Simplicity and boldness in one lethal combination," Lecersen said. "Who was this brilliant assassin?"

"Moff Tol Getelles."

He couldn't suppress a snort. "Really? I'd never have guessed it."

"You didn't guess right about Vansyn, either," she reminded him.

"Well played," he said, seemingly amused by the jab. "But if Fel is dead, why haven't I heard about it?"

"If you were his people, would *you* want this all over the Holonews before you'd figured out how to present it?"

"No," he admitted. "But they will figure out how to present it quickly enough. Jag does not—forgive me, *did* not—surround himself with fools."

"Which is why we will move, and move quickly, as soon as the others arrive."

As if on cue, there were several more flashes in the darkness of space. "Ah, and here are Vansyn's and Trevin's contributions," said Daala.

It was a respectable turnout. Both Vansyn and Trevin had far fewer resources than Lecersen, and their ships were of an age with the Maw Irregulars, though a few were newer, but the fleet was clearly starting to grow to something that would give any system pause. Daala counted quickly, and nodded as she realized the two Moffs had contributed almost twenty more vessels.

She felt her heart pick up, not with fear, but with a familiar anticipation. She was more at home here than she had ever been in her offices on Corsucant.

Daala hailed and spoke with both Vansyn and Trevin, a thick-set human of middle years with caf-colored skin and hair prematurely white. After exchanging pleasantries, she settled back to wait for Getelles.

The minutes ticked by, and she began to frown, drumming her fingers on the arm of her command chair.

"The man of the hour is late," commented Lecersen. She didn't bother to reply.

Seven minutes later, she was relieved that, despite the delay, the "man of the hour" arrived, with even more than he had promised:

Four Star Destroyers, a carrier, eight starfighter wings, and nearly a dozen combined frigates and corvettes.

"Moff Getelles," she greeted him. "You're late."

"With, as you see, a few more additional ships. Some last-minute maintenance was required, but I assure you, they are all battle ready."

"They are very welcome indeed. Captain Remal, open a channel to all vessels."

"Open, Admiral."

Daala let herself pause and savor this: the moment before they took their first step together toward their destinies. One, she would eventually betray; another, she might, or might not. More, many more, would be joining them. It was a splendid instant in time.

"This is Admiral Daala. In a few moments, we'll be departing to rendezvous with the next group of loyalists who, like yourselves, have chosen to follow me and what I represent. I have always been an Imperialist at heart. The order, the efficiency . . . the ceremony and history. Now that we are about to step boldly forward, I will tell you something that will hearten you even more. We are moving forward to claim something that no longer has a challenger. Chief of State Jagged Fel is dead."

"Oh, I rather think not," came an all-too-familiar-voice. "Jaina wouldn't stand for it. That girl *really* wants her wedding."

Daala's chest constricted, and for a heartbeat her head swam. She recovered almost at once and gestured for the transmission to be silenced. "Trace that transmission. Now," she snapped, then, "Open the channel."

"Open," said Remal.

"Really, Jag? I think she'd look much better in black," Daala said, her eyes on the agitated communications officer frantically, and apparently unsuccessfully, trying to determine where the hell Jagged Fel was.

"I'm not going to tell her she can't be a blushing bride, and I don't think you are, either. Admiral Natasi Daala, I am here to order you to stand down, surrender your fleet, and return to Coruscant for trial. There doesn't have to be any loss of life here."

Daala arched a red brow at the Sullustan communications officer, who shook his head miserably.

"Jag," Daala said, "I see how many vessels I have, and presumably, so do you. But apparently, you are nowhere to be found. Show yourself, and let's talk like civilized people." If he was on the *Pellaeon,* he wouldn't be able to. It had been reported as having departed the Meridan sector days before, after the "assassination."

"Oh, I don't think I'll show myself quite yet," Fel replied. "But I'll send a few friends in, just to assure you I'm quite serious."

Even as he spoke, several bright flashes of light revealed a number of ships suddenly dropping out of hyperspace, and Daala received her second unpleasant surprise of the day.

Star Destroyers. But no ordinary Star Destroyers, such as the nearly twenty she had at her beck and call. No, while these resembled their traditional Imperial counterparts, they were much more elegant—sleek and needle-like rather than bluntly triangular.

Chiss Star Destroyers.

The three were not alone; they were accompanied by nine heavy escort freighters and a dozen Nssis Clawcraft starfighters, their sleek, almost artistic curves belying how deadly they could be. The ball-shaped fuselage of the craft was still recognizable as the TIE fighter it had once been, but now it resembled a sea beast with long, elegant tentacles.

They held position, quietly. Awaiting orders.

And then, suddenly, Daala understood.

"You're being granted an honor, Admiral. You're the first to behold a secret finally come to light," said Jagged Fel's voice. "You're looking at the vanguard of the Empire of the Hand."

# Chapter Thirty-four

OF COURSE. OF *COURSE*. DAALA SHOULD HAVE EXPECTED THIS, GIVEN Fel's closeness with the blue-skinned, red-eyed, xenophobic Chiss. His bodyguard and assistant was even a Chiss. And yet—how *could* she have known?

"Admiral?" Remal's voice cut through her galloping thoughts. "Do you think they really are what Fel says they are?"

"It makes perfect sense," Daala said, recovering. The irony that the *Chimaera* had once belonged to Admiral Thrawn, for whose "hand" the Empire of the Hand was named, did not escape her. "But he may just have overplayed his hand. Shock value is a very nice thing indeed, but they are grossly outnumbered. Fire when ready."

For the first time since she had known him, Remal hesitated. "The Chiss Ascendancy—"

"Has nothing to do with those ships out there. They belong to the Empire of the Hand and obviously are Jag's pets. Now, don't make me repeat my order."

"Of course not, Admiral."

"Target the main Star Destroyer," she said. "Let's get their big boys first. Then we can—"

Whatever they could do remained unvoiced as the *Chimaera* was suddenly rocked by an attack from—

"Behind us!" cried Remal.

"Who the hell?" But of course Daala knew. She didn't know specifically yet which one of them had suddenly turned tail at the sight of the Chiss vessels, but it had to be one of the Moffs.

Remal knew exactly what she meant and barked, "Getelles!" Even as he issued orders to launch TIE fighters and Daala's three corvettes to crush the betrayers, Daala watched as the Chiss ships began to attack. The Nssisi Clawcrafts and AirStraekers targeted the TIE fighters while the massive, sleek Star Destroyer fired its masercanons directly at the *Chimaera*. More than conventional laser weapon technology, the uniquely Chiss masers utilized both laser and kinetic technology to buffet and damage at the same time.

Getelles. Daala swore softly. It all became clear now. "That traitor will be nothing more than messy particles in space by the time we're done with him. Lecersen!"

"Here, Admiral," came Lecersen's oily but welcome voice. "I've already begun targeting Getelles. At least now we understand how it was that Jagged Fel managed to escape point-blank assassination."

Daala felt heat rise in her face. She'd been a fool to trust Getelles. It was a novice's mistake, to underestimate one's foe. Getelles was obviously a more intelligent—and more devious—Moff than she had given him credit for. It was all unraveling. First Fel, then the Empire of the Hand, now Getelles.

"Indeed we do," she said to Lecersen. "Do whatever you like with him. Save the ships if we can, but don't trouble yourself overmuch with saving his crewmembers."

"Admiral, I hardly *ever* distress myself with such things."

She took a deep breath and asked for a status report. The report was not grim, not yet, but it was unpleasant. Two frigates had taken damage, and one corvette had been destroyed. Several of the starfighters were reporting in with minimal damage. Still, this was only a minor setback when all was said and done. The remaining fighters, and there were still plenty, were holding their own against the Clawcraft fighters.

"Vansyn, Trevin—move in to assist with my starfighters," she snapped. "Let's take down these Chiss ships. We'll show Jagged Fel just what the true Empire thinks of his little Empire of the Hand."

"Of course, Admiral!" Vansyn's voice was higher than normal and he sounded slightly worried, but one of the screens showed that several of his starfighters and four corvettes were already turning to obey her orders. Trevin's vessels, on her other side, also moved into position.

Daala folded her arms and nodded, green eyes narrowing both against the brightness and in satisfaction as one Chiss starfighter exploded right before her eyes. Wherever Jagged Fel was right at the moment, she hoped he was watching it, too.

And then, on the edge of the screen's image, there were more bright flashes of light, and Daala beheld a ghost from the past.

The vessel, at the head of at least another dozen ships, was another Star Destroyer, but smaller, and faster than many of the big capital ships. It immediately set to work targeting Vansyn's ships, drawing their fire away from Getelles. Other vessels materialized, as well, and joined in the fray, but Daala couldn't take her eyes off this one. She knew it . . . and felt a sudden strange pang as she recalled both the name of the ship and who had last commanded it.

The beasts for which the Star Destroyer had been named were semi-aquatic predators that could be trained as formidable mounts. They fought on after their riders were dead—as did this vessel.

"The *Bloodfin,*" she murmured. And, to herself, *Pellaeon.*

"This is Admiral Vitor Reige," came a strong male voice. For a moment, in her dazed state, Daala thought it even sounded like a younger Gilad Pellaeon. "Admiral Daala—I am commander of the *Bloodfin* and of this Imperial strike force, led by the true Head of State, Jagged Fel. Your claim to that title is that of a usurper's. Even so, Fel has instructed me to accept your surrender, with no further loss of life on either side. You have fifteen seconds to accept."

What was happening? How was Fel managing to pull this off? Daala steadied herself, realizing that half of the battle that now raged around her was psychological—and that her realization meant that Fel had just lost his advantage. Fel was deft, she had to give him that. Coming back from the dead in so dramatic a fashion, producing the

Empire of the Hand, and now sending the *Bloodfin,* surely hand-picked to rattle her.

And it had. All of it.

Her jaw set. Well, she wouldn't let him rattle her an instant longer. The numbers against her seemed to be increasing with each passing minute, but even so, she would still win.

Nonetheless—

"Send a message to Moffs Wolbam, Calron the Younger, and Malvek," she told the Sullustan communications officer. "Tell them to divert at once from the original rendezvous point and direct reinforcements here as soon as possible. The first Moff to arrive will receive my special thanks." She hoped they would not be needed, but even so, it would be worth it to show Jagged Fel just what he was up against.

"Your time is up," came the oddly Pellaeon sounding voice, and the viewport was filled once again with red and green streaks of laser fire as fighting began on a third front.

"Moff Trevin reports in that his flagship has taken damage, and he's lost half of his fleet," Remal said.

"Tell him to evacuate and head for the *Chimaera,*" Daala said. She was not close to the man, but his flagship was burning beneath his feet because of his decision to fight for her and against Fel. She would not throw him to the boarwolves.

Fel . . . *Where was he*? Something wasn't right here. She had assumed he hadn't shown himself initially because he wanted to show off the Empire of the Hand. But after that . . . why wasn't he on the *Bloodfin*? Why was Reige commanding it?

The *Chimaera* rocked as one of the Chiss Star Destroyers got in a good solid shot. "Shield deflectors have taken damage, but should hold for a while," Remal said.

For a while. Daala drew her thoughts back to Fel. Why was he not here, overseeing his victory? Where—

"Remal," she snapped. "Scan Exodo II and Boreleo. Thoroughly."

He turned to her, confusion plain on his patrician face. "Admiral? We're in the middle of a battle on three fronts. We're taking damage."

"Do it *now*!"

His face darkening with displeasure, Remal nonetheless obliged.

"And Remal—look for anything that could hide a Star Destroyer."

*"What?"* Remal now looked as if he was moments away from deducing that his commanding officer was stark-raving mad.

"He's got to be here, somewhere. Hiding on that cursed ship of his." Daala could not bring herself to speak the name of the vessel.

"How could he possibly hide an entire Star Destroyer?"

And then she got it. "The mining on Boreleo," she said, putting the pieces together as she spoke. "The moon's interior is riddled with tunnels and caves. And that recent debris we noticed—just hot enough to throw off a cursory scan." *Which ours had been.*

Comprehension and worry flitted simultaneously across Remal's face. He turned back at once to the scan, but it was unnecessary. As if Fel had somehow overheard her, or more likely simply decided it was time to unsettle her fleet with another display, the *Gilad Pellaeon,* mammoth and intimidating, emerged from the dark side of the moon.

*That trick can work only so many times, Fel,* Daala thought.

"Lecersen?" she said. "I direct your attention to Boreleo."

"I—I'm watching. That's not what I think it is . . . or who I think it is—is it?"

"It's your lucky day, Drikl," Daala said. Her glee was brittle and bitter, but fierce. "I believe you had a few special things you'd been saving for Jagged Fel?"

"Indeed I did—and do," he said, his old confidence creeping back into his voice.

"Let him have it."

"With pleasure."

Natasi Daala stood on the bridge of the *Chimaera,* barely blinking, her heart beating rapidly in anticipation. Jagged Fel had more than earned this. He'd had the audacity to name his flagship after a man she had admired and been fond of. He had taken that man's own ship and commandeered it for himself. He was corrupting, twisting, and mocking everything the Empire had stood for, even debasing it by allying with another so-called "Empire."

And at last, he was going to pay.

Her lips curled in the slightest of smiles three heartbeats later when the dark gray surface of the huge vessel suddenly blossomed with no fewer than four massive balls of deadly fire. Stories-high flame, fueled by the ship's own atmosphere, licked hungrily at the gaping holes, and black smoke billowed. Bodies, pieces of bulkheads, and other debris spilled forth, almost like a stream of blood from a wound.

Finally.

Ashik had disapproved of Jag's idea of several different stages for the battle. The Chiss's plan, sensible and sound but unimaginative, had been to simply amass every vessel Fel had at his disposal, have them all emerge together, and cripple Daala's fleet as quickly as possible.

Jag had disagreed. "I need to break her," he said, "and her Moffs, as well. Put her off balance. I need to humiliate her in front of them. We've got many things that will surprise her when she sees them, and possibly shock more Moffs than Getelles to join against her once they materialize."

"Psychological warfare," Tahiri had said, listening. "Smart. Intimidate them enough fast enough, and you won't have to kill as many of them. Not even Daala. Which is the whole point."

"Exactly."

"I do not trust Getelles," Ashik had said, frowning.

"I don't actually trust him either, per se," Jag had said. "But he knows wisdom when he sees it. And he certainly has motivation."

It had worked beautifully, at first. The Empire of the Hand, Getelles's betrayal, the *Bloodfin,* and now Jag himself emerging, ready for battle. And then the baradium missiles had all hit home.

Now the *Gilad Pellaeon* was nothing more than a deathtrap. The *Empire Maker* had been identified as Drikl Lecersen's ship, and obviously he knew what he was doing. The missiles had struck exactly where they would cause the most damage, and everyone was scrambling for the starfighters, corvettes, and freighters, as well as the escape pods. The ships that could fight, would. Others would be picked up by the *Bloodfin,* still engaged with Daala's forces.

Jag, Tahiri, and Ashik raced toward one of the hangars. Smoke had already clouded the air, and an alarm whooped at an eardrum-shattering timber. All three of them had managed to grab air masks, pressing them tightly over their faces as their booted feet rang on the metal plating of the *Pellaeon.* Many of the ships had already departed, but several yet remained. Those who did not make it onto a ship would use escape pods. Ruthless as Daala was, Jag could not imagine her destroying those. For one thing, it would be a waste of firepower, as they had no weapons.

There were eleven TIE Defenders remaining. "That's our best bet," Ashik said. Jag nodded. The things were older, but they were fast, maneuverable, and could handle fire from multiple enemies. Too, each ship could carry only one being. More targets made it more likely that they would all survive to rendezvous.

"I'd better see you on the *Bloodfin,* Tahiri," Jag said as he climbed up into the ball cockpit of the Defender. "You've still got a trial to attend. I won't take coming under fire by Daala as an excuse for you to miss your court date."

The blond woman flashed him a quick grin. "I know my parole rules," she said.

"Sir," said Ashik. There was a tone in his voice that made Jag's head whip around to regard his bodyguard and friend intently. "Remember . . . these ships have a hyperdrive."

Jag knew what Ashik meant—that if it looked as if Jag wasn't going to be able to fight his way to safety, he should drop out of the battle. Jag nodded, conveying his understanding—but not his agreement—with Ashik's unspoken suggestion. This was his battle, his place. He was not about to run.

# Chapter Thirty-five

A SCANT SEVEN MINUTES LATER, JAG'S THREE-WINGED TIE DESTROYER was under fire by no fewer than three vessels. Briefly he wondered if they somehow knew it was he, but then he saw that the rest of the ships fleeing from the *Pellaeon* were being swarmed, as well. From this distance, Jag could see the gaping holes and ravenous flames in the *Pellaeon*, but there was no time to mourn the dead—not if he wasn't willing to join them.

The Novaldex deflector-shield generators, nearly as powerful on the Defenders as on capital ships, held as he fired the L-s9.3 laser cannons mounted on the two lower quadanium steel wings. He got a clean shot on one of the TIE fighters, watching in satisfaction but not pleasure as it instantly exploded. Jag pushed forward into a dive away from the hurtling pieces of debris and swooped under two other fighters. He glanced at the stream of information coming in on his computer. The *Bloodfin* and safety were still too far away for comfort.

The other four closed in on him, flying in what appeared to be an erratic pattern behind him. Jag, however, knew exactly what they were doing. The Defender had one very nasty flaw—an aft blind spot. Jag's pursuers, also well acquainted with Imperial TIE designs, were obviously aware of that and were trying to fall into position for a clear shot.

Jag transferred power to the rear projecting deflector shields, then pulled back and soared almost vertically upward, continuing to pull hard into a loop that ended with him behind both fighters. He made short work of them, using not just the laser cannons but the two NK-3 ion cannons mounted on the upper wing. One of his pursuers exploded immediately, the force slamming debris into its companion and completely shearing off one wing; the hapless pilot went tumbling off.

The *Bloodfin* was on his screen now. Jag punched a button. "Little Boy Blue to Red Rider, my bearing is alpha seven mark two, heading your way as fast as possible."

Reige's voice replied, "We see you, Little Boy Blue, and are moving to rendezvous. We suggest you hurry."

"Any word on Ash and Dust?"

"Ash has arrived, still awaiting Dust."

The code name Little Boy Blue had been suggested by Ashik in one of his rare playful moments. Jag was, by both human and Chiss standards, rather short, and he was one of the very few beings the xenophobic Chiss regarded as akin to themselves. The code name was therefore both a jab and an honor in one. In the same lighthearted vein, Jag suggested Dust for Tahiri, who had grown up on Tatooine, and Ash for—well, Ashik. He was relieved to hear that Ashik had made it, but pressed down his concern for Tahiri. His . . . bodyguard? charge? . . . would make it, or she would not, and nothing Jag could do would change the outcome.

Two Clawcraft, gleaming and white and welcome, surged up to serve as escort just in time to attack one of the Moff's escort cruisers. They fairly danced around it, blasting it away, while Jag concentrated on his approach to the *Bloodfin,* now visible to his naked eye.

And then suddenly, not understanding what had happened, he was spiraling wildly out of control, as helpless to correct himself as a bird caught in a tornado. Huge chunks of debris, some of them as large as an entire Star Destroyer, tumbled past. Jag, still turning over and over and frantically trying to regain control of his fighter, spared only the most cursory of glances toward the debris—but it was enough for him to recognize that he wasn't looking at what was left of spacefaring vessels. A smaller chunk of the debris slammed into one of his wings and sent him hurtling off in another direction.

He finally managed to stop tumbling. Jag ran a quick scan of the ship. It showed that, incredibly, other than severe damage to a single wing, the TIE Destroyer—and its pilot—were intact.

"Little Boy Blue, we have a tractor beam lock on your fighter. Stand by to board Red Rider."

He let out a deep breath as he moved toward safety. It was then that, as he had a chance to look around, he caught sight of what looked like a broken egg in the distance. And that was when he realized what had happened.

Somehow, Daala had blasted apart Exodo II's moon.

It had been a desperate gamble, but it had bought them time. When Lecersen had initially proposed firing several baradium missiles into a structural weak point of Boreleo, she had thought him mad.

"To what end?" she had asked incredulously.

"Chaos and disorder, and many ships blown to pieces by flying debris," Lecersen replied.

Daala opened her mouth to dismiss the idea—she preferred order to chaos, and her own ships could be jeopardized—and then she understood. Quickly, she gave orders to Lecersen and Vansyn—Trevin had perished along with his flagship—and they began to shift the area of battle so that Jag's ships were between them and the soon-to-be-destroyed moon.

Lecersen had been right. It was not the most usual of tactics, but it certainly produced a great deal of chaos, disorder, and ships blown to pieces by flying debris. Daala used the confusion to send her ships in to pick off the ships that were already damaged. Jag's people would have the chance to surrender and either join her or be kept civilly as prisoners of war, but she had a feeling that few would take such an easy way out.

The casualty reports were coming in—from her own ships and from those of Lecersen, Vansyn, and Trevin. It was worse than she had thought. The multiple "surprises" Jag had thrown her way had done just what he had intended: keep her and her people off-guard. Trevin's entire contingent was nearly gone. Vansyn's had taken a beating, and her own ships were reduced significantly. Many of them were so crippled they couldn't even make the jump to hyperspace—the *Chimaera* among them. Repairs could be effected, but that would take time, and that was one thing they didn't have.

And she had heard nothing back from the other Moffs she had contacted.

She went over the list of ships, noting those that were wrecked hulks, those with minor damage, and those still in fighting form. Her eye fell on one of Lecersen's ships, and she pressed her lips together as an idea came to her. It might not work—but it was certainly worth a try.

"Contact Lecersen right away. I have a rather unusual use for his *Interdictor*-class cruiser."

As Jag strode onto the *Bloodfin* bridge, both Ashik and Vitor Reige snapped salutes. Jag returned them, smiled and nodded at Ashik, then offered Reige his hand. The dark-haired admiral grasped it firmly, his sharp blue eyes meeting Jag's evenly.

"Welcome aboard, Head of State. Your . . . charge has preceded you. She is currently in our brig."

Jag nodded; it was to be expected. Vitor Reige had been Gilad Pellaeon's protégé, and while he had been apprised of the current unique situation with Tahiri, it was no surprise that he had put the "prisoner" somewhere he deemed safe until Jag had arrived.

"You may release her back into my custody, Admiral. Thank you for your very timely rescue. What's our status?"

"We are continuing to rescue the crew of the *Pellaeon*," Reige said. "I've prepared a damage report for you. We—"

"Sir!" came a startled yelp. A young, red-haired human, presumably Reige's aide, was pointing at the viewport. "The pieces of the moon—they're moving!"

"Of course they're moving, they . . ." Reige fell silent, staring.

The pieces of Boreleo weren't moving. They were *being* moved.

Jag, Ashik, and Reige all stepped closer to the viewport, almost unaware of what they were doing. Jag watched, disbelieving, as an

*Interdictor*-class cruiser used its gravity-well projector to pull pieces of the shattered moon into various positions.

"That ship belongs to Lecersen, not Daala," said Ashik.

"And he's moving what's left of Boreleo into a blockade," snapped Jag. "He's going to barricade himself and some others inside."

"We hid inside the moon, now they're going to," Tahiri said. "That sounds like something Daala would do."

"Not if I can help it," Jag said, grimly. "Admiral, you now have one target above all others. Stop that *Interceptor*!"

Daala watched, relief battling worry as the *Kagcatcher*'s crew positioned the four gravity wells to draw pieces of a dead moon into a shield. They would be protected, but they would also be trapped, and as soon as Jag caught on to what they would doing, he would target the *Kagcatcher*. The savior ship would likely become a metal coffin, and the rest of her fleet would be bombarded, unless she surrendered.

But there had been no alternative. This at least would buy her some time and, if her Moffs did decide to stay loyal to her, could be the thing that saved them. The *Chimaera*, Lecersen's *Empire Maker*, and Vansyn's *Wyvard*, along with a not-insignificant number of the original fleet, were clustered together. Daala watched as the chunks of moon were slowly but inexorably maneuvered into position about them. They were not puzzle pieces, not quite, but the *Kagcatcher* was doing an admirable job of closing the cracks.

Outside the growing shell of a broken moon, Daala caught glimpses of the battle that still raged outside. Now and then, a few of her fleet's starfighters zipped through what openings there were. At first, they were followed by Jag's fighters, but those were easily picked off, and soon stopped coming altogether.

"Now what, Admiral?" asked Remal.

"Now," Daala said, "we wait."

"We could finish them off, sir," Ashik said. "Simply start hammering away at the pieces of the moon. They are completely trapped and helpless."

"Trapped, yes, helpless, no," Tahiri said. Jag had brought her up to speed as soon as she'd rejoined him. "I'm certain Daala has sent out a call for reinforcements. Getelles told us that this was just the gathering of her local resources. They could be here at any minute."

"At any minute, or not at all. We can do the same," Jag said. "Daala and I are facing a similar problem: Will those we've asked to come to our aid actually *do* so? I'm sure that once word gets out about the situation here, my Imperial ships are going to be needed just about anywhere in the galaxy but here." He rubbed his eyes.

Reige's aide said something to him. The admiral nodded and turned to Jag. "Your friend Moff Getelles wishes to speak with you."

"Patch him through," Jag said.

"Our plan worked admirably, I think," said Getelles's image on the screen. He was beaming, though he looked weary and worn.

"I do, too," Jag said. "I must confess, that is the first time I have ever willingly worked with someone whose first announcement of said plan was to stun me with a blaster."

"You must admit," said Getelles, chuckling a little, "that it fooled Daala completely."

"It certainly fooled me," Tahiri, standing beside Jag, said. "Good thing Jag came out of it before I came in."

Jag had awoken shortly after Getelles had completed his message to Daala. Getelles had been smart: he'd put his blaster on the table and his hands in the air as soon as Jag began to emit muffled grunts.

"I submit myself to your justice, Head of State Fel, but please hear me out first!"

Jag had grabbed the blaster and pointed it at Getelles. Tahiri, having heard the sound of the blaster—the room was *not* soundproof, as Getelles had misinformed Daala—had rushed in, lightsaber at the ready.

"Let him finish," Jag had instructed his bodyguard. "This should be good."

Actually, it was. "Daala plans to have you assassinated," Getelles had said. "And now you are. My cover will work if your people will play along with it. I'll tell you where she'll be in twelve hours. You show up, and I'll cast my lot in with you, for the same terms we discussed before."

"One more thing you should know that ought to solidify this deal," Jag said. "I do have a recording of you talking to Daala. I have another one of her talking to another Moff—Porrak Vansyn. It seems she hasn't really forgiven or forgotten you, Tol. Once her position was secure, she had planned to turn on you and give all your holdings to Vansyn."

It was amusing, Jag thought, to recall exactly the precise shade of purple-red Getelles had turned.

Jag had played the recording, lest Getelles think he was bluffing. Upon hearing it, and the contempt in Daala's voice as she spoke of him, Getelles had indeed become wholeheartedly an ally—as he had proved early in the battle.

"Now, I think, it's time to settle up."

Jag looked at him curiously. "What do you mean?"

"Well, sir, you must be aware that the sample of the rejuvenation serum I, er, accepted from you was a fake. You agreed to give me back the stolen sample as part of our bargain."

"Oh, I don't think so."

Getelles's smile faltered. "You said you would return the sample!"

"You asked for the vial on the table. *This vial, right here,* I believe were your exact words. I gave you that vial, right there."

The smile was now entirely gone. "I thought better of you, Jagged Fel. That sort of trick is beneath you!"

"And the development of this kind of illegal drug is beneath *you,* sir," said Jag, not bothering to hide his disgust. "I will keep to my end of the bargain. I will not charge you for experimenting with this sort of thing, nor will I hold any past crimes or offenses against you. By allying with me, you have helped keep the galaxy stable, and I think you have earned forgiveness with that action. But know that I will send someone to investigate the laboratories that created this serum, and everything pertaining to this experiment will be destroyed at that time if you haven't done so already. You walk out of this with your holdings, your reputation—such as it is—intact, your liberty, and your head. I think that should be sufficient. Do you agree?"

The anger had passed, and now Getelles looked merely resigned. "Yes, sir," he said, saluting. "The laboratories will be dismantled and the research destroyed upon my return to Antemeridias."

"I'm glad we understand each other. I do appreciate what you've done for me." Jag clicked off the comm, then withdrew a small vial from his pocket and regarded it thoughtfully.

"What's in there that he wanted so badly, anyway?" Tahiri asked.

Jag smiled. "Something to make a family very happy" was all he said.

# Chapter Thirty-six

JEDI TEMPLE, CORUSCANT

"HOW UTTERLY SATISFYING," GRAND LORD VOL SAID. "SOON OUR domination of this world will be compete—and from here, nothing is barred to us."

He and High Lord Ivaar Workan walked along the Great Hall of the Jedi Temple.

"I had hoped to have a map of the Temple complete upon your arrival," Workan said, "but we ran into a few difficulties."

"It seems you have run into several," said Lord Vol. Slightly stooped with age, he came only to Workan's shoulder. "But no doubt now that I am here, everything will get straightened out. You had quite the task ahead of you. Perhaps I should have come at the beginning of our infiltration."

The full, imposing, ancient beauty of the Temple had pleased Grand Lord Vol. Vol had to admit that he was glad they could occupy this ancient site of Jedi strength rather than being forced to destroy it. He thought bitterly of Tahv, the exquisite City of Glass, which now lay in melted ruins, and he regretted how harshly he had spoken with Workan before arriving on Coruscant. It was indeed a mammoth task Workan had been set, and all things considered he had done a good job.

"No, my lord," said Workan, uncertain if the comment was a peace offering. "You always choose wisely. Despite the setbacks"—he spread his arms—"here we are, in the very heart of the Jedi Temple. Soon our domination of this world will be complete. And from here, nothing is barred to us." He hesitated. "My lord, what is the word from Kesh? How fares our home?"

"Tahv has been abandoned," Vol said solemnly. "Too little remained to safely continue inhabiting there. We have not lost faith in you and this endeavor, though. And it seems that faith was justified. From the ashes of a blasted city, here I stand, victory a few hours away. In attempting to crush us, Abeloth has only made us stronger. She has delivered this place into our hands while she scuttles furtively about the galaxy, no doubt tackling worlds unable to offer true resistance to salve her ego while we grow strong."

He turned to the younger man and placed a hand on his shoulders. "High Lord Workan, you have done exceptionally well here. I will remember your fidelity and efforts."

Workan bowed deeply, his worries clearly assuaged. "I am honored. All is done for the glory of the Lost Tribe, for the Sith, and for you."

And Vol thought he actually believed that. He had chosen well in promoting this human, despite the "setbacks."

"Tell me everything about Rokari Kem," he said, as they walked.

So Workan did. He spoke of her history, her struggle to win freedom for the Jessar, her persona of a loving, gentle woman who desired no power for herself. "And yet, she is nothing like that," he finished. "She is ambitious, and arrogant, and greedy."

"Have you determined if she knows who we are?"

"No," Workan said. "But I have watched as she sways more and more of our allies by the day. My lord, I say to you truly—she is all that stands in our way. Once she is eliminated, we can openly claim this world, if you so deem. Let the galaxy know that the Sith—the *true* Sith—have awoken from their slumber and are poised to rule this galaxy, as is our rightful destiny."

"Perhaps," mused Vol. "Although there is strength in secrecy, as well. You have not tipped your hand?"

"No, my lord," Workan assured him. "No one, except perhaps Roki Kem, suspects a thing. Not even our imprisoned Jedi."

Vol eyed him, frowning slightly. This was the trouble with the young, he had found: their arrogance and enthusiasm sometimes were their undoing. Vol had lived long enough to appreciate patience.

"It is no ordinary Jedi you hold," he reminded Workan. "It is Princess Leia Organa Solo, who once helped topple an Empire."

Workan smirked. "She is sulking in a prison cell, my lord. There are no other Jedi here to rescue her. Even her husband has forsaken her. He has taken their adopted daughter offworld."

"I would not be so sure of that. But that is among the lesser of our worries," Vol added, lifting a hand as Workan started to protest. "It is well you have done nothing to jeopardize our secrecy. We should use the ignorance of Coruscant to our benefit as long as we can. I will deal with this Roki Kem. You are absolutely sure she is not a Force-user?"

Workan bridled slightly. "As I told you before, no one has been able to sense a thing. Apparently all her power comes from her ability to make people adore her while she selfishly grabs power for herself."

"That is a good skill in and of itself," said Vol. "Don't dismiss it. Nonetheless, politically powerful as she may be, she cannot stand up to *me.*" It was not arrogance. It was a simple truth. "There is a second wave of Sith, awaiting my instructions. They are poised either for attack or for continued infiltration, depending on what I deem is wisest once Kem is eliminated. Which," he added, "I shall do tonight. The Tribe has waited five thousand years for this moment; I am anxious to experience it."

"As my lord wishes," said Workan, and bowed.

He did not bother to cloak his excitement and pride, and Vol would not chastise him for it. Let him, and the other Sith, the humans operating in public and the Keshiri operating behind the scenes in secret, who had earned this, enjoy themselves before the hard work of ruling the galaxy began.

Workan decided to start celebrating a bit early. He opened a bottle of burtalle, sent to him by the ugly Sullustan senator Wuul in what was a clear attempt to curry favor. The two had clashed more than once, but Workan recognized a being determined to hang on to what he had, and so rather enjoyed the sparring. Particularly if an apology gift was as delicious as this beverage, which deserved opening a second bottle, and perhaps a third.

So it was that when the vidcall came at an obscene hour in the morning, he awoke slightly bleary and disoriented. Workan knew who it had to be, but as he sat up in bed wincing, his head throbbing and his mouth flimsi-dry, he thought that Grand Lord Vol could have waited until a more respectable hour to announce the Sith victory.

He threw on a robe and stumbled to a chair, pressing the activation button.

And grew, quite suddenly, stone-cold sober.

It was not Lord Vol. It was Roki Kem.

The large green eyes were crinkled in a smile that was languid but had nothing of kindness about it. Roki lifted a three-fingered hand and gave him a little wave.

"Good morning, Senator," she said in her melodious voice.

Had Vol not struck? Had she been alerted to the attempt? His danger sense was screaming in the back of his mind. Something had gone very, very wrong.

"It would be a better morning had I been permitted to awaken at my usual hour," he said. He kept his voice pleasant, but allowed a tinge of annoyance and confusion to creep into it.

"I'm so sorry," she said, her voice sounding genuinely apologetic. "But I stumbled across something I think belongs to you, and wanted to make sure you knew it had been found."

She held up Lord Vol's head.

The Grand Lord of the Lost Tribe had died in terror, or torment—perhaps both—it would seem, if the wide, staring eyes and gaping mouth were any indication. Unable to help himself, Workan recoiled in horror. Raw, pure terror shot through him.

"Who—who *are* you?" he stammered.

Roki's smile deepened, its sweetness obscenely at odds with the severed head she continued to hold up. "Who I am is unimportant. It's who I *will* be that should concern you. Who you will help me become."

She waited, enjoying playing him, enjoying his terror. Workan swallowed, reaching out in the Force to press calm upon his trembling body. Regaining a measure of the control that had enabled him to climb to the position of High Lord, he asked, "And who is that?"

Her smile widened, and her blue face shone with happiness. "The Beloved Queen of the Stars," Roki murmured.

He had recovered sufficiently to let out a snort at that. "What kind of title is that? You're insane!"

She shook her head, long, flowing, blue-green tresses waving gently with the movement. "Oh, no, Workan. I just see farther than you. My vision," she said, almost purring the words, "is vast. You will meet me . . . tomorrow. Yes?"

" . . . Y-yes."

This could, thought Workan, work to his advantage. With Grand Lord Vol dead, he was, effectively, the highest-ranking Sith not only on Coruscant, but in the entire Lost Tribe. It was not official, of course. But it did not have to be. He was in charge of the single most vital mission the Sith had ever embarked upon. In the absence of a Grand Lord, no one would question his stepping into the role. At least temporarily. And as Workan had cause to know, *temporary,* with the right machinations, could be anything but.

Workan did not know how Roki Kem had managed to defeat an unmatched Force-user such as Grand Lord Vol, and he could hardly ask her. He could only assume one of two things: either the Grand Lord had made a grave mistake that Roki could exploit, or else she was some kind of powerful Force-user herself. If the first, then she was merely arrogant. If the second . . . well, there was an old Lost Tribe saying: "The shadow of another keeps the sun from scorching." While it would have been immensely gratifying to have achieved adulation and fame, there was much to be said for lurking in the shadows and letting someone else be the target.

She had first warned him to stay out of her way. Now she wanted to meet with him.

*Who you will help me become.*

Now that the initial horror and shock had worn off, Workan found himself very curious as to what that might entail.

She had proposed meeting at The Nook, a fashionable little grill tucked away within walking distance of the Senate that specialized in breakfast foods. It opened at four in the morning and stayed open till noon. Considering that Workan did not think he would have gotten any sleep anyway, he readily agreed. The sun had barely lightened the always-brown sky to a lighter shade of tan when he walked into the quaint little establishment. He was welcomed by name by a Twi'lek and ushered into an out-of-the-way booth.

"Pleasure to serve you, sir," she said as she poured him a most welcome cup of steaming black caf. "Will you be dining alone, or will someone be joining you?"

"Senator Roki Kem will be arriving soon," he said. Her eyes lit up.

"Roki Kem? Really?"

He felt annoyance at being so overshadowed, but reminded himself again of the old saying. He knew the moment when Roki entered from the sudden applause that erupted. Applause for a Senator? Here in a restaurant that one might expect to have seen its share of celebrities? Workan shook his head.

"Please, please!" came the mellifluous voice, tinged with just the right amount of appreciation and embarrassment. "Thank you. I feel so welcome. Please, sit down and enjoy your breakfasts!"

She slipped into the booth across from him, and even though he knew better than to be fooled by her sweet demeanor, he found himself smiling a little at her.

"The peko peko egg omelet is very good here, and they have fresh brul juice," he told her.

"That sounds lovely," Roki said, gracing the slightly flustered server with a beaming smile. As soon as the Twi'lek server had gone, Roki turned to Suldar, and the smile turned predatory.

Shadow, indeed.

"I am glad I did not have to eliminate you, as well," she said.

"I'm rather glad of that myself," Workan replied, stirring powdered taka root into his caf. "We both have rather pressing schedules. Tell me what I can do to help you, Senator."

"Straight to the point," she said. "I like that. I have waited long enough myself. What I want is easy to explain. I wish to rule."

Workan thought as he stirred. "I can manage that," he said. "As you have no doubt suspected, it was my actions that ensured Padnel Ovin's appointment to the interim position. Once you make it known that you are running for the position, I am certain your own popularity will propel you to leadership of the Galactic Alliance."

"I want that, yes," said Roki, as if she had said she wanted both cream and taka root powder in her caf. "But I don't want to wait two months for the election. I want it now. Within the next day or so, as soon as you can arrange it."

"I, uh . . ." He blinked, his thoughts racing, but not unpleasantly so. He had made Padnel, he could break Padnel. "I . . . think so, yes. I'll get my legal scholars on it right away."

"Excellent. That's just the start."

Workan took a long sip of his caf, using the Force to keep his hand from shaking. Start? Chief of State of the Galactic Alliance was a *start*?

"I see," he said. "And what is your next goal, after that one has been secured?"

"First, Chief of State," she said, ticking them off on her three-fingered hand. "Second, as I told you—Beloved Queen of the Stars. And finally, what is my due."

She leaned forward, green eyes wide, hair curling invitingly over her bare blue shoulders.

"Goddess," Roki Kem whispered, and smiled.

# Chapter Thirty-seven

ABOARD *JADE SHADOW*

"SO," BEN SAID. "THIS IS A LOT NICER THAN ZIOST. SHIP'S TASTE IN locales is improving."

"Or Abeloth's," Vestara said.

The tension was thick on *Jade Shadow.* Chasing so many false leads had left them all feeling frustrated and as if they were wasting their time. When Natua had described the ruins of a temple that had closely matched Ben's description of where he had first found Ship, they had all felt a resurgence of hope that they might actually find that elusive and dangerous vessel. And with it, Abeloth.

This time, Abeloth would not be challenged only by Luke, Ben, Vestara, and the Lost Tribe, who'd had their own agenda. She would be opposed down to the final breath, the last drop of blood, of nearly every Jedi in the galaxy. And in that battle, even so ancient and powerful a being as Abeloth could not stand. It had taken betrayal and isolation of the worst sort to cripple the Jedi before; now, standing as a united front, they would be the victors, Ben was certain. And when they were, they would return to Coruscant and cleanse that world of the Sith infestation.

Ben was proud of how Vestara was handling the situation. And he could tell that finally, the Grand Master himself was starting to believe what Ben had known all along: that Vestara Khai, though born and raised Sith, could be—no, *had been*—persuaded to turn her back on the darkness and bravely step into the light.

Ben's arm was draped loosely around Vestara's shoulders as Natua Wan brought the Jedi fleet up to speed on Upekzar. Natua's long hours spent in the Temple library studying Sith worlds and their histories had made her the resident expert on this venture, and Luke had insisted that she be the one to brief her fellow Jedi. Vestara might know more about the Sith mind-set, but Natua had turned her fierce determination toward learning everything she could about their ancient habitations.

Ben and Vestara, along with Jaina, had been the first to hear about what was possibly the first real break they'd had in a long time. He listened with half an ear as Natua filled in the rest of the fleet on the Dream Singers, the lava caves, and the subterranean hangar that had once contained Sith training vessels—and might again.

When she had finished, Luke spoke to his Jedi. "This is not the first time several Jedi have worked together on a single goal," he said. "It is the first time, however, that so very many of us—almost our entire number—have done so. Natua has outlined our twin objectives: to explore the volcanic caves where the Sith held their rituals, and to investigate the nearby habitation where Ship might be lurking. All ships, plot a course that will place us equidistant between those two sites. We'll meet there, and I'll give everyone their orders."

He turned to the other three. "Natua, I have a couple more questions for you. Ben, Vestara, you two head to the lockers and get ready. If Ship *is* down there, we'll need to move quickly."

Although this was the third time Vestara had prepared to visit a formerly Sith-ruled world, she felt more nervous than she had anticipating landing on Korriban. One reason, she knew, was because the last time she had set foot on such a planet, she had been attacked by and forced to kill her own father.

But the second reason was because when she had visited Korriban and Dromund Kaas . . . she had been a Sith, visiting a Sith world.

And now, she wasn't sure what she was.

Vestara seldom cried. Her father had thought it weakness, so she had simply learned not to weep. That night, after his death, lying in Ben's arms, she had felt completely shattered. She had not had the strength—nor, frankly, the desire—to shut herself off from him anymore. He had held her while she wept and, afterward, as they drifted to sleep. There had been only kisses and loving words, nothing more; Ben would never press his advantage when she was so vulnerable. It was part of what made him Ben; what made him a Jedi.

But she, daughter of the Sith, had not been so sure that was what she had wanted. Was now not sure that any of what had passed between them that night was what she wanted.

It had felt good to truly open herself to Ben in the Force, and later, when speaking with Luke, as well. Her decision had been genuine. It was too debilitating to be a Sith, she had decided. Too hard to constantly keep her guard up, to function alone, even in the midst of a society such as the Lost Tribe. The isolation she had felt at the death of her father—

—Unbearable. As she recalled the moment when Gavar Khai had fallen beneath her lightsaber, Vestara reached out and squeezed Ben's hand. He turned to look at her, lips curving in a smile as he began to don his protective mask. She felt a wave of love and support from him; not a crashing tsunami, but the constant, gentle flow of a ceaseless tide. Vestara sent back appreciation and warmth as real as his own, then squeezed and let go of his hand. For a moment, the wavering she had felt since that awful night was steadied. She was where she was supposed to be.

"So," Ben asked Vestara as she put on her own mask, "how are you feeling about going after Ship?"

It was a fair question. Vestara collected her thoughts before replying. "As long as Abeloth is alive and has the power to command him, Ship will obey her. Therefore, he must be destroyed."

"Or commandeered," Ben said.

She gave him a sharp look. "He won't obey Jedi."

"Not even if we bend him to our will?"

"If you did that, you wouldn't be a Jedi," she said. "The only way to control Ship is through strong, aggressive emotions. Desire, anger—not very Jedi-like."

"How will you feel if we have to destroy him?"

"Honestly? I will feel regret. Ship was the—well, *entity* I guess is the word—who took me off Kesh for the first time in my life. Can you imagine being planet-bound until you were fourteen, Ben? Never seeing your world from anything but the back of a winged creature? And being told that your fate, your destiny, was not on a single world, but hundreds?" She shook her head. "Ship changed my life, Ben. Yes, if we destroy him, I will feel regret. But I'll still do it."

He had paused in his preparations and now simply stared at her, his blue eyes crinkling with the smile his mask hid.

"I wish Dad could hear you say that."

"He won't have to," Vestara said, adjusting the last snap. "I'll show him."

It was almost like hitting a physical wall.

They all felt it, down to the last Jedi Knight. Luke could sense the dark side here more strongly than anywhere else he could recall. And even he found his stomach clenching and his skin erupting in goose-flesh; he, who had looked into the face of the dark side and defeated it more times than he could recall.

The evil was not merely ancient. It was—

"Distilled," Jaina said, stepping beside him as they looked at the ruins of the city before them. Directly above the city and the dormant volcano a mere three kilometers away roiled an ugly black cloud. No simple storm, this; it did not drift from its site, and its gray-black depths occasionally flashed with blue Force lightning. Wind blew from the city, strong and foul smelling and cold. The storm, and the dark-side energies, were here.

*Just* here.

"A good word," said Kyle Katarn. "It's . . . coalesced here, somehow."

"Well, Natua did say that this was the main city, and the cave system their primary ritual site," Jaina offered.

Luke shook his gray-blond head slowly. "Then why didn't it concentrate behind us, in the tunnels, as well? Why here, specifically—in such a clearly defined area? You can feel it—it's like standing with your back to the summer and your face toward the winter." Every instinct, developed over forty years of doing battle with the dark side in one form or another, was screaming at him to be careful. He had a very bad feeling about this.

"Perhapz Ship'z presence has awakened something long asleep," offered Saba. She stood at her full imposing height, eyes narrowed, all her senses extended.

"That's a cheery thought," muttered Kyp Durron.

"But a wise one," Jaina said. "Booby-trapping an abandoned city sounds exactly like something the Sith would do."

Natua had speculated that the rhak-skuri were found only in the tunnels, but Luke saw no point in taking any risks. He had ordered that they all wear masks. Now they stood in a small crowd, facing the abandoned city of the Sith and the towering mountain that had, tens of thousands of years before, been an active volcano.

Ben and Vestara stepped quietly beside him. Vestara glanced around, seeing more Jedi gathered in one spot than she had probably thought existed in the whole galaxy. Even as she watched them with eyes of aspiration, Luke sensed the unease fluttering inside her. He knew what the pair wanted of him. They wanted him to give them an important role—something that would show the dozens of Jedi gathered here that their Grand Master trusted the former Sith.

He wanted to do that, too. But Luke knew he couldn't.

Luke called for their attention, then began splitting up the Jedi into small groups and giving them instructions. He said nothing to Vestara and Ben. They waited with admirable patience for their instructions, and when none came, Ben approached his father. Two-thirds of the Jedi who had landed were moving off toward the northeast, while the rest returned to their vessels.

Ben strode up to his dad and pointed at Kyp Durron, who was already powering up his StealthX. "What's going on? Where are they going?"

"To provide air support, should it be needed. If Ship is here, and manages to defeat us, we'll need a second line of defense. Under no circumstances can he be allowed to return to Abeloth."

"Okay, that makes sense," Ben said, glancing between his father and Jaina. "So I guess you want Vestara and me to go with the rest of the Jedi."

"No," Luke said. He could almost feel Vestara's heart sink. "I need you, Natua, and Vestara to start exploring the caves. You might find something that could help us."

Natua smiled pleasantly. "Vestara will be of great help if we come across anything written in the ancient Sith language," she said. "And she might recognize many things that would mean nothing to the rest of us."

"In other words," Ben snapped, "you don't trust her, so you're finding a job that doesn't force her to choose between us and Ship."

"That's not true," Natua started to say, but Vestara placed a hand on the Falleen's arm.

"Yes, it is," she said, looking at Luke evenly. "And he's right to do so. You can't risk anything going wrong if you run across Ship. And the truth of the matter is, I *can* help if we run across any Sith artifacts. I can help a great deal. So the logical position for me is to send me with a small group to explore the caves, where I can be an asset, rather than track down Ship, where I might be a liability. I would have made the same decision."

"Yeah?" Ben was still upset. "Well, *I* wouldn't have."

"You're not the Grand Master," Vestara said. "He can't afford to trust me."

"Vestara," said Luke, and his voice and demeanor were kind, "it really isn't a matter of trust—not this time. Nor about your feelings toward Ship."

She gave him a skeptical glance. "Think about it for a moment," he continued. He wanted her to understand why he was doing this; if she understood his reasoning and agreed with it, she would take another step along the path to the light. "We all know how seductive the pull of the dark side can be. And you grew up steeped in it. Now you've made the decision to turn your back on the dark side—and I know, believe me, how hard that can be. If I let you come with us, you're going to be tempted as never before. It's not just Ship—it's the whole miasma of the place. I've never seen anything like it, and that makes me very wary of it."

"I have been to Korriban and Dromund Kaas," she said. Her voice was calm, but Luke could feel her disappointment, her—shame?—at being thought so weak and untrustworthy. "I did not falter there, did I?"

"No," Luke agreed readily. "You didn't. And that's why I'm giving you a chance at all to become a Jedi. But this isn't a fair test of your will—not right now. It would be like asking a newly recovering spice addict to go to a party where the stuff was everywhere."

"I will have to do so eventually, if I am to become a Jedi. I cannot—I will not—hide away simply to avoid challenges."

"You're not. You've already faced two very strong tests. You knew that even Master Kyle Katarn fell to the dark side on Dromund Kaas. It's because I *do* believe you have a chance that I don't want you anywhere near that place. I don't want to set you up to fail. Trust me, the last thing I want right now is to have to cut you down in front of my son—or have Ben forced to make that choice."

Vestara turned to look at Ben. He didn't flinch from her brown gaze. They all knew he would indeed do so if it came to it.

"You can't run before you can walk," Luke said. He made sure there was no censure in his voice or expression or, indeed, even in his Force presence. "And I would be a poor teacher if I asked that of you. I agreed to train you in the ways of the Jedi. If you still wish me to do so, then consider this your first order from your Master."

She bit her lower lip, then she nodded. "I do not like it, but—I understand. If I was willing to obey Lady Rhea when she was my Master, who cared nothing for me other than how she could use me, I will certainly obey you."

Ben's pride in Vestara was like a small sun. She still stood at attention, but Luke saw her lips curve in the slightest of smiles.

"Obedience is seldom fun, but it is necessary," he said. "Knowing that you, Ben, and Natua will be away from this . . . maelstrom of energy . . . eases my mind. Thank you for understanding, Vestara. We'll comm you if anything happens. And keep us posted if you find anything that will help us."

"Of course, sir." She nodded at him. Luke gave Ben a final concerned, affectionate glance, then started off with his Jedi.

Toward a city more full of concentrated dark-side energy, of hate, and anger, and fear, and violence, than anything Luke Skywalker had known before.

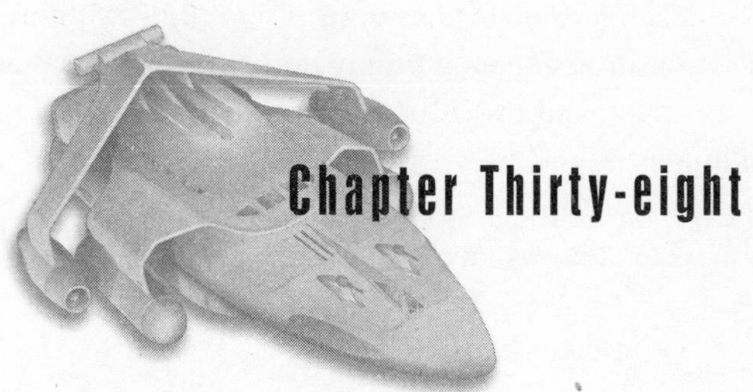

# Chapter Thirty-eight

"I DON'T KNOW ABOUT YOU TWO, BUT I FOR ONE AM QUITE CURIOUS TO see what is down there," Natua said. "After studying the Sith so intensely to help Master Luke, it is exciting to perhaps be the ones to stumble onto something."

"I don't remember you as being such a scholarly sort," Ben said. He set his shoulders, clearly trying to shake off the unpleasant conversation with his father, and the three of them turned and marched toward the cave opening.

"I'm not," Natua said. "At least, I didn't think I was. History seemed very dry to me. But having to do this research in order to help with something that was going on right now—that made me feel that I could do something." She looked over at both of them. "As you can imagine, I don't harbor a lot of warm and fuzzy feelings toward Abeloth."

Vestara thought of the first time she had penetrated Abeloth's illusions, of the hideous thing that had been the reality; of the sickness of Sarasu Taalon and the unhinging of her father's mind.

"Neither do I," she said. "Neither do I."

Worn surprisingly smooth by the flow of lava millennia past, the caves had a geometric beauty to them that seemed more than random. The glow rods provided light, but also cast strangely shaped shadows, illuminating some areas and leaving others pools of darkness. A few stalagmites and stalactites impeded their progress, but it was clear the passage of liquid, not the shifting of the planet, had made the volcanic tunnels.

The caverns had very few narrow passages, so most of the time they could walk three abreast. Vestara could sense that Ben was still put out with his father for removing them from the real action. She, however, was more or less resigned to it, and when Natua paused and shone the glow rod into an offshoot cavern, all three of them came to a dead stop.

Thus far all they had seen was what nature had wrought. Now they peered into what could only be called a "room." It felt as though the temperature had dropped several degrees, but the chill was not entirely physical. The walls—which bore delicate writing—floor, and ceiling were even and flat, not curved. There were remnants of what appeared to be rugs, cushions, and tools. And over in one corner, covered with droppings, debris, and dust, were—

"Lightsabers," Natua breathed.

"They surrendered their weapons here before going on," Vestara said.

"You guessed that?"

"I read it," Vestara said, pointing to the writing on the wall. She took a step inward, feeling the chill wrap around her like a cold mist. She knew Ben and Natua sensed it, too; this little pocket was steeped in dark-side energy. The initiates who had come here had been afraid—and judging by the number of abandoned lightsabers, rightfully so.

"What's it say?" Ben stepped next to her, touching her lightly on the shoulder. She knew what the contact meant: *I am here. I believe in you, even as we stand awash in dark-side energy.* And Vestara felt a little—a very little—warmer.

"'Initiates, you who would master the dark side, prepare yourselves. Leave your weapons, and your former selves, here in this chamber—or depart now and forever in shame, before it is too late to turn back.' "

"They were allowed to go?" asked Ben.

Both Natua and Vestara shrugged. "It probably wasn't like walking away from a sabacc game," Natua said. "They would be, as it says, forever shamed. I'd bet that included exile."

"Or some type of particularly vicious punishment, or ritual suicide," Vestara said. "Whatever the case, they wouldn't live long afterward."

"Do you think the lightsabers were left by the ones who were too scared to go through with it?" asked Ben.

Vestara turned to him. The dark-side energies here, old and patient, were too familiar for her liking, and she knew she had dropped into her former coldness as she responded. "No, Ben. I think if you refused to complete the ritual, your lightsaber was taken and given to someone more worthy. I think these lightsabers were left by owners who didn't survive the initiation."

Natua looked at the weapons and grimaced. "To reinforce fear and apprehension," she said. "Sounds like the Sith for sure. They don't even really take care of their own."

A cold, unhappy pang shot through Vestara, but she kept her expression neutral. "No," she said. "They don't."

"I'm going to make some recordings," Natua said. "We need to document everything we find."

Vestara and Ben stepped back into the main tunnel to give her room to work. "Hey," Ben said gently. "You doing okay?"

She smiled uncertainly. "For the most part," she said. "I think I'd honestly prefer to be fighting Ship than be down here with all this."

"I know. I wish we were. This stuff seriously creeps me out."

Vestara didn't answer. It creeped her out, too—but it also stirred up an unexpected longing. She was between worlds now. She had turned her back on her culture, her people, and their ancient rituals. Soon, she would be embraced—she hoped—by the Jedi, and belong to their culture, and experience their rituals. But now, she felt adrift. The feeling surprised her, and she found herself reaching for Ben's hand.

They stood in silence for a while, hands clasped, until Natua emerged. “Let’s keep going,” the Falleen said. “This is fascinating, and important data to have, but I’d just as soon not linger.”

The tunnel curved slightly, and the three of them followed the path, staying alert for any other signs of ancient Sith activity that had survived the eons. There was no more writing on the walls, or caverns carved into the stone. There were, however, fragments of old bones, scattered pieces of what was clearly equipment, and an increasing sense of unease as they traveled deeper into the heart of the planet. The bones they examined carefully; some of them turned to dust in their hands, but others remained semi-intact.

“Human?” asked Natua.

“Impossible to tell without analyzing them,” Ben said. “We only know of the tiny hallucination-inducing bugs. All kinds of animals could have made this their home over the centuries.”

“You don’t need to protect me, Ben,” Vestara said. And from the quick flush of embarrassed compassion, she knew she was right. “If the Sith left those who had failed where they fell, surely it doesn’t matter anymore.”

“You wouldn’t want to—you know, bury them? Or do whatever the Lost Tribe does with their dead?”

“I’m not a member of the Lost Tribe anymore. And if that Sith’s own people didn’t care, why should I?”

She had intended it to sound as though she wasn’t upset. Instead, she knew it came out sounding brutally uncaring, and she frowned a little. “I didn’t mean that to sound as harsh as it did.”

“This place is unsettling us all,” Natua said, smiling kindly. “I think we’ve learned about all we can without getting hopelessly lost.”

It was a white lie. Vestara could sense that Natua wanted to continue for at least a bit more and was cutting the exploration short in order to make it easier on Vestara.

“Please, neither you nor Ben need to coddle me,” Vestara said. “If you want to continue, let’s continue. It’s better than sitting outside twiddling our thumbs while Luke and the others take down Ship. At least we’re doing something useful.” She strode forward purposefully. And because they couldn’t argue with her logic, Ben and Natua fell in behind her.

The tunnels continued on. And on. As long minutes passed with no further discovery, Vestara herself started to wonder if perhaps they had indeed discovered all there was to find. It made perfect Sith sense: provide a single chamber to collect the weapons and warn the initiates close to the entrance, then turn them loose to meet the Dream Singers, letting them lie where they fell. Her steps slowed and she came to a halt as the tunnel opened up into a large, naturally formed chamber, with smaller tunnels leading in different directions.

She had just turned around, her mouth open to suggest they retrace their steps, when they all heard the sound.

It was so soft at first that for an instant Vestara wondered if she had imagined it. But Ben and Natua were listening intently, as well.

"Were there any descriptions of sounds?" Ben asked Natua. "I don't know my geology that well. Maybe caves make noises?"

It came again, a soft, low groaning, and Vestara's stomach clenched. The air suddenly grew cold, as it had in the chamber they had first encountered.

Wordlessly the three activated their lightsabers and dropped their glow rods, automatically moving so their backs were against one another and they faced outward.

"What was that you asked earlier about animals, Ben?" Natua said. Ben didn't answer, and neither did Vestara. She was too busy dealing with the sudden wave of dark-side energy that crashed over them like the ghost of the lava that had formed these tunnels so long ago. The shadows, black as full night and dancing now from the glow of the lightsabers as she and the two Jedi moved them about slowly, seemed like living beings as they surged forward and back.

And then one of the shadows reared above them, and for a second Vestara wondered if her protective mask had somehow been damaged. For surely this . . . *monster* could only come from the darkest corners of a deranged mind's nightmares.

Well over two meters tall, its shiny, sectioned body a deep blue-black, the thing gazed down at them with two pairs of glowing red compound eyes. Its mandibles clacked as ooze dripped from them. Lashing behind it were two extensions looking like a double tail. Each one ended in pincers that looked as if they could lop off an arm with no effort.

Vestara noted all this in the space of half a heartbeat as it descended on them. Four of its six arms, each ending in a hook, reached out to swipe at them while the hideous head darted with shocking speed toward—

"Ben!" Vestara cried. Ben dived away as the mandibles scraped at his mask, rolling on the cave floor and coming up fighting. The instant he moved, Vestara laid into the creature, her red blade sizzling as it bit into the hard substance that protected its body. Natua Wan charged at it as well, and the two women moved swiftly so that the creature was being attacked on two sides.

One of the tail pincers snapped at Natua, taking a huge chunk out of her leg. The Falleen hissed in pain but faltered only a little, renewing her attack while Ben dived at the creature from behind. It let out a terrible, screeching wail as Ben's lightsaber struck at the pincer, burning and blunting it but doing far less damage than it should have, and then whirled to again target the young Jedi. Their blades seemed to have only minimal effect. When the lightsabers struck the creature, their glow dimmed, somehow, as if the thing was draining energy from the blades.

Vestara extended a hand, trying to Force-shove the creature away from Ben. To her astonishment, the creature merely stumbled a little and continued its onslaught. Ben grunted in pain as slaver splashed down on his arm, burning it like acid.

Vestara felt a wave of pain at Ben's injury—a deep, dull ache in her chest—and growled furiously as she charged forward, her lightsaber almost musical, singing an angry song—

—singing—

The realization struck her so hard she stumbled and lost a precious second. How had they been so stupid!

She knew what the monstrosity before them had to be. They had been unbelievably, unforgivably complacent to think that simply because nothing had been recorded about these tunnels and what dwelled within them, there was nothing they needed to fear.

The monster that had come out of the shadows—which was now attacking Ben—was a mutated rhak-skuri.

Once it had been only a few millimeters in length, a harmless, natural being, but centuries of exposure to the Sith and the energy of dark-side rituals—and quite possibly deliberate alchemical efforts—had transformed it.

"Rhak-skuri!" she shouted. "Come for me!"

It knew its name.

It paused, ever so briefly, in its assault on Ben, whirling to stare at her with its glowing, multiple eyes, its antennae waving as if in agitation—or pleasure. It Force-shoved Ben and Natua back without removing its attention from Vestara, and for a second she felt heavy and sluggish.

. . . *Ssssssiiithhh* . . .

The word, spoken in her mind, was like a cold hand clamping down on Vestara's heart.

No. She wasn't a Sith, not anymore, she—

. . . *Ssssssiiithhh* . . .

It was not harming her, and without knowing how she knew, she understood what it wanted.

It had gone from a simple insect to this monstrous entity over centuries. By exposure to the dark side; by honoring rituals in which it had been encouraged to unleash nightmares. And it had learned not to give without taking.

Somehow she understood that it would not harm her. She was Sith. She was one of the *things-that-make,* and long, long had it been since the Dream Singer had encountered the Makers. But it needed a sacrifice.

It would feed, and remain strong, and serve the dark side.

As would she.

*No!* Vestara summoned all her energy and renewed her attack. She realized suddenly that only two were attacking the Dream Singer—herself, and Natua.

Ben stood stock-still, ignoring the acid eating into his arm, his eyes wide, his mouth open—

—his mouth—

Vestara realized with a shock of horror that Ben's mask had been ripped away by the rhak-skuri's last attack. He had inadvertently inhaled the pheromones and was now experiencing horrors that even she could not imagine.

And she understood just how the rhak-skuri fed.

It was a living being. It would consume flesh. But it would also be sated by the victim's terror.

*Like Abeloth.*

For a fraction of an instant that lasted an eon, Vestara stood as if paralyzed.

Ben was out of the fight, eyes shut, convulsing in terror. He would pass out soon, if his heart—or his mind—did not give out before then. She and Natua were by no means weak in the Force. But this thing was ancient. And evil. Fed by centuries of terror and thoughts of violence and darkness, it was much stronger than the tuk'ata or other Sith "demons" she had encountered. It had grown powerful on sweeter food.

It wanted her to ally with it. And Vestara knew that unless she and Natua could defeat it, it would have its sacrifice—with or without her aid.

And the sacrifice it wanted was Ben.

# Chapter Thirty-nine

THE GROUND BENEATH THEM TREMBLED AS THE JEDI STRODE, PREPARED for battle but with calm in their hearts, toward the ominous cloud that hovered over the city. In the air that stirred their hair like a vile caress, in the very soil beneath their feet, they could feel the dark side.

"Well," said Jaina, "I can't sense Ship specifically. But I'm sure that if even the whole Lost Tribe were gathered in one building raising a toast to Abeloth, I wouldn't be able to sense them, either."

"None of us could. It would be like trying to pick out a single flower in a field full of them," Luke replied. All his senses were alert, but that did not distract him from continuing to work things through in his head. "Natua didn't mention anything like this concentration of dark-side energy in her briefing. This . . . is new for this world."

"I think perhaps Saba had the right of it," Octa Ramis said, falling into step beside them. Like all the Jedi, she held her lightsaber, but it was not ignited. "Maybe Ship is here, and he's stirred something up."

"Some*things*," Luke amended. Now that he was growing at least somewhat used to the particular nuances, the swirls and eddies of the dark side as it manifested here, he realized that it was not a singular energy they were sensing.

Barv, mitigating his stride so that his friend Yaqeel could keep up with him, grunted that he, too, seemed to think it was an awful lot of somethings, but that he was completely confident it was nothing the Jedi couldn't handle. After all, they *were* Jedi, and they stood for the light side. Yaqeel looked up at him with soft, affectionate eyes, then away. Luke sensed that she, like himself, wasn't quite as certain as Barv of the eventual outcome.

"Then why haven't they attacked?" Kyp asked. "If these things are ghosts of Sith past, we're practically sitting on their doorstep."

"Perhaps they can't," mused Kyle. "They might be imprisoned—servants chained long ago by the Sith, only able to do a master's direct bidding."

"That doesn't make sense," Jaina said with her usual bluntness. Even in this moment of tense awareness and uncertainty, constantly keeping the darkness from seeping into him, Luke smiled. The conversation was good for them. It helped them feel more in control of the situation. Now was most definitely not a time for feelings of revenge, anger, or a desire for victory at all costs. It was a time for calmness, and tranquillity, and rational thought. These were their greatest weapons.

"Think about what we saw on Korriban," Jaina continued. "The Sith are notorious for leaving guardians or traps behind. To chain a whole bunch of dark-side entities and essentially only give them orders to 'sit' and 'stay' is . . . well, it's a stupid use of resources, and one thing the Sith aren't is stupid."

"This one agrees," said Saba. "Though it would make our roles as Jedi easier if the Sith were stupid."

Yaqeel snorted, then quickly looked away.

*Good,* thought Luke. He had never been prouder of his Jedi than now, with Jaina's smart-mouthed but logical comment, and Yaqeel's smothered laughter. They were walking, together, into darkness, and able to think and laugh. In a way, whatever happened next, they had already won.

They paused as they approached a wall that enclosed the city. This place did not have the imposing architecture of a fortress. It was both functional and decorative, but did not seem designed to impose fear and awe on the beholder. The wall was covered in faded designs of hideous, red-eyed, multilegged monsters, images of Sith meditating and sparring, and other designs that Luke didn't recognize. He wished for a moment he had dared bring Vestara, but that would have been far too risky. Natua was a second-best choice, with her newly acquired knowledge, but she was needed where she was. The gateway was a simple metal portcullis. Luke wondered at that, and spoke into his comlink to the other Jedi.

"Stop at the entrance," he said. Gateways, entrances, anything that denoted a crossing from one space to another—these were places of power. Innocent looking—well, innocent looking for a Sith construction anyway—though it might be, he needed to proceed with utmost care.

He reached out in the Force, probing for an increase in the power of the dark side here, or even a change or shift in the nature of the energy. There seemed to be nothing unusual. Now more curious than wary, Luke lifted a hand.

The portcullis rose easily, grinding slightly with eons of disuse.

"Oh, I really don't like this," Jaina said.

"Neither does this one," murmured Saba, her eyes narrowing. The Barabel's tail lashed.

"Come on," Luke said into the comlink, and the Jedi obeyed. Cautiously they moved into the city proper, all of them looking around, their senses alert to any shift, any change, any danger more immediate than the constant, oppressive hatred that poured from the dark side.

Once the last of them had entered, the portcullis dropped with a loud clang. The sky suddenly darkened, and thunder rumbled. The temperature dropped and the wind picked up. Luke glanced upward at the unnatural cloud that squatted angrily over the city, and saw quick flashes of Force lightning in its depths.

"I'm waiting for the welcoming committee," said Jaina, her voice soft but her body tense and ready to spring into action.

"Yeah," said Seha Dorvald, standing beside Octa. "I'd like for something to *happen* already."

"Keep your focus, Jedi," Luke said, projecting calmness. "I'm sure it will come, but you must be prepared to meet it. If you are spoiling for a fight, you give it the advantage."

"I am sorry, Master Skywalker," Seha said.

"No need to apologize. Just do it," Luke replied mildly.

The buildings, like the wall, seemed designed more to protect and shelter the inhabitants than to make a show of fearsome power, although they showed the wear of time in the lack of roofs and other disrepair. Other than the increased hostility of the dark-side energies, which seemed curiously still but, like hunting nexu, straining at the leash, there was nothing obvious to denote that Sith had been the former inhabitants.

"This was not a martial world," Saba said. "Their focus was different."

"The tunnels," Jaina said, and Luke felt a flicker of unease from her. "Their whole culture was centered on those rites conducted in the lava caves."

"They focused on the metaphysical, not the material," Luke said, and something settled into place. He was on the right track. "They were not warriors focused on conquering and weaponry, Saba, because they didn't have to be."

"Oh, that sounds wonderful," Kyp drawled.

Luke paused for a moment, closing his eyes and dropping deeply into himself. He extended his perception. They were close to the center of the darkness; close to what this place and these enslaved energies were hiding. A place deep in the planet, close to the mysteries these Sith found so compelling.

What they sought was there. And it knew they were coming.

He opened his eyes. "It's in the center of the city," he said. "The underground hangar. And something is definitely there. Activate lightsabers, and prepare for battle."

As he spoke those words into the comlink, the ground trembled again, more violently this time. Several of the buildings crumbled.

"And whatever it is, it really doesn't want us to find it," said Jaina.

Luke gave her a serene smile. "We're more than a hundred Jedi. Would you?"

She gave him an uncertain grin in return and, igniting her own lightsaber, moved forward. With each step, Luke felt, and knew the others felt as well, the dark side pressing in on them, trying to push them back. He steeled himself and kept moving forward, sending waves of reassurance to those Jedi less certain than himself. There was no censure in it. None of them had been trained to stand against something like this. He was extremely proud of them, and felt them rally at his touch in the Force.

Their path led them to a large open area. Luke recalled what Ben had told him about discovering Ship. Ben had commanded Ship to appear, and it had done so, forming a crack in the surface of the planet and climbing out.

Luke wasn't sure it was Ship in there. But there was definitely a presence. This was where the energies were concentrated. They had cornered their foe in its lair. Dark-side energy, focused and contained, pulsed hatred at him so intently he could almost feel his flesh burn with it.

Luke, like his son, would order whatever was in there to appear. But unlike Ben, he did not need to speak to it in a language it understood in order to be obeyed.

"Everyone, get ready," he said. "I'm bringing it out."

They all dropped into combat poses, each according to his or her individual strengths. The Jedi ships now flew into formation above them, awaiting orders to attack, defend, or retreat.

Luke extended a hand.

*Come forth.*

*No.* If coldness, and terror, and pure malice had a voice, it would speak like this.

*You will.*

*I will not.*

Luke frowned and put more persuasion into his words.

*Come. Forth!*

The ground bucked. A crack appeared in front of them, angry and zigzagging and bespeaking nothing of order, only wildness and chaos. The gap widened, huge chunks of stone falling down into the chamber below or else hurling themselves at the Jedi, who easily turned the objects away. Luke gripped his lightsaber in one hand, the other extended, staring down at the darkness and bracing himself for the sight of the hideous form this dark-side entity—*entities,* he amended—would assume.

A pale lavender face peered up at them. It would have been attractive, had it not been swollen with bruises and sliced with cuts. The figure, female, was bound hand and foot. A cord arched her body painfully, so that if she struggled, she would choke herself.

"Help me!" she cried. "Please!"

For a precious second, Luke was taken completely off-guard. A Keshiri Sith? Imprisoned and clearly tortured? Yet it was plain that she was the source of all this dark-side energy. What was going on? He felt almost battered by the confusion of his fellow Jedi.

"It's got to be a trick, Uncle Luke!" Jaina cried.

"A trick," said Luke, "or a test?" His mind was racing. If they killed this Sith without ascertaining she was their enemy, all of them—the entire Jedi Order—would have taken a huge step toward the dark side. And nothing would please Ship or Abeloth, or indeed the Lost Tribe, more.

"Please," grunted the woman. "She took away my powers. She left me here to die . . ." Tears formed and slipped down her cheeks, making tracks in the dust that paled her face.

"Who are you?" Luke demanded.

"T-tola Annax," the Keshiri woman said. "I served under Gavar Khai. I got his command when he died, but Abeloth decided she didn't need me anymore."

"Where is she?"

"I don't know," the woman cried. "Please . . ."

A sliver of darkness appeared along her skin. For a second, Luke simply thought it another track of her tears, revealing darker skin beneath the white dust.

But then he realized what it was.

They couldn't help Tola Annax anymore. She was already dead.

The crack widened, and more darkness was revealed—darkness that was luminous, pulsating. Abeloth had somehow managed to harness all, or close to all, the dark-side energy that permeated this world, and compress it into this one pitiable being. What had once been Tola Annax now contained unfathomable dark-side energy waiting to be released. It had been both a trick *and* a test. Had they attacked her, leaping into the pit and slicing her to ribbons with lightsabers, they would have been at the center of the explosion. No one would have survived—and they might yet not survive.

All this registered in a fraction of a heartbeat. "Retreat!" cried Luke, wasting no more breath on words, instead sending a shock wave of urgency in the Force and an image of their initial landing area. There was no time to comm Ben; instead Luke focused on visualizing his son and sending him the same urgent missive: *Retreat. Get to safety. Get out.*

Everyone responded at once, without question or hesitation, and began to race back toward the gate. The ground began to shake again, yet more violently, and Luke heard the sound of laughter—Abeloth's laughter—following them as they ran for their very lives.

The cloud above them changed. Force lightning struck the ground, struck the ships in the air, struck the Jedi using the Force to give them added speed and distance as they ran. All around them, buildings crumbled to dust. Luke deflected a chunk of a wall hurtling toward him, directing it to slam into another boulder that was heading straight for Seha.

Saba was a few meters ahead of him as they ran. The ground cracked open a scant step in front of her. Without breaking stride, she Force-leapt easily over the suddenly manifesting chasm, landed on the other side, and kept going. Luke, Jaina, and the others did likewise.

The explosion behind them hurled them all into the air. Luke himself had to scramble so he didn't land hard. Even as he twisted to land on his feet, he reached out in the Force and cushioned the fall for some of the less experienced Jedi Knights. He ended up facing back the way he had come, and his eyes widened at what he beheld.

The dormant volcano was dormant no longer. Gouts of orange magma spewed kilometers into the air and rained death down along the side of the mountain. It was a terrifying sight, but what alarmed Luke even more than the racing lava was the cloud above it. It looked like smoke, churning and billowing, gray and thick, but it was nothing so benevolent as mere choking ash. He knew what he was looking at.

Rock so hot it had turned into foam five times hotter than boiling water, moving at more than a hundred kilometers an hour. If this pyroclastic surge overtook them, they would be incinerated instantly, their bodies turned into charcoal.

And it would overtake them within minutes.

Their masks prevented the inhalation of the poisonous gases and thick, blinding ash, but could not cool the suddenly superheated air. Luke used the Force to cool it as best he could as he inhaled. Beside and in front of him, he saw two Jedi suddenly start clawing at their throats, falling an instant later. They had inhaled without cooling the air, and Luke felt sympathetic anguish at the agony in which they had died, drowning in their lungs' own fluid. He squeezed his eyes shut and created a barrier around them with the Force to protect them, running forward now using only his other four senses and the Force.

Fear, determination, pain—all arose around him as the Jedi raced to outrun the cloud of dark side oblivion that was hard on their heels. Some of them would not make it—some already had not. But most of them would.

He forced his eyes to open briefly. Saba Sebatyne, the one with the longest legs of them all, had already reached the gate. Not bothering to raise it, lest it be lowered again on them, she had simply blown the durasteel portcullis apart with the Force. Jedi raced through the hole, even as the walls that held it started to crumble.

Joy and gratitude washed through Luke as he saw dozens of vessels landing and taking on the nearly exhausted Jedi ground force. Others kept going, heading for their own StealthXs. He reached for his comlink, shouting to be heard over the rumble.

"Ben! Ben, can you hear me?"

There was only silence. Luke cursed, clicked the comlink again. "Raynar! Can you take on more passengers?" Most of the Jedi had flown in their own StealthXs, but there had been several larger ships included in the fleet. Raynar had piloted one such, and could get to the tunnels before Luke even reached the *Jade Shadow.*

"Yes, Master Luke, where do you wish me to go?" Thul's voice, calm as ever.

"Go to the entrance of the caves. Get Ben, Vestara, and Natua. Right now!"

"Adjusting course, Master Skywalker."

"Thank you," said Luke, permitting himself to feel a slight sense of relief. Just as he clicked off the comlink, a sudden vision flashed into his mind: the image of the multilegged, red-eyed creature carved onto the ancient wall. He suddenly realized what it was, and a new, horrible apprehension for Ben's safety seized him.

*Find my son,* he thought desperately, as he ran with flagging strength toward where he had left the *Jade Shadow.*

*Find my son.*

# Chapter Forty

THE LAVA TUNNELS OF UPEKZAR

THE CHOICE WAS MADE IN AN INSTANT.

Vestara loved Ben. The Dream Singer would *not* have him. And Ben would never have to know what she did for him. As certain about this as she had ever been in her life, Vestara whirled to attack. She lifted her lightsaber high, the glowing red light illuminating a face contorted in anger and determination, and brought it down.

The crimson weapon slashed through Natua's mask.

Taken completely by surprise, the Falleen stumbled backward, turning shocked eyes on Vestara. Vestara snarled and began attacking her. To Vestara's own shock, Natua didn't seem affected by the pheromones.

Of course . . . Natua was a Falleen . . .

Fear shot through Vestara as Natua, recovered from the unexpectedness of the betrayal, fought back fiercely.

"I knew we could never trust a Sith!" Natua snarled as her lightsaber danced and clashed with Vestara's.

Vestara parried and thrust and slashed, her blade making a sharp sound as it cut air and sizzled against the Jedi's lightsaber. Natua *would* fall, resistance or not. She could not stand against the creature and a Sith both.

And then it happened. Natua stumbled, lowering her lightsaber, and began to shriek. She started fighting again, her blade slashing empty air, and Vestara was able to dart in easily and cut a furrow across her torso.

Natua fell to the floor, flailing and screaming, her lightsaber making futile burns in the rock. Vestara stood over the spasming body, her own lightsaber lowered, sweat sheening her brow. She met the creature's compound eyes and felt their kinship. It dipped its head in—gratitude? acknowledgment?—and moved forward onto Natua. Its feelers extended, running over the thrashing form in a vile caress as it fed deeply on the Falleen's terror.

Vestara could tell the exact minute when Natua's mind finally snapped. Her eyes widened, and then her body grew limp, though she continued to breathe. The creature looked up from its feeding and regarded Vestara.

*. . . Ssssssiiithhh . . . Cooooome . . .*

Vestara heard movement behind her and a soft groan. Ben was awakening. With a slow smile, she leapt at the Dream Singer, attacking it with all her strength.

"Vestara!" And then Ben was on his feet, stumbling into the fray.

He was safe. Natua was dead.

It couldn't possibly have gone more smoothly.

The terror still shuddered through Ben, even as his body struggled against a second bout of unconsciousness. He had no way of knowing what was real and what was an illusion, but after he realized what was happening to him, Ben knew what he had to do. What his father had taught him, what his namesake had taught his father.

*Trust your feelings.*

He trusted his love for Vestara. He trusted his friendship with Natua. And he trusted that if he was determined enough, strong enough, he could still fight and not fall prey to the terror that seemed to flow through his blood with every beat of his rapidly pounding heart.

He couldn't tell if it was truly a monster, or another sentient being, or what. He couldn't tell if Natua was really dead, couldn't tell if that was really a lightsaber slash across her torso or part of the pheromone-induced illusion. But he could *feel* the evil roiling off his adversary, and could no longer sense Natua in the Force, and that was enough for him to charge in fighting.

The ground suddenly shook beneath their feet and he and Vestara, both caught off-guard, had to act quickly to prevent being hurled to the stone floor. Ben, his senses still bedazzled by the attack, heard Vestara grunt and looked up to see a huge stalactite hovering only a few centimeters above his head. She threw it away with the Force, and he heard it crack as it landed.

Vestara grabbed and shook him. "Ben! Listen to me!"

He blinked, trying to focus on her. She *looked* like Vestara, and she wasn't terrifying the life out of him—

"We have to get out. Now. The tunnels are collapsing."

"Natua—" He whirled, turning to where the creature was. It was nowhere to be seen, nor was Natua. It had used the distraction of the quake to escape. His gaze fell on a bloody smear that disappeared into the darkness.

"It's too late for her," said Vestara, shaking his arm again, "and it's going to be too late for us if we don't hurry!"

He nodded, finding his mask and putting it back on. Just in case. "Yeah. Let's get out of here!"

They raced back the way they had come, reaching out in the Force to try to sense the instant before another great, bucking shudder racked the ground and bracing themselves accordingly. Now that they were no longer exploring in a leisurely manner but quite literally running for their lives, the distance seemed much shorter to Ben. They passed where they had encountered the old, brittle bones, crushing them to dust beneath running feet. They had almost made it to the chamber where they had found the lightsabers when Ben sensed another quake about to occur.

Ben grabbed Vestara and Force-hurled them both back down the tunnel. He angled himself so that she fell on top of him, sparing as much energy as he could to lessen his own fall.

The roaring sound nearly deafened them, and it seemed to go on forever. Ben clung to Vestara, and she clung back. After what felt like an eternity, the tunnel was still.

And dark.

"You okay?" Ben asked.

He felt her pressed against him, felt her breathing, felt her heartbeat. "Yes," she said, climbing off him carefully. "Thank you."

"My pleasure."

She laughed, shakily. "I've—lost my lightsaber."

"Me too. Maybe they just got knocked from our hands." Ben's ribs were bruised from the hard landing, but he managed to sit up. He winced, knowing Vestara was as blind as he right now.

He held out his hand. It didn't matter where the lightsaber lay. He imagined how it would feel in his hand—the coolness of the metal, the familiar weight. And an instant later he felt a gentle smack in his palm as the lightsaber returned to it. Grinning despite his pain, he activated it. The first thing he looked for was Vestara's face, bathed in soft blue light.

She was not looking at him. She was looking over his shoulder, in the direction they had been heading.

Ben turned to follow her gaze—and saw that they had been sealed in.

"Bloah," he said glumly.

They stood staring for a while, then Vestara sighed. "This would go faster with two lightsabers, but let's get started. We might even get out of this alive if we do."

"Oh, we will," he said.

"You sound pretty certain."

"I am," he said. "You just recently turned toward the light side of the Force. I promised I'd watch you become a Jedi, remember?"

With her mask on, he couldn't read her expression, but she reached over and silently squeezed his arm. He sent her a warm brush of confidence and affection, and went to work on the stones.

They quickly fell into a rhythm. Ben would cut the stones. Vestara would use the Force both to move the carved-out pieces safely behind them and to keep the "wall" of remaining stone from collapsing in on them. A few more tremors came, but between the two of them the wall held.

At one point, after several minutes of this, Ben's breath started to become labored. He thought the mask wasn't functioning, and started to remove it.

"Don't," cautioned Vestara. "The air . . . it's running out. And it feels . . . hot. Use the Force to control your breathing."

He nodded. He did not speak, not after that warning, and did as she suggested—used the Force to make his body absorb as much oxygen as it could from the slow breaths he permitted himself to take.

After about half an hour, Ben stuck a hand in one of the cracks. "We're almost through," he said.

Vestara waved him over to her, indicating he should stand beside her. He did. She looked straight ahead and mimed pushing. He understood at once and nodded. She lifted her hand and counted down: *One. Two.*

*Three.*

They Force-shoved with all their strength. The wall of wedged rocks exploded outward as if a thermal detonator had been set off. For a moment, they stood staring at the gaping hole, then started laughing and hugging each other.

"Quit snuggling, you two," came a voice. They looked up, shocked, to see Corran Horn. His eyes over the gas mask looked both amused and impatient. "The volcano erupted and you need to get out with me *now.* Oh, and Vestara—"

He tossed her an unlit lightsaber.

"I believe this is yours."

# Chapter Forty-one

OFFICES OF MERRATT JAXTON, CORUSCANT

MERRATT JAXTON, FOR ALL THAT HE ENJOYED BEING THE CENTER OF attention, found that when he needed to he was very good at keeping his head down.

He'd started to wonder if something was going wrong when Lecersen fell silent. He'd *known* something was going wrong when Bramsin died of so-called natural causes and Treen left within hours of his death.

And when Parova's body turned up . . .

He, who had sent the fake Jedi after Admiral Nek Bwua'tu, did not believe it was the work of Tahiri Veila. Or any other Jedi.

There were only two of them left. Three, if you counted Suldar, who was supposed to have been the "new boy" and who had suddenly seemed to be running the show and reducing the number of people he needed to deal with right and left.

He'd liked it when Lecersen was the head of the whole thing—well, the titular head, though Jaxton knew that the whole thing had been Senator Treen's idea. Now that neither of them was reachable, Jaxton was starting to feel very, very insecure indeed.

He stared at his comlink, turning it over and over in his hand, then finally clicked it.

"Yeah," came the cold, metallic voice.

Jaxton hesitated. He didn't know what he was going to say.

"I don't like this."

"What don't you like?"

"Parova and Bramsin are dead?"

"And we're alive, so?"

Did General Stavin Thaal just not get it? "And what makes you think we won't be next? These blasted Senators, thinking they can control us . . . No word from good old Palpatine, either," he added, recalling with distaste the costumed meeting where Lecersen had shown up as Emperor Palpatine.

A pause. "You know, you have a good point. Let's get together and discuss it."

"Where?"

"I'll find you."

*Click.*

Jaxton stared at his comlink, and for no reason at all, he felt a chill.

The rest of the day passed without comment from Thaal. Jaxton went to a local cantina for a drink, then to a restaurant he was known to frequent for dinner, then came home and poured himself a nightcap. He nursed it, watched some holonews, and found himself relieved that no one he knew was reported dead.

There came a knock on his door. He let out a sigh of relief. There was the man, finally.

"Stavin," he said cheerily as he opened the door, "you are one mysterious—"

Stavin Thaal was indeed standing outside his door. So were two other men. Jaxton looked askance at them, and then looked back to Thaal. "Personal bodyguards," Thaal said. "You can't be too careful these days."

"You're telling me," said Jaxton, and waved the men in. "Can I get you something to drink?" he said, heading to the bar. "I've got a fine selection of—"

"Merratt," said Thaal, his mechanical voice oddly quiet.

Jaxton turned around. The two men were standing pointing small, handheld blasters at him. "Fine, fine, I'll bring out the good stuff," he laughed. "Not all that funny, Stavin," he went on, refreshing his own drink.

"I'm afraid it's not really funny at all," Thaal said. "Come sit down at your desk. You're going to take dictation for me."

"You're serious," Jaxton said. Thaal nodded, unsmiling. The men did not lower their blasters. Thinking he could find a way out of this or talk Stavin out of . . . whatever plot he had in his head, Jaxton obeyed.

"I've got a datapad here—"

"I'm sure you can find some flimsi and a stylus," Thaal said. Jaxton rummaged around his desk and, sure enough, came up with the requested items. With a shaky hand, using the unfamiliar stylus, Merratt Jaxton began to write.

" 'I leave this note for whoever finds me,' " said Thaal.

Jaxton had gotten as far as *whoever.* He froze. "What does that mean?" He knew, of course, but he didn't want to believe it. Couldn't believe it.

"Why, son, I'm going to kill you once this note is done."

Jaxton looked up at Thaal and the two other expressionless men. "If I know I'm going to die, then why should I write this note?"

"Because you're going to have a choice about how you die," said Thaal in his horrible droid's voice. "You finish that note for me like a good boy, and I'll make it quick and easy for you. You fight me, your suicide will be so agonizing people will admire you for having the guts to actually go through with it. It's up to you."

Jaxton hesitated, then began to write again. Thaal nodded. "Good. Now, where was I? Oh, right. 'This began as a noble crusade, for a noble cause, at least as far as I was concerned. To topple the unjust government as embodied in Natasi Daala. I joined forces with Senator Fost Bramsin and Admiral Sallinor Parova to bring this about.' "

Jaxton paused and looked up at Thaal. "I don't know why this even matters to me," he said, "but for some strange reason, it does. I know why you want me to leave you off the list. But why not implicate Treen and Lecersen, since you're naming names?"

Thaal chuckled. It came out horribly artificial sounding.

"Because they're still alive. If they keep their mouths shut, so will I. Don't even really know what's up with Lecersen, and Treen's a sharp old woman."

Jaxton licked his lips. " . . . *I* could keep my mouth shut."

Thaal shook his head, almost sympathetically. "No, you couldn't, son. Besides, that's a nice tidy list of conspirators right there. Three sounds about right; a Senator and two chiefs—all the bases covered. And all three dead makes it tidier still."

"We can work something out," stammered Jaxton.

"No, son, we can't. It just wouldn't work. It's my business to know beings, and I know that much about you."

He thought about asking Thaal if he could talk to someone, but even as the thought formed, he realized there was no one to talk to. No one who would miss him. He didn't even have a blasted *pet* that would miss him, like Dorvan did.

"Keep writing," said Thaal.

"'I cannot continue living, knowing that my fellow conspirators have died for what they believe is right. Soon I will join them.' Now sign it."

"No one's going to believe this," said Jaxton, even as he affixed his signature. "They'll know it's a murder, and they'll find you."

Again Thaal laughed, and Jaxton found himself cringing, ever so slightly, at the sound. "You may be right. Then again"—he nodded to one of his men—"you may not be."

The man leaned down and to Jaxton's shock, offered him the blaster. He stared at it as if it were an exotic animal. He could take it, and probably get off two shots—at least one good one to Thaal—before they took him down. Thaal's tidy little plan would completely unravel and become most untidy indeed.

And that was when Jaxton knew, down to his marrow, that he was a coward after all. Thaal was right. He couldn't have kept his mouth shut if he were interrogated. He'd have cracked, and cracked completely.

He wished desperately now that he'd just walked into Wynn Dorvan's office, sat down, and spilled everything. Cooperation could have saved him. His ambition and ego had doomed him. At least the ones he was implicating were already dead. There was something to be said for that.

He took the blaster and held it quietly, awaiting instructions.

"Now, put it in your mouth," said Thaal. "And then, when you're ready, pull the trigger."

Jaxton stared at the blaster, then slowly did as he was told. His breathing came quick around the muzzle, and he tasted and smelled the tang of metal. Odd, how sharp his senses were, now that they would never be used again. He looked up and straight into Thaal's pale, cold eyes.

Thaal nodded. "I'll watch you go," he said, his voice as gentle as it could be made, hearing the unspoken question.

Jaxton pulled the trigger.

Leia couldn't sleep. She hadn't slept much since they'd placed her in this cell. The mattress was lumpy and old and uncomfortable. Still, she knew that wasn't why she lay awake. She had slept on harder ground, softer hammocks, even in trees and in another, more antiseptic and evil prison.

She couldn't turn off her brain. She kept going over what Eramuth had said about "Club Bwua'tu." About how they thought there were conspiracies—plural—afoot. Eramuth said that both she and Han were now "members of the club," and that she should not despair. "One way or another, my dear," the old Bothan had rumbled, "we're getting you out of here. Do not doubt that."

She didn't. But she doubted that they would uncover the conspirators in time. She doubted that Padnel Ovin would see what was right there in plain sight. She doubted—

Leia heard noises, and saw the darkness in the hall lighten slightly. Someone was coming—two someones, two sets of footsteps—and they had glow rods. She sat up, straining to listen.

" . . . highly unusual, sir," said someone.

"So is the situation, guard," came Padnel's gruff voice. "And Jedi Solo is a highly unusual being. Now open the door and leave us alone, or you'll be looking for new employment."

They appeared at the door. The guard, an annoyed-looking Sullustan, shut down the force field, permitted Padnel to enter, reactivated the field, gave them both dirty looks, and departed.

"Rank hath its privileges," said Leia. "What brings you here at this hour? Good news, I hope?"

Padnel, carrying the glow rod, began to pace. "Not at all, really, though it may be good news in the end. For you, at least." He paused and looked at her solemnly. "You think I don't listen. Sometimes I don't. Sometimes I do. I thought about what you said, and all that has gone on recently. And I shared your concern with Dorvan. There's apparently a sort of . . . club that's sprung up around such concerns as you raised."

Hope rose in Leia, warm and rich and fierce. "Club Bwua'tu," she murmured.

He nodded. "I don't know much about it; don't need to know. Enough that Dorvan and the admiral are involved. Better that way. They share your opinion. About a conspiracy. They had discovered some kind of connection among Bramsin, Lecersen, and Jaxton—"

"The poisoning!" Leia remembered her conversation with Javon Thewles. "It was designed to discredit the GAS. And Parova—"

"Put her people in instead," Padnel finished. "And now she's dead, Bramsin is dead, and Treen and Lecersen have disappeared. That leaves only one."

"General Jaxton," breathed Leia.

Padnel nodded. "That was enough to convince me to plant a small listening device in Jaxton's office. One sensitive enough to catch both ends of a comm conversation. And this afternoon, before Jaxton left for the evening, I recorded a very interesting conversation. I was only able to listen to it just a short while ago."

"What did he say? Who did he talk to?"

"They spoke about Bramsin and Parova being dead, the 'blasted Senators,' and someone he called 'good old Palpatine.' They were going to get together tonight to discuss things. Unfortunately, the person Jaxton contacted was not named, and he used a droid voice to disguise his—or her—own."

"It's got to be Suldar," said Leia. "With everything else that's going on—"

"My thoughts exactly. There's enough on here to bring Jaxton in for further questioning at least."

Leia made a face. "If there was enough for me to be brought in, then yes, I agree."

Padnel looked remorseful and put a hand on her shoulder. "I never doubted you, Leia," he said, "I just thought you were mistaken about the conspiracy."

"That's doubting," Leia said. At the look on his face, she softened. "I understand why you did, though. It sounded almost as ludicrous as the charges brought against me."

"I'll let you know what—" His comlink beeped. "Excuse me a moment," he said, speaking into it. "Ovin. What?" He listened, and his eyes widened. Softly he growled. "I see. Be respectful of the body, but bring it in to the Galactic Senate Medcenter for immediate autopsy. No, no, you were right to contact me. Keep me posted."

Leia grew cold. "Jaxton," she said. He nodded. "Murdered, like Parova?"

He shook his head. "Looks like a suicide. But I don't believe that for a minute."

"Nor do I."

Padnel turned to her and took her hands in his. "Leia, I'm sorry. You shouldn't ever have been brought in here. I thought I was doing the right thing by going along with the Senators and observing, but I should have stopped this the minute I smelled something rotten."

"You did what you thought was best. Who knows, perhaps you actually got me out of harm's way," she said.

"I'd like to hope that. I'd like to think I did something right. But now I intend to *keep* you out of harm's way." His olive-green flews pulled back from his sharp, jagged teeth in a chilling smile. "I've heard it said that being the Chief of State means when you speak, they have to be quiet. Tomorrow I intend to make them quiet long enough to repair some of the damage I've done. And then—I'm going to knock some heads together."

Despite the direness of the situation, Leia found herself smiling. "You sound just like Han," she said.

"That is perhaps the finest compliment I have ever received," said Ovin. And Leia had to agree.

# Chapter Forty-two

HIGH LORD WORKAN WAS RATHER PROUD OF HIMSELF.

This political system was so easy to manipulate. One could be physically weak, even unable to use the Force at all, and still rise to power based on being popular and gathering enough beings in one's corner. There were loopholes everywhere, if one knew where to look, and like a pack of anoobas, Sith excelled at finding weaknesses and using them to destroy. What Roki Kem wanted him to do was not only fairly easy, it was even *legal.*

The Senate had the ability to appoint whomever they chose as interim Chief of State until such time as a formal election could be held. Workan had persuaded the Senate to appoint Padnel Ovin a short time ago. All he needed to do was introduce the motion to appoint Roki Kem instead. With the Jessar's charisma, fame, and the path of goodwill she left everywhere she went, as well as his own resources, he would easily be able to get the three-quarters majority necessary to replace Ovin.

Then it was on to making her Beloved Queen of the Stars, whatever *that* meant. Workan would, as he always had, handle that as he came to it.

If all went according to plan, and there was no indication that it wouldn't, he would secure the position of Chief of State for Roki Kem by the end of the day. Which would definitely win him favor in her eyes.

Workan had admired and respected Lord Vol, but he had to admit he was enjoying the new turn of events.

The current chair of the Senate, a Chagrian named Nensu Kaatik, stepped forward and read the agenda. Workan sat with his eyes closed, extending himself in the Force, letting it flow through him and carry him to touch each Force presence in this vast chamber. He listened, and when the last item was read and the chair inquired if there was any further business to be put before the Senate, he rose.

"May it please the Senate," he said, fighting the desire to use the Force to make his voice carry and relying solely on technology. "I have urgent business to place before this Senate immediately."

The chair frowned. "The chair recognizes the honorable Senator Suldar from B'nish."

Workan inclined his head and moved his hoverdais forward. He thought, not for the first time, that with the lighting and the uniform color and shape of the daises, from a distance the Senate chamber looked like a massive scaled beast.

"It is established that in times of crisis, when an interim Chief of State is in power, the Senate has the right—nay, the duty—to challenge its leadership and put in place whomever this august body determines is best suited to navigate the crisis," Workan said. He could hear the murmuring already and smiled to himself. "We faced such a crisis recently, and it was I who put forth the motion to nominate an outsider, whom I thought would bring a fresh perspective." He looked around with mock regret. "Unfortunately, I believe that this being, Senator Padnel Ovin of Klatooine, is not the right choice for this time. His connections with the Jedi, and with terrorist activities—I had hoped he would overcome them. But with the recent murder of the acting chief of naval operations, the mourned death of our beloved Senator Fost Bramsin, and the regrettable resignation of veteran Senator Haydnat Treen of Kuat, I believe it is clear that he is not the appropriate leader for such a time. I put forth the motion that we dismiss

Senator Ovin and replace him with someone who still brings the freshness of an outside perspective, but who has proven herself a superior, and beloved, leader. I nominate Senator Rokari Kem."

Some several meters away in her own dais, Roki Kem managed to look both honored and shy. She rose, smiling, projecting the perfect combination of determination and caring.

What a fine little actress she was.

"The chair recognizes the honorable Senator Rokari Kem of Qaras. Senator, your name has been put forward to assume the office of interim Chief of State of the Galactic Alliance. Do you accept this nomination?"

"If it pleases the Senate," she said, her voice sweet and sincere, "I came to Coruscant to serve. Not just my own people of Qaras, but everyone I *can* serve. Whatever knowledge, wisdom, and experience I have—if the Senate wishes me to serve in this role, then serve I shall, humbly, gratefully, and as well as I possibly can."

"May it please the Senate!" came a voice. Workan frowned. It was Luewet Wuul, the Sullustan. He was recognized, and continued speaking. "The Galactic Alliance should not discard one it has elected like a piece of clothing we don't fancy anymore. Padnel Ovin has only been in office a short while. He's barely had time to move datapads across his desk, let alone make sweeping changes. I move this motion be struck down."

"The chair agrees with you, Senator," said Kaatik, "but legally, the motion has been introduced and must go forward."

"Then I propose, due to the extraordinary nature of the situation, we make the vote at least four-fifths majority rather than three-quarters."

"The chair agrees. All in favor of four-fifths majority, cast your votes now."

Workan gritted his teeth. He had been confident of a three-quarters majority. But there were several empty seats here today. He was not at all certain he could get the votes if it was upped to four-fifths.

But he would have to, or they'd find him dead on the steps of the Jedi Temple. Or worse.

The vote was approved—startlingly quickly. Workan needed more time. He had to notify some of his followers, tell them to come *now*, vote *now*, or—

"Permission to address the Senate!" came a deep, gruff voice. A ripple of surprise fluttered through the room. Padnel Ovin himself was present. He was standing next to Wuul on the Sullustan's hoverdais, his hands on his hips, and he looked like he was ready to tear the throats out of the entire Senate.

"The chair recognizes the interim Chief of State," said Kaatik.

"Esteemed Senators," said Padnel, "I have just learned that a motion has been put forth to remove me from my office."

"The chair reminds the Chief of State that he has no vote in this matter," said Kaatik, looking uncomfortable.

"This is true," Padnel continued. "But there is a clause stating that I have the right to address the Senate prior to a vote."

It was true. He did have that right, but it was a formality. No one ever expected a being in this position to try to influence the Senate. It was considered crude and rather oafish. The acting Chief of State was expected to endure the vote in gracious, stoic silence.

But, Workan reflected, Padnel *was* crude and rather oafish. And he just might inadvertently have bought Workan enough time to call in a few favors.

"By all means," Workan said earnestly, "I would never deny the Chief of State—excuse me, interim Chief of State—any rights he wishes to exercise."

"The chair then recognizes the right of the interim Chief of State to address the Senate."

Padnel inclined his head graciously. "Thank you. My fellow Senators," he said, looking out over the vast collection of beings, "I know you think you know me. But most of you may have heard rumors about my behavior, or about my brother and his organization. Let me dispel some of these before you vote on my ability to lead the GA. I will start with the history of my people, and the Treaty of Vontor."

It was going to be a long, long speech. *Talk all you wish, Ovin,* Workan thought, and picked up his comlink.

If there was one thing Padnel Ovin was good at, Wynn Dorvan thought as he entered the now-empty office of the Chief of State, it was stubbornly standing his ground. Padnel would likely be holding the Senate captive for the entire day and perhaps well on into the night. If all went well, though, Dorvan would only need the Senators distracted for an hour. He made sure the door was locked, then drew the curtains and turned toward what looked like a plain blank wall.

More knew about this secret exit than he would have liked, but it was still not common knowledge. He tapped the code, and the outlines of a door materialized, then slid open.

He had never had to use this door before, but he had access to the blueprints of the labyrinthine corridors it opened into, and knew exactly where he was going.

It was dimly lit, and dusty. Dorvan made a mental note to tell whoever eventually became Chief of State—he would be content with whomever the Senate chose; he had grown to respect Padnel and, like everyone else, thought Roki Kem was an amazing being who would do just fine—that these corridors needed to be cleaned and all the doors checked to make sure they were still properly functional. A secret escape pathway would do no one any good if they couldn't actually get out.

Dorvan moved swiftly, not quite running but not quite walking, down flights of stairs and through long corridors that had not been used in years, if ever. Mentally he ticked off each turn and exit, until finally his path took him upward.

He reached the door he wanted. It was unmarked save for a number. Another safety redundancy—those who knew the numbering system knew which door led where. Intruders would be at a disadvantage.

Dorvan took a deep breath, and slid open the door.

He found himself staring at three huge blasters.

"Gentlemen, please put those away," Dorvan said. "If you kill me, you'll never find your way around."

"Like I'm ever trigger-happy," said Han Solo. Lando Calrissian rolled his eyes.

"Man's got a point," said Zekk. "I had no idea there was a secret entrance in the Temple garden that led to the Chief of State's office."

"Now that you do, Jedi Zekk, I encourage you to forget about it as soon as possible. Let's go, gentlemen. The Princess is waiting."

They followed at once, bristling with enough weapons to equip a small army. "Let's go over the plan one more time," Dorvan said.

"We went over it six times already," said Lando.

"Redundancy is never a bad thing," said Dorvan. "Tell me what the plan is."

Lando frowned and growled a little, but complied. "We follow you till we get to the prison section. No one knows about the entrance—you can't even see it from the other side. A patrol of three guards comes past it every seventeen minutes. It's a blind corner with no vid-cams. We listen for their approach, pop out, knock them on the heads, and take their uniforms and key codes."

"Excellent," Dorvan said. "Now, Captain Solo, what's next?"

Han shot him a blistering glare. "Dorvan, anyone ever tell you you are incredibly annoying?"

"Frequently, sir, but that doesn't change the fact that I need to make sure everyone knows the—"

"Okay, okay, if it'll shut you up. We—"

"We're here," Zekk said. Han looked relieved. Sure enough, they were at door 41-A. Han motioned for silence, glanced at his chrono, and placed his ear to the door. They stood for a long moment, waiting. Finally, Han nodded and held up his fingers, counting down. *Three. Two.*

*One.*

Dorvan punched the button and the door slid open. The poor guards didn't stand a chance. They whirled, drawing their blaster pistols, as three large men materialized seemingly out of nowhere and took them down with the experience of long years of practice.

"Well done, gentlemen," said Dorvan, gazing down at the three unconscious bodies. "But we seem to have a problem."

Before them lay a male human, a male Falleen . . . and a female Chadra-Fan.

"Stang," said Han.

"Time for Plan B," said Dorvan.

The Bothan chief of security looked up, did a double take, then bolted out of her chair. "What is the meaning of this?" she demanded. "Where did you find him?"

Wynn Dorvan stood in front of her desk, hands clasped before him, looking as mild-mannered as he always did on the holovids. With him were two guards carrying an unconscious male human dressed in brown and tan robes. He was obviously a Jedi, but fortunately, one unable to harm anyone right now.

"Found him during a patrol in the corridor," one of them said. "Don't know how he managed to break in. But it's a Jedi, all right."

"Well done, Chief Lua'wan," said Dorvan. "I daresay that with a capture of a Jedi hitherto unknown to be on Coruscant, all of you are due for promotions. I have here an order from the Chief of State regarding this . . . being's . . . incarceration."

Lua'wan read the order. "He's to be put in the same cell as Jedi Solo?"

"Of course," said Dorvan. "It places less of a strain on the law-abiding, taxpaying citizens of Coruscant. I was just coming down to question the Jedi prisoner Solo when I came across the takedown. I'll speak to the Chief of State personally about how well all of you handled the situation."

Lua'wan had been upset, but now was starting to become calmer. This was a good thing. Another Jedi behind bars, she and her team praised for the incident . . .

"Thank you, sir. There's a pair of cuffs over there if you—"

The other guard chuckled. "Trust me, he's out like a light," he said. "He'll be waking up in a prison cell."

Lua'wan shrugged. "As you wish," he said. "You brought him down in the first place. I'll log in your visit, Chief of Staff Dorvan. I'm glad to confirm that security is operating up to your expectations."

"Indeed it is," said Dorvan. "Indeed it is."

Leia had sensed her husband's Force presence almost from the minute he entered the building, and shortly afterward realized that Zekk, Lando, and Dorvan were with him. When they approached her cell, dragging an "unconscious" Zekk between them, she smiled at them, folded her arms, and simply said, "What took you so long?"

"Short guard" was all Han said. He deactivated the force field, took two long strides forward, and swept his wife up in his arms for a deep kiss.

"Not to intrude, ma'am," said Dorvan, "but time is of the essence."

Leia pulled away, her hand still on Han's chest. "Of course," she said. "What's the plan?"

"This," said Lando. He tossed a small datachip to Zekk, who caught it. The two men immediately began opening cell doors, and Leia sensed joy and relief from her fellow inmates. Most of them were, like her, unjustly being held. But not all.

"We can open twelve cells with these, including yours," Lando said. "That's going to make for a very good distraction."

"Follow me," Dorvan said. Alarms were starting to ring now. Han grabbed Leia's hand and together, they all raced down the corridor. Zekk and Leia used the Force to gently—and sometimes not-so-gently—shove aside the throngs of their fellow escapees. Finally Dorvan skidded to a halt and turned to face—

"—a blank wall," Leia said, but as soon as the words left her lips, she knew she was wrong. She could sense openness on the other side. "A hidden door."

"Exactly," Dorvan said. He pressed something to the door, and its outline appeared for a moment before it slid open. Just as they moved to go through, they heard someone yell, "Hey! A door!"

Han swore, turned around, and fired his blaster into the crowd. Three beings dropped unconscious. Leia motioned as well, sending two beings hurtling backward to smash into several others. Then they were through, and the door was closed.

"Now," Dorvan said, a few hairs slightly out of place but otherwise looking as calm as ever, "this is where we part company. The door to the Jedi Temple gardens is four-one-A. It's a bit tricky to get to, but just keep going down the way we came until you find it. I must return to the Senatorial debate."

"Thank Padnel for us. That's a long time to talk about whether or not to put a tax on exotic fruit."

Dorvan sobered slightly. "His . . . speech is actually somewhat different than we had planned on. Senator Suldar has challenged his ability to continue in office. He's nominated Roki Kem."

"I'm surprised," Han said. "I'd expect that sleemo to nominate another one of his hangers-on."

"I did, too," Dorvan said. "But either way, Ovin is talking to buy you time. Use it well."

"Thanks, Wynn. I won't forget this," said Leia, squeezing his hand.

Han clapped him on the back. "Beneath that neatly pressed exterior, you've got the heart of a rogue and a pirate, Dorvan," he said.

"Please, Captain Solo. There's no call for insults."

Han grinned, then the four of them headed toward freedom.

Dorvan watched them go. He'd done a good day's work here. Tonight he would sleep better than he had in a long, long time. Padnel Ovin, Roki Kem—either of them was better than Daala. They'd start straightening things out.

He turned and began the task of navigating the multitude of corridors. Left, right, up stairs, left, up stairs, right, right, up one more flight. He glanced at his chrono: the entire thing had taken only fifty-four minutes. All would be well.

He reached the secret entrance to the Chief of State's office and took a moment to compose himself. Calmly, he pushed open the door.

And stared at three extraordinarily handsome men and women, all carrying red lightsabers.

"How did Dorvan manage this without a datapad?" marveled Lando as they kept taking turn after turn.

"Man's a bureaucrat," Han said. "They like details like this."

"He might be a Force-sensitive and not know it," quipped Zekk. "Takes something extra not to get lost here. Speaking of which . . ." He slowed, frowning. "I don't think this is the way we came. I think we should have gone left back there."

"Numbers were wrong," Han said. "It was this way."

Zekk followed, but his frown deepened and Leia sensed he was not at all certain Han was right.

"Honey, are you sure?" she said to her husband. "It's difficult not to get lost here."

"Numbers are starting to go up," Han said. "We're on the right track."

"Go *up*?" asked Lando, coming to a full halt. "Han, we were only looking for the forties."

"No, no, Dorvan said four-one-eight," Han said impatiently.

Leia looked at the numbers. They had been descending stairs at every opportunity, and the numbers had gone from the single digits to the three hundreds. Her stomach sank.

"Han," she said, "Dorvan said four-one-A, not four-one-*eight*."

"Nah, he didn't." Han paused. He stiffened, and turned around with an almost comical look of mixed hope and defiance. "Did he?"

"I'm afraid he did, pal," Lando said wearily. "And I think I may be getting too old to climb up all those flights of stairs again." Han closed his eyes miserably. Leia touched his arm gently.

"It's okay, buddy," Lando said, trying to sound bluff. "No one knows we're even in here, and they sure won't be able to find how to get in from the outside. Those doors just vanish. We can take our time, take a break, then—"

"No," Leia said suddenly. Her eyes met Zekk's and he nodded. "We can't. Someone's following us."

"Bloah," swore Han. "This is my fault."

"That's a first," said Lando, but Leia waved him to silence.

"Hang on," she said. She Force-leapt up the stairs the way they had come, unfastening her hair as she did so. Landing lightly, she chose a door at random, and dropped the barrette in front of it. Her hair would be in her face for a bit, but their pursuers would head off in the wrong direction—for at least a while.

She dropped back down. "I've laid a false trail," she said. "Pick a door, and let's go."

"But we don't know—" began Lando.

"She's right," Han said. "Anything's better than this. Besides, I'm sick of stairs."

He went to the nearest door, pushed it open, and they all rushed out.

Into the undercity.

Leia and Han had watched the segment on *The Perre Needmo Newshour*. They had seen how the place had fallen even farther into violence and chaos. But the *Newshour* vidcrew had failed to capture the enormity of the sudden spurts of plant growth. They were everywhere.

Every ramshackle building was nearly choked by the living green carpet. Vines seemed to be moving almost of their own accord, but Leia could see that there were gangs moving through the growth. The place was so strong with fear, despair, and an almost unnatural sense of malice that she had to quickly shield herself from it in the Force.

"Lovely," Zekk said. "So nice to see healthy growing things."

"Hey, I'd rather fight my way out than be hunted," said Han.

"I've got a lightsaber," Zekk said.

"I've got the Force," Leia said.

"And we've got blasters," Han said. "Let's go."

# Chapter Forty-three

"HOW MANY?"

It was the seventh time in the last hour Roki had commed Workan, inquiring how many votes he could put forth.

He forced his voice to sound pleasant and agreeable as he replied. "We're waiting on two more, then we should have the four-fifths."

"I don't like to wait, Suldar."

"I know, my lady." The term always seemed to mollify her. "But they will be here soon."

"They had better be. We have so much to do. This is only a stepping-stone, and I am anxious to move forward."

"So you have said, my lady. They should be here any minute."

Lady Enara Massar looked at him. She knew about Roki, of course. Once he had chosen to throw his weight behind her—not that he had been given much of a choice—he had informed all the Sith who answered to him that they would now do likewise. There had been a few who had objected. They had been sent to explore the depths of the Jedi Temple, and no one had heard from them since.

"I do wish she were a trifle more patient," he told Enara. "Not all spiders venture forth and hunt their prey. Some of the most successful simply spin their webs and wait for their future dinners to stumble across the sticky strands. Is a few hours of gracious waiting too much to ask when I'm about to make her Chief of State?"

"So it would seem, sir," Enara said, commiserating. "Though to be fair," she added, "listening to Padnel Ovin hold forth for an hour would test a Grand Lord's patience."

"You have me there," he admitted.

The Klatooinian had been droning on about his history and that of his world for the past—he checked—hour and seventeen minutes. Now he was starting to address the issue of his brother's martyrdom.

"By dinnertime, he'll have gotten to his arrival on Coruscant," Workan muttered. "I do wish there were some way to get him to hurry up."

" . . . He knew, that with his death, others would be inspired to follow the cause," Padnel was saying. His posture was still rock-steady. The rules dictated that he not sit and not leave. Once he did, his time would be considered over. More than Kem and Workan were fidgeting; no one had expected it to go half this long. And Padnel showed no signs of slowing down. Even his voice showed no strain. "Those who died in the incident were fellow warriors—the military. Not civilians. Grunel went to great lengths—"

"Sir," said Enara, sounding very pleased. "Senators Sh'klaa and Onoru have reported in. They're moving to their seats now. They'll be ready to cast their votes in five minutes."

"Excellent," said Workan. He clicked his comlink.

"Roki Kem," came the bright voice.

"My lady," Workan said, allowing a trace of smugness to enter his voice, "I am delighted to report that the last two Senators have entered the building and are moving to their daises. Once Padnel Ovin has wound down—and he has to use the refresher *sometime*—your ascension to Chief of State will be secure. Our worries are over. I suggest you sit back, relax, and enjoy the last we will see of Padnel Ovin."

"It will indeed be the last we will see of Padnel Ovin," Roki agreed, "but I'm quite tired of waiting."

A chill went through Workan at the iciness in her voice. What did she—had she gone mad? Hired an assassin to strike right in the middle of Ovin's speech, or done something else equally as outrageous? He sat up, eyes fastened on the Klatooinian still holding forth. Even as he watched, Padnel stopped midsentence. He grunted, then stumbled a step.

". . . Sand Panthers avoided . . . t-taking civilian life . . . may I have some water, please?"

And then Workan understood. Oh, she was good. Very good. Somehow she'd hidden her Force abilities from him completely. And obviously also from Vol, until it was too late. Perhaps this was how she had been able to influence her fellow Jessar to love her so well during and after their world's crisis. And now, of course, she stood staring at the soon-to-be-ex-Chief of State, a hand to her mouth, her eyes wide with horror, the very picture of compassionate sympathy.

Kaatik handed Ovin some water, looking at him with concern. "Sir," he said, "I think you have stated your case very well. Perhaps you should—"

"No!" snapped Padnel, glaring at him. "I'm not done yet! I'm allowed to speak as long as I wish, and speak I—"

His hand went up to his chest and clutched it. He started to gasp. Then, in full view of several hundred beings and millions more watching the coverage live, Padnel Ovin, interim Chief of State of the Galactic Alliance, collapsed.

Chaos erupted. Everyone watched raptly as medical droids appeared and began their work. Kaatik returned to the mike, his blue skin paler than it had been a few moments before. "Everyone, please, we must have *order*! This Senate is still in session! Padnel Ovin is unconscious but his situation has stabilized. He is being taken immediately to the Galactic Senate Medcenter."

"I motion to postpone the vote until Chief of State Ovin has recovered." The motion came, not unexpectedly, from Senator Wuul.

*No!* Workan thought. If Padnel died before Roki was confirmed, legally the office would go to Wynn Dorvan. And that would be a disaster.

Workan leapt to his feet. "I motion that the vote be pushed through!" he cried. "Of course, like all beings here, I hope for a full recovery for Senator Ovin. But the fact remains that if he survives, he will still be the same being he is—and his leadership has been challenged. I say it is even more important now than ever to decide if he or Roki Kem will lead the Galactic Alliance!"

Nearly all decorum and seemliness had flown out the window. The chair seemed to recognize it, for he didn't rebuke either Wuul or Workan for speaking out of turn.

"I agree with the honorable Senator from B'nish," Kaatik said, looking shaken. "Cast your votes now."

Workan sat down. It could all still fall apart. Most of his "supporters" were not Sith. They were simply gullible newcomers, looking for someone to point them in the right direction. If they got rattled by Padnel's collapse and decided to err on the side of Dorvan rather than risking a chance on Kem—what would she do? Give *everyone* a heart attack?

He realized she might.

Quickly he punched in his YES vote and sat back, using the Force to calm himself. Others hurried to vote, eager to have this over and done with, eager to have some direction, any direction.

The chair seemed to be recovering as he perused the votes. Finally, he looked up. His face gave nothing away, but Workan could sense his disappointment and worry in the Force.

The question was—who had disappointed him by winning?

"By a vote of four-fifths majority, with twenty-four abstentions," Kaatik said, "the Senate is honored to announce that the Senator from Qaras, Rokari Kem, has been—"

The rest of his announcement was lost in a wild cheer. Surprised by how relieved he felt, Workan rose to his feet, applauding along with the rest of them. He felt Roki brush him in the Force—praise and pleasure, rather like one might show to a pet who had performed a trick exceptionally well. Workan made sure his irritation was not sensed.

She moved her dais forward, waving to the crowd. Not everyone was happy, but most were. And why should they not be? Rokari Kem was a legend, a role model, someone to admire and emulate. And she was now going to lead them out of this place of fear and worry.

"Thank you so much," Roki said, her voice thick with emotion. "As you know, the Jessar do not speak things that are not true. And so you may take it as the pure truth when I say that your faith in my ability to lead you well and courageously honors me beyond words."

There was more applause. She was telling them exactly what they wanted to hear, no doubt taking her inspiration from what she sensed from them in the Force. Again, he exerted a tight rein on his anger at being fooled by her.

"My first act as your interim Chief of State is to commandeer the use of the now-abandoned Jedi Temple as my house of operations," she said. Workan was surprised. They had discussed her moving in eventually, but right away?

The cheering crowd seemed confused, but continued to listen. "They have decided to sever ties with the Galactic Alliance. Surely in their absence, I, as the head of the GA, can put the resources to better use. It will show to the Jedi that they cannot make such decisions lightly. If they wish to leave, of course they may. But they should not expect us to welcome them back with open arms. One must answer for one's decisions."

He felt it nudging against him, like Dorvan's pet chitlik seeking a treat—her gentle Force brush. He grinned, knowing what she would sense, knowing that she was reaching out to everyone in this huge chamber and touching them in the same fashion. Not overtly, just enough to make them believe they agreed with her.

"The continued incarceration of Jedi Leia Organa Solo, and the rumors of other Jedi still here such as escaped convict Tahiri Veila, concerns me greatly." And oh, she did sound so very concerned, so very worried for her people. "Movement has not been made toward bringing Solo to trial. I will recommend that the Senate subcommittee consider the alternative, bitter a remedy though it might be. If the Jedi do not wish to be here, then when they break our laws, they should face execution."

That was pushing things too far, Workan thought. He felt the shift in the room. Imprisonment was one thing, but execution? Roki sent waves of soothing calm, and to Workan's disbelief, he could feel at least some minds changing.

"It has been a trying day for all of us," she said, "and I suggest, with the Senate's approval, of course, that this session be terminated and you all return to your duties. I, meanwhile, will go to the Temple, so that everyone will see that my protection of my people against the Jedi is sincere. Thank you again. I promise, your trust in me is not misplaced!"

She whispered to her assistant, who began to move the hoverdais back to its dock. Frowning, Workan clicked his comlink.

"I think this a mistake," he said. "You should go to your new offices and start discussing your responsibilities with Dorvan. You need to at least keep up the appearance that you are working for the beings who elected you!"

"I think this is perfect," said Roki. "I need to present a picture of the new path the Alliance is going to be taking. Think how striking it will look on the holonews when I sweep into the bastion of the Jedi!"

He realized she hated the Jedi almost as much as the Sith did. And for some reason, that unsettled him.

Thirty-seven minutes later, the steps of the Jedi Temple were thronged with holojournalists. The Keshiri Sith currently in residence there had made themselves scarce lest some more creative reporter catch a glimpse of a beautiful lavender face, and Workan had sent ahead what human Sith he could contact to prepare at least somewhat for the Chief of State's arrival.

She had insisted he accompany her, establishing their friendship in the public's mind. So it was that High Lord Ivaar Workan strode beside Rokari Kem as they ascended the Temple that had once belonged to their enemy, and now belonged to them. It was a giddy, heady moment, the delight dampened for Workan in that he wished his Grand Lord could have seen it.

But then again, he wouldn't be with Roki Kem if Vol were alive.

She did not grant interviews, smiling apologetically every time a reporter shouted out something to her, moving steadily up the steps in a long, shimmering dress that looked like flowing water. They reached the top, then turned around and looked down.

So much adoration in the faces as they looked up at her. So much faith, and trust, and hope. And she—her face alight with love, if completely false, for the people she had been chosen to guide.

It occurred to Workan that it might not be such a big step to "goddess" after all.

With a final wave, Roki turned and entered the Temple. Several Sith stood at attention. Among them were Senators, business owners, holoanchors, security chiefs. They all were beautiful, and ready to serve, and Workan was terribly proud of them.

One of Roki's assistants was speaking into a comm. She clicked it off, approached her mistress, and bowed.

"I have news, my lady, both good and bad," she said. "First, I am pleased to report to you that as of two minutes ago, Senator Padnel Ovin is dead."

Roki smiled her falsely sweet smile. "I knew that already," she said, and actually giggled a little. "What is the rest of your news?"

The woman hesitated. "Well," she said, "unfortunately, it appears that Jedi Solo escaped before we could move her to a more secure location to await her execution."

The blue-green brows drew together, and even Workan had to brace himself against the fury he knew was coming. "An escape? She is gone? Who did this? I will find and destroy them!"

"My lady," the woman kept insisting, "please—we were able to capture one of those who had assisted with the escape. We have arranged for him to be brought here, assuming that you would wish to see him and . . . attend to his punishment yourself."

Workan felt the storm of Roki's anger subsiding before the prospect of torturing one who had displeased her. "You assumed rightly," she said. "Bring him before me. Now."

The woman bowed again and hurried off, speaking into her comlink. Workan turned toward Roki. "You do realize that Leia and her rescuers couldn't possibly have known about your, ah, new policy toward the Jedi," he said. "This is simply an unfortunate coincidence."

She jerked her head to look at him. "Unfortunate for them," she said. "They will regret ever knowing her by the time I am through with them. But I will learn what I want to know."

Workan wondered who had dared break Leia out of prison. Whoever it was, her husband certainly had to be among them. He wondered where Leia's adopted daughter was—Amelia, he believed her name to be. If they could find her, that would certainly be excellent leverage.

The assistant was returning. With her were two human males. Between them, they half carried, half dragged another male. His head was covered by a hood and his hands were tightly, obviously painfully, bound. The guards brought their prisoner up to Roki and stood, awaiting their orders.

She addressed the prisoner first. "Kneel," she ordered. "Show proper respect to your Beloved Queen of the Stars."

The prisoner didn't move. One of the guards shoved him down, and he grunted as his knees struck stone.

"Remove the hood," Roki said.

They had thrown the hood over him the second he had appeared, tackling him and literally beating him into submission. Dorvan had passed out and had only recent awakened to find his wrists tied together and the hood still firmly in place over his head. When they pulled it off him, the light was so bright it hurt his eyes.

His vision cleared, and he found himself looking up into a blue, beautiful, female face.

Rokari Kem. He blinked, utterly disbelieving. Surely he was still unconscious.

"Wynn Dorvan," Roki purred. "I confess, this is a surprise. But a happy one. You have served two Chiefs of State. And, I think, others, that we do not know about. Yet."

Still smiling, she bent down and cupped his battered face in her hand, turning his head up to face her. "You know things, don't you? Things that may prove very useful to me. Do be sure, Wynn, that I will learn what you know, who you know, what you have seen . . . one way or another. I may even permit you to live . . . if you learn to love me."

Her smile, beautiful and sweet and kind and an utter lie, widened.

And widened.

It stretched across her face, too large for it, nearly reaching her ears. Her skin paled, her eyes began to sink back into their sockets. Her hair turned from blue-green and shiny to pale yellow, growing long, longer, all the way down to her feet. The hand that grasped his chin in a grip that would not release became slick, tiny tentacles forcing him to stare into her eyes. Eyes that looked like tiny stars in a black hole.

And he understood the full disaster that was about to unfold.

Abeloth and the Lost Tribe of the Sith had come to Coruscant—and were running the Galactic Alliance.

ABOARD THE *JADE SHADOW*

Vestara thought at first that part of her was forcing the numbness upon her. That perhaps what she had done was so heinous, so abominable, she couldn't let herself feel the true impact of the choice she had made only a few hours earlier. Because she felt certain that she should be racked with guilt, horror, and self-loathing, and . . . she wasn't.

The whole thing had taken on the quality of a dream. A bitter smile curved her lips at the irony as she lay staring up at the ceiling of the *Jade Shadow,* her thoughts racing as fast as the ship itself. A dream; a nightmare caused by the rhak-skuri? No, there was no such convenient and exonerating excuse for what she had done.

She, Vestara Khai, had murdered a Jedi Knight. And she had done so coldly, deliberately, and with full knowledge of her choice. It couldn't even really be said that her act was as merciful as simple murder. Vestara had not merely executed Natua Wan. She had knocked off the Falleen's mask, knowing that doing so would cause Natua to experience the terrifying hallucinations, and that the Jedi Knight's horror would placate the rhak-skuri.

Vestara's mask had been firmly in place the whole time.

The creature had wanted Ben, and she was not willing to let it have him. There was no other choice.

But that thought was as pleasant a fiction as telling herself she had been affected by the rhak-skuri's pheromones. There was always a choice. She and Natua could have stood side by side, a Jedi Knight and a future Jedi Knight, fighting the creature. Maybe they could even have defeated it.

But she hadn't taken that road. And even now, Vestara wasn't wishing she had.

Search her feelings and thoughts as she might, she knew that given the same set of circumstances, she would make the same decision again. And she also knew that Ben, if he ever knew about it, would despise her for that choice. He would rather have died, horribly and in the grip of madness, than have an innocent's blood on his hands.

Vestara supposed that it was a good thing the blood was on her hands. Ben need never know.

Never know that she had turned her back on the Jedi path and embraced the Sith method of handling such a painful decision.

She heard again the creature hissing in her mind and turned over, at last feeling something, even if it was vague unease. It had called her. It had wanted her to come with it.

Vestara hadn't. Again, a choice, and she had chosen to stay with Ben.

She punched the pillow angrily. What did any of this matter? She had done what she had done—she had saved Ben. She did this because she had wanted to stay with him and become a Jedi.

And then she realized the bitter, inevitable, unforgiving illogic of the thought.

She would *never* be a Jedi. She would never learn to think like them. Never learn to think like Ben. Even at a point in her life when Vestara had thought she knew what she wanted, she had so easily, so familiarly, chosen the Sith way of getting it.

Vestara had never desired anything so badly in her life as to be with Ben Skywalker. And yet, the full spectrum of the love he offered her terrified her on some level. He was willing to give completely, utterly of himself, and she knew that so much vulnerability would destroy her. If he would only turn to the dark side . . .

He could never be a Sith. He would never learn to think like them; never learn to think like her.

So be it, then. Vestara Khai was a Sith, and as she lay looking at the stars streaking past her window, she made a Sith's choice. She would stay with Ben, as long as she was able to. She would give him all she could of her heart, which would never be enough for him. She would do these things until one day, when their paths inevitably diverged, lovers would become enemies.

And then, when that day came, her heart would break into a thousand pieces as she killed him.

# About the Author

CHRISTIE GOLDEN is the *New York Times* bestselling author of nearly forty novels, including *Star Wars: Fate of the Jedi: Omen* and *Star Wars: Fate of the Jedi: Allies*. Other media tie-in works include launching the Ravenloft line in 1991 with *Vampire of the Mists,* more than a dozen Star Trek novels, and the Warcraft novels *Rise of the Horde, Arthas,* and *The Shattering: Prelude to Cataclysm.*

www.christiegolden.com

Read on for an excerpt from

*Star Wars*™ *: Fate of the Jedi: Apocalypse*

by Troy Denning

THE PILLARS STOOD SCATTERED ACROSS THE DISTANT MOUNTAINSIDE, their pale shafts cropping out of the blue-gray dust like cliffs of white larmelstone. They looked a hundred stories tall, and whatever mysterious edifice they had been erected to support remained hidden beneath a kilometer-high mound of silt. No road crossed the endless sweep of scrub-dotted plain that surrounded the dust-mountain, and no craft was to be seen streaking across the orange sky above it. And yet, the pillars were the sole hint of civilization in the Reo System—in the whole Maraqoo Sector—so this had to be the place.

Raynar Thul eased the landspeeder forward. Though he had played an important part in several recent Jedi missions, he did not feel ready for this one. Master Skywalker had asked him to return to the Killik Colony he had once led as the Joiner UnuThul. But Raynar had literally not been himself back then. He had been a wounded combat survivor who had allowed himself to become lost in the shared mind of a Killik hive. It was an experience that had totally destroyed his sense of identity and left his mind a shattered wreck, and Raynar continued to feel tenuous and incomplete in his recovery.

But now the Jedi were facing an enemy as enigmatic as she was powerful, and their only hope of survival was to coax some answers from the jumbled hive-minds of Killiks. *Someone* had to convince them to reveal everything they knew about the mysterious Celestials they had once served, and Raynar was the only Jedi who could do it. So he had accepted the assignment and promised to succeed . . . even if it meant losing the mind he had spent eight long years trying to reassemble.

As the landspeeder drew closer to the mountain of dust, Raynar saw that the giant pillars were decorated with reliefs of winged beasts and horned fiends. Twined around the feet of these figures were ropy shapes that might have been serpents or vines.

Lowbacca, two-and-a-quarter meters of Wookiee, hunched in the front passenger seat with his knees in his chest, growled the opinion that the vines were a good sign.

"I quite disagree, Master Lowbacca," C-3PO said, speaking from directly behind the Wookiee. "In this context, the tendrils are symbols of inevitable destruction. If the ruins weren't so obviously deserted, I would suggest that we turn around immediately and erase them from our memory chips."

"I think Lowie means that we're in the right place," Tekli said. Sitting in the passenger seat behind Raynar, the furry little Chadra-fan was probably the only one in the crowded landspeeder who was even remotely comfortable. "The vines suggest that we've finally found a hive with a direct association to Abeloth. But the winged figures are something new. Is there a record of ophidian grotesques appearing with other symbols?"

"Not in my data banks," C-3PO assured her. "And I have cached every available reference to the subject. In fact, I have available two point three million articles and seven point one million images—"

Lowbacca interrupted with an impatient rumble.

"No, I would not prefer to ride on the stowage cover," C-3PO replied. "Do you have any idea what all this dust would do to my servomotors?"

Lowbacca rumbled again.

"I am not experiencing a problem with my vocabulator, Jedi Lowbacca," C-3PO answered. "And even if I were, I assure you that more dust would only make it worse."

Raynar chuckled, glad to have his friends along to keep his mind off his fears. Officially, Master Skywalker had assigned Tekli and Lowbacca to the mission as its medic and technical officer. But Raynar was pretty sure their most important duty was to keep him sane—at least, he *hoped* it was. C-3PO was on loan to serve as a translator, so it wouldn't be necessary for Raynar to become a Joiner again just to communicate with the Killiks. Whether it was part of Master Skywalker's plan or not, the droid had also acted as a constant annoyance—and a diversion. The three Jedi had been living in close quarters for over a month now, and C-3PO had given them a handy place to redirect any irritation they felt with one another. It was a job at which the droid had never failed to excel.

The landspeeder was still a kilometer away from the mountain when dark specks began to appear in the spaces between exposed pillars. At first, the flecks seemed to be some sort of decoration, but as the companions drew closer, the shapes grew more square-like, then swelled into distant window openings. A path appeared in the dust at the base of the mountain, running through a narrow channel toward a tall black arch that looked a lot like an open gateway.

Deciding the black arch *was* a gateway, Raynar turned toward it and felt a cold prickle of danger-sense race up his neck. He expanded his Force-awareness and felt something much nearer, a huge hungry presence moving toward the landspeeder almost as fast as the landspeeder was moving toward the mountain.

The sensation made no sense. There was a steady breeze blowing across the plain, raising a thin veil of smoke-blue dust that hung about a meter above the ground. But visibility was still close to three hundred meters, and the presence was a lot nearer than that. Raynar brought the landspeeder to a halt.

"I feel it, too," Tekli said. "Something is eager to get at us, before we reach the mountain."

Lowbacca groaned a question.

"Well, I can't see anything except the back of your enormous and furry head," C-3PO answered. "Perhaps I would be of more use if you didn't insist on making the droid ride in the back."

"I don't think it's an illusion," Tekli said, ignoring C-3PO and replying to Lowbacca. "It can be sensed only through the Force. And any illusion that can be sensed only through the Force won't turn away many threats."

Lowbacca moaned his agreement, and the hungry presence continued to draw nearer. Raynar popped the canopy latch on his side of the landspeeder—and then saw the soil settling and understood. He put the landspeeder in reverse and pushed the throttles to maximum.

Too late.

Twenty meters ahead, a giant pair of serrated pincers burst from the ground and spread apart, revealing a slimy red maw about twice as wide as the speeder. The maw led into a long sinuous throat lined by concentric rings of spines. Out of the depths of this cavern shot a spray of gray, ropy tongues that slapped down on the front end of the vehicle. The pincers snapped shut against the body, burying their tips deep in the side panels.

The landspeeder started to slide forward. Raynar pushed the throttles past maximum to overload, clear to the end of the lever guides. The vehicle continued to slide toward the fang-filled maw.

"Out!" Raynar yelled.

Lowbacca popped the latch on his side. He exploded from his seat so swiftly that he caught the canopy bubble on his neck and shoulders, snapping it off at the hinges. Tekli yelled that she was also free. By then, Raynar was already pushing off the steering wheel, using the Force to send himself tumbling out of the landspeeder. He came down five meters away, landed on one foot, then cartwheeled two full rotations before he finally brought his momentum under control.

When he looked back, the maw had engulfed the landspeeder almost to the passenger compartment and was dragging it down into the dusty pit from which it had emerged. Still in the back, C-3PO was leaning away from the ropy tongues, waving both arms at Raynar.

"Jedi Thul, why are you just standing there? Please *do* something quickly!"

The landspeeder passed over the edge of the pit and tipped forward.

C-3PO pointed down into the pit. "I suggest that you kill it *now*!"

Killing the creature was out of the question—and not only because of its size. Instead, Raynar extended a hand and used the Force to lift the droid out of the landspeeder—then found himself struggling against Lowbacca, who'd had the same idea.

Raynar released his Force-grasp. C-3PO went sailing, then hit Lowbacca in the chest, bounced off, and landed in the dust at the Wookiee's feet.

Lowbacca dropped his chin and studied the droid for a moment, then moaned a question.

"I could not possibly know that yet," C-3PO replied. "I'm still running my diagnostics!"

Lowbacca shrugged and set the droid on his feet, then growled and rubbed his chest.

"It's not *my* fault my elbow gave you a bruise," C-3PO said. "I was merely trying to minimize my own damage."

The shriek of folding metal sounded from the pit. Raynar stepped to the edge and, through a veil of blowing blue dust, saw a huge heart-shaped head poking out of the bottom. It was rolling the crumpled landspeeder around in its mandibles, using its mouth to tear off pieces and crush them into meter-wide spheres—which it quickly found unpalatable and spat out.

A small hand grasped Raynar's arm and tried to pull him away from the pit. He pulled back just hard enough to stay where he was, and Tekli stepped to his side.

"Raynar?" Tekli whispered. "Is it really wise to stand where that thing can see you?"

Raynar shrugged. He wasn't sure what that thing was, but there was a reasonable chance it was some variety of Killik. He took a deep breath, both calming himself and filling his lungs, then raised both forearms in greeting.

"Thuruht?" he called.

The insect stopped chewing and pushed its head another meter out of the pit, revealing a huge bulb that was probably a vestigial eye. The ground trembled beneath Raynar's feet, and he felt a faint rumbling deep in his stomach.

"Oh my!" C-3PO said, speaking from three meters away. "She

would like to know who is asking, and why you are disturbing her work."

Raynar smiled as much as the flesh of his burn-scarred face allowed. "Tell her I'm an old friend," he said. "UnuThul needs help."

"Jedi Thul, I'm not sure that's wise," C-3PO said. "Killiks rarely cooperate with liars, and you haven't been UnuThul for quite—"

Lowbacca growled, warning C-3PO to be careful about what he said.

Raynar glanced over at the droid. "Tell her, Threepio."

Before C-3PO had a chance to obey, the ground trembled again. The droid cocked his head, then said, "As it happens, that won't be necessary. Thuruht comprehends Basic quite well. She has invited us to the Celestial Palace."

Raynar looked into the pit and dipped his head. "We're grateful."

The ground trembled in reply, and Raynar led the way around the pit and started toward the palace. The air was arid and choking hot, and with a haze of blue dust obscuring everything below their waists, it was difficult to find the best path across the plain. Twice, Raynar sank to his thighs when he inadvertently stepped into another pit.

Several times, Raynar glimpsed a ridge rising in the dust ahead as one of Thuruht's giant guardians burrowed across the plain to greet him and his companions. Usually, the greeting consisted of little more than coming alongside them and emitting a subterranean rumble so deep they felt it in their stomachs. But about three hundred meters from the palace, a huge head burst from the ground, blocking their way and clacking its mandibles.

It had been a long time since Raynar had been part of a Killik hive mind, but he didn't think the creature was trying to threaten them. He motioned his companions to lower their weapons and stepped forward. Keeping his prosthetic arm at his side, he raised his flesh-and-blood hand in greeting. The insect responded by dipping its head and rubbing its wormlike antennae across his forearm. Then it emitted a soft, muffled *boom* and withdrew.

As soon as the creature vanished into the ground again, Tekli stepped to Raynar's side. "You'll be coated in pheromones now," she observed. "You still have your nasal filters in place, yes?"

Raynar sniffed hard. Finding it difficult to draw air, he nodded.

"No worries," he said, starting toward the palace again. "No one who's been a Joiner wants to become a Joiner again—including me."

Lowbacca observed that no one ever wanted to become a Joiner in the first place. The pheromones just made it happen.

"We'll be okay," Tekli assured the Wookiee. "Even if the filters overload, the counteragents will give us enough protection to get through a week of exposure."

Lowbacca turned to Raynar and growled a question.

"Hard to say," Raynar answered. "But a week is probably long enough."

"And if it isn't, I have more counteragent aboard the *Long Trek*," Tekli said. "We can always return and take another injection."

Lowbacca glanced over his shoulder, looking back toward the distant ridge where they had landed the scoutship, then grumbled unhappily.

"I quite agree," C-3PO replied. "That's a very long walk, indeed. My actuators simply won't tolerate it."

"You won't need to," Raynar said. "Pheromones don't affect droids. You can just wait with Thuruht."

"Alone?" C-3PO objected. "I'm quite sure that's not what Princess Leia had in mind when she offered to send me along."

"Probably not," Raynar agreed.

As they entered the channel at the base of the dust-mountain, Raynar realized that the scale of the place was even larger than it had appeared from the landspeeder. The channel stretched two hundred meters to the gate, and its walls were easily seventy meters high. The archway at the far end was large enough to accommodate a Lancer frigate, and the enormous support columns flanking the entrance rose a hundred meters before vanishing into an overhang of wind-packed dust.

The figures on the pillars were largely hidden by the dust. On the left-hand column, all that could be seen were a pair of sharp-taloned feet dangling beneath the overhang, tangled in the coils of what was either a serpent or a tentacle. On the right-hand column, even less could be seen, only a single wing dipping out of the dust, wrapped in what was either a length of vine or rope.

The air grew dank and humid as they drew within two dozen steps of the archway. Raynar sensed the fused Force-presence of a group of Killiks loitering in the passages near the entrance, and his pulse started to pound in his ears.

"Don't worry," Tekli said, stepping to his side. "We're here with you."

Lowbacca added his own reassurances, promising to drag Raynar out by his feet at the first hint he was becoming a Joiner again. The words were offered in kindness, but Raynar found them to be little comfort. There *was* something to fear. If becoming a Joiner again was the only way to learn what Thuruht knew of Abeloth and the Celestials, then become a Joiner he would. And he knew the same was true of Lowbacca and Tekli. The Order needed the intelligence they had been sent to gather far more than it needed them.

The trick, of course, would be making sure that at least one of them stayed sane enough to report back to the Council.

Together, the Jedi stepped through the archway into the cool darkness of the ruins. Raynar heard the clatter of approaching insects, and a moment later he began to feel their antennae brushing over him. They were careful to avoid the prosthetic arm, however. Killiks did not like artificial body parts. The devices blurred the line between living being and droid, and Killiks did not like droids. Droids were alien and never to be trusted, because droids never became Joiners.

As his eyes adjusted to the darkness, Raynar found himself facing a trio of Killiks with mottled-blue exoskeletons and four delicate arms. They had the same heart-shaped heads as their giant hive-mates outside, but they were only about one-and-a-half meters tall and lacked the huge mandibles of the guardians. When they saw Raynar studying them, all three folded their arms against their thoraxes and dipped their heads.

"Ruur ubb unuwul burur," said one. "Uru rur rruru bub."

"Thuruht welcomes the wise UnuThul and his followers to the Celestial Palace," C-3PO translated. "The hive is honored that he has chosen to rejoin the Kind through them."

Lowbacca let out a quick growl, informing Thuruht that they weren't there to join anything.

"Are you certain you wish me to translate that, Jedi Lowbacca?" C-3PO asked. "You're actually being rather—"

Thuruht interrupted with a short thrum, and the droid turned to face the insect. After a moment, he looked back to Lowbacca.

"Thuruht says it doesn't matter why you came, the hive will be honored to have you." He shifted his attention to Raynar. "We are asked to attend the Queen in her chamber."

Had his burn scars permitted it, Raynar would have raised his brow. Modern Killik hives were no longer organized around a queen, but he supposed it only made sense that Thuruht's social structure would reflect its great age. He inclined his head to the blue insects.

"If you'll show us the way."

All three turned and led the way up a stale-smelling passage that ascended along the outer walls of the palace. The climb was steep and lonely, rising in a rough spiral that felt five kilometers long.

They frequently passed through musty-smelling areas where a side tunnel led into the depths of the palace. The few insects they encountered seemed to be wandering about aimlessly rather than executing the business of the hive. Most of the time, the balls of luminescent wax hanging along the walls were too dim to see much more than the silhouettes of the three guides ahead. Every so often, however, they would pass one of the huge windows they had seen from outside, and the light would spill in to reveal archways decorated with bas-relief carvings of plants and animals from a thousand different worlds.

But it was the panels between the arches that put a flutter in Raynar's stomach. The images depicted the grandeur of deep space, always with some peculiar twist that seemed unlikely to occur in nature. There was a supernova exploding in only one direction, a ring of nine planets circling their sun along a single orbital path, a nebula hanging like a curtain between two star systems. Finally came a scene that looked all-too familiar—a system with five planets orbiting the same star in very similar orbits, with the third and fourth planets locked in a tight twin-planet formation.

Raynar stopped and asked, "What's that picture?"

The insects answered without stopping or looking back. "Urrub."

"Our work," C-3PO translated. The droid paused, waiting in vain for a more thorough explanation, then said, "I'm sorry, Jedi Thul, but Thuruht doesn't seem to be in a very informative mood right now. Perhaps they've been offended by Lowbacca's rudeness."

Lowbacca moaned a half-hearted apology.

Thuruht continued to ascend the corridor. Raynar remained where he was and called, “Is this one the Corellian System?”

The insects stopped five meters up the passage, then reluctantly turned around. “Buurub uu ruub ur ru ub.”

“Thuruht wouldn’t know what it is called by lesser beings,” C-3PO translated. “But to Thuruht, it is known as Five Rocks.”

Tekli stood on her toes, reaching up to wipe the dust away from the twin planets, then asked, “Does Thuruht know its original purpose?”

“Ub.”

The insects turned and walked on.

“Thuruht said *yes*,” C-3PO translated. “May I suggest we follow? They seem to be growing impatient with us.”

Lowbacca shrugged and started up the passage. Raynar and Tekli fell in behind the Wookiee. A few minutes later they turned toward the center of the palace, traveling down a long hall even larger and more ornate than the one they had just ascended. The air grew warmer and more humid. The glow-balls started to shine more brightly, and they began to see more worker insects, scurrying in and out of side passages carrying tools, bales of a stringy yellow fungus, and waxy orbs of one of the Killiks’ favorite nourishment, golden membrosia. Raynar started to feel thirsty, and he noticed Lowbacca eyeing a membrosia bearer as she crossed the corridor ahead.

“*That* I miss about being Taat,” Tekli said. Taat was the hive she and Lowbacca had inadvertently joined years before, after Raynar had summoned them to help the Killiks fight the Chiss. “It will almost be worth the trip to have some again.”

“They sell it in Restaurant Galatina on Coruscant, you know,” C-3PO offered helpfully. “I understand the Horoh is especially fine this year.”

“And a thousand credits a liter,” Tekli said. “I’m a Jedi Knight, not an investment banker.”

They reached the end of the hall, where two huge guardian insects stood to either side of the corridor, their long mandibles locked across an entrance ten meters wide. The insects looked much the same as the one that had eaten the landspeeder, except there was nothing vestigial about their eyes. The pair glared at the procession as it approached, and Raynar began to fear that he and his companions would not be permitted to enter the queen's chamber.

Then a deep drumming sounded from the interior. The guardians lifted their mandibles, and the guides led the way into a vast chamber containing hundreds of empty floor pits. In a healthy hive, the pits would have been filled with incubation cells. But the deep drifts of dust in the bottom of these suggested they had not been used in centuries. Unlike the rest of the palace, the room was well lit, the sun's orange light spilling in through a transparent membrane stretched across the vaulted ceiling.

The guides stopped a few steps inside, leaving Raynar and his companions to continue down a large center aisle toward the queen. Almost as large as the entrance sentries, she lay stretched across a massive dais, with six sturdy legs curled against a Bantha-sized abdomen and a mouth flanked by a pair of multi-jointed mandibles. Standing on the floor in front of her were four guardians identical to those outside the entrance.

Closer to the dais were a pair of floor pits filled with the familiar comb of incubation cells. Raynar saw no more than thirty compartments, and only three nursery Killiks to attend them. The hive wasn't quite dead, but it wasn't thriving, either.

As Raynar and his companions passed the last nursery pit, the guardians shuffled away from the center of the dais, revealing a wide set of stairs. The queen's abdomen rippled, filling the chamber with a long, low rumble barely audible to human hearing.

"I must say, this is quite unexpected," C-3PO said. "The queen is inviting Lowbacca and Tekli to groom her."

Lowbacca emitted an uncertain groan.

"It means you remove her external parasites," Raynar explained. Lowbacca and Tekli's old hive, Taat, had been much more egalitarian in social structure, so they had probably never participated in the ritual. "It's an honor. Yoggoy used to groom me—"

Lowbacca huffed in disgust.

"Just think of it as a medical procedure," Tekli whispered. "And remember why we're here."

The Wookiee sighed and dropped his head, and the group ascended the stairs. An attendant emerged from behind the queen, appearing atop her giant abdomen with a bucket in one hand and a cloth and bottle of antiseptic spray in two of her other hands, then motioned for the groomers to join her. As former Joiners themselves, Lowbacca and Tekli had enough experience to realize Killiks weren't shy about crawling over one another, so they scrambled up to join the attendant.

Raynar watched them ascend, then stepped over to present himself to the queen. Her head was small compared to the rest of her body, but it was still half the size of Raynar himself, with eyes as big as shockballs and slender mandibles the length of a Wookiee's arm. Raynar raised his flesh-and-blood hand in greeting. In return, the queen dipped her head, then rubbed a feathery antenna along his wrist.

"Wuur uu rur uu," she thrummed. "Ubub ruub uru."

"Thuruht welcomes you back to the Kind," C-3PO translated. "The hive will be honored to have you."

Raynar felt a nervous flutter in his stomach. Lowbacca had clearly stated they had not come to join the hive, yet Thuruht was speaking as if it were already fact. All Killiks had a tendency to confuse belief with reality, so the queen might simply be saying she believed the three Jedi would eventually become Joiners again. But her tone was insistent, and it struck Raynar as an assertion of will—a warning that Thuruht would not be defied.

Raynar continued to hold his arm aloft until the queen withdrew her antenna, then said, "You know we are not here to join the hive."

The queen lifted her head above his, then clapped her mandibles together and let out a short rumble.

"Yes, but it *will* happen," C-3PO translated. "She seems quite sure of it."

Raynar let out his breath, taking a moment to calm himself, then looked into the queen's nearest eye. "That can't happen," he said. "You remember last time, when I became UnuThul."

The queen dipped her head a little, and let out a series of soft booms.

"You won't make the same mistake again," C-3PO translated. "You have grown in years and in wisdom."

"It doesn't matter," Raynar said. "The Chiss wouldn't like it. They would go to war."

The queen's reply grew a little softer.

"What the Chiss don't know will never hurt us," C-3PO said.

"They already know."

A low rumble sounded from the insect's thorax, and C-3PO translated, "You told them?"

Raynar shook his head. "No, but they have spies everywhere." As he spoke, he was trying to figure out why Thuruht seemed so determined to have him as a Joiner. Visitors became Joiners after they had been exposed to Killik pheromones for enough time. But hives rarely engaged in deliberate recruitment—not unless they were in need of something a new Joiner could provide. "If I don't return to the Galactic Alliance soon, the Chiss will mobilize for war—and they *will* attack the Kind."

The queen studied him for a long moment, then tipped her head and rumbled a question.

"Thuruht asks why you came, if your presence is such a danger?"

"Because a greater danger threatens the Galactic Alliance, and we need Thuruht's help to defeat it," Raynar explained. "We need to know everything Thuruht can tell us about the Celestials—and a being who calls herself—"

The queen's entire body shuddered. "Ruur ub?"

"It seems we're in luck, Jedi Thul," C-3PO said. "She asks if the name is Abeloth."

Raynar nodded. "Then you know who Abeloth is?"

The queen gave several short, nervous booms.

"Indeed she does," C-3PO responded. "Thuruht is the one who imprisoned her."

Raynar's heart began to pound. "Good. The Jedi need to know everything Thuruht can tell us about her."

"Ub?"

Raynar needed no translation. "Because Abeloth has escaped," he said. "And we don't know where she went."

The queen raised her head and let out a rumble so thunderous that Raynar's own torso began to reverberate. Workers started to pour into the chamber from all sides, some bearing orbs of membrosia and others rushing to clean the dust from the cell pits in the floor. The nursery attendants dropped into the nearest clean pit and began to exude wax, creating a comb of fresh incubation cells.

Raynar turned to C-3PO, who was watching the sudden flurry of activity with an attentiveness that suggested a major portion of his processing power was engaged to make sense of it.

"Threepio," he shouted, trying to make himself heard above the rumbling queen. "What's all the booming about?"

"I'm afraid it makes no sense, Jedi Thul," the droid replied. "I must be misunderstanding."

"Tell me anyway," Raynar ordered.

"Very well," C-3PO said. "Thuruht keeps saying that the hive must spawn and prepare."

"Spawn?" Raynar echoed. "Prepare? For what?"

"That's the part that makes no sense, considering her determination to restore her hive," C-3PO answered. "Thuruht keeps saying that the galaxy is dead. She keeps saying that the end of times is here."

## About the Type

This book was set in Galliard, a typeface designed by Matthew Carter for the Mergenthaler Linotype Company in 1978. Galliard is based on the sixteenth-century typefaces of Rober Granjon.